2299003, 46½9

WILDE WEST

WILDE WEST

WALTER SATTERTHWAIT

St. Martin's Press

NEW YORK

Production Editor: David Stanford Burr

Design by Glen M. Edelstein

Library of Congress Cataloging-in-Publication Data

Satterthwait, Walter.
     Wilde west / Walter Satterthwait.
        p.   cm.
     "A Thomas Dunne book."
     ISBN 0-312-05997-3
     I. Title.
   PS3553.A764M4   1991
   813'.54—dc20   90-28738
                                                          CIP

First Edition: August 1991

10 9 8 7 6 5 4 3 2 1

This is dedicated to Jon Richards and Claudia Jessup, with thanks and love. The bears are for them.

ACKNOWLEDGMENTS

In the States, thanks to Scott and Donna Anderson, Reagan Arthur at St. Martin's, Dick Beddow (again), Dana and Nancy Bramwell, Richard Brenner, Yiorgo Chouliaras, Marilyn Copp, Valerie DeMille, Dick and Dottie Gallegly, Cathleen Jordan and Holly Wallinger and Judy Downer of *Alfred Hitchcock's Mystery Magazine*, Doris O'Donnell, Diane Moggey at Worldwide Mystery, Sara Nakian, Karla Satterlee, Shirley Sweeten, Duke and Martha Schirmer and Kate Whelan. Thanks, also, to the many people in Leadville who offered kindness and information, particularly to Georgina Brown and to Patty McMahan at the Silver Dollar Saloon.

Here on Paros, thanks to Jim Clark, David and Vanessa Grant, Vicki Kondili, Jack Neale, John and Jane Pack, Bill and Helen Riding, Angelos and Yianni Spyridoyiannakis, and Sabine Scholtyssek-Aoki. (*Guten tag,* Sabine.)

In Athens, thanks to Mano Ignatiadis and Lelli Rallis.

In Frankfurt, thanks to Klaus Schomburg.

In Edinburgh, thanks to Dr. Olga Taxidou.

In Amsterdam, very special thanks to Elzo Wind and Carola Van Doremalen.

Anyone who reads both this book and Richard Ellmann's magistral biography of Oscar Wilde will at once perceive the debt which the former owes to the latter. I've also plundered shamelessly from *The Queen City* by Lyle W. Dorsett and Michael McCarthy, and from *Leadville: Colorado's Magic City* by Edward Blair. I've played fast and loose with facts and dates, however (the Leadville Crystal Palace, for example, wasn't erected until 1896), and I'm totally responsible for all errors, exaggerations, and outright lies.

People are strange
when you're a stranger . . .
        —*Jim Morrison*

Under normal circumstances, sexual desires become stabilized as
soon as they meet adequate satisfaction. . . . Freud describes a case
in which the husband and wife had reached an exceptionally high
level of perversion before they met (they had practiced every
perversion in the book); it was a completely happy marriage, which
ended only when the husband was arrested for the murder of a rich
American woman.
        —*Colin Wilson*, Order of Assassins

Prologue

S HE STALKED IN the darkness past the tiny scurrying forms of the Chinese, through pockets of their mindless squealing chatter, he inhaled the stench of old fish and of human excrement, the reek of rotting fruit, the stink of the unnamable herbs and spices with which these people cooked their wretched food.

But he delighted in them, those smells; almost giddily he sucked them in and played them along the back of his throat. They provided proof that tonight, once again, his senses were preternaturally acute.

Not that he needed proof; no.

He needed nothing, lacked nothing. On a night such as this he was complete, he was whole. The boundaries of his interior self had expanded, miraculously, to meet exactly the boundaries of his physical body; he could feel, all over, his spirit pulsing just beneath the taut surface of his skin. He moved within the center of a perfection.

No, he needed nothing.

Wanted, yes. There was something, there was one small thing, one small tasty thing, he wanted. And this, by right, he would soon have. This he would soon take.

(*Yes.*)

The fog tonight was everywhere. It blurred the glow of the streetlamps, swirled around the corners of the tiny huddled shops, curled like smoke across the wooden sidewalk, whirled and eddied behind the clattering wooden wheels of the carriages and wagons. It comforted him, yes, of course, it assured him that the very elements, air and water, would collaborate with him in his quest: would give him the secrecy he required, would hide him.

But it was chill and it was damp. It hung about his clothes and pressed dense and clammy against his face, like the touch of a snail. It seeped through the dank leather of his gloves and it numbed his fingers.

But was this not merely another example of the heightening, the intensification, of all his senses? Yes, surely. Smell, taste, touch: each had been brought to a supreme throb of awareness by the diamond-like clarity of his purpose.

Vision, too: he saw things that others did not, could not. Looking into the faces of the people he passed, he could detect, as clear to him as the outline of their fragile skulls, the cramped futility of the souls trapped within, the pathetic emptiness of their lives.

He very nearly felt sorry for them.

None of them would ever know for themselves the heights to which he had soared: those luminous ethereal reaches of experience and insight. None of them had bathed in that pure white infinite radiance. None had ever sensed the presence, the approval, of the Lords of Light.

Yes, that tingling, that numbness at the fingertips was a small price to pay for the life of marvel and wonder he had been granted.

And in any event, he would be warming those cold hands soon enough.

(*Oh yes.*)

He felt anticipation curl down his spine and ball itself like a cat at the base of his belly. He smiled.

(*Oh yes.*)

2

The area he wanted, and had at last found, was on the fringes of Chinatown, near the docks. Here the seamen's bars crouched along narrow side streets, the dim light behind their small square windows casting a sickly yellow pall out onto the slowly swirling mist.

And here the whores walked.

Now that he had arrived at the hunting ground, his clothes seemed to fit more tightly on his body; his chest felt confined within shirt and vest, jacket and topcoat. It was as though the purpose, the power, that filled him had swelled his frame, had engorged bone and muscle and ligament.

He shivered, almost shuddered, with pleasure.

And no one, not one of them, would ever guess his secret.

How uncanny it was that he could present such a show of outward normality—could appear as insignificant to the others as they were in fact themselves—when inwardly his soul hummed with this awesome, irresistible strength. Outside, a simple mortal, unprepossessing; insignificant even. Inside, the same boundless energy that could furl tumults of storm cloud across a bloated moon, send lightning bolts crashing through the black sweep of rain. The energy of the Lords, the dark, forgotten gods who held sway over storm and fire.

The common run of man, given sudden dominion over this enormous power, would topple to his knees, wailing and gibbering; or all at once explode.

How uncanny that he could dissemble so; that through his own skill and cunning he had mastered the force within, learned to conceal it.

And how delicious—that, too. Really: how delicious.

In the air was the tang of stale urine, and of brine from the Bay, smelling of tears and phlegm. The night was sliding toward dawn and the streets were nearly deserted. No carriages rattled here, few pedestrians passed; beneath the faint yellow blur of the streetlamps, the empty pavements disappeared off into darkness and fog.

Only a handful of the creatures would be left, of course. But he knew that among them he would find the one he wanted. As surely as he sought his destiny, his destiny sought him.

Lurching from a doorway just a few steps away came the first of them. It saw him, cocked its big head, smiled its predatory red smile. "Lookin' for a piece of pie, handsome?"

(*This one.*)

It was a big blowsy thing in its early twenties, bloodshot blue eyes and bright clownish lipstick smeared beyond the outline of its thin lips. It evidently took some pride in its hair, for this, blond and shining, was left uncovered and pulled back neatly into a heavy bun. In a sullen, bovine way the thing was almost handsome. But it was too bulky, too boxy, too heavy with meat.

(*Take her.*)

And it was too young by far. It hadn't reached yet that peak of ripeness he required.

(*Take her!*)

It didn't, finally, deserve his attentions.

(*TAKE her!*)

He shook his head abruptly and stepped around it, careful not to touch it. He heard it bray with laughter behind him.

(*Coward! Gutless spineless WRETCH!*)

The chill in the air was stronger; he drew his topcoat more tightly about himself.

(*She frightened you! Too big, too strong!*)

He shoved his gloved hands into his pockets. Soon. He would find the right one soon. It was a certainty; it was fated.

(*Soon! Soon!*)

One block farther along, he saw the second whore.

It stood just within the murky light of the streetlamp, leaning against the alley-side corner of a two-story brick building. Its eyes unfocused and its mouth slack, it wore a dreary black bonnet set askew above a damp disheveled tangle of red hair. It noticed his approach and it blinked several times, with an obvious effort gathering together the tatters of consciousness. Then it pushed itself off the wall, took a step, tottered, righted itself. Clutching

4

a small purse down at its thigh with the stiff, exaggerated care of a drunk, it stumbled toward him.

He knew, by the sudden growing heaviness below his belly, that this was the one.

(*Yes. Yes.*)

The creature leered, swaying slightly. "You want some pussy, honey?" It ran a lewd tongue over its lips. "You want some, Flower's got it."

(*Yes!*)

Thin and angular, perhaps thirty-five years old, perhaps forty-five, it gave off the stink of old sweat and cheap whiskey and cheaper perfume. The features of its face were regular, but the skin was lined, crow's-feet at the eyes, deep furrows bracketing the wide red mouth. Beneath caked white powder, its cheeks and thin nose were blotched with ruptured veins. It wore a frayed red sweater over a drab green dress, the sweater open and the dress cut low to parade the sagging breasts, gray and goosefleshed, marbled with blue.

(*Now!*)

He smiled at the creature.

"Two dollars," it told him. "Best pussy you ever had. You want French, that's three."

He told it what he wanted.

Its body wavered slightly, buffeted by the breezes of alcohol, and it leered again.

(*You see: She wants it too, she wants it.*)

It said, "You wanna knock at the back door, honey?"

(*Bitch! Foul filthy strumpet!*)

He nodded.

Leering still: "Sure. Sure. We'll have us a good time." It swayed again, blinked, closed its mouth and sucked vaguely on its tongue, concentrating. Its eyes narrowed shrewdly. "Be three dollars, honey, and a dollar for the room." Blearily it looked up and down the empty street. "You're in a hurry, we can use the alley."

(*Loathsome despicable slut!*)

5

It leaned unsteadily toward him, put out a hand, touched him. "Feels like you're in a hurry, honey." It laughed—it barked—into his face, and its breath was pestilential: liquor, garlic, moldering teeth. "Come on, we'll take care of that. We'll do you, honey, we'll do you right."

(*Trollop! Pig! Vile stinking hole!*)

It slipped its arm around his and on wobbly legs it led him into the unlighted alley.

(*Take her take the rotting slut now!*)

A part of his mind was dancing, whirling, amid a bright interior radiance. Stars erupted. Comets fizzed and glared. The power, held in check for so long now, shook the walls of his flesh.

And yet such was his command, his mastery, that he could still savor the warmth and tenderness he felt for the squalid thing beside him; a vast fondness; almost, indeed, a gratitude. The creature shared his destiny; it *was* his destiny. The two of them had glided on their separate lives down through the arc of years to arrive together at precisely this place, at precisely this time: so that together they might partake of this unique moment of power and glory. Of transcendent grace.

(*Take her take her TAKE her . . .*)

It stopped, its head loose atop its neck. In the gray half light, its face was a blur. "Fine here, honey, no one ever comes through the alley. Flower's private place." It touched him again, stroked him.

(*TAKE HER!*)

The power clogged his chest, clotted in his throat; he could barely breathe.

The creature released his arm and bent down to gather up the hem of its dress.

(*NOW NOW NOW!*)

The power drummed against his ears, against his eyes. He took his hands from his pockets and removed his gloves. He noticed—as though from very far away and through undulating curtains of light, a flickering aurora—that his hands were steady; and, remotely, he was pleased. He folded the gloves and put them carefully in his pocket.

6

(*NOW NOW NOW!*)

The creature turned its back to him, its lifted skirt bunched in its right arm. Bending toward the wall, legs apart, head drooping, left forearm braced against the brick, it presented itself.

He reached into the topcoat and found the handle of the knife.

(*NOW NOW NOW!*)

The creature turned its head, slurred over its shoulder, "Do me, honey. Do me."

(*NOW NOW NOW!*)

He stepped forward, left hand moving for its hair, right hand moving for its throat. And as he did, all the scattered shimmering brightnesses that swam within him—incandescent streamers of mist, fiery reeling stars and comets—merged at once into a single roaring flame that blazed with a hard white insuperable light.

The creature yelped as his fingers snared its hair, and its body stiffened, tried to arch away; and then the knife, a benediction, floated through its throat; and the white flame suddenly flared across the universe; and, scorched, blinded, he himself spurted at exactly the same moment that the creature spurted out the tumult of life it held within.

He caught the body as it slumped, quivering; he supported its limp heaviness as it spattered the ground with its saps. Then, murmuring, whispering, he lowered it gently, carefully, onto its rump. Reverently he drew back its dress and tenderly he laid the folds across its breast, its face.

Still murmuring and whispering, and cooing now, he set to work, his hands busy, the knife hissing.

His hands were no longer cold.

BOOK ONE

From the Grigsby Archives

February 15, 1882

DEAR BOB,

Everyone here is well and the children send their love. Little Bob loved his birthday present but Bob I wish that you would not send him toys like that. I gave it to him against my better judgment. If you had not hinted at it in your last letter to him I would have thought seriously of keeping it hidden. I know you did that on purpose Bob. Very clever. I know how unhappy he would be if he did not receive a present from his father. I had my fill of guns while you and I were together Bob and now every time I try to read little Bob runs around the house waving that thing like he was a Comanche and shouting Bang Bang at the top of his lungs. It makes me worry about his future and it is also extremely annoying. And now Sarah wants one too. Do not send her one Bob. I am serious.

Last night I went with Molly Sebastian to Platt's Hall to listen to a lecture by Mr Oscar Wilde the famous English poet and esthete. It was his first visit to San Francisco. He was not like I expected. First of all he was young I guess about twenty

11

five years old. Second he was very tall at least six feet four inches and good looking in a bulky way. Like an overgrown boy. His hair was long almost to his shoulders and he was very dandified in knee britches and stockings. He talked in that "refined" way that Englishmen have that makes you think they know every word that William Shakespeare ever wrote by heart. And maybe Mr Wilde really does.

He was very interesting as he talked about what made up an artistic type of house. Some of what he said made sense but you would need a lot of money to make all the changes he talked about. Wainscoting and such. Only rich people can afford to have good taste I guess. Molly was very taken with him. I think she has a bit of a "crush." He is giving another lecture there tomorrow night and she wants to go to that one too. He is also going to Denver in March Bob so you will have a chance to see him yourself. I know you are very fond of poetry and art. Right Bob?

I am sorry. I do not want to be mean to you. I guess I am in a bad mood because of the news in all the newspapers today. There was a horrible murder here last night. Some poor woman was killed down by the docks and they say that the murderer must have been a maniac. They say that after he killed her he mutilated her terribly with a knife. Who would do such a thing? The police have no idea who was responsible. I suppose she was "a lady of the evening" but no one deserves to die like that.

I hope you are well. Are you drinking these days? I hope not. I know you are a decent man at heart when you are sober and I only wish for your sake that you would be sober a little more often. I know you do not believe me but maybe if you had been drunk a little bit less we would still be together today. And Bob you are getting to be of an age where you can no longer abuse your body like you have your whole life.

I can just see you reading this and grinning like an old fool while you pour yourself another drink. You are hopeless Bob.

Oh well there is no use crying over spilled milk. You are

who you are and I am who I am. Sometimes love just is not enough. I guess we discovered that together.

Please take care of yourself and I hope you will write to me again. I always enjoy hearing from you.

Love,
Clara

CHAPTER ONE

STATELY AND PLUMP, OSCAR FINGAL O'Flahertie Wills Wilde lightly with the pale tips of spatulate fingers pressed aside the wooden batwing doors and, regally blinking, sailed forward into the gaudy gaslight glare. Banners of blue smoke, cigarette and pipe and cigar, coiled and slowly uncoiled at the ceiling. The crowd droned. A tinny piano hammered. Somewhere, stage right, a woman shrieked: perhaps in laughter.

Along the dark sweep of cherrywood bar, and duplicated in the bright silver sweep of mirror beyond it, a row of Stetsons swiveled. Beneath their brims, eyes widened in surprise or narrowed in puzzlement.

Languidly plucking the cigarette from his lips and exhaling a billow of clove-scented smoke, Oscar paused for a moment, as much to savor the reaction of the crowd as to determine his own.

Pleased. Yes, he was pleased. The huge saloon was packed, a gratifying turnout, every table surrounded by a clutch of cowboys and miners and shopkeepers and giddy gaudy women, all of the men wearing hats and all of them (and some of the women, it seemed) sporting identical handlebar mustaches, like walruses.

14

And at the moment, all of them, men and women both, were gaping at Oscar.

His clothes tonight were subdued, somewhat. No cape, no knee britches. He wore pale yellow patent leather boots, lime green twill trousers, a white silk shirt with a flowing Byronic collar loosely secured by a broad silk cravat whose yellow exactly matched the boots, and the three-quarter-length velveteen dinner jacket he had ordered shortly after he arrived in New York City. He had specified that the jacket bc the shade of a lake beneath moonlight; but, as he admitted (although only to himself), its hue more closely resemblcd the dull gray of a field mouse's rump. Still, it was beautifully cut; and if perfection were in fact an impossiblc destination, then we must learn to enjoy the achievements which present themselves along the way.

In the boutonniere at the jacket's left lapel was a small red rose. This flower struck a bit of a false note—roses being after all rather vulgar—but Henry had told him that just now there were no lilies to be had in all of Denver. The entire town was lilyless. The undertakers had cornered the market, said Henry. A recent rash of hangings and gunfights. Although perhaps not in that order.

Really, the florists should have been better prepared. Hangings were reportedly a commonplace. And gunfights were evidently the local equivalent of cricket. Certainly, from what Oscar had heard, the earnestness of the players and the zeal of the audience were much the same. But cricket, of course, was far more deadly.

Oscar smiled. Not half bad. He must remember that.

He glanced around. The audience, his no longer, had returned to its cards and bottles and conversation. Time to move along.

He saw the Countess and O'Conner sitting with von Hesse at a small round table on the far side of the room. He took a puff of the cigarette and ambled across the hardwood floor, sauntering around the tables, carefully picking his way over the tawny drifts of sawdust and the occasional dark suspicious stain on the oak planking. (Not all the saloon's patrons understood the purpose of a spittoon, or had any interest in learning it.) Behind him he trailed a most satisfactory wake of murmurs and mutters.

15

O'Conner raised a glass of whiskey in salute as Oscar approached. Wearing his inevitable rumpled brown suit, an item which would have sent a shudder of horror rippling down Bond Street, the newspaperman sat slouched in one chair with his feet propped upon the rung of another, his left side and left elbow braced against the table. "Hail, O Poet," he said, and leered. He was drunk, but he had been drunk since joining the lecture tour in San Francisco, over four weeks before; and probably for twenty or thirty years before that. Every day, slowly but relentlessly, he consumed at least a quart of bourbon whiskey. Amazingly, his hands never faltered; he never lost his lucidity, never slurred his words. Perhaps he became bumbling and incomprehensible only when sober. Unlikely that anyone would ever know.

Oscar nodded to him. "O'Conner." It never hurt to be pleasant to a representative of the press. Particularly when the representative was covering this lecture tour for the *New York Sun* (circulation 220,000).

"Where's your protégé?" asked O'Conner.

"Young Ruddick, you mean?" said Oscar. "I've no idea."

"Oscair," breathed the Countess in her voice of smoke and honey, "how adorable you look tonight. I admire very much the cravat. Do you think I should look presentable in that shade of yellow?"

Oscar smiled. "I venture to say, madame, that you should look presentable in whatever you chose to wear."

"Or chose not to," said O'Conner, leering over his whiskey glass and interrupting before Oscar had a chance at cleverness himself.

O'Conner's remark was a trifle coarse, but it was apposite. (And also perhaps usable, sometime in the future.) The Countess was undeniably a handsome woman. A rosy complexion, only a few lines at the corners of her hooded blue eyes, thick tumbling ringlets of blond hair untouched by gray (but lightly touched, no doubt, by an occasional application of cash). She was wearing a dress of black tulle, gathered at the shoulders, sleeveless, plunging dizzily in a décolletage which would have occasioned her

16

arrest almost anywhere in England, and possibly in even a few remote corners of France.

O'Conner had been attempting to seduce her since the tour left San Francisco. The Countess's virtue, such as it was, had apparently remained intact. Oscar suspected that the Countess's virtue, like the mortgage on the chalet she owned in Plaisir, had been several times renegotiated over the years. Still, her sleek white arms demanded admiration, and the alabaster swell of those round white breasts . . .

Oscar's reverie was broken as von Hesse stood up from the table. His back straight, he made a small stiff formal nod. Somehow the dark gray suit he wore contrived to resemble a military uniform. The effect was heightened by his hair: shiny pink scalp gleamed beneath a close-cropped bristle of white. "Please, Mr. Wilde, you will join us?"

"Delighted," said Oscar. He pulled back a chair and sat down. Von Hesse sat opposite him, his spine never once veering from the vertical.

Von Hesse smiled his small crisp smile and asked him, "You are, as they say, out on the town tonight? On your own, eh?"

Oscar nodded. "For a bit, yes." He looked around for an ashtray, saw that the table held only a whiskey bottle and three glasses, and so tapped the ash from his cigarette onto the floor. When in Rome. "Later this evening I'm to pay court to the man who owns the Opera House here. A chap named Tabor. The good Mr. Vail arranged it. Evidently, Tabor's a man who's dug tons of silver out of the ground and converted them into tons of gold." He inhaled on the cigarette. "Or perhaps it was the other way round. The intricacies of high finance have always escaped me."

"Silver mines," said O'Conner, sipping at his whiskey as quite openly he ogled the sweep of aristocratic breast offered by the Countess. "He owns the richest silver mines in Colorado."

"Ah."

"He is married?" asked the Countess.

Oscar smiled. He found it endlessly endearing, this tendency she had in any conversation to deflect it suddenly, and with an

17

utter lack of self-consciousness, toward herself and her concerns. It was a trait with which he sympathized. "All successful men are married, Countess. Society inflicts marriage upon them as a punishment for their presumption."

She returned the smile. "And what of yourself, dear Oscair?"

He laughed. "Ah, well. My own presumption, alas, continues to outpace my success."

"Tabor's married, all right," said O'Conner. "But while the wife's stuck back in Leadville, old Horace is here in Denver, playing house with Baby Doe."

"And what, pray," said Oscar, "is a Baby Doe?"

"Elizabeth McCourt Doe. Baby Doe. A real beauty, they say. A knockout. She came here from Virginia with a husband in tow, and dumped him when she decided she wanted a silver baron of her own. She latched on to Tabor a couple years ago."

The Countess blinked quizzically. "A baron?"

O'Conner leered. "Not a real one, Countess. You outrank him." His glance dipped again to her breasts.

"As you would," said Oscar, "even if he were a prince, and genuine."

O'Conner frowned slightly at Oscar and sipped at his whiskey. "Anyway," he said, "if you're meeting Tabor tonight, you'll be meeting Baby Doe too. He doesn't let her out of his sight. He may be an old fool, but he's not stupid."

"Now, now, Mr. O'Conner," von Hesse said, running his hand lightly over his scalp. "Let us not judge others, lest we ourselves be judged."

O'Conner shrugged. "Part of my job, General. The laborer is worthy of his hire."

Von Hesse smiled. "I was never a general officer, Mr. O'Conner. And does not a reporter's job consist of determining the truth in a given situation, and presenting only that?"

O'Conner grinned again. "Depends what you mean by truth, doesn't it? Truth's a pretty slippery thing. Ask Pilate. Ask any politician."

Von Hesse nodded thoughtfully. The man was seldom less than thoughtful. "You subscribe, then, to a sort of relativism. I

18

believe, myself, in the existence of an objective truth. What about you, Mr. Wilde?''

Oscar inhaled on his cigarette. "I think that truth is greatly overrated, *mein Herr*. Lies are infinitely more entertaining. Anyone, after all, can tell the truth. But only an artist can create a beautiful lie.''

"I disagree," said von Hesse. "Art, I think, must always at base be concerned with truth. Art, like religion, aspires to the Infinite.''

"Ah," said Oscar, "but only Art stands a chance of actually arriving there." And then, recognizing an exit line when he heard it, he stood up. He dropped his cigarette to the floor, stepped on it. "I'll fetch us something else to drink, shall I?''

The bar was still crowded; but, toward its center, his back to the room, stood a single individual who was bracketed on each side by an empty space. The man was slender and, like most men, shorter than Oscar, perhaps five feet, seven inches tall. He wore black trousers and a nicely tailored black frock coat, nipped in at the waist. He was hatless, unusual here in the West where males kept their heads covered from the moment they arose until the moment they went to bed, and conceivably beyond.

Oscar glanced in the mirror opposite and saw that the man, lost in thought, was staring down at his whiskey glass. His thick black hair was combed back in soft waves from a high, intelligent forehead. Thin eyebrows arched gracefully over large dark brown eyes. Below the narrow pointed nose and draped neatly over the sensitive, almost feminine lips was a carefully trimmed handlebar mustache. The man wore a slim black bow tie and a starched white shirt and a snugly fitting waistcoat ornately brocaded in gold silk. Oscar rather envied him the waistcoat.

The barman—barkeep, they called him here—approached, a tall slender man drying his hands at the hem of his once white apron. "What'll it be, sport?''

"Have you any tea?" Oscar asked him.

"*Tea?* This is a saloon, sport.''

"Whiskey, then. A bottle.''

The barman handed Oscar a clean glass and a full bottle of

whiskey (Old Harmony, The Finest Bourbon Whiskey West Of The Pecos). As Oscar turned to leave, his elbow accidentally bumped into the shoulder of the man standing beside him.

"Terribly sorry," Oscar said, and smiled pleasantly.

The man turned to him. His eyes weren't brown. They were black: as black as the outermost regions of the night sky, and at least as empty and as cold. Staring into that emptiness, Oscar all at once felt as though the ground had shifted beneath his feet. For a moment, it was as though a sudden seismic shock had splintered the reality he knew and given him a glimpse, unwonted and unwanted, into an awful Secret that yawned, fathomless, beneath it. The skin of his face went abruptly chill and he realized, with no small surprise, that he was frightened.

It was for only an instant, a few seconds, but they were the longest seconds he could remember living, because he knew—knew without knowing how he knew—that he had never come so close before to Death.

And then the eyes narrowed fractionally, a microscopic tightening at the delicate folds of skin that held them, and the man spoke. "You're the poet," he said. His face was expressionless and his voice was low and soft, a whisper.

"Yes," Oscar said, and his own voice was absurdly thin and reedy, the piping of a rodent. He cleared it. "Yes," he said again. "The poet. Wilde. Oscar Wilde." He shifted the empty glass into his left hand and held out his right. Americans loved shaking hands.

Those black empty eyes peered down at the hand for a moment that seemed like several years, and then at last the man reached forward and took it in his own. The fingers were long and slender, like those of a pianist or a surgeon, but they seemed fleshless, frigid, a clutter of bones. Even so, ridiculously, Oscar felt a relief so strong that he fancied it might actually be rising off him visibly, a white vapor streaming from his ears.

Had it been necessary, he would have clutched the other's hand all night long, but the man released him after only a brief brisk shake.

"John Holliday," said the man in that soft uncanny whisper. "Saw you at Platt's Hall in San Francisco." Nothing in his face or voice told Oscar what the man had thought of the lecture, or that he had given it any thought, or that in fact he ever thought at all.

"Ah," said Oscar. "Did you? San Francisco, eh?" He was acutely aware that he was babbling, trying desperately to plug the vacant space between them with sound, any sound. This would never do. Fortunately he had something prepared. San Francisco: debutante. "I rather enjoyed San Francisco," he said. "It has an impudent self-consciousness which reminds one of a debutante in her first gown."

Holliday's expression, or lack of it, didn't change in the slightest. His empty eyes stared emptily into Oscar's. Oscar abruptly experienced that feeling which obtains at the top of a stairway when one takes, clunk, that extra step which remarkably is not there.

Another tack, then. He inhaled deeply, filling himself with as much bonhomie as he could muster. Then, holding up the bourbon bottle, cheerily he said, "Fancy a drink?"

Once again Holliday's expression remained unchanged. But he nodded his head—once only, and so slightly the movement might have been imaginary. "Obliged," he whispered.

Oscar set the glass down on the bar top and uncorked the bottle. Carefully, he filled Holliday's glass and then his own. He put down the bottle and raised the glass ceremoniously. "To what shall we toast?" Oscar asked.

Holliday lifted his glass and for the first time his face showed some animation. Faintly, and for only an instant, the right corner of his mouth twitched upward, behind the handlebar mustache. It could have been a smile; it could have been a nervous tic. Oscar believed it to be a smile—unlikely that Holliday possessed any nervous tics. To be burdened with such, one must first be burdened with nerves.

Holliday said softly, "To dying in bed."

Reflexively, Oscar began to say, "And to living in it, too."

21

Immediately he decided against this. "To dying in bed," he repeated, and clinked his glass against Holliday's. The two men tossed back their whiskey.

Oscar had drunk bourbon before, although never with much pleasure; this particular brand was exceptionally repellent. It was harsh, oily, and probably toxic. What little actual taste it provided was doubtless a result of the membranes in his mouth dissolving. But he didn't flinch as the vile stuff seared its way down his throat. He smacked his lips appreciatively and announced, "Delightful."

"It's donkey piss," whispered Holliday.

"Ah," said Oscar, caught once again off guard. "Yes. Donkey piss. But I like to think that there's room in this world even for donkey piss. I expect that donkeys like to think so, too."

Holliday's black empty eyes turned to him, moving swiftly, mechanically, as though set on gimbals, and they looked into Oscar's. For a split second Oscar thought that reality might splinter again; but then Holliday's mouth twitched in another quick ghost of a smile and he said, "You in town for long?"

Relaxing again, Oscar said, "For two days. And then off to Manitou Springs, and then a place called Leadville. And you?"

The thin shoulders shrugged lightly. Very lightly: merely a flicker of movement. "Don't know."

"Ah. Well, perhaps we'll meet again."

A faint nod.

A splendid idea, the whiskey: the man had grown positively garrulous.

"I hate to rush off," Oscar said, "and I hope you'll forgive me, but I've some friends waiting. You know how friends are."

Again the man's head moved slightly, but this time in a muted negative motion. "Nope," he said.

Was the man having him on? Was there possibly a glimmer of amusement floating somewhere in the depths of those dark eyes?

Impossible to tell.

"Well," Oscar said, "it's been a great pleasure chatting with

22

you like this, and I certainly hope we can do it again sometime in the very near future." He held out his hand again and Holliday, expressionless, took it. "Goodbye, then," Oscar told him.

"Be seeing you," Holliday said.

Walking back to the table, exhaling elaborately, Oscar discovered that his silk shirt was damp with perspiration. Remarkable.

"Oscair," said the Countess as he sat down again, "who was that gentleman at the bar? The one you were talking with?"

"Ah. Chap named Holliday. Interesting fellow."

O'Conner's glance shot toward the bar and his eyebrows floated up his forehead. "Jesus," he said.

"No," said Oscar. He uncorked the whiskey bottle. "His first name was John, actually."

The Countess laughed softly. Von Hesse appeared vaguely puzzled. Oscar poured himself another drink.

The reporter leaned toward Oscar and whispered urgently, "Jesus Christ, Wilde, do you know who that is?"

"I'm afraid not." He smiled. "But evidently you do."

"That's *Doc* Holliday, man."

"A doctor?" He took a sip of the whiskey. Wretched. "He didn't mention a medical background."

O'Conner shook his head, annoyed. "He used to be a dentist. But he's a gambler now, and a gunman. One of the worst. He's a killer, Wilde." Having looked into those empty black eyes, Oscar had no difficulty believing this. "He's famous for it," said O'Conner. "Last year in Tombstone, he and the Earp brothers gunned down the whole Clanton family. Killed every one of them. The gunfight at the O.K. Corral. It was in all the papers."

"Somehow it escaped the *London Times*."

"He's quite good-looking," said the Countess. "Is he married?"

Oscar smiled at her, much entertained. "I wouldn't know, madame. We didn't broach the subject." He turned back to O'Conner. "The *Earp* brothers? Rather an unfortunate name."

"Jesus, Wyatt Earp's a legend. So is Holliday."

23

"Legend or not, I found him utterly charming. I'm sure that if he killed this Clanton family, as you say, they must have been dreadful people."

"Come, come, Mr. Wilde," said von Hesse. "Surely no one deserves to be murdered."

Oscar made his face go thoughtful. "It would depend, of course," he said, "on his table manners."

"Ah," said von Hesse, nodding in understanding. "You make a joke."

"So what'd he say?" asked O'Conner. "What'd the two of you talk about?"

"My goodness, O'Conner. It was a private conversation. I really don't think it would be fair to Mr. Holliday—to Dr. Holliday—to use it as a diversion for your readers."

"Okay, okay. Off the record."

"We discussed poetry."

O'Conner frowned, dubious. "Poetry?"

"Yes. Doctor Holliday was of the opinion that Shelley was a poet superior to Keats. I suggested to him that this was absurd. Shelley had of course some talent as a versifier, and certainly he possessed enthusiasm, but he lacked finally the maturity which true poetry—"

"Wait a minute," O'Conner said, eyes narrowed, head cocked to the side. "Hold on. You told Doc Holliday that what he said was absurd?"

"Well, I could hardly let him get away with that, could I? I mean, one has only to place their poems side by side to see—"

O'Conner was frowning. "How come I'm having a hard time believing all this?"

"Your innate skepticism, perhaps. You've only to ask Dr. Holliday." Oscar smiled. "I'm sure he'll verify what I've said."

O'Conner looked at him for a moment and then he grinned. "You're good, Wilde. I've gotta hand it to you. You're good. And whatever else happened, there's no denying that you had a drink with Doc Holliday."

"Or that he," said Oscar, "had a drink with Oscar Wilde."

From the Grigsby Archives

February 25, 1882

DEAR BOB,

How are you, you old bastard?

We been busy here in El Paso. We had a killing here night before last, one of the local hookers. Susie Morris, maybe you remember her, the redhead with the big honkers worked at Sadies place. Come to think, I believe you had her once yourself—that time you was here to pick up Sid Carver & we spent all of Saturday night & most of Sunday at Sadie's? I never drunk so much rotgut whiskey or dipped my wick so many times ever in my life. Its a wonder the two of us are still alive. Anyway, Susie isnt, shes dead as a doornail.

I never seen anything like it before. I still get sick just thinking about it, & you know how I got a pretty strong stomach. He used a knife on her, whoever it was did it. Doc Amundson figures on account of the blood that he cut her throat first & thats what killed her, but then its like he went crazy. He took a knife to her innards, filleted her like a catfish, & tossed everything out onto the ground. All her parts,

I mean. Well, not all of them, because according to Doc, he walked off with her privates. Just cut them out & maybe stuck them in his pocket & sashayed out of there. This was in the alley around the corner from Sadie's place, by Buchanon's livery stable.

Did you ever hear of such a thing?

We dont got no idea at all who done it. Probably it was some hopped-up Mexican from across the river, which means well never get him. Makes me madder than hell that some loco bastard could do that to poor Susie & get away with it. I been in this law & order business too long, maybe.

Your friend Doc Holliday is in town this week, gambling over to the Longbranch. I had me a talk with him, warned him I didnt want no trouble, & he just nodded & looked right through me with them funny black eyes of his. He is one spooky son of a bitch, Bob. I wont be sorry to see him leave, Ill tell you.

We had another famous visitor this week, that English poetry fellow, Oscar Wilde. Maybe you heard of him. He gave a lecture on art at Hammersmiths. I didnt go myself, but Connie did, & she says he was smart as a whip. I met him at the Mayor's house & he looks like a pansy-boy to me, if you want the truth. He acts like one too, very lah di dah. But hes sure a big one—must be six foot four or five. I reckon pansy-boys can come in just about any size, though.

Well, time for me to mosey on. You take care of yourself. When are you heading down this way again? You let me & Connie know & well fix up the spare room. (Ill let Sadie know too, so she can warn the girls!) Are you writing to Clara these days? If you are, you send her our love & tell her from me & Connie that we hope the two of you can work things out & get yourselves back together. Youre too old & ornery to be on your own.

Sincerely,
Earl

CHAPTER TWO

NSIDE THE NARROW HORSE-DRAWN CARRIAGE, swaying an irritating beat or two behind the sway of the carriage itself,
beginning to feel like a strand of seaweed tugged left and right
by the rhythms of a relentless tide, Oscar Wilde was displeased.

"Look, Vail," he said, "couldn't we just give all this a miss?
There must be some more engaging way to pass the time. Peeling
an orange, say."

"Peeling an orange," repeated Vail, and chuckled. In the
dimness, magically, he would slowly disappear and then slowly
reappear as bars of light, cast through the carriage windows by
the streetlamps, slid obliquely across the interior. Business manager for the tour, he was a squat plump man who spoke in hearty
gusts through snow-white dentures clenched around a squat
plump, and now unlighted, cigar. His head was round and lumpy
and it was topped with a gray toupee, flat and shiny and seamless,
which curled upward at the sides and back, making it resemble
a halibut in rigor mortis. At the moment, fortunately, this was
entombed beneath a squat plump derby hat. "You kill me, Oscar.
You really do. You think these things up ahead of time, or do
they just come to you?"

27

"Henry invents them for me. He writes them down on my cuff."

" 'On your cuff,' " Vail repeated, and chuckled again. " 'Henry invents them.' " He shook his head in admiration. "You kill me."

"I mean, is this visit really necessary?" Oscar asked. The carriage swayed again, bypassing some obstacle in the road. A cadaver, no doubt. Another gunfight victim.

"You handle the Art, Oscar boy, and you let me handle the business. This Tabor guy is the big cheese around here. Richest guy in the state. Used to be lieutenant governor. Won't hurt to butter him up some."

Oscar nodded. "Now there's an image to conjure with. A lieutenant governor dripping butter, like a scone."

"Not *Left*-tenant," Vail said. "*Loo*-tenant."

"According to O'Conner," Oscar said, "he was never elected to office. Some other fellow died and this Tabor bribed his way into the post."

Vail shrugged. "A lieutenant governor's a lieutenant governor. Listen, Oscar boy, you got a real future on the circuit. You could go a long way. I mean it. You got class, you got wit. The way you wrap these yokels around your little finger, that's a real talent you got. So this guy wants to shoot the breeze with the famous poet. What's the problem? A little shoulder-rubbing never hurt anybody, right? You give him a couple minutes, you keep him happy. No big deal."

Oscar smiled. "I appear to be dripping some butter myself."

"Hey, I mean it. Sincerely." A pale rectangle of light glided over and illuminated a pair of eyebrows knotted sincerely together below the derby's brim.

Oscar said, "There's a name, you know, for the sort of person who makes someone happy for a few minutes in exchange for cash."

His sincerity evidently spent, Vail was looking out the window at the houses slipping past in the night. "Yeah? What's that?"

"Business manager."

Vail looked at him, blinked, and then chuckled. "You kill me, Oscar."

"How, exactly, do I address him?"

"Huh?"

"Tabor. What do I call him? Lieutenant?"

"You call him Governor."

"Bit of a misnomer, isn't it? He was never actually a governor, and he was only the lieutenant thing for a few months."

Vail shrugged. "Respect for the office." He sat back and clasped his hands together atop his round stomach.

"Why not Your Highness? Or Your Majesty?"

Vail considered this for a moment. "Nah," he said finally. "That's overdoing it some."

Oscar laughed.

It was a genuine liveried butler, the first Oscar had seen since London, who opened the front door to Tabor's huge brick sprawl of a mansion. Tall and thin, middle-aged, he stood with stiff, typically butlerian arrogance; but when he spoke—"Yes, gentlemen?"—it was with the nasal twang of an American, and Oscar very nearly giggled.

Vail took the cigar from his mouth. "Jack Vail and Oscar Wilde, the poet, to see Mr. Tabor."

"Yes. Mr. Tabor is expecting you. May I take your coats?"

"Long as we can get them back," said Vail, and chuckled around his cigar. His elbow thumped merrily into Oscar's liver; he wasn't tall enough to reach Oscar's ribs.

At Vail's remark, the butler produced a smile whose wan politeness managed to convey bottomless depths of contempt; no British butler could have done it better. Vail, naturally, never noticed. He handed the man his topcoat, as did Oscar, and the butler draped them on a towering rack that could easily have held the coats of the entire House of Commons. Vail gave the man his derby; in the lamplight his toupee shone with a soft piscatorial glow.

As they followed the butler down the hallway, Oscar leaned to Vail and whispered, "Poet isn't a tradesman's title, you know, like plumber."

"It pays to advertise," said Vail from the side of his mouth.

The breeze outside had ruffled Oscar's shoulder-length hair. He ran a hand back over it—wouldn't do to meet His Royal Governorship in a state of dishevelment—and looked around him.

The house was obviously new—the smells of cut lumber and varnish still laced the air—but it had been designed to impersonate a Georgian manor.

They'd got it all wrong, of course. The scale was off, for a start; everything was overlarge. The entryway was too wide, the ceiling too high: the place was cavernous.

And the colors were not only dreadful in themselves, they defied probability and clashed with each other. The carpet that ran (for far too long) down the parquet floor was a dreary brown, like dead leaves in an autumn rain; the flocked wallpaper (*flocked*, no less!) was a particularly hideous green.

Past the entryway, across an expanse of foyer the starkness of whose white marble floor was somewhat softened by a few passable Oriental rugs, an enormous wooden stairway with ornately carved mahogany balusters and handrails climbed upward to meet a wide landing, then divided at right angles into two, one rising off to the right, one to the left. The carpeting that angled up the treads and risers was a red plush which would have been more appropriate in a bordello. The stairway, by itself, occupied as much space as most London houses.

At the bottom of the stairs, the butler turned right.

So, thought Oscar: too big, too gaudy. The home of an extravagant giant. An extravagant giant who lacked taste.

Mr. Horace Tabor may have lacked taste, may have been extravagant; but in person he was no giant. A short man running to fat, he sprang up almost greedily from a red leather wingback chair in the library. Grinning beneath a mustache that was a good deal wider than his egg-shaped face and that looked like a sparrow frozen at the moment of taking flight (and so provided an intriguing contrast to Vail's defunct halibut), he held out a plump

30

eager arm to Oscar. "Mr. Wilde! *Good* to meet you." Pumping Oscar's arm enthusiastically. "A real pleasure."

He seemed atumble with nervous energy: wide darting eyes, busy hands, that ridiculous grin. Anxious to please, like a shopkeeper on the verge of bankruptcy. (Which, according to O'Conner, he had once been.)

"How do you do," said Oscar. "You know Mr. Vail, of course."

"Sure, sure. How are you, Vail." He shook Vail's hand with the same exuberance. Like a child, really. American men remained adolescents until the age of sixty. (At which time they became toddlers.) "Listen," said Tabor, "grab a seat, take a load off. Baby'll be down in just a minute." With an expansive gesture, like a music hall conjurer, he indicated the two chairs opposite his, and identical to it, across a square of carpet that might have been a genuine Persian. Still grinning beneath that paralyzed black sparrow, he shook his head and said, "Women. Why do you figure they like to keep us waiting?"

Oscar said, "It's the revenge they take upon us for our insisting that they be beautiful." He sat down and the taut new leather chirped beneath him.

"I get you," said Tabor. The man's grin was capable of expressional nuance: all at once it became knowing, and, inexplicably, he winked.

Tabor turned to the butler, who stood off to one side, practicing his disdain. "That's okay, Peters. You can take off now. I'll pour."

The butler nodded and padded silently away. The moment he disappeared, Oscar could no longer remember what he looked like. The mark of a first-rate butler, he decided. Good: *remember that*.

"Get you a drink?" Tabor grinned at Oscar. "Whiskey? Brandy?" The man hadn't stopped grinning since his guests had arrived; any moment now his cheeks would cramp. And what had been the significance of that wink?

"The brandy's the real thing," Tabor said. "Coniac. Direct from Paris, France."

Pity the Countess wasn't here; she'd enjoy this little man. "By all means, then, the brandy."

"Vail?"

"Same for me." Vail sat back comfortably and crossed his legs. Nothing pleased him more, Oscar had noticed, than relaxing in the homes of the rich and powerful. Truth to tell, Oscar didn't at all mind it himself.

Tabor scurried to the serving table and splashed three or four ounces of amber liquid from a crystal decanter into each of two large balloon glasses.

Oscar glanced around the library. One more wingback chair remained, sitting expectantly upright beside a small Hepplewhite table that separated it from Tabor's. This chair, doubtless, was Baby's. (How on earth could anyone live with an adult person named Baby? How could any adult person named Baby live with herself?) The four walls were lined with leather books that had been carefully arranged by the color of their bindings: there were blocks of blue, blocks of red, blocks of green. The chromatic approach to literature. The brown block was the largest, filling whole shelves, and here the books had been arranged by size, from tallest to shortest. He wondered whether anyone had ever actually read any of them. Or, for that matter, opened them.

Tabor returned and handed a glass to Oscar, another to Vail. He sat down opposite them, lifted his own glass from the table to his right. Leaning forward eagerly, elbows on his thighs, the balloon glass in both hands between his knees, and still grinning (amazing, that), he said, "So tell me, Mr. Wilde. What do you think of Denver?"

"Most impressive." He sipped his cognac. It was indeed French, and quite good. Perhaps there was hope for Tabor after all. If only he'd stop baring his teeth.

Tabor nodded as though he had expected nothing less. "Population now is over sixty thousand. We've got over a hundred hotels, more than a hundred restaurants, six newspapers, and at least ten railroads, last I counted."

"The mind boggles." Curious how Americans were so fascinated by these statistics, the dull arithmetic of progress.

32

Tabor's grin became rueful, almost embarrassed. "Course, it's not London yet, or even New York." The grin grew hearty again. "But if things keep up like they're going, who knows? Why not? Anything can happen." He took a sip of brandy and was able—quite a trick—to maintain his grin without spilling a drop.

"I had thought," said Oscar, "that the American ideal was a kind of pastoral existence, a sort of enormous garden spot, a demi-Eden, inhabited by honest, independent yeomen."

Grinning, Tabor shook his head. "Those days are gone. Progress is the thing today. Industry. The railroad, the cotton gin, the steam tractor."

"The road to Hell," Oscar said, "is paved with good inventions."

Tabor's grin began momentarily to falter; Vail said quickly, "So everything's arranged for Wednesday, Governor? The train and all?"

"Yep," said Tabor, and his grin returned. "You bet you. I've got a first-class compartment for six, and a second-class seat for the valet." He turned to Oscar and the grin became knowing again. "Say, you mind if I call you Oscar?"

Very much, Oscar thought, but smiled graciously. "Not at all. Tell me something, Mr. Tabor."

"Horace."

"Yes. There won't be any trouble, will there, about my valet? He's a black man, and we had some difficulties with the train authorities in—where was it, Vail? West Carolina? East Virginia?"

"South Carolina."

"Wherever. They refused to let him eat in the dining car."

"No problem at all," grinned Tabor. "Long as he can afford to pay. Say, they tell me you're traveling with a countess?"

Oscar nodded. "Countess Mathilde de la Môle, of Plaisir." He smiled. "That's not terribly far from Paris, France."

Tabor winked again. "A real looker, they tell me."

With some difficulty, Oscar ignored the implication, and the lickerish gleam, behind Tabor's wink. "A most attractive

33

woman, yes. She's traveling with her escort, a Colonel von Hesse."

"Von Hesse? A Dutchman, huh?"

"He's a German."

"Like I said. How come—" Tabor, glancing over Oscar's shoulder, suddenly cut himself short, set down his glass, and bounced to his feet. *"Baby!"* he said, and his grin was abruptly wider than before, which should have been physiologically impossible.

Both Oscar and Vail stood up, both turned toward the library door.

"What's this I hear about a countess?" she said. She stood smiling at the entrance in a gown of scarlet and gold that was as bright and festive, and as undeserved, as a Christmas gift. The shimmering silk clung to haughty breasts and arched rib cage and flat stomach, and then, below the voluptuous flare of hip, belled out and fell in flounced tiers, billowy with hidden petticoats, to the floor. Without actually being tall, she gave the impression of regal height: she held her slim imperious body gracefully erect, her head proudly poised atop the long slender Nefertiti neck. Her hair was red—no, russet—no, auburn—a lovely, deep mahogany shade that gleamed and glistened in the yellow lamplight. And there was a mass of it, there were piles of it, rich and shiny, there were glittering titian curls of it cascading down to outline the strong feline curve of her cheeks and spill out across her firm square shoulders.

Oscar realized, all at once, that he was gaping. She was quite simply the most beautiful and the most utterly sensuous woman he had ever seen.

"My dear, my dear," said Tabor, bustling across the room, his grin gleaming at her. (The presence of this remarkable woman here in this house—for that matter, the fact of her existence anywhere in the world—went a long way toward explaining that perpetual grin.) He held out his arm at a stiff officious angle and she placed her slender hand upon it. He put his own atop hers, protectively, and led her into the room, his entire body, scalp to toes, clearly turgid with pride.

34

"Gentlemen," Tabor announced, his eyes beaming, "allow me to introduce Elizabeth McCourt Doe. My fiancée."

Her large radiant eyes were the color of violets, and dancing behind them was an unmistakable intelligence that recognized exactly the effect she produced, and found it—what? Entertaining? Amusing? The gown left bare her throat and her long slender arms, and her skin was as smooth as Parian marble, and as white and poreless (and as peerless, Oscar appended later, when all his faculties had returned). Her nose was straight and strong, with finely sculpted, slightly flaring nostrils. Her mouth was just a whisper too wide to be considered perfect by classical standards; but, canted softly in its faint Gioconda smile, it was a lush red remarkable mouth that, all by itself, dramatically and conclusively proved that classical standards, perhaps all of them, were wrong.

"My dear," said Tabor, "this is Mr. Oscar Wilde."

She removed her hand from Tabor's arm and held it out to Oscar. He took it—and felt an erotic shock, swift and startling, dart through his loins. He blinked in surprise and alarm. (Surely everyone in the room had sensed that jolt leap through him? Surely she had?) Quickly he bent over the hand, which was warm and dry against his own clammy, traitorous palm.

"Madam," he said. His voice was unusually thick, a stranger's. He forced himself, an act of conscious will, to look up into those extraordinary violet eyes—much the way, in Germany, in the Harz Mountains, he had once forced himself to peer over the edge of a ragged windswept abyss. He felt now precisely what he had felt then, a sudden wild urge to jump, to leap, to plunge headlong and heedless, wailing with terror and exaltation, down into the giddy depths.

Those eyes narrowed and she smiled her small ironic smile. "I've read your volume of poetry, Mr. Wilde."

"Ah," he said, straightening his back, standing up to his full height, which was all at once too tall. "Have you." He was speech-less if not speechless, and this for the second time in a single night. That grim killer, that Holliday, he too had possessed extraordinary eyes. But those were empty, hollow, ghastly. These were—what *were* they? Worry that out later.

Her hand still lay in his. She said, still smiling, "I think you must be a very wicked man."

He said, "One can only hope so, madam."

He said it without thinking—he had said it, or something like it, many times before—but she laughed easily, tossing her lovely head lightly back as the muscles of her throat played beneath the surface of that smooth incomparable skin. Her white even teeth were small and slightly pointed. Lamplight glinted, gold and copper, along her hair. And Oscar realized that he would be quite ridiculously happy for the remainder of his life if he could spend it making this woman laugh.

"You tease me, Mr. Wilde," she said, her eyes sparkling at him, that amused light dancing behind them. "But may I call you Oscar?"

He inclined his head. "So long, madam, as you call me often." If she wanted laughter, he would provide it.

And, gratifyingly, she laughed again; and then finally, yet still too soon, she slipped her hand from his.

"And this," Tabor told her, "is Mr. Jack Vail. The business manager."

Oscar looked at grinning Tabor with mild surprise; for a few moments he had totally forgotten that the man was there.

Good Lord. She *lived* with him.

Bit of a snag there.

Almost physically, he felt something leave him, flutter like a bird from his breast: a possibility, a hope. A dream.

So much for a lifetime of laughter.

An abrupt and altogether absurd sadness settled over him. (Or was this simply petulance, masking itself as something less trivial?)

She passed in front of Oscar, offering her hand to Vail, and he caught the fragrance of her perfume, something dark and complex, herbs and flowers in a matrix of musk. Even in his preposterous melancholy (or petulance), he found it intoxicating. Preposterously.

Where women were concerned, Vail normally demonstrated the sensitivity of a turnip. But even he was obviously impressed,

36

possibly even intimidated, by Elizabeth McCourt Doe. He had plucked the cigar from his mouth, and now, his brow furrowed, his glance shifting nervously as it looked everywhere but into her eyes, he took her hand and mumbled, "Pleased, I'm sure."

"Come, my dear, come," Tabor told her. "Sit."

With lamplight rippling down the sleek red silk, she moved across the carpet, Tabor at her side. She turned and sat, her back upright, her ankles crossed.

Oscar and Vail returned to their seats, the two of them suddenly an audience.

"Brandy, my dear?" Tabor asked her.

Oscar discovered that he was leaning forward; he sat back.

"Yes, please, Horace," she said. "Thank you." As he busied himself with the brandy bottle, this unlikely fiancé of hers (wasn't there already a Mrs. Tabor lurking somewhere in the wings?), she turned to Oscar. He could feel the weight of her glance along the skin of his face; those bright violet eyes transfixed him. "Now," she said, smiling. "Please. You must tell us about your countess."

Lightness. Lightness is all. "There's very little to tell, madam," he said. "All of us, of course, are in search of something. I, in my humble way, am searching for beauty. My good friend Mr. Vail, like Diogenes, and with as much luck, is searching for an honest man. Colonel von Hesse, the Countess's escort, is searching for God. The Countess, as it happens, is searching for real estate." Specifically, a large productive piece of it firmly attached to a reasonably presentable (and himself unattached) rich man.

"She's traveled with you from New York?"

"From San Francisco."

She smiled. "I imagine that countesses must be very beautiful. Like the princesses in fairy tales." (Princesses: courtly. Yes.) She took the brandy snifter from Tabor, thanked him, turned back to Oscar. "Is she very beautiful, your countess?" she asked as Tabor sat down, grinning, beaming at her with naked and really rather embarrassing adoration.

"I had thought so," Oscar said. "But that was before I met

37

you, madam. Since then, of course, I have reappraised all my notions of beauty, and found them wanting."

Courtly.

She laughed. A wonderful sound: relaxed and musical. Oscar's sadness—if such it had been—was beginning to lift, a mist blown away by the breeze of her laughter. Or by the silent storm of his effort.

"A flatterer, too," she said. "You *are* a wicked man."

"That may be," he said. "But it would be abjectly wicked of me not to give beauty its due."

From the corner of his eye, he had been watching Tabor, trying to gauge the silver baron's reaction to all this. Occasionally Tabor would shoot a quick look at Oscar and at Vail, as though to reassure himself that his guests were still there, still happy; but always he returned his gaze, puppylike, to the woman. The grin never left his face. The man was besotted. Understandably.

She sipped at her brandy. "Is that the only form of wickedness you recognize?"

"For me," he said truthfully, "the only true wickedness is cruelty."

She raised an eyebrow, at once amused and challenging. "And what, then, of Sin?"

"The only true sin," he said, and, to punctuate the statement, sipped at his brandy again, "is boredom."

"A dangerous philosophy." She smiled, the smile hinting that she had a secret fondness for dangerous philosophies. She sipped from her snifter. "I fear you'll corrupt us all."

Oscar returned her smile. It was wonderful, really, this move and countermove behind the brandy snifters. "Nothing would give me greater pleasure," he said.

She laughed again. "I see that I mustn't expose myself to your influence too often."

Off to the left, Vail was fidgeting: legs restlessly moving.

Oscar glanced at Tabor: still mooncalfing. "Then, madam," he said, "by your cruelty to me, you should yourself be guilty of wickedness."

Another laugh. She turned to Vail. "Tell me, Mr. Vail, does your poet always carry on like this?"

Vail shifted in his seat. Eyes dim, mouth tight, he no longer looked comfortable. "He's a great little kidder, ma'am," he said, with a peculiar emptiness in his voice.

She turned back to Oscar. "I read in the newspapers that you met Mr. Walt Whitman at his house in New Jersey."

Oscar nodded. "I did. I admire him very much."

"The man or his poetry?"

He shrugged lightly. "For me, the two are inseparable."

"I've never met him, of course, but I enjoy the poetry. I find it so very"—she cocked her head lightly, smiled—"physical." And so she would've found the man: for two hours old Walt hadn't taken his thorny speckled hand off Oscar's knee. "Don't you?"

"I make no distinction," Oscar said, vaguely aware that Vail was squirming in his seat and digging plump fingers into the snug pocket of his waistcoat, "between the physical and the spiritual."

Vail had produced his watch. "Gee," he announced with elaborate regret, "look at the time. I'm real sorry, folks, but I got to get Oscar here back to the hotel."

Oscar frowned, surprised. "Come now, Vail."

"Nope," said Vail, and stood up. "Sorry, Oscar boy, we got a matinee tomorrow, and then another lecture tomorrow night. And then on Wednesday we got Manitou Springs." He turned to Tabor and Elizabeth McCourt Doe and he made a quick awkward shrug. "You folks understand how it is."

"Sure, sure," said Tabor, grinning as he rose from his chair. "I know how you artistic-type people need your rest." Not at all displeased to see them leave.

Well, to be sure: he had the woman; what did he need with poets and business managers?

Presented with a fait accompli, Oscar pulled himself slowly and reluctantly to his feet. As he did, he looked over at the woman and saw that her glance was traveling, calmly, reflectively, up the length of his frame. When the glance met his, she smiled.

Electricity surged up his spine. His face, he realized, was flushed and taut, flesh suddenly too full for skin.

Betrayed once again by his treacherous, ungainly body.

The woman turned to Tabor. "Perhaps Mr. Wilde can join us tomorrow for breakfast."

For the first time, Tabor's grin vanished. "Gosh, Baby, I've gotta leave early in the morning. That cattle thing, I told you. But *hey*." He turned to Oscar, the grin suddenly back in place. "*You* could come, couldn't you, Oscar? Baby loves company in the morning. Be a real favor to me if you stopped by and joined her. What do you say?"

Oscar looked at the woman, who sat there smiling faintly up at him, violet eyes sparkling over the rim of her brandy snifter.

From the Grigsby Archives

DEAR MARSHAL GRIGSBY,

I understand that you knew my predecessor, the late Mr.
Henry Bettinger, former Sheriff of Leavenworth, Kansas. You
no doubt have heard of his unfortunate and untimely death.
Two months ago the good citizens here appointed me his
successor. I am sure that you and I will enjoy the same
friendly relations that existed between yourself and Mr.
Bettinger while he was alive.

The reason I am writing to you is this. Two nights ago, on
the 1st of March, a young woman was murdered here in
Leavenworth. Her name was Carolyn Mullavey and she was
the wife of Thomas Mullavey, who operates the general store
here. Mr. Mullavey informs me that his wife has a brother, a
Mr. Benjamin Whelan, who lives in Denver. I would be
grateful if you would verify this statement for me, and if you
would verify for me that Mr. Whelan was in Denver on the
night of April 1st, when Carolyn Mullavey's homicide was
perpetrated. If he was not, I would be grateful if you would

41

ascertain his whereabouts on the night of March 1st. If you have reason to believe he was here in Leavenworth, Kansas, I would be grateful if you incarcerated him.

So far, of course, Mr. Whelan is not actually a suspect. But in policework, as you know, it is always necessary to eliminate the innocent in order to determine the guilty.

I have sent a telegram to the Chief of Police there in Denver, Mr. William J. Greaves, which contained a similar request, but so far I have had no response. I have heard some unfortunate stories about Mr. Greaves and so I took it upon myself to write to you, in your capacity as Federal Marshal.

I enclose a clipping from the *Leavenworth Sentinel* which gives some details as to Mrs. Mullavey's death. The actual facts were even worse than those reported there.

If Mr. Whelan, the brother of the deceased, was actually in Denver at the time of the murder, please extend to him my deeply felt sympathy and assure him that I am fully confident we will bring to justice the madman who perpetrated this heinous crime. Scientific policework and careful investigation will produce results every time. As you know, of course.

Thanking you in advance, I am

> Your humble servant,
> Lawrence Draper
> Sheriff of Leavenworth

MUTILATION ON MAIN STREET!
Woman Found Butchered!

A Leavenworth woman, Mrs. Thomas Mullavey, was found savagely mutilated early Thursday morning in the alleyway between Mullavey's General Store and Harper's Hardware Empo-rium. The body was discovered by Cecil Cooper, of Leavenworth, an unemployed house painter who often utilized the alleyway as his "sleeping quarters."

According to recently elected Sheriff Lawrence Draper, Cooper stumbled upon the unfortunate woman's horrible remains at three o'clock on Thursday morning. He immediately notified Deputy Sheriff Orville Cleaver, who, after viewing the mutilated body, promptly roused Sheriff Draper from sleep. Cooper is not suspected, Draper says.

According to Draper, Mrs. Mullavey and her husband had attended last night's lecture by Oscar Wilde, the celebrated English esthetical poet, at the newly built Leavenworth Opera House (see story on page 2), leaving the hall at ten o'clock. She and her husband, the owner of Mullavey's General Store, then returned to their home on Sheridan Street. At twelve o'clock, Mrs. Mullavey, discovering that she and her husband were out of whiskey, left the house with the intention of procuring a bottle from their store on Main Street. Witnesses, said Sheriff Draper, have testified that they saw her walking along Main Street unaccompanied. She was never seen alive again.

Her husband, meanwhile, had fallen asleep and was unaware of the fearful fate that befell his wife until awakened and informed of it by Sheriff Draper.

Dr. Hiram Buckley, who examined the body of Mrs. Mullavey, said that her death apparently was caused by a single wound to the throat, such as might be made by a long-bladed butcher-type knife. Asked to respond to reports that the body had been brutally mutilated, Dr. Buckley declined further comment. Sheriff Draper also refused to discuss the nature of Mrs. Mullavey's dreadful mutilations.

The husband of the deceased was unavailable for comment. Witness Cooper, however, interviewed at the Blarney Stone Pub on Grant Street, provided additional information regarding the mutilations. "It was awful," he said. "He chopped her up like a hog. There were parts of her lying all over the alley." Mrs. Mullavey's ferocious wounds were of such gruesomeness that they cannot be described in a family newspaper.

Mrs. Mullavey, with her vivacious ways and her flaming red hair, was well liked here in Leavenworth, to which she came five years ago from St. Louis, Missouri. Neighbors and friends, all outraged at this despicable act, agreed in describing her as outgoing and gregarious. "She was a swell gal," said neighbor Kathleen Krebs. "Sure, she liked a good time. Don't we all? But there wasn't a mean bone in her entire body."

While admitting that no arrests had been made as yet, Sheriff Draper asserted that several suspects had been interviewed, and he vowed a speedy solution to the case. "I personally promise the good citizens of Leavenworth that I will apprehend the craven coward who perpetrated this horrendous crime. Murderers such as he stand no chance when confronted by the irresistible juggernaut of Scientific policework."

CHAPTER THREE

THE JUNIPER LOGS BURNING in the cast-iron stove had warmed the air in the room and spiced it with the delicate peppery smell of woodsmoke.

"I think the chartreuse," said Oscar thoughtfully. "Yes. Definitely, the chartreuse."

His left arm extended to display the four draped cravats—blue, mauve, chartreuse, and red—Henry Villiers nodded his long black solemn head. He plucked away the chartreuse cravat and hung it carefully over the back of the wooden chair. He slid his right hand under the other cravats, deftly slipped them off, and then turned and carried them back to the closet.

Sitting in the room's only comfortable chair, his legs crossed, wearing black leather slippers lined with rabbit fur and, over his saffron yellow cotton pajamas, a black dressing gown of Japanese silk, Oscar enjoyed his first cigarette of the day.

The night had been lovely and restful, his sleep artfully interwoven with dreams, forgotten now but for the lingering impression of a slow deliberate sensual surfeit. Languorous, pleasantly sated, he sat and watched his exhaled smoke roll into the golden light slanting through the opened lace curtains and become, mag-

45

ically, a precisely defined, incandescent slab of bright white whirls and swirls and spinning convoluted arabesques.

Henry called from the closet, "You be wantin' the green jacket, Mistuh Oscar?"

"Indubitably," said Oscar, and exhaled another elaborate rolling plume. Silently, brilliantly, it flared in the sunlight.

What a truly glorious morning this was. How absolutely top drawer.

It was the sort of morning when even a rustic Denver hotel room could seem as hallowed and sacred as a Doric temple. The sort of morning when the simplest, most mundane objects—the round white porcelain water basin atop the pinewood dresser, the plump white porcelain pitcher beside it, the squat black woodstove, the round red bedposts gleaming in the sunstream— abruptly acquired a profound beauty and significance. Each of these, by its very uniqueness, its irreducible singularity, was suddenly numinous, suddenly resonant with import. Each in its own way was flawless, and each by its perfection implied a higher Perfection which, however transcendent, still somehow lay, miraculously, just within the scope of human understanding and achievement.

Everything this morning, including Oscar, was divine and immortal.

Henry emerged from the closet carrying the green velvet jacket and a white silk shirt with a ruffled front. "You be wantin' the knee britches?"

"Trousers, I think," said Oscar. "The black ones. And the patent leather shoes. Black stockings." Conservative, subdued. Mustn't overwhelm the woman on our first rendezvous.

Henry nodded, set the jacket and shirt upon the quilted bedcover, then returned to the closet.

Had she appeared in his dreams, this miraculous Elizabeth McCourt Doe? Had she stalked through them like a red tigress, those violet eyes glowing in the night?

What a thoroughly stunning, what a remarkable, woman.

And soon, in only an hour or so, he would see her again.

46

Poor Vail had been entirely against this breakfast tryst. Outside Tabor's mansion, climbing into the carriage behind the business manager, Oscar had asked him, "Why the sudden departure? I thought we were supposed to charm this Tabor fellow." He pulled the carriage door shut.

"Yeah?" said Vail. He plucked the cigar from his mouth and turned to him. "You figure raping his doxy, that's gonna charm the guy?"

Oscar was clapped back against the seat as the carriage lurched forward. "Raping? What on earth are you talking about?" But glad that the darkness hid the sudden blush that bloomed across his face.

Vail shook his head. "Jesus Christ, Oscar, I gotta tell you, I never saw anything like it. The two of you were going at each other like a pair of minks. Right in front of the guy. Another five minutes and you would of been humping right there on the floor. Yeah, that would of charmed him pretty good, I guess."

Oscar made his voice curdle with disdain. *"Humping?"* (But, unbidden, inescapable, the vision flashed across the back of his brain: he and the woman atop the Persian carpet, a tangle of white arms and legs, a tumble of red hair.)

"Look," Vail said. "You got to forget this breakfast deal tomorrow."

"Don't be absurd. I've already told them I'll be there. He asked me himself. You heard him."

"Oscar, I'm telling you, the woman is poison. Poison. You get involved with her and Tabor's gonna find out. Nah, you think. Not him. Sure, right, he looks like a dope. He acts like a dope. He *is* a dope, prob'ly. But he's rich, Oscar boy. He's powerful. And people like to tell stuff to rich folks. The servants, the neighbors. Believe you me, he'll find out. And he's not gonna take it kindly, you putting the hose to his chippy."

"Putting the *hose?*"

"He could hurt you, Oscar. Hurt you bad."

"The man is three feet tall, Vail. What will he do, kick me in the shins?"

47

As the streetlight passed across Vail's face, his eyes narrowed. "What do you figure it costs, a town like this, filled with six-guns, for him to get someone to plug you?"

"I couldn't begin to imagine."

"About thirty-five cents."

"This is ridiculous," Oscar said. "I'm merely going to breakfast. Nothing more."

Vail shook his head firmly. "You got to forget it."

"Now see here, Vail. When it comes to my business dealings—costs, finances, guarantees—I'm perfectly happy to listen to your no doubt sage advice. Providing sage advice is what you're paid for, after all. But outside the framework of commerce, my life is my own. I've been asked to breakfast with Mrs. Doe. I am going to breakfast with Mrs. Doe. Is that understood?"

"Oscar boy, there ain't nothing at all that's outside the framework of commerce."

Oscar frowned in annoyance. "A typically American remark. In Europe, even in England, we understand that life isn't merely a matter of shopkeepers and tradesmen. There is, thank goodness, an entirely separate universe. Of Beauty. Of Truth. Of Compassion and Nobility."

"Yeah, well, first of all, this ain't Europe. And second, I notice you generally got a pretty good idea, every night, what the receipts are gonna be. Down to the penny. You count the house pretty good for a poet."

"Poetry," Oscar announced, "is by no means incompatible with arithmetic. Look at the ancient Greeks."

"Jeez," said Vail, "that's all we need, the ancient Greeks again."

Oscar stared at him. "And what does that mean?"

Vail shook his head, waved his hand. "Nothing, nothing."

"Are we back to young Mr. Ruddick now?"

"I didn't say a word about the fella."

"I know your feelings on the subject."

"Look, all I said was that maybe he was a bit on the lavender side. I didn't mean nothing personal."

48

"Mr. Ruddick is an extremely sensitive young man. He shows great promise as a poet."

"Right. Right. He's swell. You want him along on the tour, he comes along. I'm flexible, right? I can compromise. So how come you can't? Oscar boy, for your own good, you got to forget about seeing this chippy tomorrow."

"Permit me to determine where my own good lies. I was invited. I am going."

Sadly, Vail shook his head. "She's poison, Oscar. I'm telling you."

"Perhaps, but the fact is, I'm not having *her* for breakfast."

Vail frowned glumly. "Yeah, well. We'll see about that."

And they had sat in silence, the light from the streetlamps ticking slowly over them, until they returned to the hotel.

Now, sitting in his room, Oscar blew another stream of smoke at the slab of sunlight.

Poor Vail. Impossible, of course, for him to comprehend how two souls might come together in a companionship that was spiritual, literary, Platonic.

The poor man would never understand that each soul possessed, as it were, its own distinctive vibration. That when a particular soul—through one of those lovely tricks of frivolous Fate—came upon another which vibrated at the same frequency, it began at once to hum. Like two tuning forks of identical pitch—which need never actually physically touch each other—the two souls beautifully resonated in sympathy.

So it had happened with himself and Elizabeth McCourt Doe.

Oh, no question that the woman was attractive. Yes, that lavish titian hair, those uncanny violet eyes, those wide red lips, those firm full breasts, that unsullied skin, that long lithe body so exquisitely and extravagantly sensual . . .

No question at all.

But of course it was not this which fascinated him. Well—he smiled—to be entirely honest, it was not this only.

No, far more than her undeniable physical beauty, it was the beauty of her soul, incandescent behind those uncanny violet eyes, that drew him irresistibly to her. It was her soul's obvious

49

compatibility and harmony with his own that drew the two of them irresistibly toward each other.

Poor Vail. A decent enough chap. Good hearted even if mercantile. But of course the union of two pure souls was something he could never fathom.

From the closet Henry came carrying the boots, the socks, the black trousers, and a pair of black silk undershorts patterned with grey fleurs-de-lis. He set the boots on the floor and arranged the rest on the bed beside the other clothing. "Anything else, Mistuh Oscar?"

Oscar blew another cone of smoke. "Could you hire up a carriage and have it waiting outside in, say, forty-five minutes?"

Henry nodded his white-haired head.

"And could you tell Mr. Ruddick that I won't be joining him this morning for breakfast?"

"Mistuh Ruddick," Henry said, "he already left. He say he goin' up to the mountains, talk to the wildflowers."

Oscar smiled. "How very fortunate for the wildflowers. They're certain to find Mr. Ruddick's conversation stimulating."

Henry nodded again, his black face, as always, expressionless. "Yes suh."

"Thank you, Henry. I'll see you at twelve-thirty then, before the matinee."

"Yes suh, Mistuh Oscar."

As Henry left the room, Oscar stubbed his cigarette out in the ashtray. He stood, untied the silk belt at his waist, slipped off the robe, lay the robe across the chair, unbuttoned his pajama top, stripped it off, lay that over the robe. He untied the string of his pajama bottoms, awkwardly stepped out of them, lay them over the rest, and then naked he padded over to the full-length oval mirror.

Frowning in disapproval, he looked down the length of his pale reflected body. Doughy flesh, podgy breasts, slack saddles of meat slung over broad hips, white stomach sagging over the presumptuous thatch of black hair and that limp comedy trio dangling below, Freddy Phallus and the Testicle Twins.

Ah well.

What we have here is not precisely the classical ideal. Not precisely Adonis.

Narcissus, yes, perhaps; but a Narcissus working under enormous handicaps.

Good shoulders, though. And rather shapely legs.

It was possible, of course, that she liked shoulders and legs; that she favored them.

It was possible, of course, that she did not.

A new regimen, perhaps. Brisk walks in the morning.

Perhaps a change of diet. Something Spartan. Watercress and champagne. An occasional stalk of celery.

For a few weeks. For a few days, anyway. To see how it went.

He turned sideways, sucked in his belly. Better. With a little imagination, and perhaps a little myopia, he might pass for a prizefighter. One of those dim pugilists who pounded each other to bare-knuckled oblivion amid cigar smoke and shouted wagers in the London clubs.

He put his fists up in approved pugilistic fashion, moved them in determined circles.

He frowned again.

Charming. Here we have a poet, a playwright, an Aesthete, the heir apparent to Ruskin, to Pater, who at his very best resembles a modern-day gladiator, soft and seedy and sad.

He lowered his hands, turned to face the mirror, permitted his stomach to slide back to its natural position. Then, stepping lightly forward with his left foot, swinging his long right arm in a graceful sweep, he presented himself an elaborate formal bow.

He looked up into the mirror and broadly smiled. "Madam," he intoned, "we who are about to die salute you."

<hr />

No butler this time; she opened the door herself. The elegant tumble of red hair shimmering about her oval face like an aura, she wore a green satin dress that was, technically, an extremely proper affair: gravely long-sleeved, severely buttoned up the bodice to a trim, prim collar. But from waist to arch of throat the fabric embraced her flesh as though she had grown into it, com-

51

pleting the process only moments before; and proudly, mockingly, it revealed all the magnificence it pretended to conceal. Her red lips smiled faintly, her violet eyes glittered. "Oscar," she said. "Come in." By daylight the color of those eyes was even more extraordinary.

He stepped into the hallway and she closed the door behind him.

"I gave the servants the day off," she said, smiling still.

"Ah," said Oscar.

He thought suddenly, *Ah?* What a brilliant rejoinder.

He could smell her fragrance again, the musk, the forbidden spices, the pale white flowers that bloomed only in the light of the full moon; and perhaps it was this that had made his head suddenly drain itself of thought, become as taut and buoyant as a soap bubble. Soon it would pop off his neck and go sailing up to bounce lightly against those dreary nailhead moldings along the ceiling.

"Come along," she said. Lightly she touched his arm: beneath her fingers, fire flashed along his skin.

He followed her down the hall as though leashed to her by that dark sweet streamer of scent.

Suddenly he remembered seeing once, in Ireland, in late summer at Lough Bray in the Wicklows, the neighbor's collie loping behind his father's setter bitch, the male dog's thin aristocratic nose twitching behind the other's frisking rump, the two dogs trotting in file through the angled amber light of early evening to disappear among the long purple shadows of the forest.

The setter's fur had been red as well.

The recollection of that moment, its resemblance to the present one, did not even slightly distress him; indeed, and rather to his surprise, it inflamed him all the more.

At the base of the broad stairway, she stopped and turned to him. Smiling, she put her hand atop the mahogony rail. "Are you terribly hungry?" she asked.

In fact he was famished. The mere idea of living on watercress and celery had generated a ravenous appetite. And yet some spirit within him, some guardian angel more wily than he, counseled a show of indifference.

"Not terribly, no. Why?" My *God*, but she was beautiful.

"Horace won't be back till late this afternoon."

"I see." He didn't, really; just then he could recall only vaguely who Horace was.

"We'll have breakfast later," she said. She smiled. "Afterward."

"Ah." Afterward?

And then she was coming closer, the luminous violet eyes peering up at him, the red lips of her smile slowly parting, the slender hand rising to his face.

For the briefest of instants he hesitated. For perhaps a second, thoughts of Dishonor and Disgrace, Sin and Six-guns chased like collies and setters around his brain, collided, rocked and scuffled one atop the other.

And then the hand was settling at the back of his head, like a door closing to shut out the cold, and the lips were against his, soft and moist; and then a slick, knowing, pointed tongue was tapping, teasing, at his teeth.

All at once, as though toppling from a precipice down through perfumed clouds, he surrendered to this amazing moment, telling himself that soon it would be a part of the past, over with and done. The past could be managed; it was only the future that presented difficulties and decisions. Later, afterward—yes, at breakfast—his life would continue its familiar forward march.

Set suddenly free of his will, his hands moved on their own and slipped around her narrow waist and slid down the electric smoothness of the satin to cup her sleek round buttocks. The nerve endings along his fingertips had multiplied a thousandfold: they could detect, and celebrate, every individual silken thread of the dress; and, still more remarkable, every individual tingling atom of the firm straining flesh beneath.

Her breasts were cushioned against his chest, her leg was nuzzling between his. Her tongue roiled in his mouth. The air was dense with the dusky intoxicating smoke of her scent.

53

His body was adrift, bobbing on a tropic sea where the woman's deep sultry currents met his own, the two giddy streams merging to carry him off, blindly, relentlessly. From a distance, far back in the remaining sliver of mind that still watched and noted and judged, he had no idea, none at all, where they might sweep him. Nor did he care.

Swept away, he thought.

Dear God, he thought, *a cliché*.

Her hand snaked up his thigh and found him, and he stopped caring about this as well.

From the Grigsby Archives

MARCH 15, 1882

TO:
U.S. MARSHAL ROBERT J. GRIGSBY
FEDERAL BUILDING
DENVER, COLORADO
VICTIM FEBRUARY 14 KNIFING DEATH HERE
PROSTITUTE SALLY ZUVAH STOP AMERICAN BORN
GERMAN DESCENT 40 YEARS 110 LBS 5 FOOT 4
INCHES STOP YES RED HAIR STOP SINGLE THROAT
WOUND NEARLY SEVERING HEAD CAUSE OF DEATH
STOP VISCERA REMOVED PLACED BESIDE BODY
PRESUMABLY BY KILLER STOP UTERUS EXCISED
AND UNFOUND STOP PLEASE EXPLAIN SOONEST
YOUR REASON FOR INQUIRY

FROM:
DETECTIVE INSPECTOR CARL LOGAN
SAN FRANCISCO POLICE DEPARTMENT
SAN FRANCISCO, CALIFORNIA

CHAPTER FOUR

"THE REAL POWER TO create," Oscar pronounced, "lies with the artisans, the people that work for you and make things for you. The great trouble in America is that you give your work over to mere machines. Until you change this you will find little true art."

How many times had he delivered this lecture? Fifteen, twenty?

However many it had been, he had never delivered it before with such élan, such effortless consummate skill.

Earlier today, the matinee had gone badly. After his morning with Elizabeth McCourt Doe, his knees had been weak, his delivery weaker. The thin crowd had been restive, distracted, and he had plodded through the English Renaissance like a mule through a bog, thinking only of its end.

(Afterward, a sour and suspicious Vail had asked him how the breakfast had gone. "Dreadful," Oscar had told him. "The local minister was present, and also three ladies from the Women's Temperance Society. My eyes glazed over so badly that for several moments I thought I had gone blind.")

But Oscar had napped before supper, a light, restful sleep threaded with vivid visions of his morning, and now he felt

56

expansive, weightless and airy, and yet somehow more charged with himself, with his own unique potency, than he had ever been in his life.

This was something more than mere self-confidence. It was a feeling almost blasphemous, something akin to what a god might feel when, out of ennui perhaps, he visited the shrine where he was worshiped.

And, strangely, it enabled him to see the text of his lecture with new eyes. He detected in the sentences and paragraphs subtleties of thought, felicities of expression, which for some reason had escaped his attention till now.

And it enabled him, as he delivered the lecture, to play with the thing. He paused now, and he emphasized, where before no emphasis or pause had existed. He teased out the length of vowels, clipped the consonants, rolled the words up from his diaphragm to his throat and then down along his tongue. Tonight the words were notes of music; tonight he was the instrument and the musician who played them.

The nap had helped him, certainly. But more important, *she* was here tonight.

"The basis of our work in England is that we have brought together the handicraftsman and the artist. Think not that these can be isolated. They must work together. The School of Sculpture in Athens and the School of Painting in Venice kept the work of these countries at the head of the world."

She sat, she and Tabor, in the box seats at stage right. Behind them in the box were a few other Denver luminaries, four men looking as stiff in starched collars and black ties as Indian maharajahs. Perhaps they were bankers, or perhaps they were dead.

Tabor was not grinning tonight. He sat in his red plush chair with the epic seriousness of a monumental bronze, his lower lip protuding thoughtfully below the stuffed sparrow of a mustache, his balding, egg-shaped head nodding from time to time in ponderous approval.

Tonight she wore a flounced dress of gray satin, a broad bonnet of matching silk, a stole of elegant ermine, white as a snowbank below the Titian fall of her hair. She sat demurely, her hands clasped together on her lap, and no one who observed her now could possibly imagine that only this morning those hands had been stroking and kneading his trembling flesh and groping between his legs. Oscar could scarcely imagine it himself.

But on her red lips played that small, knowing, Gioconda smile.

"All the arts are fine arts. There is no art that is not open to the honor of decoration and the rules of beauty."

Her white breasts are perfectly rounded at the bottom, and they slope down along their upper surface in a graceful arc to broad, pale pink, puckered aureoles and stiff fragrant nipples the thickness of fingertips; and, kneeling upright and naked on the huge four-poster bed, her long body at once lean and voluptuous, she offers them to him cupped in slender hands as he buries his head between them and inhales the impossible dizzying scent. Moans like small trapped animals move in his throat. Neither of them has said a word since her "Afterward" and his "Ah."

"Think of those things which inspired the artist of the Gothic school of Pisa. The artist saw brilliantly lighted palaces, arches and pillars of marble and porphyry. He saw noble knights with glorious mantles flowing over their mail as they rode along in the sunlight."

He lifted the glass from the lectern, raised it to his mouth. As he sipped—the water was cold and tasted faintly but not unpleasantly of sulfur—he glanced around the dim opera house.

The room was full tonight, row after row of silent disembodied heads and shoulders rising in tiers to the shadows at the far wall; more people, these equipped with arms and legs, crowded the aisles.

And they were enrapt, all of them, gazing up at him as though mesmerized.

And it was not the message (despite its patent brilliance and profundity) that so bedazzled them; it was the messenger. He

58

could have—had he chosen to—declaimed a string of non-sense syllables. For some of them, doubtless, he was doing so now.

There was this to be said about an audience: it reflected back to the speaker his own excellence, his own power. Like a mirror. Like a lover.

For the first time, Oscar understood the terrible addictive intoxication of the actor, the priest, the demagogue.

"He saw, too, groves of oranges and pomegranates, and through these groves he saw the most beautiful women that the world has ever known."

Astride him, the slick strong walls of her sex gripping at his stiffness, her red hair draped in curtains along his face, she turns her head slightly to the right and sucks in through pursed lips and clenched teeth a long shivering sibilant breath. He lifts his own head from the satin pillow and locates her wide wet mouth, her adroit slippery tongue. His hands, amazed at their good fortune, stagger across the opulence of pliant, and compliant, flesh. He can feel his spine becoming molten as, too soon, too soon, unstoppable, his climax builds.

"One of the most absurd things I ever saw was young ladies painting moonrises on a bureau and sunsets on a dinner plate. Some consideration of the use to which the article is to be put should enter into the mind of the artist. It is well enough to have moonrises and sunsets, but we are not particularly pleased to dine on them."

Appreciative laughter rippled through the audience—followed, as often happened on the tour, by the isolated lunatic chortle of some buffoon who had finally seen the point, or finally seen that he was supposed to. (Perhaps, lecture after lecture, dogging him from city to city, it had been all along this same buffoon.)

He glanced at her theater box, casually, not lingering on any of the faces, even hers; the lecturer calmly surveying his audience.

Her smile had widened now.

He felt a tremor of pride and triumph. And felt also, under his knee britches, behind the providential shelter of the lectern, a stiffening in his crotch. He took another sip of water.

Pity he couldn't dip behind the curtain and douse poor Freddy.

"These things, and many others, are what your schools of art should teach your young people."

Afterward, his mind is fragmented. An inchoate surge of feelings—none of them attached to any rational thought—lashes around the rubble like waves around splintered rocks. Gratitude and awe seem to be the major streams, but there is also disbelief and guilt and even a small measure of unease.

She lies beside him curled in a comma, head on his shoulder, leg across his stomach.

"I am," he says, "astonished." His voice is not yet his own.

Along the skin of his upper arm, he feels her lips move in a smile. Then she turns her head and her small pointed teeth bite lightly into his flesh. "It was Fate," she says.

He smiles; he shares the sentiment, of course. "But which, exactly, was fated? My astonishment? Or this?" He waves a hand to indicate their bodies, the bed, this particular moment into which the storm of previous moments has swept them, driftwood, jetsam.

"Both," she says. "All of it. Everything."

"I know that this is absurd," he begins. "We met only yesterday. But I really must tell you—"

The tip of her finger lands softly atop his mouth, closing it.

"Don't," she says. "I know already. Don't say it. If you put it into words, it will start to die."

"We will teach our youths to love nature more. When we can teach them that no blade of grass and no flower is without beauty, then we will have achieved much."

60

She is sucking his left nipple, her tongue moving in small, even, maddening circles along its compacted crust. Taut thin ligaments within his body, their existence previously unsuspected, connect this nipple to the back of his neck, to his spine, to his groin, to the soles of his feet.

While she silently suckles, he silently sulks. He is still smarting at her prohibition. There is so much nameless new emotion dawning within him. There is so much to be said. And how will he ever know what all this actually is, unless he shapes it with language?

Words for him are toys, tools, currency, plumage; they are his métier. Denied them, how will he win her?

Could he ever really wish to win someone who refuses him the means to do so?

For the moment, the answer clearly is yes.

Her soft thick hair trails against his chest as her mouth licks and nips and sucks down along his belly. Chills unfold at his back. Finally, she engulfs him.

"What you have daily before you, what you love most dearly and believe in most fondly, that is where your art may be found. All around you lie the conditions of art. No country can compare with America for its resources of beauty."

She is sprawled across the satin coverlet, her arms outstretched atop the red gleaming outspread fan of hair, her legs apart, one knee drawn up. His kisses explore the crook of elbow, furrow of rib, hollow of throat, swell of shoulder, curve of jaw. The vulnerable V formed by opened lips at the corner of her mouth. The cunning coil of cartilage at her ear.

His heart pounding against his temples, he does things he has never done before, because they were forbidden; does them now because they were; because somewhere they still are.

With his tongue he licks the salt from her armpits, traces and retraces the tufts of her hair. He savors the taste of her navel. He tastes the savor of her toes. (At *this little piggy stayed home* she sighs his name; and that portion of his soul not suffused with lust suddenly fills with manly pride.) His fingertip pries and prods between the cleft of her globular buttocks. His face roots in the fur and the folds at the juncture of her legs and he swallows her sweet astringent juices. Soon he employs not only tongue and lips but also nose and chin and fingers: a mole. He is crawling, Good Lord, back into the womb.

She moans and her hands clutch at his hair.

"Oscar," she says, and her voice is frayed, hurried. "Come inside me. Please. Now."

"Let it be for you here in America to create an art by the hands of the people that will please the world. There is nothing in the world around you that art cannot ennoble."

Their mutual rhythm grows more rapid as their bodies, locked at the hip, buck and wallop. Her legs are coiled around him, her fists grasp at the sides of the pillow as though she fears she will soar off it into the air. Her lower lip is caught between her teeth and she is panting, her chiseled nostrils flared.

He is climbing, climbing. Once again that invincible energy begins to coalesce in the pockets and burrows of his body, the secret vents and channels. Soon, soon, soon.

She moans from low within her throat, moans once, then moans again, longer this time and at higher pitch. The moans become a wail, a slowly rising keen as she arches her body toward his, as tense as a hunter's bow.

And he is there to meet her. Ball lightning rumbles down his spine and up his legs, trembles for an instant at his center, then all at once, as he lunges deep deep deep inside her, into her very

62

core, it erupts through him in an explosion of infinite overwhelming sweetness and power that shatters the structure of his being and sends shards and shreds and blistered fragments spinning out across the universe.

The applause began off toward the left of the auditorium—curious how it arose each time from some new locus—and then undulated to the right, growing in strength.

He stepped aside from the lectern and with slow solemn dignity he bowed once from the waist toward the crowd.

The applause thickened most satisfactorily.

He turned to the left, to the box that held a handful of beaming frontier nonentities in formal wear. He bowed.

He turned to the right, toward the box that held her and Tabor and the local eminences. Tabor had rediscovered his grin and he was clapping his small hands with a furious delight. The eminences, while showing somewhat less exuberance, in their stiff way still seemed eminently satisfied.

And she, she was smiling widely as daintily she clapped, as her violet eyes met his.

He bowed. And although he took care not to bow even a millimeter more deeply than he had before, this time as he bent forward his blood rushed, hot and thick, to his head.

CHAPTER FIVE

A LURID GLARE SPILLED FROM the windows of the saloons, splashed across the crooked wooden sidewalks, sputtered through the churning crowds that bumped and jostled him as they babbled by.

The smells here were worse than any he had ever encountered. The sour, feral odor curling off the unwashed bodies of the gaunt-faced cowboys and the grime-coated metal workers. The stinking sulfurous smoke of the smelters, hanging overhead in a low gray perpetual cloud, blotting out the stars. The reek of blood and manure and animal terror drifting from the nearby stockyards. And—dense, vile, almost palpable—the mephitic stench of raw sewage floating from the river.

More intense even than the smells was the endless noise. Freight cars rumbled, locomotives groaned and hissed. Horses clopped, carriages rattled. Children bawled and whooped and screamed; grown men chittered and chattered, bellowed and roared.

It was all too much: the crowds, the stink, the confining walls of clatter.

The garish light.

He needed the darkness. His work demanded the darkness.

The dirt street on which finally he found himself was narrow and dim, lighted only infrequently by gaslamps overhead. On each side of it, wooden shacks and shanties stood in low, cramped, uneven file, like a row of worn and rotten teeth. The smells still lingered—the slaughterhouse, the smelter, the sewage—but here only a few people moved about, drunks and derelicts slowly puzzling their way through the desolate shadows.

Where is the whore?

Soon, soon, he assured the sudden harsh voice within him; and he smiled.

This was a new and astonishing thing: a benefaction. The entities who shared his dominion over the primal forces, the Lords of Light—they now communed with him directly. They permitted him, at last, to hear their speech, low and guttural yet thrilling. In recognition of his own authority, his dedication, his adamantine purpose, they had granted him this unique gift.

There were two voices, one basso profundo, resonant, gravelly; the other, higher in pitch, slightly less raspy. One day he would work out their exact connection to each other, and to him. One day that might be amusing.

Astonishing that they would finally speak; yes, but he had of course not been astonished. When first heard, they had come to him as naturally, as inevitably, as the sound of his own breath. He had been—all along, but unwittingly—preparing for them; he realized, at the first moment he heard them speak, that all along he had been expecting them.

He was grateful for their presence. For lately he had been— not confused, no. But lately the cloudy moments—those periods when time itself somehow guttered out and a blackness engulfed his mind—those moments seemed to be growing longer and more frequent. One moment he would be walking calmly along, wrapped securely in the familiar pretense of day-to-day, hiding,

65

hidden; and then suddenly, unaccountably, the blackness would sweep over him. Later, ten minutes, half an hour, he would abruptly find himself, as though hurled there by some silent and invisible tempest, in a different neighborhood, on an unfamiliar street.

It never happened during the quest itself, of course. While he was stalking, nothing at all could diminish the power of his concentration: this was as focused then, and intense, as the hissing white barb of a welder's torch.

No, only during the dismal day-to-day, when discretion demanded that he mask himself, masquerade as merely one more puny, ineffectual nothing, indistinguishable from the others.

It was the result, no doubt, of the massive, superhuman energy he expended during the quests. No one, not even he, could share the furious energy of the gods, meld his own flame with the Infinite Flame that roared at the core of the cosmos, without somehow suffering.

He was prepared to suffer—had he not suffered for years? Had he not undergone exquisite torments of flesh and spirit? The flails, the belts, the ropes that dug into his skin until it sweated pus and blood? Chafing in his own foul excrement, blistering in the sting of his own sour urine. And hearing all the while, in the background, the mocking laughter of the Red Bitch.

The suffering had strengthened him. Yes: purified his will, cleansed him of the dross, the pollution, that held mere mortals captive, earthbound.

If need be, he would suffer again. He would survive it; he would prevail.

But the voices helped. They strengthened his resolve, refined his purpose.

Not that his purpose had ever faltered. Not that he had ever, even for a moment, doubted the necessity, the urgency, of his mission.

No, but by their presence the voices added strength to a strength that was already incalculable.

Where? Where is the whore?

66

It was near now, the creature destined for him: he knew this. Already he had seen others of its kind, only a few feet from the sidewalk, leaning out the windows of their squalid shacks, their slack faces feigning desire, their flaccid breasts draped like rotting fruit between the open folds of their gowns.

Perfect. The night was perfect. Only a few souls stumbled through the streets, and these were debased, furtive beings so blinded by their own sordid lusts that he would be invisible.

Oh, it *was* delicious, was it not? Could anything, could even the ritual itself, the joining, the union, could even that be sweeter than this triumph of secrecy? To walk as softly as a shadow among them, unknown, unsuspected—

The whore!

Yes, yes. Yes.

This one!

This one, yes, was perfect.

Its face grotesquely powdered and painted, it leaned toward him from its window, its fat red mouth twisted in a leer. A small oil lamp on the sill beside it cast a trembling yellow light that seemed to set the creature's bright red hair aflame.

"Only three dollars," it said, its voice tattered from a lifetime of debauch. "Ten dollars gets you all night."

He glanced up and down the street. No one watching.

Dare he do it?

Always, before, in the alleyways, in the dim sidewalk alcoves rank with the fumes of rotten garbage, he had found union quickly, performed the ritual as swiftly as possible. Detection loomed in every passing moment, in every approaching footfall. He had never been allowed—he had never permitted himself— to prolong it. To bring it to a level of perfection, of artistry, about which, he now suddenly understood, he had always dreamed.

Time, then, would become irrelevant. There would be no limits, no boundaries at all. Except those which in the process he set, or discovered, for himself.

The slow unhurried opening of flesh into blossoms of scarlet; the slow unhurried scrape of knife against pink bone,

The prospect made him breathless, dizzy.

But dare he do it?

Do it. Do it. Take this one.

Yes.

Yes.

He stepped to the entrance and knocked. The pinewood door, thin and shabby, rattled in its frame.

BOOK TWO

CHAPTER SIX

THAT WEDNESDAY MORNING, as usual, Grigsby woke up and wished he was dead.

It was dawn. Even with the curtains drawn, the light a blurred uncertain gray, he knew it was dawn. Since Clara left, no matter how much he drank the night before, no matter how early or how late he went to bed, he always awoke at dawn. It was as though some pain-loving, pain-seeking part of him insisted on his being present at sunrise, so he could suffer through every single long aching moment of daylight.

His lips were parched and cracked; overnight his tongue and teeth had produced a fine thick crop of moss His lungs were clotted with phlegm—it had been their rattle, as they lurched for breath, that snapped him awake, hurled him back from oblivion into a world, and a life, and a bed, in which he had virtually no interest.

Stale fumes of cheap perfume made the air seem like some dense substance too thick to sustain life, certainly too thick to breathe. The smell was sickly sweet, spiky with the sharp, sour-oatmeal tang of dried sweat. The sweat might be his, it sometimes was, but who belonged to the perfume?

71

He turned his head to the left—slowly, cautiously, so that it wouldn't split down the middle.

Above the brown woolen blanket poked a bundle of blond hair, showing an inch or so of gray roots on either side of a ragged part.

For an empty moment he had no idea whose head it was.

And then, his heart dipping in his chest, he realized.

Brenda.

Jesus.

Had he really been drunk enough to fuck Brenda again?

At the thought of drink, or maybe at the thought of fucking Brenda, his stomach reeled; hot bile foamed at the back of his throat. He swallowed it down, tossed aside the blanket, and slowly pulled his big weary frame upright. Carefully, he swung his legs off the mattress. Bones creaked loudly in his left knee— his body reminding him, once again, that it was turning into stone.

He was wearing his union suit, so maybe he hadn't actually fucked Brenda after all.

He was exhausted. Sleep no longer comforted; it left him more weary than a day in the saddle.

His stomach heaved again.

He stood, swayed slightly, and then staggered from the bedroom that he and Clara had shared for four years, tottered down the hallway where Clara had sometimes sung softly to herself as she passed through on her errands, where the children had run and played and hooted. Bits of grit clung to the cold soles of his feet. He stumbled into the bathroom that Clara had kept spotlessly clean—this had been one of the first houses in the neighborhood with indoor plumbing—and he hobbled over to the toilet.

The curtains were open; gray light seeped into the room. In the toilet, circling the bowl at the waterline, was a ragged ring of brown fur. The moment he saw it, his stomach erupted.

➤   ➤

He felt flimsy, fragile, made of sticks and string and rice paper. His skin itched, not on the surface, but below it, as though the

72

hair on his body was growing backward. His shoulders were slumped, his head was bowed as he sat on the rim of the bathtub and stared down at the tile floor. Yellow splotches at the base of the toilet bowl. Small spidery coils of gray hair scattered about.

Clara had been so damn proud of that floor—it was crazy, the way she'd carried on. *Real* tile, she'd grinned proudly, her big brown eyes wide and excited, her face slightly flushed.

As though it was silver or gold.

Maybe he should rip it out and send it off to her. They'd paid for it with money from her inheritance. It really belonged to her.

He could box it up, freight it by train to San Francisco. With a note. Here, Clara, take the fucking floor, you've got everything else, you might as well have this too.

He didn't want the fucking thing.

When you came right down to it, he didn't want the fucking house.

He should've moved out. At the beginning, as soon as she left. (She wasn't coming back, not ever—it was time to face it.) Should've sold the place, got himself a room at one of the hotels. Fresh linen. Maid service. (And some of the maids, he knew, had a pretty broad-minded notion of service.) A good restaurant downstairs, tablecloths, smiling waiters who served up fried eggs and crisp bacon in the morning.

His stomach twisted.

He stood, opened the medicine cabinet with a trembling hand, groped past the cough elixir (unused, untouched since the children left), and plucked out the pint of bonded bourbon.

He uncorked the bottle, raised it to his mouth, took a swallow, felt the whiskey scald its way down his throat. As the warmth went glowing out along the old familiar pathways, his stomach gurgled and cooed like a baby at the breast.

He looked at himself in the mirror.

His eyes were rimmed with red, as though someone had poked at them—someone with a sharp stick and a mean streak. His gray hair was matted. (Clara had always made fun of his hair in the morning, the way sleep had poked it into fuzzy tufts at the back.) His skin was gray and blotched and lined; along his cheeks

73

and nose, narrow red veins traced whorls and curlicues. His stubble was pure white now, an old man's, not a speck of black in it anywhere, not a one.

One day you wake up and you look in the mirror and you discover that you're an old man.

And one day you wake up and you discover that you're dead.

He said aloud, "Grigsby, you are one pathetic son of a bitch."

He took another swallow of bourbon.

Better. The whiskey was driving its core of warmth down through the hollow center of his being.

He was beginning to feel half human again. Half human was about the best he ever managed.

Now if he could get himself cleaned up and dressed and away from the house before Brenda figured out that he was gone.

➤   ➤

She came into the kitchen while he sat gulping his coffee at the table. Making the coffee had been a mistake.

She was wearing an old pink bathrobe of Clara's, one that Clara had left forgotten at the rear of the bedroom closet, and for an instant Grigsby wanted to leap up and rip it off her back.

His fury surprised him. And then somehow, in the midst of his surprise, the anger dissipated.

These days none of his emotions lasted for very long. Not fury, not surprise.

Self-contempt—but that wasn't an emotion.

Fuck the robe. What difference did it make if Brenda wore the damn thing?

He set the coffee cup down atop the red and white checkered oilcloth that covered the table. (Clara would've hated it, but it was easier to keep clean than wood.) He lifted his cigarette from the ashtray.

Brenda smiled at him—she was a bit blurry, like a photograph not quite in focus—and padded around behind him, put her heavy arms around his neck. "How's my big man this morning?"

Sucking on the cigarette, he concealed a cringe of distaste. This was what she always said in the morning, whenever he had

74

been lonely enough, desperate enough, drunk enough, to bring her here for the night.

He grunted then, his standard morning greeting, deliberately cool, almost gruff. He always hoped that by refusing her any real conversation, she would one day stop trying to have one. So far, this had never worked.

She put her cheek next to his. Her hair was stiff and prickly against his skin, like dried grass. "Let me fix you up some food," she said. "You're a growing boy, Bob. You need your vittles." Her cheek pillowed out against his as she smiled.

This was something else she always said.

And that was the problem with Brenda. (One of them, anyway.) Give her the same damn situation and she would say exactly the same damn thing. Every time. Regular as a banker's bowels. And whatever it was she said, you could tell from her smile, all sugary and pleased with herself, that she still thought it was cute as kittens. The first time, maybe it had been. (He couldn't remember, but he doubted it.) Now, after ten or twenty or fifty times, whenever she did it he wanted to scream.

He told her, "I'm not hungry." And then—reluctantly, because her pitiful gratitude at his small kindnesses always shamed him—he added, "Thanks."

She squeezed his neck and again he felt her smile against his cheek. "Yeah," she said. "I reckon maybe you had your fill last night."

Jesus.

He *had* fucked her.

He sighed. He lifted his cup and took a bitter, penitential swallow of coffee.

" 'M I gonna see you tonight?" she asked him.

Not if he stayed sober. "Don't know," he said. "Lot of work to do."

"Well, you know where I live."

He grunted. He was able to make each grunt identically non-committal to the grunt before.

She smiled again. He thought, I'll keep the home fires burning.

She said, "I'll keep the home fires burning."

He grunted.

She chose to take this particular grunt as an endearment, and nuzzled her nose into his neck.

That was another problem with Brenda. She saw anything short of a punch in the gut as affection.

And even if he were the kind of asshole who punched out women, how the hell do you punch out a woman who was hurting so badly for some kindness? Any kindness at all? Be like kicking a little puppy dog.

The main problem with Brenda, when you got right down to it, was that she wasn't Clara. And he couldn't really blame her for that. Wasn't her fault.

The main problem with him was that he deserved Brenda, or someone like her, more than he had ever deserved Clara.

He finished off the rest of his coffee. "Gotta go," he said.

She stepped back as he stood up, and just then someone knocked at the front door.

Grigsby frowned. Doors that got knocked on at six in the morning never opened up onto anything good.

He turned to Brenda. "Stay here," he told her.

She curtsied, smiling. She was too big a woman to pull off a curtsy—too big and too old a woman to do half the cutesy little-girl things she did. His feelings moved through their old familiar dance, shuffling from embarrassment to irritation to shame.

She said, "Your wish is my command, sire."

He nodded, looked grimly away. Jesus.

His clothes from yesterday, and hers, were flung about the parlor—pants on the floor, shirt draped over the armchair. Her corset wrapped around his other pair of boots. Her stiff petticoat standing upright, like a squat teepee, in the center of the carpet.

He and Brenda had done themselves proud, looked like. No wonder he was so damn tired. He couldn't remember any of it, but probably that was a blessing.

He opened the front door.

Officer McKinley stood there in his blue Denver Police uniform, looking fat and ill at ease. He glanced quickly up and down the empty street, as though he suspected that spies watched him

76

from within the small frame houses or from behind the hedges and shrubs. He tapped the brim of his cap. "Mornin', Marshal."

"Morning, Tom." Grigsby yawned. The air was cold; he felt its chill through his woolen shirt, his leather vest. Behind McKinley the houses were taking on form and color in the early morning light. There had been a time once when Grigsby had actually enjoyed this part of the day.

"Grady tole me to come talk to you," McKinley said. "He said you wanted to know if sumpin happens to a hooker." He looked off warily to his right.

Grigsby was suddenly wide awake. "What happened?"

"Molly Woods." He looked off warily to his left. "You know her? She got cut up sumpin awful, Grady says. They already sent for Greaves."

"Molly Woods? Lives down by the river?"

"Yes sir. You hurry, you can get there before he does."

Grigsby nodded. "I owe you, Tom."

McKinley shook his head. "Jesus, Marshal, how'd you know?"

"Hunch."

"Grady says he never saw anything like it. He says there was pieces of her all over the place, like—"

"All right, Tom. I'll be going now."

McKinley remembered himself, looked furtively down the street again. "Greaves asks you, it wasn't me what tole you. Right?"

"Absolutely. I'm obliged, Tom. You get on back now."

As McKinley bustled off, obviously relieved to be leaving, Grigsby closed the door. He lifted his gunbelt off the coatrack, slung it around his hips, buckled it closed. Reflexively, out of years of habit, he adjusted the big Colt in its holster, slid it out a few inches, let it fall back, loose and ready.

He slipped his sheepskin jacket from the rack, wrestled it on.

Brenda wandered into the parlor. Grigsby had completely forgotten that she was in the house.

"Who was it, Bob?" she asked him. She drew the front of the robe more tightly around her heavy breasts.

77

"Business," he told her.

"You're leavin' now?"

"Yep," he said, hooking the last of the leather loops over the topmost staghorn button.

She nodded. " 'M I gonna see you later?"

He frowned. "You already asked me, Brenda. I don't know. I got a lot of work."

"Sure," she said. "Sure, Bob. I understand." She shrugged. "Well," she said. "You know where I live." She smiled a small smile, somehow sad and hopeful at the same time.

Grigsby put on his hat. Sooner or later he had to end this thing with Brenda, once and for all. For her sake. "Right," he said. "See you."

It took Grigsby five minutes to reach the livery stable, another five to saddle up the big roan.

The shantytown along the North Platte was a part of Denver that the men of the Chamber of Commerce never mentioned in those advertisements they took out in the eastern newspapers. Most of the eastern travelers passing through town never saw it, never knew that it existed. The locals knew, but except for those who lived in it, and who had no choice, none of them ever came here.

It was a neighborhood for people who had no choice—people who had run through all their choices, or tossed them all away, or people who had never had much of a choice to begin with. Italians recruited by the railroads, paid a starvation wage for a while, and then laid off. Negroes escaping the South and discovering, years after the War, a new kind of slavery. Swedes and Norwegians and their families who came looking for work and for clean mountain air, and who found typhoid, cholera, and pneumonia. And the women: widows, abandoned wives, unwanted daughters, farm girls who had once been pregnant and desperate and who now, after years of abuse, weren't girls any more and didn't have the energy to be desperate.

Gathered here, huddled in ramshackle shanties of tarpaper and

78

scrapwood, they were the refuse tossed aside by the city as it grew fat and sleek on the money from the mines and the ranches, the smelters and the stockyards.

Grigsby hated the place. Here the light never grew brighter than the bleakness of dusk: day and night a blanket of smelter smoke obscured the sky. Soot lay everywhere, clung to everything; in winter the snow was the color of ashes. In summer the winds brought the grime and the dust billowing up off the rutted roadbeds in choking black clouds; in spring and fall the same roads became narrow swamps of black glutinous muck.

The last rain had been a week ago, but the hooves of Grigsby's horse made dull sucking sounds as the animal plodded down Curlew Street. Trash littered the mud: tin cans, whiskey bottles, scraps of paper, a dead cat. Thin, whey-faced children, bundled up against the cold in tattered rags, watched him from the sidewalks with big dark eyes that were as shiny, and as blank, as marbles. The adults—some of them trudging slowly past, some stiffly leaning, arms folded, against the greasy wooden walls— had eyes that were blanker still.

Three Denver policemen stood huddled together on the sidewalk outside Molly Woods's small frame shack, the blue of their uniforms looking black in the murky light. They were silent, their hands buried in the pockets of their coats, their breath puffs of white in the chill, still air. None of them looked at the others.

A small knot of shantytown locals, four or five battered-looking men, two battered-looking women, everyone dressed in shades of gray, stood off to the left, watching and waiting.

Grigsby reined in the roan, swung himself down, felt the mud squirm beneath his boots. His right leg wobbled slightly—the hip was acting up again, pain knifing from the pelvis down the thigh bone. Pretty soon his riding days would be over. It would be buckboards for him then, and then the rocker on the front steps, and then the coffin.

He tied the reins to a sagging wooden rail and, holding himself deliberately upright, walking through the pain, climbed up onto the sidewalk.

The three policemen nodded; they all knew him.

"Gerry," he said, nodding first to the oldest, Sergeant Hanrahan. Then, to the others, "Zack. Carl."

The sergeant spoke for all three: "Bob. How'd you hear?"

"Little bird told me. Greaves get here yet?"

Hanrahan shook his head. His round face was red, but not from the cold. It was always red. "Hill's a long way off," he said. Capitol Hill, where Greaves lived, was Denver's most expensive residential district. " 'Specially this early of a mornin'."

Grigsby jerked his head toward Molly Woods's shack. "Bad?"

Hanrahan took in a deep breath, blew it out between pursed lips, shook his head. "Jesus, Bob. He was crazy, whoever did it. Ye can't even tell who she was. *What* she was. Ye knew her, did ye?"

"To talk to."

The sergeant shook his head. "Makes it worse."

Grigsby glanced at the other policemen. Zack Tolliver was all right—slow, no genius, but honest and dependable. And he hated Greaves. Carl Hacker was one of Greaves's pets, a bootlicker and a liar. But he was gutless. Without Greaves around, he was no threat and no problem. Grigsby looked back at Hanrahan. "I'm going in."

Out of the corner of his eye, he saw Hacker turn to the sergeant.

Hanrahan's face was expressionless. "Now why is that, Bob?"

"Somethin' I'm working on."

Hanrahan shrugged. "City business, Bob. No federal jurisdiction, don't ye know. Greaves won't care for it."

Grigsby smiled. "Guess I just don't give a shit, Gerry."

Hanrahan looked at him for a moment, finally nodded. "Guess ye don't." He pulled a small tin flask from his pocket, held it out. "Better have yourself a taste first. Ye'll be needin' the help of it."

Grigsby accepted the flask and unscrewed its cap. He drank some of the whiskey—Irish, and good—then screwed the cap back and handed the flask over to Hanrahan. "Thanks. I won't touch anything in there."

Hanrahan returned the flask to his pocket. "I know that, Bob."

Grigsby nodded again, then turned to the door of Molly Woods's shack. The doorknob was cold. He twisted it, pushed open the door, and stepped inside.

CHAPTER SEVEN

THAT WEDNESDAY MORNING, WHEN Oscar awoke, he wished
that he were dead.

His mouth was dry and grainy, his forehead felt heavy and
hairy and sloped and hideously ridged at the eyebrows, like an
orangutang's.

With the window shade down, the curtains drawn together,
the room was dim and funereal. Which suited him perfectly.

Another night with Elizabeth McCourt Doe like last night, and
probably he *would* be dead.

She and Tabor had come to the dressing room after the lecture.
She had looked—impossibly—even more ravishing and radiant
than he remembered her, and Oscar had marveled that the
cramped little room could contain, without bursting, two souls
so extraordinary as his and hers.

He had marveled, too, when he discovered that his own ebul-
lient good nature extended even to Horace Tabor. Tonight the
silver baron seemed so amiable, so childlike and uncomplicated,
so exuberant about the lecture (which surely suggested a sliver

or two of sound taste buried beneath that awful American vulgarity), that only a boor could have disliked the man. A bit on the uncomplicated side, certainly. But that was nature, not nurture; and none of us can choose our parents. And if he were perhaps a tad preoccupied with the world of commerce, he was also honest, forthright, and totally without malice. Not a bad sort at all. Salt of the earth, actually.

What a wonderful world it was, brimful with people who were either fascinating or genial; or with people who, like himself (and Elizabeth McCourt Doe, of course), were both. The best of all possible worlds it was. Poor Pangloss was right.

And the best thing of all in this best of all possible worlds was the secret love he shared with Elizabeth McCourt Doe. And precisely because it was secret, isolate, it would remain forever pure.

When she shook his hand in farewell, she pressed into it a folded square of paper. He pocketed the paper by reaching into his jacket pocket for his cigarette case, as smoothly as if he had been doing this sort of thing all his life.

After they left, and while Henry, behind him, cleaned away the dressing table, he removed the paper and opened it.

Tonight at one-thirty. The north corner of Lincoln and Washington Streets.

Inside Oscar's tweed trousers, Freddy Phallus stirred expectantly.

He had supped with von Hesse and the Countess—selecting from the limited menu a rather dismal ragout (one more bloodsoaked steak and he would begin to howl like a wolf) and he had been brilliant. The Countess had laughed merrily as she tossed her shiny blond curls, and even von Hesse had interrupted his methodical chewing and permitted himself a crisp Teutonic smile or two. After the German left the table to use the washroom, Mathilde had leaned toward Oscar and put her delicate hand along his arm.

"Oscair," she smiled, "you are a veritable devil. You must tell me. Who is she?"

He hid his surprise behind a frown, "Whatever do you mean?"

She smiled again. "You know very well what I mean. *La Femme*. Only a woman could have produced this remarkable change. You are positively *enthusiastic*. I find it charming, of course, but also entirely intriguing."

"My dear Countess," he said, looking levelly into her eyes, "if I act any differently tonight, this is only because the evening lecture went so well. There is no woman, I assure you." He smiled ruefully; a nice touch, he thought. "Would that it were so."

"Ah," she said. "I understand. She is married. Wonderful! Not another word, then. Only this." She leaned still closer, lowered her voice to a smoky whisper, and murmured in French, "Always continue to deny. Even if he confronts you, the brute of a husband. Even if he discovers you *en flagrante*, you understand me? If you never waver, even for a moment, he will begin to doubt the evidence of his own eyes. I promise you that this is true."

Oscar laughed.

Later, as he lay fully clothed atop the bed in his room, he teased and tortured himself with memories of Elizabeth McCourt Doe. Visions, pink-tipped and titian-tufted, twirled across his brain. He heard her laughter, her sighs and moans. He felt the shiver of her flesh.

And when he opened his eyes, found himself alone in the small, drab room, he experienced within an aching emptiness, a pain at once appalling and delicious. Before he met her, he had thought himself whole, entire; now he discovered that he was merely half a being, a tattered fragment of a soul, yearning wildly, desperately, for that which would complete it.

The refrain of an old Irish love song kept repeating itself back in some musty, misty corner of his mind. *Do not forget, love, do not grieve, for the heart is true and it can't deceive. My heart and soul I will give to thee, so farewell my love and remember me.*

Irish love songs. Nothing in the history of literature was more perfectly contrived to bring a tear to the eye, or a sneer to the lip. He was becoming pathetic. Soon he would be plucking the petals off daisies, loves me, loves me not, and walking blindly into walls.

He was mooning and swooning about like a provincial schoolboy.

He was twenty-seven years old, a grown man in full possession of all his limbs and organs (indeed yes!) and all his faculties.

But, God in heaven, the woman was like no other he had ever met.

He slipped her note from his pocket. He opened it, inhaled the dark, exhilarating, remembered scent that clung faintly to the paper.

Tonight at one-thirty. The north corner of Lincoln and Washington Streets.

(He had possessed the foresight to ask the desk clerk—with a towering nonchalance—where these particular avenues might happen to converge.)

Her unparalleled grace and intelligence were obvious even in this simple missive. Not a word wasted, each doing its job in a simple, straightforward manner. The *north* corner: how sublimely specific. Really, how altogether admirable.

And the handwriting itself—it was as uncluttered and spare, as pure of line, as Japanese calligraphy.

He tugged free his pocket watch. Eleven-thirty. Two hours yet.

Where was she now? What was she doing at exactly this moment? Why was it necessary for them to wait until one-thirty? Why was his mind suddenly achurn with idiotic questions?

How wearisome this love business actually was. The endless waiting, the endless wanting, the endless futile fantasizing. No wonder that lovers were forever quaffing poison and leaping from bridges. Anything to relieve the tedium.

Would she like London?

Of course she would. A woman of instinctive cultivation, of natural, inborn refinement, how could she help but like the most

85

cultivated and refined city (excepting Paris) in the world? And together the two of them would become its leading lights—arbiters, because paragons, of fashion. They would amaze and dazzle with their taste and flair. Their house, perhaps a small Georgian on Grosvenor Square, would become a legendary gathering place for the *cognoscenti*.

A few small obstacles did loom on the horizon, admittedly.

Money, for a start. Where exactly would they find the lucre to support this enlightened existence?

Two can live as cheaply as one.

Yes, so long as one of them doesn't eat.

His play. *Vera*. It *would* be produced. All he needed was the agreement of that wretched woman in New York who labored under the misapprehension that she was an actress.

First New York, great success, his name emblazoned across the marquee, Jimmie Whistler gnawing his liver in a paroxysm of envy back in London; and then the West End. Money gushing into Grosvenor Square. He could burn the stuff to light his cigarettes.

Yes. Convince her. Tonight. Convince her to leave Tabor, a decent chap certainly but clearly wrong for her. Convince her to leave Denver, come along to finish up the tour, and then sail with him for England. Together, they would burn their bridges behind them.

But what about Mother? How would she react to a daughter-in-law who was not only American, which was accidental and therefore possibly forgivable, but also penniless? Which to Mother was an indication of willful stupidity.

We'll burn that bridge when we come to it.

He smiled. He rolled over, lifted his fountain pen from the notebook lying atop the mattress, opened the book, and wrote:

Burn that bridge when we come to it.

At one-thirty he had been waiting on the north corner of Lincoln and Washington Streets for three quarters of an hour. It was an empty, cold, and exceptionally inhospitable intersection. The wind moaned over the rooftops of grim brick buildings, mournfully, drearily, as though it had been reading Dickens. The air was chill. A skein of hard white stars winked overhead: so distant, so frigid, so utterly indifferent to the fate of Man that finally they had become quite irritating.

He heard the hurried clop of horses' hooves against hard-packed earth, heard the clack and rattle of a carriage. Looked up and saw the animals, two of them, suddenly appear at the corner in an insane gallop. Coal-black flanks agleam in the yellow light of the streetlamp, they dragged behind them a small black hansom that careened to the left as it reeled in its turn.

The driver, Oscar saw as the vehicle approached, was swathed in a long black topcoat and muffled about the face with a long black scarf that concealed his face and trailed over his shoulder. A black hat, flat-crowned and flat-brimmed, was pulled low over his head, its shadow masking his face.

Just before the carriage reached Oscar, the man reined in the horses and pushed down the wooden brake lever with a booted foot. Silently he nodded, tapped the gloved forefinger of his left hand against the brim of his hat, and then indicated, by a curt swing of his whip, that Oscar should enter the cab.

"Ah," said Oscar. Elizabeth McCourt Doe had apparently laid on transport.

But he hesitated. He peered inside the carriage. Empty. He looked up at the driver. Extremely romantic, to be sure, bundled up like Dick Turpin; but what guarantee was there that the woman had sent this chap? Who knew what sort of villain he might be? A genuine Turpin, perhaps: a real highwayman. Plotting to cart Oscar off and plunder him at gunpoint in some dusky deserted alleyway.

But highwaymen, if memory served, didn't drive carriages. Carriages were what they robbed. They rode horses, or they bounded out of bushes.

Perhaps this was something else they arranged differently in American cities. A lack of suitable bushes.

The driver leaned over and impatiently slapped the carriage door with the tip of his whip.

87

"Are you quite sure," Oscar asked the man, "that you've found the right party? Mr. Oscar Wilde?" The impoverished and entirely harmless poet, he almost added.

The driver nodded, a single brusque movement, and then again, brusquely, smacked his whip against the carriage side.

My heart and hand I will give to thee . . .

Sighing sadly, Oscar opened the door and stepped into the cab.

Even before his other foot had left the ground, the driver cracked the whip and the horses bolted forward. Oscar's shoulder slammed onto the seat's back as his knee smashed against its front. His breath suddenly gone, he wrenched himself awkwardly around, clutched for handholds along the carriage's side. The carriage lurched to the left and he was thrown against the door, which sprang open and, for a frantic moment before he jerked it shut, revealed an expanse of dark, disagreeable roadway racing away below.

The carriage bounced and bucked, leaped and bounced as it plunged along. Oscar attempted to support himself, hands braced against the sides of the vehicle, feet braced against the opposite seat, while the darkened city of Denver hurtled by the windows. Dry goods stores, blacksmiths' stables, laundries, warehouses, small obscure factories, even a church or two skittered past. Conceivably, someone out there witnessed this mad dash through the empty streets; but no one called out, no one tried to save him.

At last, in a dark and dismal neighborhood of small, mean wooden houses shouldering each other along the narrow street, the carriage began to slow. Frowning out the window at the desolation around him, Oscar rearranged his cravat.

The vehicle stopped before a house that seemed somewhat larger than the rest, a two-story building looming up out of the starlit shadows. Its windows unlighted, its façade dark and blank, the place appeared abandoned.

Which showed, Oscar felt, excellent judgment on the part of the abandoners, whoever they might have been.

The carriage dipped as the driver vaulted to the ground. Peering

88

out the window, Oscar saw the man's dark form glide through the gloom to the front door.

There must be some mistake. Surely Elizabeth McCourt Doe would never orchestrate a meeting in a place like this.

Suddenly a pale yellow strip of light pitched across the weedy lawn. Silhouetted against the opened door, the driver waved an impatient, beckoning arm.

Once again, Oscar hesitated.

The place could be thick with desperadoes. Thieves, thugs, cutpurses and, worse, cutthroats.

And if she *were* there? Surrounded by assassins, gunmen, skulking felons?

Enough of this.

Perhaps these louts imagined that an Irishman, and a poet, would be easy pickings. They deceived themselves. The blood of Cuchulain surged in his veins. And he knew a thing or two about the Manly Arts. Self-defense was something a poet quickly learned in an Irish public school.

He did rather wish, however, that he possessed somewhere on his person a small but powerful handgun.

He unlatched the carriage door, pushed it open, stepped down. Head held high, he stalked across the lawn to the house.

The driver watched him approach, then turned and entered the building.

Oscar trailed resolutely behind.

Just to the left of the door, startling Oscar by his presence, stood a small Chinese man in sandals, black silk pants, a black silk top, and a round, black silk skullcap. He might have been thirty years old; he might have been fifty. Grinning with enormous enthusiasm, bowing as rhythmically as a metronome, he shut the door behind Oscar and gestured for him to follow the driver.

Oscar did so, feeling as disoriented as if he had somehow entered into another universe. The hallway was broad and airy. The floor was oak, spotlessly clean, draped along its center with a runner of Oriental carpet, black and scarlet, so perfect in its elegance and simplicity that it must be authentic. Brass sconces along the walls provided a soft gentle light. The walls themselves, unadorned, were wainscoted with some dark, rich wood, teak or mahogany.

There was a smell in the air of jasmine—incense, doubtless— and of something else, something darker, heavier, more penetrating.

Oscar followed the driver's back. The hallway ended where it met, perpendicularly, another passage. Here a small alcove set into the wall held a wonderfully wrought bronze Buddha.

The man turned to the right, down a hallway longer than the first. His boots thumping on the carpeting, the driver passed several closed doors, stopped at one, opened it, and stepped inside.

Behind him, Oscar entered the room.

It was a large, uncluttered space. White walls, white ceiling, a gaslight softly glowing overhead within a white paper globe. Bleached oak floors, a strategic scattering of Oriental carpets in subtle shades of cream and pearl. Against the far wall, where the window might be hidden, a tall and broad Chinese screen displaying painted vistas of dreamy mountains strung with waterfalls, steep remote valleys draped with mist. Against the wall to the left, a large double bed framed in brilliant red-lacquered wood, covered by a quilt of red embroidered silk. Against the wall to the right, a low, red-lacquered table, atop which sat a slim ivory-colored vase containing (Good Lord!) a single white lily. Lying beside the vase, a teakwood box and a long narrow smoking pipe of elaborate Oriental design. Next to these, a silver salver holding two crystal tulip glasses and an iced-champagne bucket; inside this, a bottle of Krug.

Very inviting, very charming, all of it. But it lacked, manifestly, one rather important item.

Elizabeth McCourt Doe.

Where was she?

Oscar looked at the driver. Silently, churlishly, shoulders hunched, hands in the pockets of his coat, the man stood with his back to Oscar.

Really, this was too much. The fellow's maniacal steeplechase through the streets of Denver had been bad enough. But this insolence was altogether intolerable. The oaf deserved a thrashing. And unless he produced an explanation, and right now, Oscar Fingal O'Flahertie Wills Wilde was just the person to give it to him.

Abruptly, the man turned and tore from his head the broad, flat-brimmed hat. Rich red glistening curls cascaded down his shoulders, and his bright violet eyes sparkled, and suddenly he was a she, and she was laughing.

Over the course of the next few hours, he had somehow neglected to ask Elizabeth to leave Tabor and come away with him. At first, the hurry of passion had distracted them both. She was naked beneath her disguise, no underclothing whatever, her lambent skin once again a revelation; and as soon as he could wrestle the denim trousers from her long elegant legs, the two of them collapsed like felled trees to the red silk quilt.

Later, the novelty of smoking opium had diverted him. With the quilt wrapped around his middle and falling in Neronian folds from his shoulder, Oscar sat plumped against the headboard as Elizabeth McCourt Doe, perched cross-legged atop the mattress, prepared the pipe. She still wore her man's denim shirt—its metal snaps had been ripped apart during the proceedings (by him, by her, who knew?), but the shirt had remained on her shoulders— and in its opened front her bare breasts swayed slightly, teasingly, as she moved.

The smoke from the drug was thick, milky, at once sweet and acrid, and it seemed to insinuate itself almost immediately into the joints and interstices of his body. Soon a warm luxurious languor had settled over his entire frame. His mind was lucid and buoyant and utterly relaxed. The colors in the room, he noticed, had somehow acquired a clarity and an intensity that he had observed before only in dreams, but which he had not realized, till now, that he *had* observed in dreams.

"You like it?" she asked him.

"Ah well," he said gravely, "I am morally compelled to.

91

Look at Coleridge. Look at Poe. At Baudelaire. The modern poet must know as much about opium as he knows about dactyls and iambs." He smiled suddenly. "How convenient. Making a vice of necessity."

She laughed and held toward him his glass of champagne. "Try another vice."

"You tempt me, madam." He took the glass.

She smiled. "My intention exactly."

"And whatever shall I do with all these new temptations?"

She put her hand along his naked thigh. "I believe that the only way to remove a temptation is to surrender to it."

He laughed.

Another bout of passion provided an additional distraction. He had become persuaded that he was too deeply sunk in this marvelous lassitude ever to function sexually again, ever to want to; but Elizabeth McCourt Doe, with her cunning fingers and skillful mouth, proved him mistaken. Freddy rose, as it were, to the occasion and performed prodigies of valor and endurance.

Later, drained, growing a bit muddled, he had become distracted by their conversation.

He had said, almost to himself, "But I still fail to understand how all this happened."

"I felt," she said, "when I met you, that I already knew you completely."

He smiled. "To be known completely is what everyone tells himself that he most desires. And what everyone, of course, secretly most dreads. You knew me from my poetry?"

"From your eyes."

Again, he smiled. "Eyes can lie. They often do."

"So does poetry."

He laughed. "And what did you know from my eyes?"

She lifted his hand from her knee, kissed the knuckle of his thumb. "That you carried within you a great sadness."

"Really?" he said, surprised and delighted. "You knew that?"

Now, lying in his bed at the hotel, he could recall that he had been so taken by her insight that he had prattled on for an hour, ecstatically, about his great sadness. He had talked about the deaths of his sister, his half sisters, his father; about his loneliness at public school, at Trinity, at Oxford. Finally he had become— how dreadful—almost maudlin. He was still sadly babbling away when they dressed; still babbling as they went back to the carriage.

He had grown silent only when he was alone in the carriage as she drove it—more sedately this time—through the gray light of early dawn. He had, now, only the vaguest memory of that journey; could recollect only in disjointed fragments his actual return to the hotel.

Had he in fact made a fool of himself? This would have been, in any circumstance, a disaster; in her presence, it would have been a catastrophe.

Or would it? For some reason he couldn't bring himself really to care.

How astounding. Had his love died so quickly?

He searched within himself for the passion, the heights and depths of it, that he had felt so strongly last night. He found only a dull lifeless discomfort that might have been merely the residue of the champagne. Or the opium.

Was passion like currency? Once spent, forever gone?

Perhaps this was the catastrophe.

Whatever the truth might be, certainly this morning he felt catastrophic. Parts of his body that had never experienced pain before experienced it now: his hair, for example; his eyelashes.

Fortunately he delivered no lecture until this evening. If he wished, and he wished it most fervently, he could stay in bed all day. He could lie there and attempt to reason out the peculiar evanescence of rapture.

Just then, as though to disprove this, a loud unpleasant rapping suddenly sounded at the door.

Henry? But he had told Henry he wouldn't be needing him until this evening.

The rapping came again. So emphatic it was that Oscar felt as though someone were pounding a fist against his temple.

Rapping, rapping at my chamber door. Quoth the raven, "Nevermore."

He sat up, swung his legs off the bed, slipped his feet awkwardly into his slippers, fumbled his arms into the dressing gown.

Who would be so barbaric as to come calling at—he glanced at the clock on the dresser—nine o'clock?

Bang, bang, bang.

"Yes, yes, yes," he mumbled, tying the gown's belt. He shuffled over to the door, unlocked it, jerked it open.

CHAPTER EIGHT

RIGSBY WALKS INTO MOLLY WOODS'S room and closes the
door behind him. The air is heavy with a dank, slaughterhouse stench. He looks around him and for a moment he
cannot comprehend what it is he sees. For a moment, his mind
is unable, or it refuses, to recognize what lies before it.

Something awesome and fearful sprawled upon the narrow
blackened bed. Limp strips and bits of something strewn around
the tiny room. Fragments of something clinging to the walls, the
oval mirror, the sides of the rickety wooden dresser.

And when, abruptly, it all comes into focus, when he understands, his legs buckle and the blood drains from his face; and
he knows, with an absolute conviction, that his life is forever
changed. He knows that this room and the horror it holds will
be with him, will reappear in sweat-soaked dreams and unbidden
memories, until the day he dies.

He closes his eyes. He wants nothing now but to sink into the
embrace of his absent wife, bury his face in her neck. He hears
himself mutter her name: "*Clara*."

He forces himself to open his eyes. To look again.

The thing on the bed, its upper half propped against the wall, was once Molly Woods. The thing wears a petticoat, pushed back to its waist, and its legs are drawn up. There is no skin or flesh on the legs: glistening white shinbones, a pair of round white kneecaps, white thighbones. Only the feet, splayed out against the bed, are intact. Each toenail, he notes, is painted red.

The flesh has been stripped, too, from the ribs, and between white arches of bone he can see a dull film of pink tissue.

The arms are peeled as well, from shoulder to wrist. The curled fingers of both hands—these, like the feet, intact—have been placed at the black savage rent in the belly, as though to make it appear, obscenely, that they are drawing back the wide lips of the awful wound.

The face is gone. The thick red hair, falling to the exposed shoulder bones, frames a leering skull from which empty sockets gape.

Grigsby takes a low shallow breath through his mouth. Deliberately, he moves his glance around the room.

The strips lying about are ribbons of flesh. They are everywhere: stuck to the walls, piled atop the mattress, dangling from the knobs of the dresser, arranged in careful coils along the floor, Four or five of them hang from the rim of the mirror like meat left to dry.

Grigsby looks at the table to his right. Exactly in its center is a small mound of flesh. It is a woman's breast. On either side of it, stuck to it with blackened dried blood, is a human ear.

Grigsby has seen enough. Has seen far too much. He stumbles to the door.

When he stepped outside, Grigsby sucked in a long deep breath. After Molly Woods's room, even the sooty, sulfurous air of Shantytown tasted as sweet as spring water.

Without a word, Hanrahan held out the tin flask of whiskey. Grigsby took it, unscrewed the cap, raised the flask to his lips and drank, holding his throat open so the liquor could reach his stomach more quickly. He lowered the flask and his body made a small, quick, involuntary shiver.

96

He could feel the watchful stares of the younger policemen. It was as though they were waiting for the words that would explain the violated thing lying on the bed inside, and the crazed, inhuman violence that had created it.

The words that could explain this, Grigsby knew, didn't exist.

He said to Hanrahan, "Need to talk to you for a minute, Gerry."

Hanrahan glanced at the other policemen, turned back to Grigsby, nodded. Together the two of them walked away from Tolliver and Hacker until they were ten or twelve yards distant.

"Anybody see anything?" Grigsby asked.

Hanrahan shook his head. "You know better than that, Bob. No one ever sees nothin' in Shantytown."

"You covered the street?"

"Not all of it. Waiting for Greaves now, we are."

"He'll try to keep this under his hat."

Hanrahan nodded. "Bad for business, a thing like this gets out."

"You send for Doc Boynton?"

"I did."

"Tell him I'd like to hear from him afterward. Soon as he finishes."

Hanrahan nodded. "Greaves won't like it a-tall."

"He won't if he knows about it."

For a moment Hanrahan pursed his lips thoughtfully together. Then, "What's yer interest here, Bob? Where's the federal side come in, exactly?"

"Like I said, somethin' I'm working on."

"And might ye be sharin' that with us one day?"

"When I got somethin' to share."

"Playing it a bit close to the vest, ain't ye, Bob?"

"The way I always play it, Gerry."

Hanrahan glanced back at Tolliver and Hacker, looked again to Grigsby. "Right you are, Bob. Time being, then, it's yer deal."

Grigsby nodded. " 'Preciate it, Gerry."

97

Hanrahan shrugged. "I owe ye one. Ye'd best make tracks, though. Before—ah, well. Too late. Here's himself arrivin' now."

Grigsby turned. Drawn by four large black geldings whose sleek coats had been brushed until they gleamed like patent leather, the big black carriage rumbled down the narrow street. On the vehicle's door, gilded in ornate gothic script, were the words CHIEF OF POLICE, CITY OF DENVER.

The carriage stopped ten feet away from Grigsby and Hanrahan. The door opened and William J. Greaves stepped out. He was tall and broad-shouldered and, even now, despite the extra weight that good living had added to his frame, despite features that had somewhat blurred and thickened, he was still a striking man. His jet black mustache was artfully waxed and his curly black hair was theatrically silver at the temples, a color that was precisely matched by the fur lining at the collar of his elegantly tailored black wool topcoat.

He looked like everything a chief of police should be, very smart, completely fearless, and totally incorruptible; and he was, Grigsby knew, only very smart. In Denver, Grigsby had once told Clara, it wasn't just the cream that rose to the top. The scum did, too.

Greaves glanced down at the muddy ground, grimaced with distaste, looked up and saw Hanrahan and Grigsby. The grimace became an angry frown.

Stepping down from the carriage behind him came Harlan Brubaker, assistant to the chief. Brubaker was Greaves's bagman. He collected the protection money from the saloons and gambling halls, the brothels and opium dens. He was a short, officious, ferret-faced man who was wearing a fur-lined topcoat identical to Greaves's. The two men were the same age, midforties, but the difference in their size and the similarity of their dress made them look like prosperous father and promising son.

Greaves stepped onto the sidewalk and stalked up to Hanrahan. Pointing a blunt forefinger at Grigsby, he demanded, "What is this man doing here?"

"We were just discussin' that, Chief," said Hanrahan.

"This is city business. He has no jurisdiction here."

Hanrahan nodded. "Exactly, Chief. I just got finished explainin' that very thing."

Greaves's eyes narrowed. "You and Grigsby go way back, don't you, Sergeant. Rode for a while together. Texas Rangers, wasn't it?"

Hanrahan shrugged. "Years ago, that was. Can't hardly recall it a-tall now, Chief."

"I certainly hope so. That dime-novel nonsense, cowboys and Indians and the wide open prairies—those days are gone, Sergeant. You're supposed to be a policeman now, working for the City of Denver. I hope, for your sake, that your loyalties haven't gotten confused."

Grigsby, looking on, thought that Hanrahan's face might have grown a shade redder. But the sergeant's voice was level and unemotional when he said, "Nobody's ever had cause to doubt me loyalties."

Grigsby said to Greaves, "She was one of my informants."

His face tight with displeasure, Greaves turned to him and looked Grigsby slowly, coldly, up and down. Finally he said, "What?"

"The prostitute. Molly Woods. She was one of my informants."

Greaves snorted. "*Informants.* Is that what you call them now? What'd she inform you about? The price of pussy?"

Behind him, Harlan Brubaker chuckled.

Grigsby took a step toward Greaves and Hanrahan interposed his bulk between the two men. To Greaves he said, "I already explained to Marshal Grigsby that this here's a city matter. He was just leavin', Chief."

"See that he does. And Sergeant, if I find out that this man, this old *buckaroo* of yours, has interfered in any way with a municiple investigation, I'm going to hold you personally responsible. Is that clear?"

"Absolutely, Chief."

With another quick cold glance at Grigsby, Greaves turned and stalked away. A smirking Harlan Brubaker followed him.

99

Watching the two march toward Molly Woods's shack, Grigsby said, "You shoulda let me slam him one, Gerry."

Hanrahan shook his head. "Too many witnesses. He'd be off in a flash to see Judge Sheldon, and between the two of them they'd have yer job by lunchtime." He grinned. "Besides, these days an old codger such as yerself is like to get sorely hurt in a donnybrook."

Grigsby smiled. "The day I can't take a bag of pus like Billy Greaves is the day I toss in my badge." He watched as Greaves and Brubaker entered the ramshackle building.

"Ah," said Hanrahan, "yer only thinkin' that, ye see, 'cause yer still livin' in those famous dime-novel days of yers. How was it he put it now—cowboys and Indians and wide open prairies."

Grigsby looked at him, smiled again. "Maybe so," he said. And added, "buckaroo."

Hanrahan grinned. "I'll talk to Doc Boynton. Prob'ly he can get to yer office this afternoon."

"Good, Gerry. 'Preciate it."

Just then there was a sudden bang as the door to Molly Woods's shack flew open and Harlan Brubaker came reeling out. His face white, he pushed aside Officer Hacker, staggered to the edge of the sidewalk, bent forward at the waist, and vomited into the street. The two city constables looked away.

Grigsby sympathized. The interior of that room was a vision he wouldn't wish on anyone, even someone like Brubaker.

Hanrahan shook his head sadly. "Ye know, the pity of it is, that's the first time I ever seen the fella show a single solitary spark of humanity."

The thing on the bed, its upper half propped against the wall, was once Molly Woods. The thing wears a petticoat, pushed back to its waist, and its legs are drawn up. There is no skin or flesh on the legs . . .

Grigsby took another sip of whiskey and closed his eyes.

"No steak this mornin', Bob?"

Grigsby opened his eyes and looked over the bartop at Conlan, the beefy Irish barkeep. "No, Tim. Not today."

Polishing a glass with a bright white rag, Conlan said, "Well then, listen, I made up a nice hot batch of porridge this mornin'. Fresh as mother's milk. Why don't I fetch you a big bowl of the lovely stuff?"

Grigsby sipped at his shot glass of whiskey. "You know, Tim, one day you're gonna make some lucky cowhand a wonderful wife."

Conlan smiled, shook his head, shrugged his meaty shoulders. "Ah well, Bob, you have it your own way, then. You usually do." He turned and ambled down the bar.

Grigsby stared down into his shot glass.

Wilde. It all came back to Wilde.

In three cities where Wilde had given one of his talks—three that Grigsby knew of; there might be more—hookers had been murdered and cut up.

So far as Grigsby knew, he was the only person aware of the connection between Wilde and the killings. He had learned only by accident, through the crazy coincidence of those letters, from Clara, from Earl in El Paso, from the spit-and-polish new sheriff of Leavenworth. And, technically, he had no jurisdiction in any of the murders; each had occurred in an area with its own local police force, its own local courts.

Technically, he should give what he had to Greaves.

But, Jesus Christ, the idea of handing a murder investigation over to Greaves—Grigsby just couldn't do it. Even if Greaves managed to get together enough evidence to bring Wilde to trial, he'd only use it to line his own pockets somehow. Wilde was in tight with Tabor, and Tabor had money. Greaves goes to Wilde, Wilde goes to Tabor, Tabor goes to Greaves with a handful of cash. And Molly Woods's murder goes unsolved.

The ribbons of flesh are everywhere: stuck to the walls, piled atop the mattress, dangling from the knobs of the dresser, arranged in careful coils along the floor, Four or five of them hang from the rim of the mirror like meat left to dry.

The man who did that, who *could* do that, was crazy. Worse

101

than crazy. He was evil in a way that Grigsby had never encountered before.

Grigsby knew he should wait for a while. Sober up some. Get his balance back. He knew that he was too angry, too stricken by what he'd seen, to conduct an intelligent, rational investigation.

But the crazy bastard who sliced up Molly Woods—he wasn't rational either.

Fuck it. Let's go. Let's do it.

Grigsby pounded on the hotel room door. *Bang bang bang.*

He waited. Nothing.

He pounded again.

The door finally opened and he saw, standing behind it, a lumpy young man wearing a black dressing gown over a pair of sissy-yellow pajamas. He was at least as tall as Grigsby—big enough, definitely, to handle Molly Woods—and his brown hair hung in disheveled tangles to his shoulders. His face was round and pasty, his eyes were puffy, and Grigsby immediately wanted to ram a fist into that thick, wide, sensual mouth.

"You Wilde?" he said.

CHAPTER NINE

THE MAN WHO STOOD outside the hotel room door was a tall and bulky cowboy, or at any rate a tall and bulky individual who chose, for some obscure reason of his own, to dress like a cowboy. He wore scuffed leather boots, denim pants, an ancient holster containing an enormous pistol, a stained brown leather vest, an open sheepskin jacket that had seen better days (many of them), and a hat that was—certainly at this hour—truly ludicrous. The white, conical, comical crown rose a good foot from the elaborately curled brim, like a snow-covered Kilimanjaro from the rolling hills of Africa.

But if the hat was comical, the man's face was not. The skin was lined and weathered and blotched, the narrow gray eyes were rimmed like wounds with red flesh, the mouth was set in a bitter and perhaps permanent scowl.

"You Wilde?" the man said. He was, Oscar realized, nearly as tall as Oscar himself, and quite a bit wider. He smelled, very strongly, of whiskey.

"Usually, yes," Oscar told him. "But I really couldn't swear to that just now."

"Grigsby," the man said. "Federal marshal. I got some questions for you."

103

"Ah." Federal Marshal? Another tiresome newspaper? "Would it be possible, do you think, to write them down and leave them? I've a really wretched headache this morning, you see. I'll be delighted to get them back to you sometime later today."

"Right here," said the man, the words clipped and cold. "Right now. Or else we go down to the federal lockup and you give me the answers there."

A federal lockup, whatever it might be, sounded not at all inviting. "Well, then," said Oscar, "by all means, do come in."

He stepped back and Grigsby shouldered past him, stalked across the room to the window. Oscar shut the door and said to the broad sheepskinned back, "Would you mind terribly if I sat down? Gravity and I are not getting along this morning."

Grigsby jerked at the window shade and the thing zipped up with a loud snarl and a final brittle slap. Sunlight toppled between the curtains. Oscar blinked in the glare; a small poisonous pain began to flicker at his left temple.

Peering out the window, Grigsby put his big hands in the pocket of his coat and said over his shoulder, "What'd you do with the knife?"

Oscar was still standing; his astonishment at the man's behavior had rendered him immobile. He said, "I beg your pardon?"

Grigsby turned. His face was hard, his features set. "The knife. What'd you do with it?"

Oscar frowned, puzzled. "Has someone misplaced a knife?"

Grigsby stared silently. A muscle fluttered elaborately along his cheek. Oscar wondered, idly, how he accomplished this.

He said, "You know, if you don't mind, I really must sit down. Either that or fall down." He waved his hand toward the room's other chair. "Please. Feel free. Make yourself comfortable." He shuffled to the chair, sat down, sighed expansively, crossed his legs knee over knee, arranged the folds of his dressing gown, and looked over to the second chair. It was empty. He looked back at Grigsby. The man hadn't moved.

Grigsby said, "What time did you get back to the hotel this morning?"

Oscar frowned again. "Is this in reference to the knife you mentioned?"

"What time?"

"Perhaps you could explain to me what this is all about. I mean, I'm perfectly willing to help in any way I can, of course." Fellow was obviously drunk, probably deranged as well; humor him. "But I should tell you at the outset that I know nothing about knives. A gentleman never does. If one's gone missing, I'm afraid you'll have to ask someone else." He reached into the pocket of his gown for his cigarette case and the box of matches, and Grigsby's right hand leaped from the pocket of his jacket and darted toward the holster on his hip in a movement too swift and blurred to be broken down into individual components, and then abruptly the hand was holding his pistol and the pistol's muzzle, only two feet away and as wide as a tunnel in the Alps, was pointing directly at Oscar's forehead. Oscar heard a cold metallic *snick* as Grigsby thumbed back the hammer.

Grigsby said, "You move real, real slow now. But whatever it is you got in that pocket, you fetch it out of there."

Oscar's heart thumped in an irregular trot against his ribs. Carefully, slowly, he withdrew his hand, bringing along the cigarette case and the box of Vespas.

Grigsby looked at them, said nothing. He still aimed the gun at Oscar.

"Mr. Grigsby," Oscar said. He was surprised—and rather pleased—at how perfectly normal his voice sounded.

"That's *Marshal* Grigsby." Drunk or not, the man held the gun with a hand that was as steady as a rock.

"*Marshall* Grigsby. Yes, of course. Marshall is your first name?"

"Marshal is who I am. Federal lawman."

"Ah." Oscar opened the cigarette case, took one out, then held the case toward Grigsby. His own hand was trembling, but the tremor was so faint that he doubted Grigsby could see it; he knew, without precisely knowing how, that this was important. "Fancy one? They're quite good. Virginia and Latakia with just a hint of clove. Chap in Piccadilly makes them up for me."

Grigsby said nothing. The gun still hadn't moved.

Oscar closed the case, tapped the cigarette against its monogrammed silver top. "Marshal Grigsby, if you've resolved to use

105

that weapon, then there's probably very little I could say to dissuade you. You're obviously a man of determination, and naturally I find that altogether commendable. In England, one sees so little determination these days. Except, of course, among the mothers of marriageable daughters." He put the cigarette to his lips. "But I do think that before you plug me—do I have that right? plug me?—you ought, at the very least, give me some clue as to why."

"I know about the woman," Grigsby said.

Of course. Tabor had sent the man. Tabor had learned somehow about last night's tryst with Elizabeth McCourt Doe and, no doubt vomitous with rage, he had dispatched this federal lawman lout to terrorize the adulterous poet. Or, as Vail had warned, to kill him.

Only thing to do was follow the Countess's advice and deny everything. Brazen it out. He plucked a match from the box, struck it, held the sputtering flame to the tip of the cigarette. He puffed. "And which woman might that be?" he asked. He inhaled deeply and then turned his head slightly sideways to exhale the cloud of smoke—just in case blowing smoke down the barrel of a gun was considered, in these parts, bad form.

"Molly Woods," Grigsby said.

Oscar frowned. Molly Woods?

"I know about the others, too," said Grigsby. "In San Francisco. And El Paso. And Leavenworth. Guess you figured no one would ever tie it all together. Looks like you were wrong, scout."

Oscar was baffled. He inhaled again on his cigarette and said, "Would it be at all possible to convince you that I have no idea what you're talking about?"

Grigsby shook his head. The barrel of the gun never wavered.

"Well, then," said Oscar, "suppose we do this—just as a sort of exercise, a way for the two of us to get to know each other better. Suppose you explain what it is you believe that these women and I have done, and then we continue from there. What do you say to that?"

What Grigsby said to that was nothing. He did appear, however, to be considering the proposition. Or considering something: his eyes had narrowed still further, speculatively. Oscar took heart.

"And really, Marshal Grigsby, I don't mind admitting that your revolver is an extremely impressive weapon. And I don't doubt for a moment that it's in excellent working order. But it looks rather a heavy piece of equipment. Wouldn't you be more comfortable if you returned it to its saddle, or holster, or whatever you call it?" He smiled—winningly, he hoped. "I know that *I* would. And I assure you that even without it, you will have my undivided attention."

A moment passed. Then, faintly, slightly Grigsby nodded. He said, "You got some balls. Say that for you."

Oscar sensed that this—just now, anyway—was perhaps the highest compliment that Grigsby could have paid him. He inclined his head. "I'm very gratified that you should think so."

Grigsby stared at him for a moment more, and then suddenly swiveled the gun's barrel toward the ceiling. He eased down the hammer, frowned once, as though debating whether this were actually a good idea, and then returned the gun to its holster.

"There," said Oscar, carefully preventing the enormous relief he felt from seeping—flooding—into his voice. "Isn't that better? Now why don't you sit down and tell me all about these women of yours? I'd offer you tea, but I'm afraid I've given my valet the morning off. Besides, I've discovered there isn't any in this hotel."

Grigsby didn't sit. He hooked his thumbs into the pockets of his jacket—which positioned his hand only inches from the butt of his pistol—and he asked, "What time you get back to the hotel this morning?"

"Quite late, actually. Around six, I believe."

Grigsby nodded. "I talked to the clerk who worked the desk last night. Six, he says."

For a moment Oscar was tempted to inquire why, if Grigsby had already known the answer, he had bothered to ask the question. Then he realized that the man had wanted to learn whether Oscar would essay a lie. And realized, too, that Grigsby was also informing him that very possibly he already knew the answers to any other questions he might ask. "Yes," Oscar said. "Six."

"He says you left at twelve-thirty. So where were you between twelve-thirty and six?"

107

"Wandering about," Oscar said smoothly. "I often wander about in the early hours."

"Where'd you wander to?"

Lightly, Oscar shrugged. "I couldn't begin to say. Here and there. Up streets and down them." A bit of flattery, perhaps: "I was, I must say, extremely taken by the size and sophistication of your fine city."

"It's not my city," Grigsby said, curt and abrupt. "You talk to anyone? You see anyone?"

"No one at all. I prefer solitude on my rambles. This is, of course, why I conduct them at night."

Grigsby said nothing.

"But really, Marshal Grigsby, I thought you were going to tell me what all this is about. Women, you said."

Grigsby peered into Oscar's eyes for a moment, as though his stare could somehow lance through them and snag the thoughts skimming beneath their surface. Then he said, "Hooker got killed last night."

"Did he," Oscar said. "I can't say that I know the gentleman."

Grigsby was watching him closely. "Not a he. A hooker. A whore. A prostitute."

Oscar nodded. One could never tell with American slang. "And she was killed, you say." Surely the man would get to the point soon.

"She was gutted. Whoever did it cut her up like a side of beef. Worse. He scraped the meat off her bones. He sliced it up into strips, like jerky, and threw it around the room. He scraped off her face. Her nose, her mouth, everything. He—"

"Wait!" Oscar interrupted him, wincing in horror as he held up a shaking hand. "Stop!" He was ill. "Why are you telling me this?"

Still watching him, gauging him, Grigsby said. "That was Molly Woods."

"Molly Woods? *That* was Molly Woods?" And then he realized: "And the knife. You think—Good Lord, you think that *I* did that?"

Grigsby said nothing, merely stood there, watching.

108

Oscar remembered: "And *others*, you said? There were *more* of them? Like *that*? In San Francisco?"

"And El Paso," Grigsby added evenly. And Leavenworth. All of them killed off when you were there, giving one of your talks."

"But that's impossible. That can't *be*." He shook his head. Stunned, disbelieving. "No. No. A coincidence. A dreadful coincidence."

Grigsby shook his head. "All of them cut up the same way. All of them hookers. No coincidence."

"Someone is following the tour. Some madman."

"And why's that?"

"How should I know? How should anyone? A madman's logic is impossible to fathom. Yes, that's it, that must be. That explains it. A madman."

"Sonovabitch is crazy. But following this tour of yours?" He shook his head. "Don't see it."

"Have any of these killings taken place in towns where I haven't lectured?"

Grigsby frowned. "I'm lookin' into that."

Oscar sensed a possible momentary advantage here. "Because if even one of them has, don't you see, this would mean that the killer is someone unconnected to the tour."

"If," Grigsby said.

"But it must be. A madman. Someone completely unconnected. It's the only possibility that makes sense."

"Nope," said Grigsby. "Not the only one."

"Mr. Grigsby. Marshal Grigsby." Oscar leaned earnestly forward. "You don't know me. I understand that. But if you knew me even slightly, even in the most peripheral, insignificant way, you would realize that what you're suggesting is utterly impossible. It's absolutely preposterous. I literally would not harm a fly. I've been known to catch them in teacups—*Sèvres* teacups— and ferry them to the nearest window, so they can flutter off and merrily live out their little fly lives."

Grigsby nodded. "So you're still sticking to this story that you were out walking last night."

109

"Yes, of course." It was unthinkable, whatever the threat to himself, that he mention Elizabeth McCourt Doe.

"From twelve-thirty till six."

"Yes."

"Why'd you ask the desk clerk how to find Lincoln and Washington?"

"Pardon me?" *Dear God, yes, why?*

"Lincoln Street and Washington Street. You asked the desk clerk where they were. How come?"

"Ah. Yes. They were presidents, you see."

Grigsby frowned. "Presidents."

"American presidents. It's a caprice of mine. A whim. Whenever I'm in a new city, I like to visit streets named after American presidents. I'm enormously keen on American history. Especially the presidents."

For the first time since entering the room, Grigsby smiled. It was a faint smile, and one that held less amusement than it did a weary, distant scorn. "You got some balls, all right."

Oscar produced an elaborate frown. "How do you mean?"

"You really figure I'm gonna buy that."

"If by *buy it*, you mean *believe it*—then, yes, certainly." Sincerity without indignation: don't overplay the part.

"What other streets you visit here in Denver that got the name of presidents?"

"Ah, well, none as yet, I'm sorry to say. I've been terribly busy."

"Name me some presidents."

"Excuse me?"

"You know your presidents. Name me some."

"Ah." He inhaled on the cigarette, exhaled. "In chronological order?"

Grigsby smiled the faint smile again. "Any ole way you want, scout."

"Well. Let me see. There was Adams. And Jefferson. Then Madison, of course. Monroe. Then another Adams."

Grigsby's smile had faded.

"One of my particular favorites," Oscar said, exhaling ciga-

110

rette smoke, "is Jackson. It's the log cabin, I expect. Such a nice rustic touch. But on the other hand, I imagine that being born in a log cabin must be an extremely limiting experience. One is compelled, evidently, to become the president of the United States. Like Lincoln, for example. I think this quite unfair. What do you think, Marshal?"

Grigsby frowned. "I think I been sandbagged."

"Sorry?"

Grigsby nodded once. "You made your point. You know your presidents."

As Oscar noticed a droplet of perspiration prickling down his side, he sent up a silent blessing to whatever gods had provided him with that wretchedly written little pamphlet on American history he'd glanced at before leaving London. And a blessing, as well, to his own superbly retentive memory.

Grigsby said, "You got people traveling with you on this tour."

"That's right. Yes."

"Who?"

"Marshal Grigsby, I can assure you that none of them could be responsible for this . . . horrible thing."

Grigsby nodded. "S'pose you give me the names."

"But honestly—"

"One way or the other," Grigsby said, "I'm gonna find out who they are. Save us both some time."

Oscar inhaled on his cigarette. "Very well," he said, exhaling. "But none of these people could have done this."

Grigsby nodded. "The names," he said.

Oscar sighed. "First of all, there's Mr. Jack Vail. My business manager." He stubbed out his cigarette in the ashtray.

"He been with the trip since San Francisco?"

"Since the beginning. Since New York. We began the tour in New York, and that more or less establishes his innocence, doesn't it? I mean, none of these dreadful murders were committed before San Francisco."

Grigsby shook his head. "Don't know that."

Oscar frowned. "You mean there might be still *more* of them?"

111

"Maybe."

Oscar winced again.

"You started the trip in New York?"

"That's correct, yes. New York."

"When was that?"

"January."

"When you get to San Francisco?"

"Toward the end of the month. I don't have the exact date. I'm afraid I'm not much good with dates. Vail would know."

"You were in El Paso, Texas, on February twenty-fourth."

Oscar nodded. "Very likely."

"And Leavenworth, Kansas, on March the first."

"If you say so."

"If you went as far east as Leavenworth, how come you came back this way afterwards?"

"An excellent question, one that I've frequently asked Mr. Vail myself. It has to do, apparently, with the availability of the lecture halls."

Grigsby nodded. "Okay. Vail. Where's he stayin'?"

"Where's Vail stayin'?"

"Here. In the hotel."

"Which room?"

"203."

Grigsby nodded. "Who else?"

"Colonel von Hesse. Wolfgang von Hesse. A retired Prussian military officer. It would be absolutely impossible for him to have done this."

Grigsby nodded, his face empty. "How long's he been with the trip?"

"Since San Francisco."

"How come he's travelin' with you?"

"He's acting as escort to Countess de la Môle."

"Who?"

"Countess Mathilde de la Môle. From France."

"She joined up with you in San Francisco?"

"Yes."

"How come?"

112

"She introduced herself. She knows some people I know in London. She was traveling across the country and asked if she might join the tour."

"Where they stayin'?"

"Here in the hotel. We're all staying here."

"Room number?"

"She's in room 211. He's in room 210."

Grigsby nodded. "Who else?"

"O'Conner. David O'Conner. A reporter for the *New York Sun*."

"Joined up in New York?"

"San Francisco. He's covering the tour for his newspaper."

"Room number?"

"207, I believe."

"Who else?"

"Wilbur Ruddick. A poet from San Francisco. But really, the idea of young Ruddick doing anything so dreadful is completely absurd."

Grigsby nodded. "Room number."

Oscar sighed, resigned. "Room 208."

"Who else?"

"No one."

"You said a valet. A servant."

"Henry? But Henry's been with me since New York. Henry Villiers. He's a dear, sweet man."

Grigsby nodded. "Which room?"

"214. But really, Marshal—"

"That it? Nobody else?"

Oscar sat back. "No one else."

Grigsby nodded. "You givin' another talk tonight?"

"Yes."

"Tomorrow?"

"Tomorrow we go to Manitou Springs. I give a lecture at some private mansion there."

"The Bell mansion?"

"Yes. And from there, the next day, we go on to Leadville."

"Train or stage?"

113

"Pardon?"

"To Manitou Springs. You takin' the train or the stage coach?"

"The train."

"Noon train?"

"Yes."

Grigsby nodded. "You got a list of the places where you gave talks? Since you started?"

"Why? Oh. Of course." He frowned. "To determine whether there were any more of these killings. No, I haven't. Vail does. I can obtain it from him, if you like."

Grigsby made a slight negative motion with his head. "Get it myself."

"You'll be talking to these people? All of them?"

Grigsby nodded.

"They'll all be very disturbed by this," Oscar said.

"Not as disturbed as Molly Woods."

Oscar frowned. "Yes, of course. Of course. But at the risk of repeating myself, I'd like to say that not one of them could have been responsible for any of this. I should be happy to swear to that. I've been traveling with all of them for weeks now. I know them. I've eaten with them."

Grigsby shrugged. "Even a crazy person's gotta eat."

"But it's *impossible*."

Grigsby said, "One of them didn't do it, then you did."

Oscar raised his eyebrows. "Marshal—"

"You listen to me," Grigsby said. "Someone killed those hookers. Way I figure it, the bastard's got to be one of you people. One of the seven. Now maybe it wasn't you. And then again maybe it was. You know your presidents, maybe, but that story about the streets, Washington and Lincoln, that story is bullshit. So I want to tell you this. I'm gonna be all over you and your people like ugly on a hog. You take a drink, any one of you, and I'm gonna swallow. You fart, and I'm gonna smell it. If it was you who did it, I'm gonna find out. We clear on that?"

"Yes, certainly, but—"

"Good." He stalked to the door, opened it, and strode out, pulling it shut behind him.

114

CHAPTER TEN

GRIGSBY STOOD FOR A MOMENT outside Wilde's door. His hip was throbbing—all that standing—and he was still shaky from pulling the gun. He had moved reflexively, without thinking—the moment Wilde reached into his pocket, Grigsby's hand had jumped to the Colt, surprising him as much as it had Wilde.

Jesus, he hadn't drawn down on anyone for years. No call for it. Now, alone in the hotel corridor, he could feel the tension percolating from his body. He'd held it in, ignored it, while he talked to Wilde. But now it was trickling away like sap from a tree, leaving him limp and weak.

He took a breath, let it out.

He smiled. One thing, though—he was still pretty goddamn fast. Not as fast as he used to be, naturally. Not after all the years, all the wear and tear, all the booze. But still pretty goddamn fast.

He adjusted his gunbelt with a self-satisfied tug.

Not bad for an old man.

By god, that deserved a drink.

115

Sitting in the empty bar downstairs, staring at his glass of bourbon, Grigsby frowned.

Could Wilde have done it? Killed and cut up Molly Woods and the others?

He was a nance. Looked like one. Acted like one. All soft and fluttery, talking through his nose with that airy-fairy accent. Grigsby was convinced that Englishmen—he had met a few—only talked that way out of spite. If you woke them up in the middle of the night, caught them off guard, they'd talk like normal people.

Now nances, it was a well-known fact, didn't like women. Hated them. Jealousy.

But you wouldn't think that a nance would have the balls to cut a woman up like that.

But you wouldn't think that a nance would have the balls to light up a cigarette, bold as brass, while someone was holding a loaded Colt to his forehead, either.

Grigsby had seen the faint shaking of Wilde's hand as he held out the cigarette case. It hadn't lessened his respect for the gesture. Anyone who didn't get a bit edgy when someone pointed a gun at him wasn't right in the head.

No, Wilde had some balls, all right. For a nance.

Well now. Be fair. Lot of normal men wouldn't have the balls to light up a cigarette with the barrel of a .45 looking up their nose.

But did Wilde have balls enough to commit four cold-blooded murders?

That wasn't balls. That was craziness, pure and simple.

Wilde had seemed surprised when he heard about Molly Woods. Surprised, hell, he nearly shit in his pants.

But that could've been playacting. Nances were good at playacting. Lot of stage actors were nances. Came from playing at being women, maybe. Or playing at being normal. And Wilde was smart enough to pull it off—look at the way he'd come up with that story about the streets. Smooth as a snake oil salesman.

But the corner of Lincoln and Washington was a good two miles from Molly Woods's shack. So why the story?

A boyfriend? He met up, maybe, with another nance?

It was smart, too, for Wilde to ask about killings in places where he hadn't given one of his talks. Got to check on that.

First, though, talk to the valet. The servant. When you want to know about the boss, you ask the hired hand.

➤   ➤

"No suh," said Henry Villiers. "I never heard no prostitutes got kilt in those cities."

Grigsby sat in one of the two unsteady chairs in the valet's tiny room. He was sitting down because his hip still ached, and because the ceiling was so low it bumped against his hat. The room had probably been a storage space, maybe even a broom closet, before the Laidlaw brothers, the owners of the hotel, got greedy and crammed the bed and the chairs in here. The only other furniture was a small pinewood dresser. There was no window. The wallpaper, muddy green, trembled in the pale yellow glow of a small oil lamp.

"Where were you at last night, Henry?" Grigsby asked.

"With Mr. Oscar. At the Opera House."

"Until when?"

"Until after the lecture."

"And when was that?"

" 'Bout ten o'clock."

"Where'd you go afterwards?"

"Went for a drink."

"Where?"

"The Red Eagle Saloon."

Grigsby nodded. The Red Eagle was one of the few downtown saloons that served coloreds. The Red Eagle served everyone. Except for the Chinese, naturally. No one served the Chinese.

"What time you get back to the hotel?"

" 'Bout twelve."

"Anyone see you? Clerk at the front desk?"

Henry shrugged. "Don' know. Maybe."

117

He was a small slender black man, fifty or so years old, with white hair and a long narrow face. He wore a neat black suit, a white shirt, a black bow tie. His features were even and regular, and so far they had been completely without expression, revealing nothing at all of what went on behind them.

"How you gettin' along with Mr. Oscar, Henry?"

"Jus' fine."

"You figure he's a little strange, maybe?"

"Strange how?" The features didn't change.

Grigsby grinned, man to man. "C'mon now, Henry. You know what I mean."

Henry shook his head. "No suh."

Grigsby generally liked colored people—their good humor, their innocence, the easy unthinking rhythm of their simple lives—and although occasionally, like now, they were a little slow on the uptake, generally he got along just fine with them all. Some of them were shiftless, sure—but, hell, when you came right down to it, so were some of the whites. Most of them were hard workers, good providers, men who knew their place in the scheme of things, and stayed in it. There weren't a whole lot of uppity coloreds here in Denver—one way or the other, uppity coloreds didn't last long.

And all the coloreds in town knew that Grigsby might be hard, but he was straight. He gave a man a fair shake, black or white.

If only he could get Henry here to see all this.

Grigsby said, "You married, Henry?"

"No suh."

Grigsby nodded. "So I guess maybe, being a normal kind of fella, every so often you get yourself a hankerin' for a woman." Grinning again, Grigsby winked. "Know what I mean?"

Henry shook his head. "No suh. Don' really have no time for the women."

"Well, sure, Henry. You got responsibilities. But I mean, if you had the time, you'd probably get yourself a woman every now and then, right?"

Henry shrugged. "Yes suh. Prob'ly."

"Sure you would. And all I'm askin' is, you figure that Mr.

118

Oscar does that? Get himself a woman now and then?'' Or a nancy boy, maybe?

Henry shook his head. "Wouldn' know 'bout that."

"Yeah, but Henry, you see him every day. You'd know if he was out tomcatting, am I right?"

Henry shrugged. "See him in the morning. See him at the lecture. Don' see him at night, mostly."

Try something else, Grigsby told himself.

"Who takes care of Mr. Oscar's clothes, Henry? Gets 'em to the laundry and all?"

"I do."

"You ever noticed anything strange about Mr. Oscar's clothes?"

"He got a lot of them," Henry said. "Lot of different colors."

They were like children. You had to lead them along, step by step. "No, Henry," Grigsby said patiently, "what I mean is, you ever noticed bloodstains or anything on Mr. Oscar's clothes? Or maybe they were damp, like he'd tried to wash 'em off himself?"

Henry shook his head. "No suh."

"You see what I'm getting at, Henry?"

"No suh."

Grigsby sat back. He plucked the sack of tobacco from his vest pocket, opened it. You just had to be patient, was all. "You smoke, Henry?"

"No suh."

Didn't use tobacco. Didn't use women. Maybe Henry was a nance himself. Nances were popping up all over the place.

Grigsby poured tobacco into the curled sheet of paper, rolled the paper, licked it, stuck the cigarette between his lips. He struck a match with his thumbnail, lit the cigarette. Exhaling, he said, "He hired you, Henry? Mr. Oscar?" He stuck the tobacco pouch back in his pocket.

"No suh," Henry said. "Mistuh Vail."

Grigsby nodded. "You get along okay with Mr. Vail?"

"Yes suh."

"You ever notice anything strange about Mr. Vail?"

119

"No suh."

"What about the others? The newspaper reporter. O'Conner. Anything strange?"

"No suh."

"And the German? This colonel fella."

"No suh."

"And who's the other one? The poet?"

"Mistuh Ruddick. No suh."

"Everybody's one hundred percent normal and okay."

"Yes suh."

Grigsby took another puff. "Well, Henry, I don't think so. I think one of these fellas is crazy. Evil-crazy. I think he's killin' hookers. I know he is. So I want you to do me a favor. You don't mind doing me a favor, do you?"

"No suh."

Grigsby nodded. "You do me a favor, maybe I can do you a favor. You come through for me, maybe I can slip you a few dollars. How would that be?"

Henry nodded, still expressionless. "Be fine," he said.

"We can all use a few extra dollars, right?"

"Yes suh."

"Okay, so what I want you to do, I want you to keep your eyes open. You see anything strange, you let me know. Anything at all, okay?"

Henry nodded. "Yes suh."

Grigsby stood. "Good. We got a deal then?"

"Yes suh."

"Just between us, now. You and me. No point in lettin' anybody else know."

"No suh."

Glancing around the room, for the first time Grigsby noticed the book lying atop the pinewood dresser. "That yours, Henry? The book? You can read?"

"Yes suh."

"Hey, that's great. Here in Denver, not many of the coloreds can read. You ought to be proud."

"Yes suh."

120

"What's the book?"
"The Red and the Black."
"Yeah? Any good?"
"Yes suh."
"Well, that's great, Henry. Great. You keep it up."
"Yes suh."
"And you let me know, you see anything strange."
"Yes suh."

Back downstairs in the bar, Grigsby sipped at his bourbon. All in all, he thought he'd handled Henry pretty well. Patient and friendly, no strong-arm stuff, no threats. Straight from the shoulder, one regular fellow to another. Even complimented him on his reading. (*The Red and the Black?* What was that? Some kind of history about Indians and coloreds?) Anyway, he figured that he and Henry were real solid now. And maybe, to get the money Grigsby had offered, Henry would come through with something new.

Probably not, though. Henry wasn't exactly the smartest colored that Grigsby had ever met.

He took another sip of bourbon. Who's next?

"Wait a minute," said Jack Vail, suddenly sitting back in his chair. "Let me get this straight. You're saying someone's been killing off hookers in the cities where Oscar's been giving lectures?"

Grigsby, sitting opposite the business manager, said, "Yeah."

Vail's room was three times the size of Henry's, and bigger even than Wilde's. Being a business manager paid pretty well, it looked like.

"On the same days he was there?" Vail asked.

"You got it."

"Jeez. Don't tell O'Conner."

"How come?"

Vail raised thick eyebrows almost to the rim of one of the

121

worst wigs that Grigsby had ever seen. Gray and shiny, smoothed down flat at the top, it looked like some kind of dead fish curling up in the sun. "How come?" Vail said. "He's a reporter, that's how come. Soon as he knows, he'll try to get it in every newspaper in the country. It'll kill the tour."

"Uh-huh. Tell you the truth, I got a bigger problem here with the hookers gettin' killed."

"Hey. Sure. Naturally. I can understand that. But you got to understand my position also, Marshal. I got to make sure everything goes smooth on the tour. This gets out, I'm gonna lose bookings like crazy, all over the place."

He was a typical Easterner, talking mile-a-minute from the corner of his mouth. Maybe forty-five years old, he wore a suit of brown and mustard yellow plaid that reminded Grigsby of the tablecloths in cheap restaurants. He was round and tubby, with two or three shiny chins.

"So where were you last night, Mr. Vail?" Grigsby was getting a headache. From staring at Vail's suit, probably. He needed a drink.

Vail sat back in his chair and pointed a plump forefinger at the center of his chest. "*Me? You* talking about *me?*"

"You're the one I'm lookin' at."

"Hey now, Marshal. Hold on there. You don't think that any of *us* knocked off these hookers?"

"You got a better idea?"

"Sure I do. It's obvious. There's some bastard out there trying to sabotage the tour."

Grigsby smiled at the notion. "Yeah? Who'd do a thing like that?"

"How do I know? I got a lot of rivals. And I'll tell you this. It's a rough business, Marshal. Ferocious. You wouldn't believe it if I told you. I know a guy—I'm not mentioning names now—but I know a guy, an actor, he burned down a theater in Buffalo because another actor got the part he wanted. Burned it to the ground. In *Buffalo*. Like Buffalo really *counted*, right? Can you believe it?"

122

"Never been there," Grigsby said. "So where were you last night, exactly?"

"Here. I was here. But listen, Marshal—"

"All night?"

Vail shook his head. "Jeez. You don't give up. I went over to the Opera House at nine, to check the receipts. Got back here around nine-thirty, quarter to ten."

"You see anybody? The desk clerk?"

"I had a drink downstairs. Talked to the bartender for a while. Came up to my room about ten-thirty."

"And stayed here?"

"Yeah. Went to sleep around eleven."

Grigsby nodded. "Tell me about the other folks on this tour of yours."

"Hey. Really, Marshal. You're barking up the wrong tree. Couldn't of been any of them."

"Let's start off with O'Conner," Grigsby said.

"Jeeze," Vail said, and shook his head again.

"What kind of a fella is O'Conner?" Grigsby asked.

Vail shrugged. "He's a reporter. He drinks. So what else is new."

"He ever disappear at night?"

"How would I know? I'm in bed by ten-thirty, usually. But lookit, Marshal. O'Conner's not your man. I'm telling you, it's somebody trying to screw up the tour."

"What about the German? Von Hesse?"

Vail leaned forward. "Lookit, Marshal, you gonna have to talk to O'Conner about all this?"

Grigsby nodded.

"I just had a thought, see. Follow me on this, okay? If O'Conner puts this in the paper, it's gonna kill the tour, am I right?"

"That's not my problem."

"Yeah, but see, maybe it is. 'Cause if it gets out in the newspapers, then this guy of yours, the guy who's killing all the hookers, he's gonna know you're wise to him, am I right? And

123

he's gonna hide out, right? He's gonna lie low. And you're never gonna find him.''

"I'm talkin' to all the people on this here tour. The sonovabitch I want is one of 'em. He's gonna know, straight off, that I'm wise to him.'' And for all I know, Grigsby thought, you're the sonovabitch.

"Right, sure,'' said Vail, without missing a beat, "but if the tour gets canceled, everyone's gonna take off on their own. They'll be all over the place. See what I mean? He'll be gone, he'll be in New York or Chicago or Philadelphia. Wherever. Somewhere you can't get hold of him. But if the tour stays together, see, he stays with it. He's got to, 'cause if he leaves now, he's gonna draw attention to himself. Am I right?''

"You figure I should let him kill off another hooker?''

Vail's eyebrows soared up his forehead. "Jeez, no, o' course not. I look like Attila the Hun to you?'' The eyebrows lowered. "No, see, what I was thinking, you keep digging around for him, see? And I cooperate, you know? I mean, I help you out any way I can. Maybe you're right, maybe it's one of these guys on the tour. Now I think about it, it makes sense to me. Sure it does. It's obvious, right? So I keep an eye peeled, I watch these guys like a hawk. And I let you know if I pick up anything. But the thing is, we keep the whole business under wraps, see? So the papers don't catch on.''

"And how'm I gonna stop O'Conner from writing it up? Shoot him?''

Vail was leaning forward now, enthusiastic. "You do a deal with him. He'll love it. You tell him you're gonna give him an exclusive, see. You tell him that once you find the guy—and I got a lot of confidence in you, Marshal, I know you're gonna find the guy, you and me together—and once we find him, you're gonna give O'Conner everything you got. All the facts, see? All the background stuff.'' Vail sat back. "He'll love it, Marshal. Trust me.''

Grigsby had learned over the years that it was generally a pretty good idea not to trust anybody who said "Trust me.'' He said, "He'll still be writing it up afterward.''

124

"Yeah, but see, by then it'll all be over. You follow me? I mean, you'll *have* the guy. It's not like the women who come to the lectures—and, see, the women, they're three quarters of the audience, probably—it's not like they're gonna be afraid to come. Which they would be, see, if they knew he was out there, running around loose. But *afterwards*, after you catch the guy, well, jeez . . ." Vail sat back and looked off thoughtfully. "You know," he said, "publicity like that, it'd send the receipts right through the roof, probably. You couldn't *buy* publicity like that." He looked back at Grigsby. "So whatta you say, Marshal? We got a deal?"

Vail didn't know it—if he had, most likely he wouldn't have been so eager—but what he'd just offered was a solution to a problem that, somewhere behind Grigsby's dull headache, had begun to nag at him. If Greaves learned about the other killings, he'd weasel his way into the investigation. He'd try to edge Grigsby out, he'd try to gouge a few bucks out of this for himself.

But if Grigsby could keep everything under wraps, Greaves would never know.

He nodded to the business manager. "I reckon. Long as you do your part. Long as you cooperate."

"Hey," said Vail, holding out his hands, palms upward. "Didn't I say I would? And you ask anybody in the business. Jack Vail says he's gonna do something, that thing is as good as done."

Grigsby nodded. "So why don't you tell me about this von Hesse fella."

Vail grinned and pointed his finger at Grigsby. "See? That's what I like. You just don't give up. You got that incredible persistence. Jeez. It's amazing." He sat back, shook his head in admiration. "You know, I got to feel almost sorry for this guy you're looking for. I mean, with you after him, he's as good as dead already."

"Uh-huh," said Grigsby. "And von Hesse?"

Vail waved his hand lightly, dismissively. "Nah. Not a chance. No way could he be your guy. I mean, he's an officer and a

125

gentleman, you know? Besides, he's also like deeply religious. He's reading these religious books of his, all the time.''

"If he was a soldier," Grigsby said, "he'd know how to use a knife.''

"Yeah, well, sure. But a soldier, wouldn't he use a gun instead?''

"Depends.''

Vail shook his head. "Nah. Not von Hesse. All you got to do is talk to the guy and you'll see what I mean.''

"What about this fella Ruddick?''

Vail hesitated. For an instant, his eyes went shrewd—and then, all at once, they became innocent and open. It was the same swift change of expression that Grigsby had seen in bad poker players when they picked up a pat hand.

"Well now, Marshal," said Vail. "You ask me about Ruddick. Now naturally I don't think he could of done these terrible things you're talking about. And naturally I don't want to say anything bad about the guy. I mean, live and let live, that's my motto. But I got to admit that Ruddick, he's a strange one.'' He leaned forward and lowered his voice. "Just between you and me, I think he's kind of a swish. A nance.''

Grigsby nodded. "And that's how come he's traveling with Wilde? The two of them together?''

Vail frowned. "What?'' He sat back suddenly and he laughed. "You think Oscar's a swish?'' He laughed again. "Nah. That's just part of the act. It fooled me too, the first time. I thought, jeez, whatta we got here? What kinda pansy-pants is this guy? But you should see him with the women, Marshal. They eat that stuff up. They're crawling all over him, like snails on a tomato. And Oscar, I'm telling you, he loves it.'' He leaned forward confidentially again. "The fact is, I happen to know personally that Oscar gets more beaver than John Jacob Astor.''

Grigsby frowned. The idea offended him. Not because it meant he was wrong about Wilde. (Wilde was a nance, whatever Vail said.) But because it suggested that he was wrong about women. Grigsby would bet his life savings—not much of a wager, admittedly—that real women didn't go for the lah-di-dah sissy

126

types. Society women, maybe. All stiff and dried up, like last year's roses. Smelling of dust and talcum powder. Them, maybe. And them, Wilde was welcome to.

But not real women.

He said, "So you figure I oughta talk to Ruddick?"

Vail held up a hand. "Don't get me wrong. Like I say, hear no evil, speak no evil. All I'm telling you, he's a strange one."

Grigsby nodded. "What about this Countess?"

Vail lowered his head skeptically, multiplying his chins. "Hey. Come on. You don't think a woman could of done that?"

Grigsby shook his head. "She's travelin' along with the rest of you. Maybe she saw somethin'."

Vail pursed his lips. "Well. Maybe. But lookit, Marshal, if you talk to her, could you do me a personal favor and break it to her gentle like? I mean, she's a real lady. A real aristocrat. She's not used to all this kinda stuff."

Who was? Grigsby wondered. "She's travelin' with von Hesse?"

"Yeah, sure," said Vail, "but nothing like you think. He's her escort, like. They're friends, is all."

Grigsby nodded. For the first time, he found to his surprise that he was almost liking Vail. At least the little man tried to look out for this Countess of his. "How's she get along with Wilde?"

"They're friends. Really, Marshal, she's not that kind. She's a real lady."

Vail reached into his vest pocket, pulled out a gold watch. "I don't wanna rush you, Marshal like I say, I'm happy to help out any way I can. But is that it, pretty much? I mean, there's some things I got to take care of."

"I need a list of all the places where Wilde gave his talks. Since he left New York."

"Sure," said Vail. "No problem."

127

CHAPTER ELEVEN

ANDS IN THE POCKETS of his overcoat, lips puckered, Oscar pondered his way down the wooden sidewalk of Main Street. He had been unable to remain in his room. After Grigsby's visit, the place had become abruptly smaller; he had felt hemmed in, oppressed. Quickly, ignoring the bright filaments of pain that trembled and twitched against the inside of his skull, he had done his toilet and dressed himself. In basic black, as seemed fitting—although, having no suitably somber topcoat, he had been obliged to wear the ankle-length green velvet coat he had brought from London. Its collar and cuffs, at least, were black.

What he had wanted to do, still wanted to do, was trot off to Elizabeth McCourt Doe. His strange, traitorous doubts had vanished. The dull vacuum he had discovered within himself when he awoke—this had suddenly been filled, swollen, by an almost overwhelming need.

But she might not be at the mansion. Or Tabor might be. And so might the servants . . .

And so Oscar was, once again, alone.

Curious how aloneness could remember only itself. The easy, commonplace joys of friendship, the wild joys of love: it could recall none of these. One felt, experiencing it, as though aloneness were the fundamental reality; as though the rest were mere illusions.

He looked around him.

Within the few minutes since he left the hotel, the sun had vanished. The sky now was overcast, crowded with gray brooding clouds so close to the earth that they seemed to scrape along the rooftops of the bleak brick buildings.

Appropriate. Nature mirroring a state of mind. The clouds a reflection of the clouds that lay over his tour. Over his life.

He walked on, looking down again at the sidewalk, oblivious to the passersby.

Four women killed. Mutilated. What kind of madman could do that?

Grigsby was wrong. He must be wrong. Impossible that one of the others could be responsible. A madness so extreme, a madness so patent, surely by now it should have revealed itself in a word, a glance, a gesture?

"Ah, Mr. Wilde."

Oscar stopped, looked up from the gray wooden slats at his feet.

Colonel von Hesse stood before him, as military as ever in a long gray topcoat and sharply pressed gray slacks. Under his left arm, holding it at an angle of forty-five degrees from the horizontal, he carried a large book with a worn brown leather cover.

"What excellent luck," said von Hesse. "I was hoping to meet with you. Tell me, how would you translate the word *abgeschiedenheit*?"

Oscar frowned. "I beg your pardon?"

"*Abgeschiedenheit*. You would translate it how?"

Translating from the German was perhaps the last thing Oscar wished to do at the moment. But the good Herr von Hesse was, as always, so relentlessly earnest that Oscar found it difficult to dismiss him. (He had often suspected that this earnestness was something that good people relied upon, in much the way that beggars relied upon their rags.) "Detachment, I should say. As in a dwelling. Isolation. Separateness."

129

"Ah," said von Hesse, nodding. "In the spatial sense, yes? I would translate it in this manner also. But Eckhart, you see"— he tapped the book with the forefinger of his right hand—"uses the word in quite a different manner. I should translate his use of it as meaning *disinterest*. He puts it into the psychological, eh? And it is fascinating, I find, that he ranks this *abgeschiedenheit* higher even than love in the scales of virtues. The highest of all, he ranks it, in terms of approaching to God."

Oscar decided that the two of them could discuss God some other time. "Look, Herr von Hesse, obviously you haven't heard about these murders."

Von Hesse blinked, startled. "What? Murders?"

Oscar glanced around, suddenly realized that the sidewalk was crowded with people. He took von Hesse by the arm. In German he said, "Come along. I'll explain."

"But this is horrible," said von Hesse.

The two of them sat over cups of muddy coffee at a corner table in a small gray restaurant (EATS, the sign outside had grimly promised). The floor here, like the floors of most of the saloons and cafes in Denver, was ankle-deep in sawdust. Only two of the remaining five tables were occupied: one by an elderly man drooped inside a limp black suit, the other by a pair of grizzled, dour, and spectacularly dusty cowboys.

"Yes," said Oscar, "but perhaps the most distressing aspect is that this Grigsby is firmly persuaded that one of us is responsible."

Von Hesse, sitting as usual with his spine perfectly vertical, nodded thoughtfully. "Well, of course, this is possible."

Oscar sat back in his uncomfortable chair. "Come now. It would mean that one of us is not only a madman, but a madman capable of masking his madness so well as to make it undetectable."

"But perhaps," said von Hesse, running a hand along his scalp, over the furze of closely cropped white hair, "perhaps he masks it so well that even he cannot detect it."

130

Oscar frowned. "Which means what, exactly?"

Von Hesse took a sip from his coffee cup. "May I tell you a story from my life?"

Oscar shifted slightly in his chair; other people's accounts of their lives often seemed to last as long as the lives themselves. "Yes, certainly."

"Once," said von Hesse, "when I was in the army, it came to my attention that graves in the nearby area were being desecrated. Not far from Coblenz, this was, in a small town. The mayor came to me and asked me for my help. The graves were always those of women. Their coffins had been disinterred and broken open, and the condition of the corpses indicated that they had been assaulted."

"Assaulted?"

"Sexually assaulted."

"Good Lord."

Von Hesse nodded. "It was horrible, yes."

"The women had died recently? They were young?"

Von Hesse cocked his head slightly. "This would make a difference?"

Oscar frowned. "Well, if they *had* been young, and beautiful, then perhaps understanding the man's motives might not require such a leap of the imagination."

"It requires, always, a leap of the imagination to understand the motives of another. This is what compassion is, no?"

"Ah, well. I should say, rather, that compassion is the recognition that another is as important an entity as we are ourselves." Oscar smiled. "*As* important, perhaps, but not more so. Sympathizing with the pain of another is one thing. Sympathizing with his success is something quite different."

"But this recognition," von Hesse said, "this is the leap, I believe. It is a leap inward, into ourselves. We contain within ourselves, all of us, heaven and hell, angels and devils. In order to understand the devils of another, we must perceive them in ourselves. For this, imagination is required."

"Yes, well," said Oscar, who felt that they were going rather far afield, "these women. They were young?"

131

"There had been three violations, which had all occurred within a week or so of burial. One of the women was young. The others were not."

"Which would lead one to believe," Oscar said, "that the attacks had less to do with the women themselves than with the fact that they were dead." Would've made a better tale otherwise, however. Reality proving itself, once again, an inept storyteller.

Von Hesse nodded. "In any event, as the mayor explained to me, the townspeople were very concerned. Very frightened, yes? They are in this part of Germany a superstitious folk, and already there was much talk of demons and evil spirits. I agreed to help. I agreed that, should another woman die, I would secretly assign a squad of men to guard the cemetery."

"Why secretly?" Oscar sipped at his coffee. The stuff was so thick that, after one blew on it, ripples remained for a time on its surface.

"I recognized the possibility that the person responsible could have been one of the men under my command. It was, in fact, more than a possibility—it was a likelihood. We had been stationed near the town for only ten months, you see, and the attacks had begun some three months after our arrival."

Von Hesse sipped at his coffee. "For a month nothing happened."

Oscar removed the cigarette case and the box of matches from his coat pocket. No one nearby pulled out a revolver and pointed it at his head.

"And then," von Hesse said, "a young girl died. A fall from the family barn. It was a particularly tragic accident, because so easily avoidable, and the reports of her death quickly circulated among the troops and within the town. She was said, this girl, to be very beautiful. She was fifteen years old."

Oscar tapped a cigarette against the case, placed it in his mouth.

"She was buried, I remember, on a Sunday evening. I assigned a squad of men to watch the cemetery that night. No one approached the grave."

Oscar lighted the cigarette, exhaled.

"The next night, I assigned a second squad, rotating them, yes? The same thing happened. Nothing. On the third night, when the first squad returned, there came a storm. The rain fell very hard, so thickly that one could not see one's own hand before one's face. The men in the cemetery were gathered together behind a large oak tree. You must picture it, Mr. Wilde. This was autumn, and the tree was empty of its leaves. Its bare branches disappeared above them in the darkness and the torrent. They sat beneath their greatcoats, soaked to the skin and of course very cold. No doubt, among themselves, they cursed me for keeping them there. For it was inconceivable that anyone would go out on a night such as this."

Oscar nodded, exhaling. "But you're about to tell me, if I divine aright, that someone did." He looked around for an ashtray, discovered (as usual) that none had been provided, and flicked his ash to the floor.

"Yes," said von Hesse. "Someone did. By midnight, the men were no longer even attempting to watch the cemetery. They were concerned only with keeping warm. And then, just as midnight passed, they heard an awful scream, a truly terrifying scream. *Unheimlich*, yes? Unearthly. Like the scream of a demon. I believe that lesser men, having heard that scream, would have deserted their post. But these were brave men, true soldiers. They ran quickly toward the source of the scream. They found an opened grave, and the corpse lying inside the shattered coffin, which was filling up with mud and rainwater. The corpse's shroud had been torn away, and, lying atop the body, unconscious, they found the man who had been committing these horrible attacks."

"Unconscious?"

"Yes. He had fainted, apparently, at the moment of his ghastly triumph. At the moment of his scream."

"And was he one of your soldiers?"

"Yes. A young corporal. One of my most promising young men. Very brave, very conscientious."

"How did he explain himself?"

"That is the point, Mr. Wilde. He did not. He could not. When he regained consciousness, he had no recollection whatever of attacking the girl. Or of attacking the others."

"Or so he maintained."

"Mr. Wilde, you fail to understand. This corporal, he was the leader of the second squad I had assigned to the cemetery. You perceive the logical consequences of this? In his conscious mind, he *knew* that the cemetery was guarded. Consciously, he would never have attempted to commit such an act."

"The night was dark. You said yourself that the rain was heavy. Perhaps he persuaded himself that he might escape detection."

"And was it to escape detection that he screamed? No, Mr. Wilde. I am convinced that he genuinely could not recall any of the attacks. It was as though his mind had somehow become split, and the hidden part of it had developed a subterranean life of its own. And it was this, this separate and unsuspected semi-being, who committed the attacks. I suspect, too, that such a phenomenon has presented itself throughout history. Perhaps it is to this we might look for an explanation of the stories about demon possession, and the many tales of werewolves."

"Werewolves," said Oscar.

"You know the legends? They are mythical creatures, half man and half wolf. Outwardly they appear normal. Indeed, for most of their lives, they *are* normal, completely. And then, during the nights of the full moon, they change. They become filled with bloodlust, with an overriding desire to kill and destroy."

"Yes. We have them in England. We call them critics."

Von Hesse smiled faintly, sadly. "Ach, Mr. Wilde. You are not serious."

Precisely what the critics had said about Oscar's poetry. "Well, let's assume for a moment that your theory is correct. That the corporal was honestly unaware of this 'other being' within him. But wouldn't the other being be aware of the corporal? Wouldn't it—or he, if you like—know everything the corporal knew? And if so, if it knew that the cemetery was being guarded, why would it jeopardize its existence, and the corporal's, which amounts to the same thing, by committing the attack?"

134

"Ah," said von Hesse, smiling slightly, "you have seized upon, I see, the most interesting question. To this I believe there are only three possible answers."

Oscar, who had believed his question so devastating that it might end the conversation, now realized that he was destined to hear all three of these. He disguised a small sigh behind an exhaled cloud of tobacco smoke.

"First," said von Hesse, "perhaps the being, this subterranean aspect of the corporal, perhaps it was *not* aware of the corporal's existence, any more than the corporal was aware of its existence."

Like a pair of lodgers in the same apartment building, Oscar thought. Different floors, different hours. Different interests, as well: one of them produced cadavers, the other swived them.

"Second," said von Hesse, "perhaps it *was* aware, but perhaps the urge to commit the attack was so powerful, so all-consuming, that nothing else mattered. The fact that the attack was committed in a terrible downpour might incline us toward this explanation."

It might indeed. Mud, rain, cold. Why not wheel the lady off to a nice warm room, light a cosy fire, open a bottle of amontillado? Romance, alas, was dead.

"And the third possibility?" he asked. *Romance was dead:* Really, under the circumstances, that was quite good.

"Guilt, Mr. Wilde."

"Guilt?"

"Yes. Perhaps at some level this being *wanted* to be discovered, wanted to be punished. Perhaps it knew that what it did was wrong, and it wanted to be stopped. And perhaps this is why it attacked that night."

"Why wouldn't it simply stop, then, on its own?"

"Perhaps it could not. Perhaps, as I said before, the attacks came out of a kind of compulsion."

"So," Oscar said. "On the one hand, you maintain, it wanted to commit these attacks. On the other, it wanted to stop committing them. Sounds a fairly muddled sort of being, doesn't it?"

"But Mr. Wilde, we are speaking here in metaphors. There was in actuality no creature, no being. There was finally only

135

the mind, the soul, of the corporal. It was divided, yes? Bifurcated. Very muddled, in fact.''

Von Hesse sipped at his coffee. "The human mind is a great mystery, yes? As mysterious finally as the universe with all its stars and its planets. Perhaps in the distant future, perhaps in a hundred years, we will better understand how it operates, its twists and its turns and its hidden secrets. But I believe this: I believe that at bottom, we are all good. We are all tiny pieces of the infinite, and so we are all connected, each of us, to all the others, and to everything in creation. I believe that deep within us, below the masks we have acquired in our individual lives, we all somehow know this. And I believe that we know that we cannot do violence to another without doing violence to ourselves. The other *is* ourself. And it is from this knowledge, I believe, that the corporal's guilt arose.''

"All right, look," said Oscar, "even supposing that you're right, you can't be suggesting we just ignore the man who's been killing the prostitutes, in the hope that somehow he'll discover a sense of guilt?''

Von Hesse shook his head. "No, no, Mr. Wilde, I suggest no such thing. I merely explain why I thought it possible that one of us could be the killer, without himself being aware of it. It was this you asked me, yes?''

"And you really believe that one of us could secretly be a madman?''

Von Hesse frowned, puzzled. "Did I not just say so?''

Oscar dropped the cigarette to the floor, stepped on it. "You can accept the idea that one of us, someone you thought you knew, has been killing prostitutes? Without even being aware of it?''

"Accept, yes, of course. What choice have I? It seems to me at least possible.''

"It seems to me distasteful.''

"Murder is always distasteful, Mr. Wilde. Would you find it any less so, if one of us were committing the murders deliberately? Consciously? This might also be possible, of course.''

"Well, at least in that case the murderer might be prevailed upon to stop."

"How would one do so? He has already killed four times. Do you believe that you might make him stop simply by asking him? Even if you knew whom to ask?"

"But we still can't say with any certainty that the murderer is one of us."

"Can you produce a more persuasive explanation than Mr. Grigsby's?"

"Grigsby." Oscar frowned, irritated. "He's not going to give way on this. He'll be underfoot forever, interfering with the tour." Playing Javert to Oscar's Jean Valjean. Making it impossible to arrange future trysts with Elizabeth McCourt Doe.

"But it is his job to determine guilt."

"I suspect that he'd be happy merely to assign it. To me, for example."

"You feel that he is biased against you?"

"I feel that we got along less than swimmingly."

Von Hesse frowned thoughtfully. After a moment he said, "You are familiar with Frederick the Great?"

Oscar looked at him, smiled. "Not intimately, I confess."

"A great tactician and strategist. Somewhere in his *Military Instruction* he says, 'It is an axiom of war to secure your own flanks and rear, and endeavor to turn those of the enemy.' "

"Grigsby being the enemy?"

"No, Mr. Wilde. Your enemy is this killer. It is his flanks you must endeavor to turn."

"By which you mean . . . ?"

"I mean that perhaps you should attempt to discover, yourself, who he is."

137

CHAPTER TWELVE

"OH YEAH?" SAID O'CONNER. "What kind of a deal?"

"The first part," Grigsby said, "is you forget you're a reporter until I nab this sonovabitch."

O'Conner grinned. "I guess," he said, "you being stuck out here in the sticks, you don't know much about real reporters, Marshal. We've got printer's ink in our blood. Even if we wanted to, we couldn't stop doing what we do."

Printer's ink wasn't the only thing in O'Conner's blood. During the twenty minutes that Grigsby had been in the small, spare room, the reporter had downed two or three ounces of bourbon. The sleeves of his pale yellow shirt folded back, his spine slumped against the headboard, he drank the liquor, straight, from the water glass he held atop his small round belly. While Grigsby sat hunched in the hard wooden chair, O'Conner lazed with his legs comfortably crossed, like a potentate's, along the bedspread. His feet were naked, bony ankles poking out below the bottoms of his brown trousers. The soles of his feet were gray.

Grigsby didn't have any reason at all to like the man—and

didn't expect to find one, even if O'Conner bothered to offer Grigsby a drink. Something that, so far, he hadn't done.

"The second part," said Grigsby, "is that later, after I get the bastard, you get the story exclusive. All the facts, straight from the horse's mouth."

O'Conner shrugged. "That's *if* you get the guy." He didn't seem too taken by the possibility. "And meanwhile, the public's being deprived of its right to know. You haven't read the United States Constitution, I guess. A free press, it says. And as long as the public's got the money to pay for it"—he grinned and took another sip of bourbon—"they get themselves a free press."

Grigsby thought (not for the first time) that one of the good things about an asshole—probably the only good thing about an asshole—was that usually he identified himself as an asshole pretty quick.

"You write about these killings now," Grigsby said, "and this tour of Wilde's is gonna get canceled. The sonovabitch who killed those hookers is gonna take off. And then you and the public don't get any story at all."

O'Conner shrugged again. "Maybe. But before that happens, I'll sell a shitload of newspapers. Look, Marshal, this is a hell of a story. Sex, murder, mutilation—Jesus, the boobs'll eat that up with a spoon. 'Cross-Country Trail of Carnage' . . ." Fingers spread wide, he moved his hand in a broad swath through the air. He grinned at Grigsby. "How's that for a headline?"

"The third part," said Grigsby, "is that you get to keep lyin' around your hotel room all day, drinkin' whiskey and makin' up headlines."

O'Conner blinked, frowned. "Yeah? As opposed to what?"

"As opposed to lyin' in a cell at the federal lockup. We don't serve no liquor there. Just broth and hardtack. On Sundays, you get chicken stew. Some of the boys, after a while, they take a real fancy to the chicken stew."

O'Conner laughed—a laugh that sounded to Grigsby a bit hollow. "You're crazy, Marshal. You can't arrest me. For what?"

"Suspicion of murder."

O'Conner snorted. "Yeah? On what evidence?" He took a quick swallow of bourbon.

"You been with the trip since San Francisco."

"So has Wilde. So has Ruddick. *And* Vail, *and* von Hesse."

Grigsby leaned a bit forward in his chair. "Yeah," he said. "But they don't piss me off."

O'Conner's face was abruptly red with anger. "What is it with you, Marshal? A couple of two-bit hookers get sliced up. One less slut in 'Frisco. One less slut in Denver. So what? Who cares?"

Grigsby nodded. "So what you're sayin' is, you're not real fond of hookers."

"Go fuck yourself, Marshal. What I think about hookers is none of your goddamn business. You come in here and start threatening me with your bullshit federal lockup. You want to arrest me? Then arrest me. I'm a goddamn reporter, you understand? For the goddamn *New York Sun*. My editor, he hears about this, he'll have a telegram on the president's desk before breakfast. The president of the United States? You ever heard of him? So you go ahead. You arrest me."

Seemed like everybody was handing out presidents today.

Grigsby ran his hand thoughtfully along his jaw. "I reckon maybe you're right. Maybe the lockup wouldn't work out. Reckon you don't leave me much choice." He reached for the Colt, slid it from the holster, cocked it.

O'Conner's face twisted with scorn. "Yeah, sure—"

The sudden roar of the big Colt was deafening in the small room. Simultaneously—or so it seemed—a flurry of plaster dust sprayed from the wall beside O'Conner's neck, and O'Conner's body sprang up, twitching, from the bed. "Jesus *Christ!*" the reporter shrieked.

Grigsby stood and stalked over to the bed, the gun pointed at O'Conner, who scurried back along the mattress toward the wall, toes spading at the bedspread. His eyes were open, whites showing all around. His shirt front was wet with spilled bourbon (good couple of shots worth, Grigsby noted regretfully), and bits and

140

flakes of plaster sprinkled his left shoulder like a nasty case of dandruff. The hand that held the empty glass was trembling.

Grigsby said, "You listen to me, you dumb shit. I'm gonna get this sonovabitch. I'm gonna nail his pecker to the wall. You stand in my way, I'm gonna roll right over you. For all I know, the sonovabitch is you. Puttin' a bullet up your snout, that'd be one good way to find out, now wouldn't it? And I'll tell you this, it wouldn't fret me one little bit. I'm comin' to think that I might even enjoy it. So you write one word, just one word, about these hookers before I tell you it's okay, you talk to anybody else about this, anybody at all, and you'll be goin' back to the *New York Sun* at the bottom of the baggage compartment. Am I talkin' too fast for you?"

Frantically, O'Conner shook his head.

"You follow what I'm sayin' here?"

"Sure, sure," said O'Conner, his voice a squeak. He cleared his throat. His Adam's apple, which resembled his ankle, dipped and bobbed. "Sure I do, Marshal. Absolutely."

"Good," said Grigsby. He holstered the Colt. "Now let's just start all over again. Let's just make like we never had this little squabble." He strode back to the chair, turned, sat down. "I reckon, a couple of sensible hombres like you and me, we can come to some kinda agreement on this business. You don't write anything till I give you the go-ahead. And then later, after I nab this bastard, you get the exclusive. How's that sound to you?"

"Terrific," said O'Conner, still backed against the wall. "Terrific, Marshal."

Grigsby nodded. "Good. Now s'pose—"

A faint, tentative rapping came at the door to the room.

Grigsby turned. "Yeah?"

From behind the door, muffled (as though its owner were standing well away from the line of fire), a voice called out, "Everything all right in there?"

"That you, Wally?" Grigsby shouted. "Bob Grigsby here. Everything's hunky-dory. Come along in."

After a moment, the door opened and the daytime desk clerk, tall and thin and bespectacled, poked his head around its edge.

141

"You're sure, Marshal? Sounded like a gunshot." His face uncertain, his glance darted to the bed and O'Conner.

"It surely was," Grigsby said cheerfully. "I was demonstratin' my iron to Mr. O'Conner here, and the damn thing went off." He grinned. "No fool like an old fool, eh, Wally?"

The clerk glanced again at O'Conner. O'Conner smiled weakly.

"Appears I did some damage to the wall there," Grigsby said, nodding toward the ragged hollow in the plaster. "You have Lonny Laidlaw send the bill over to the office and I'll take care of it. Thanks, Wally. Sorry 'bout all the commotion."

The clerk nodded, his face still uncertain, and then ducked back behind the door, pulling it shut.

"Now," said Grigsby, turning to O'Conner. "Let's talk. S'pose we start with where you were last night."

A half an hour later, down in the bar, Grigsby sipped at his bourbon and went over O'Conner's story.

Played poker at the Mad Dog Casino from eight o'clock till twelve. Lost twenty dollars. Came back to the hotel at one, didn't leave again. Went to sleep at two.

Easy enough to check on, most of it.

The problem was, the hotel had a service entrance that opened onto the back hallway, near the kitchen. The door was kept locked at night, to stop riffraff from stumbling in and pinching the salt shakers, but anyone inside could open it by turning the latch below the knob.

A round mirror above the hotel's entryway, visible from the front desk, was supposed to let the desk clerk know when one of the guests forgot to settle his bill and wandered off, luggage tucked under his arms, down the rear hall and out the service entrance. But Grigsby had already talked to Ned Winters, the night clerk, and knew that Ned had slept away most of his shift.

So O'Conner—or Vail, or Henry, for that matter—could've snuck down the stairs, snuck past the rear of the front desk, snuck into the hallway, unbolted the door, gone out into the night,

142

found Molly Woods, cut her up, and come back to his room the same way he'd left it. No one the wiser.

The only one of them, so far, who admitted being outside the hotel that night was Wilde.

Got to remember, Grigsby told himself, to ask Doc Boynton if he could figure out what time Molly Woods got killed.

He took another sip of bourbon.

O'Conner, talking about the others, hadn't been any more helpful than Wilde or Vail, or Henry. He'd turned real cooperative after he got shot at—in the mirror behind the bar, a duplicate Grigsby shared an evil grin with the original—but he'd dismissed all of them with an easy scorn, first as human beings, and then as suspects. Wilde was "a second-rate poet and a first-rate charlatan." But he'd probably keel over at the sight of blood. Vail was "a grubby little New York hustler." But too shrewd to threaten the tour by killing hookers along its route. Von Hesse was "a stiff-necked Bible-banger." But too sanctimonious, probably, to talk to a hooker, let along kill one. Ruddick was "a pimply little pansy." But too lah-di-dah to have any truck with women, hookers or not. Henry, of course, was just "a dumb nigger." Which in O'Conner's opinion removed him from any kind of consideration altogether.

Which left, when you got right down to it, O'Conner himself.

Just because a man's an asshole doesn't mean he's guilty of anything, except being an asshole. (A truth that upon many occasions Grigsby had sadly remarked before.)

But O'Conner's dismissal of the others was different somehow from *their* dismissals. Wilde and Vail (and Henry, too, in his way)—each of them had seemed convinced that none of the men on the tour could've been the killer. (Although Vail, probably for reasons of his own, had badmouthed Ruddick, the poet.) O'Conner, on the other hand, had seemed more concerned with convincing Grigsby.

He wanted to get the Law off his back so he could write up the story, maybe.

Or maybe he wanted to get the Law off his back so he could keep on killing hookers.

143

If he was the killer and he wrote up the story, wouldn't he be drawing attention to himself?

Nope. What he'd be doing, he'd be drawing attention to all the rest of them. Who'd believe that the fella who wrote about dead hookers was the same fella who was killing them off?

And O'Conner, from what he'd said, didn't much care for hookers.

Right, Grigsby told himself. Keep an eye on O'Conner.

The decision pleased him. He'd already been inclined to keep an eye on O'Conner. Fella was an asshole.

Now. Time to talk to this Ruddick.

But when Grigsby knocked on the door to room 208, no one opened it.

Colonal von Hesse then, decided Grigsby.

But no one opened the door to room 210, either.

So maybe he should talk to this French countess.

Grigsby had never talked to a countess before, French or otherwise, and he knew that the opportunity wasn't likely to present itself again.

He knocked on the door to 211 and waited. Nothing happened.

He turned, was starting back down the corridor, when the door opened a foot or so and a woman stood there. "Yes?"

She was short, maybe five foot three, and she was blond, her hair falling in long bouncy curls to her shoulders. From her brown eyes—which looked like they'd seen a few things in their time, and enjoyed most of them—she was probably somewhere between thirty-five and forty years old, but her skin was as smooth and white as a baby's. Pink cheeks, a small nose, a mouth that was just a shade or two more red than natural. (Brenda's lipstick, when she worked the saloon, was the color of boiled beets.) She wore a silk dressing gown, pale blue, clinging, belted just below a pair of breasts whose upper curves peeked out at the top, as round and plump as peaches.

"You'd be the Countess," Grigsby said.

"Yes?" Her lips went pouty as they moved around the word.

144

He tapped the brim of his Stetson. "Marshal Bob Grigsby, ma'am. Wonder if I could talk to you for a few minutes."

She cocked her head slightly. "A marshal?"

"Federal officer, ma'am. A lawman."

"Oh yes? There is some problem?"

"No, ma'am, not for you. Just need to talk to you for a bit, is all."

"I see. Yes, then, please. Come in."

She took a step back and Grigsby moved forward into a warm pocket of scent, a perfume that was light and fresh and probably expensive, and all at once he realized that most likely he smelled, himself, like the bottom of a whiskey barrel.

She smiled and held out a hand toward the pair of wooden chairs by the window. "Please. Sit."

Grigsby took off his hat, ran his fingers through the matted hair at his temples.

"Here," said the Countess, reaching for the hat. "May I take this?"

Grigsby surrendered it, and noticed for the first time that it could stand a good cleaning.

The woman turned it around, eyeing it appreciatively. "A most formidable headpiece," she said, and smiled at Grigsby.

"Yes ma'am," he said. "It's a Stetson. Out of St. Louis, Missouri."

"Admirable," she said, and indicated the chairs again. "Please."

He crossed the room, turned one of the chairs to face the other, and sat down. He crossed his legs, booted ankle atop his knee, his spur suddenly lethal, and he wondered what to do with his big heavy hands. They seemed, right now, to be located a long way from his shoulders. He crossed his arms over his chest.

The Countess set the Stetson on the dresser and then sat down opposite Grigsby. She leaned slightly toward him, her own small hands folded at her lap, and smiled again. "Now. How may I help?"

"Well, ma'am," said Grigsby, trying to keep his stare from sinking toward the soft swell of breasts, and mostly succeeding.

145

"You been with this tour of Mr. Wilde's since San Francisco, that right?"

She nodded, waiting. "Yes?"

"Well, ma'am, it looks like somebody on the tour—one of the fellas, I mean, I don't know which one of 'em—it looks like maybe he's killing people. In different towns along the way," he finished. He realized that he was sweating.

Warm in here. The woodstove.

The Countess frowned, her lips daintily bunching together. "I'm sorry?"

Grigsby tugged at his collar. He slid his hands into the pockets of his jacket. "See, ma'am, it was a coincidence, like. I got these letters, is what happened, from people in these different towns. San Francisco. And El Paso. And Leavenworth, Kansas. And see, in all these towns, somebody killed off a woman. Killed her off and, well, what he did, he cut her up pretty bad. Now the thing of it is, all these women got killed off at the same time that Mr. Wilde was there, givin' one of his talks. Hadna been for these letters, I wouldna figured it out. And now, what's happened is, just last night one of them got killed off here in Denver."

"Killed?" said the Countess, her head bent forward, her arched eyebrows moving in puzzlement. "Who was killed?"

"Ladies of the evening, ma'am. Women that were, well, no better than they had to be, if you follow me."

"Ladies of . . . ? *Poules?* Prostitutes?"

"Yeah," said Grigsby, relieved and grateful. "Yes, ma'am. Prostitutes."

"In San Francisco? The other towns? In every town where Oscair spoke?"

"Well, ma'am, I don't rightly know about every town. I'll be lookin' into that. But the thing is, they were all killed off the same way, exactly. So it's pretty clear to me that it musta been the same guy, each time. Which means—"

"Which would mean," said the Countess, "yes, that very possibly one of the people traveling with the tour, he is a murderer." She sat back. "How horrible," she said, and shook her head. "But this is ghastly."

146

"Yes ma'am."

Looking off, she said again, "How horrible."

"So what I thought, ma'am, I thought I'd come and ask you, since you been on the tour all this time, if maybe you seen anything or heard anything that might help me get a bead on this fella."

The Countess frowned again. "I'm sorry? My English. Sometimes it is inadequate."

"Not a bit of it, ma'am. What I'm lookin' for, ya see, is anything that could help me figure out who this fella is. You were in all those towns, along with the rest of 'em. Maybe you saw somethin'. Maybe you heard somethin'."

"But no. Nothing. This, today, what you tell me, this is the first I have heard of such a thing. If even for a moment I had thought—" She broke off, shook her head. She looked at Grigsby, leaned forward. "Are you quite certain, Mr. Greegsby—forgive me, it is Greegsby?"

"Yes ma'am. Grigsby."

"Are you quite certain there is no possibility of error?"

"Well, ma'am, no," Grigsby said. "I don't hardly think so."

She sat slowly back again, looking worn and drawn, and suddenly she seemed to be years older than Grigsby had first thought she was. And, strangely, this made him feel abruptly protective, almost paternal, as though by growing older, by allowing herself to grow older before his eyes, she had become vulnerable and frail, like a little girl.

He said, "Now listen, Countess. Don't you worry. I'm gonna find this fella. I'm gonna nail—I'm gonna nail him to the wall."

The Countess had been bleakly staring off, out the window, where the sky had darkened and the streets had grayed. Now she turned to Grigsby and with a visible effort, inhaling deeply, straightening her back, she brought herself back to the room, and back down the years. She produced a small, tired smile. "Yes," she said. "I am sure you will. But I am wondering whether it would be better for me if I left the tour."

"Well now," said Grigsby. "That'd be up to you, ma'am. So far, this fella, it seems like he only has it in for prostitutes, like

147

I say." But was this an actual fact? What about the woman in Leavenworth? That storekeeper's wife. She'd been hooking on the side, maybe? "And—Listen, Countess, if I told you somethin', confidential-like, could you keep it between you and me? Not let the rest of 'em in on it?"

Once more, she cocked her head slightly. "Yes, of course. You have my word." She leaned forward and softly touched Grigsby's knee with the tips of her fingers. "But please. Not Countess. My name is Mathilde."

"Yes ma'am." Grigsby was still trying, less successfully now, not to look at her breasts. "Well, the thing of it is, all these women so far, the women that got killed off, they were all redheads."

"Redheads?" Pronouncing the word like she hadn't heard it before.

"They all had red hair, ma'am. All four of 'em. Now red hair, you don't see much of that, usually. So I figure, what with all four of 'em havin' it, I figure this fella's gotta have a special kinda interest in red hair."

The Countess reached up, abstracted, and felt lightly at her own blonde curls. "And why would you not want the others to know of this?"

"Because the way I calculate it, ma'am, one of 'em is the killer. And I figure maybe it's better for me to know a little somethin' about him, about this fella, that he don't know that I know, if you follow me."

She nodded. "Yes. I comprehend. I shall not mention it. And you think that because of this, I should be safe if I remained with the tour?"

Grigsby sat back. "Well now. Safe. I don't know as I could put no guarantees on that, ma'am. But I reckon that if you kept an eye peeled, made certain sure that you didn't get yourself alone with any one of 'em, you'd be okay, prob'ly. And the other thing is, like I been tellin' all of 'em, I'm gonna be one step behind this here tour. Until I find this fella and nail him. What I mean is, I'm gonna be around. Close by. You figure you

148

need yourself some help, all you gotta do is come to me and let me know."

She smiled again, more warmly this time. "Thank you. It is kind of you to reassure me."

"My pleasure, ma'am." He nodded to her. "And now, I reckon I'll let you alone." He stood up, and winced involuntarily as the old familiar twinge shot from his hip down his leg.

The Countess looked up at him, concerned. "You are in pain?"

"No, ma'am. Touch of rheumatism, is all. Well, I'm right sorry I gotta be the one who tells you all this. And I appreciate your help."

"Not at all," she said, standing. "It is I who should be grateful." She stepped over to the dresser, picked up Grigsby's Stetson, returned and handed it to him. "And perhaps you will visit with me again one time? Perhaps, if I give thought to this, I will remember something that could help you."

"Yes ma'am. Thank you. Maybe I'll just do that." He started for the door, and then turned back to the Countess. "One other thing, ma'am. Just thought of it." Later, after he learned the truth, he would ask himself why he had.

The Countess raised her eyebrows. "Yes?"

"The reporter. O'Conner. You ever read any of his articles?"

"About the tour, you mean?"

"Yes ma'am."

"But no. How should we find a New York newspaper out here?"

Grigsby nodded. "Reckon that's so."

CHAPTER THIRTEEN

WITH A BROAD BUOYANT GRIN, hugely pleased by the brilliance and ingenuity of his Plan, Oscar swept through the door and past Henry Villiers. When he reached the middle of the room—which took no more than a single, abruptly terminated step—the grin disappeared and he looked around him in shocked disbelief.

"Good Lord, Henry. Are *these* the sort of accommodations that Vail's been providing you?"

Still standing by the door, Henry shrugged. "It's fine with me, Mistuh Oscar."

"But Henry, it's drab. It's worse than drab. It's *funereal*. That wallpaper is *grotesque*. If you continue to stay here, you'll become quite morbid. And I simply cannot tolerate morbid people—they become so involved with themselves that they ignore me altogether. I'll speak with Vail, we'll get you moved into a new room immediately."

"Really, Mistuh Oscar. No need for that. This room's jus' fine."

"Nonsense. Now, please, close the door and come along. Sit

down while I explain what I've come up with. I think you'll find it extraordinary.''

Henry did as ordered, stepped over and sat in one of the room's two chairs, both of which looked cramped and hazardous. Oscar remained standing, his hands clasped behind his back.

"Now," he began. "This Marshal Grigsby person—big brutal chap with a silly hat and a colossal handgun—has he spoken with you yet?"

"Yes suh."

"You know about the women being killed, then. The prostitutes. And you know that Grigsby believes one of us responsible."

"Yes suh. A terrible thing, Mistuh Oscar."

"Yes, yes, of course. Terrible. And I'm afraid that Grigsby may be right, that one of us is, in fact, the murderer. But it's obvious to me, Henry, that Grigsby is entirely out of his element here. Oh, no doubt he can twirl a rustler and track down a lariat, or whatever it is these frontier stalwarts do, but the simple fact is, just now he's confronted with an extremely cunning and resourceful killer. And Grigsby is hopelessly outclassed."

Oscar drew himself up to his full height. "So, what I propose to do, you see, is determine for myself just exactly which one of us is responsible."

Henry nodded. "Yes suh. How?"

"Ah, Henry. Wonderful. You leap at once to the crux of the matter. How, indeed. And I answer—by bringing to bear on this problem a talent, a faculty, that poor Grigsby lacks, one which he would be utterly unable even to imagine."

Oscar leaned forward and intoned, "I speak now of the sensibility, the intuition, of a poet."

Henry nodded. "Yes suh."

Oscar smiled happily and spread his arms. "Do you see it, Henry? Of course you do. Really, it's obvious, isn't it? Who better than a poet, with his insight into the mind and the heart, who better than he to penetrate the mask behind which this villain has hidden himself? We will uncover this man, Henry, and we will do it by a systematic application of the poetic imagination."

151

"Yes suh," Henry said. "We, Mr. Oscar?"

Oscar put his hands into the pockets of his coat. "Well, yes, of course. I'll need your assistance, Henry. One of the first things we must do is learn as much as we can about these women, and specifically about the woman here in Denver. We shall enter into the mind of the killer by apprehending the nature of his victims. What particular quality, or combination of qualities, did these women possess, such that they were chosen? This we can learn only by talking to the locals. And, naturally, being an American, you'll be of tremendous help to me in dealing with them."

"Yes suh. But Mr. Oscar—"

"And, too, bear in mind that three of the men under suspicion—Vail, O'Conner, and Ruddick—are also Americans. Here again, you'll be of enormous assistance. As distasteful as it is, we must study them, Henry. We must study not only their outward appearances and activities, but also, in so far as possible, the inner workings of their psyches. The hidden wellsprings of their lives. For I have a theory, Henry."

Oscar began to pace. One step to the left, a turn, two steps to the right, a turn. "I believe it possible that this killer may be a kind of bifurcated personality. What do I mean by this? I mean that in some manner, for some reason, the mind of this person may have become split, divided. And, as a result, one part of his mind has become a sort of subterranean self—a separate and unsuspected semi-being, if you will—and it is this being, this creature, which is committing these terrible crimes. *Without*, and this is the salient point, Henry, *without* the man himself knowing of it."

"He don' know he's killin' people," Henry said.

"*Exactly*. You grasp my meaning perfectly. I—"

Someone knocked at the room's door.

Oscar turned, frowning impatiently. He strode over to the door and jerked it open.

"Oscar boy," said Vail. "I been lookin' all over for you." He scuttled into the room, nodded to Henry, turned back to Oscar, and said, "Lookit, this yokel marshal, he talked to you, right?"

"Yes, yes. A very colorful character."

152

"Right. So you know about the hookers and all. Well, I just wanted to tell you not to worry. I got everything under control."

"Under control?"

"I went and talked to Bill Greaves. He's the chief of police here, met him the other night at the lecture. Nice guy, kinda guy you can do business with. Anyway, I asked him about this hooker thing, and Grigsby and all. And you know what I found out?"

"I will in a moment, presumably."

Vail chuckled, shook his head. "That wit you got. Okay, what I found out is, Greaves didn't know nothing at all about the other hookers. The ones in the other cities. It was a big surprise to him. And he told me that this Grigsby, he's a federal marshal, sure, but he don't have any kinda jurisdiction here in Denver. Not over this case here, the hooker who got killed down by the river, and not over the others neither. Grigsby's just an old rummy, Greaves says, who likes to stick his nose into other people's business." Vail grinned. "Greaves is really burned up at the guy."

Oscar frowned. "I'm not sure I understand. You mean that no other prostitutes were killed?"

"Who knows? Maybe they were, maybe they weren't. What's it got to do with us? *You* didn't kill 'em. I know *I* didn't."

"And the others on the tour?"

"Come on, Oscar boy. Von Hesse? O'Conner? Can you picture either one of 'em as a guy kills hookers? And besides, I got the whole thing figured out."

Oscar was frowning still. "Figured out," he repeated.

"Right. We drop 'em. O'Conner, von Hesse, all of 'em. We tell 'em to hit the road. That way, later, if it comes out about the hookers, we put out a statement, see? We say, yeah, sure, there *were* some folks traveling with us, maybe it *was* one of them who did this horrible thing, but we don't know anything about any of it, and anyway they're all gone now." Vail interrupted his explanation to frown thoughtfully. "Too bad about the Countess. She's got a lot of class." He shrugged. "But sometimes in life you got to make sacrifices."

Oscar nodded. "Tell me something," he said. He was finding

153

it extremely difficult to keep his voice even. "Why did you go to this Greaves in the first place?"

"I got to protect the tour, Oscar boy. With this guy Grigsby running around asking questions, it would of gotten out about the hookers. And that's the kind of publicity we don't need. I stalled him for a while, told him I'd cooperate, right? And then I got to thinking. How come Bill Greaves never came and talked to me about all this? Me and Bill got along real well. And who's this Grigsby guy anyway? So I went and had a little talk with old Bill."

"I see," Oscar said. He cleared his throat. "And what about the prostitutes?"

Vail looked puzzled. "What about 'em?"

"What are old Bill's feelings regarding the prostitutes?"

"Jeez, Oscar. What kinda feelings is he gonna have about a bunch of hookers got killed in some other city?"

"And the one who was killed here?"

"Okay, it's a tragedy and all, and, sure, naturally, he's gonna try to find out who did it. That's his job, right? But the thing is, Oscar boy, he knows it wasn't us. He knows we got no reason to go around killing hookers. He knows we don't need no bad publicity on the tour. And like I said, he's a guy you can do business with." Grinning, Vail winked broadly. "Him and me, see, we came to an understanding."

"An understanding?"

"Sure. He keeps quiet about the other hookers, keeps all that outta the newspapers, and he gets Grigsby off our backs."

"And in return?"

Grigsby shrugged lightly. "We slip him a percentage of the receipts. Not much, don't worry. And even at twice the price, I'm telling you, it'd be worth it. And it's only until we're out of Colorado."

Oscar nodded. "Mr. Vail," he said, "are you familiar with the word *abominable*?"

Vail frowned again. "Sure, yeah. I know plenty of big words. And what's with this *Mr.* Vail?"

"I think that what you suggest is abominable. I think it is

154

loathsome. I think it is despicable. I think that you, personally, are contemptible. No. I think, actually, that you are beneath contempt. So far beneath it as to make contempt seem like veneration. I should call you a swine, but compared to you a swine seems the pinnacle of grace and chivalry."

Vail glanced uneasily toward Henry. "Hey, Oscar boy, not in front of the troops. I mean, we got a disagreement, we can—"

"Has it occurred to you, has it even once penetrated that quagmire you call a mind, that whoever is killing these women will continue to do so, indefinitely, until someone stops him? Has it occurred to you that if the killer is one of the people traveling with us, then we, you and I, are in some measure responsible for these deaths?"

"*Responsible?* Jeez, you got to be kidding!"

"On an even simpler level, much more your style, has it occurred to you during your shabby attempts to keep this from the newspapers, that O'Conner is a reporter? If we drop him from the tour, what's to prevent him from writing about all this?"

"Hey, O'Conner's a lush. I can handle him. Or Greaves can—"

"Can what? Chop off his head? What portion of the receipts will that cost us? And has it occurred to you, furthermore, that if one of these people *is* guilty, then the rest are innocent? And that you, in your glib indifference, will be casting them to the wolves?"

"Oscar boy, we got the tour to think about."

"We are not going to drop anyone. Not O'Conner. Not von Hesse. Not anyone. No one is going to hit the road."

"Now Oscar—"

"Except perhaps yourself. I mean that literally. If you open your mouth once more before I've finished speaking, I will pick you up, walk you over to the window, and push you through it. I assure you that I'm capable of doing this with great dispatch, and with even greater pleasure."

Oscar paused. Vail, unfortunately, merely stood there blinking.

"Now," said Oscar. "I want you to listen to me very carefully. This is what you're going to do. First, you will talk to the others and make sure that they've all spoken to Marshal Grigsby and

155

given an account of their activities last night. To any who haven't, you will suggest that they do so. Grigsby may be a buffoon, but he's a determined buffoon, and he won't be satisfied until he's talked to all of us.''

Vail took a deep breath. Oscar glared at him. Vail said nothing and blinked a few times more.

"Second, you will go down to the desk clerk and arrange for Henry's things to be moved from this dreadful little crypt into an actual room. If the expense money is dwindling, then I recommend that you make up the difference by altering your own accommodations.''

Vail opened his mouth, Oscar glared, Vail shut his mouth and returned to blinking.

"Now. You mentioned that the prostitute had been killed near the river. Where, exactly?''

"How come you want—''

"*Where?*''

"Shantytown,'' said Vail quickly. "That's all I know. That's what Greaves said. Come on now, Oscar boy, this ain't right. You threatening me like that. We been through a lot together.''

"And perhaps we shall continue to do so. We'll discuss it later.''

"Yeah, but Oscar . . .''

Oscar looked at him. "Yes?''

"About Grigsby. I told you, we don't have to worry about him no more.''

"I suspect it will take more than a chief of police to stop Marshal Grigsby. For the time being, we cooperate with him. Is that understood?''

"Yeah, sure, of course. Whatever you say. Naturally. I mean, there's no need to get yourself in a tizzy.''

"I am not in a tizzy. I have never been in a tizzy in my life.''

Quagmire of a mind.

Swamp, Oscar thought. *Swamp* would've been better. *Has it even once penetrated that swamp you call a mind.*

156

Still, all in all, it had gone off very well.

Poor Vail had been absolutely terrified. As well he should've been. He had revealed himself as possessing the mind of a ferret. He deserved defenestration.

Has it once penetrated that bog you call a mind.

Swamp. Yes.

"Mistuh Oscar," said Henry. "This 'pears to be the place, ahead here."

Oscar looked. Ahead, on the right side of the narrow dirt roadway, a ragged crowd of ragged people was sluggishly milling about, slowly eddying before a tiny gray ramshackle building where three blue-clad policemen stood morose silent guard.

"Police not gonna let you in there, Mr. Oscar," Henry said.

"No, of course not. What we want now is a public house." He leaned forward and called to the driver, "Is there a saloon nearby?"

Over his shoulder, the driver grumbled in a sour voice, "And how would I be knowin'? This bein' me first time in this hellhole of a place?"

The Irish, Oscar thought. Ever amiable.

"Do you suppose you could find one?"

The man grumbled, shrugged.

Oscar sat back. If anyone could locate an establishment where whiskey was served, even in hell, it was an Irishman.

Oscar looked around. *Hellhole* was in fact an apt description.

He had been silent throughout the trip, fuming, still furious at Vail, looking up only now and then to notice vaguely that the streets were growing more narrow, the houses more slovenly and shoddy.

But this, this Shantytown, this was worse than anything in London, worse than Spitalfields or Whitechapel. There the buildings, squalid though they might be, were at least made of brick and stone; here they had been thrown together, hastily, with bits of tin and tarpaper and strips of mismatched timber clearly torn from packing crates. Some of the structures had been painted, quickly, slapdash; but all of them were coated with a dull coat of grime that seemed, despite the temporary character of the

157

buildings themselves, ageless and ineradicable. Looming in the alleyways and empty lots between the buildings were piles of rubble and rubbish—empty liquor bottles, tin cans florid with rust.

The sky overhead, which in the rest of Denver had promised rain, here threatened apocalypse. A thick, shapeless, yellow-gray fug lay over everything, leaching away the light and stinking of sulfur.

The wind had begun to blow, moaning and whistling as it swept around the shanties, sending scraps of paper tumbling down the desolate roadway; but it left untouched the blanket of gray overhead.

How, in a country so rich in resource and promise, could a place like this exist? How could anyone permit it to exist?

The carriage pulled up alongside a low rambling wooden edifice which was as dreary and dingy as the rest, but which had apparently been constructed with some small hope of permanence. A thin yellow light quivered behind the two small windows in the clapboard front. Over the door, swaying in the wind, a weathered wooden sign identified it as the Devil Dog Saloon.

The driver turned, his wrinkled red face pinched with displeasure. "Two dollars," he said.

Oscar took the money from the pocket of his topcoat and handed it to the man. "Would you mind waiting until we return?"

The man snorted. "Wait? Around here? Are ye daft? Close me eyes for a minute and some ruffian will be off with me wheels and me horse. Ye wanted Shantytown, where the poor bawd got herself killed, and here ye are, and that's an end to it. I'll be off now, and good day to ye."

Oscar smiled. "You'll be a Galway man, by your voice."

The driver narrowed his eyes. "Will I now? And just why, exactly, would you be thinkin' that?"

"I've connections there. To the O'Flaherties and the O'Flynns."

"Course you do," said the driver. "And me own bloody name is Prince bloody Albert. Pull the other one, why don't ye."

The wind snapped at Oscar's hair. "The name is Wilde. Oscar

Fingal O'Flahertie Wills Wilde. You've heard of my mother, perhaps. Jane Francesca Wilde. Speranza.''

Still dubious, the driver said, "The poet lady? Of Dublin?''

"The very one.''

"And how is it, then, that ye talk with a mouthful o' bloody English plums?''

"Ah well,'' Oscar smiled. "The result of a youth misspent at Oxford University.''

The driver considered for a moment. Then he said, "Speranza's son? You'd not be lyin' to me?''

Oscar smiled. "May the good Lord strike me dead in my boots.''

The driver suddenly grinned. "Well, why din't ye say so?'' He swiveled farther around on his seat and stuck out his hand. "O'Hara. Benjamin J. O'Hara. Of Galway and Denver.''

Oscar shook the hand and the driver leaned toward him, his face abruptly serious. "But now listen, young Mr. Wilde. This shebeen here, 'tis a nasty place, not fit for decent folk. There are hard men hereabouts, thieves and killers and the like. I've heard me some terrible stories.''

"It can't be helped, I'm afraid. I've some business to transact. But there's a fiver in it for you, Mr. O'Hara, if you'll wait the carriage for us.''

"Git away with your fiver. Take money, would I, just for standin' about? No, I'll be waitin' for ye, never fear. And if ye find yerself in some difficulty, you just give me a holler and I'll come runnin'.''

"I'm sure of it.'' Oscar turned. "Henry, shall we go?''

Henry, his face as expressionless as always, looked from Oscar to the driver and then back to Oscar. "Yes suh, Mr. Oscar.''

CHAPTER FOURTEEN

PLEASE INFORM ME ANY RECENT DEATHS PROSTITUTES YOUR AREA

Short and sweet, thought Grigsby.

He looked up from the sheet of paper, sipped at the bourbon in his half-full water glass, and called out, "Carver?"

Through the closed door, he heard a sharp clunk from the anteroom as the legs of the deputy's tilted chair slammed to the wooden floor. The chair squeaked against the floor, chalk on blackboard, and a moment later the door opened and Carver Peckingham loped into Grigsby's narrow office, brushing lank brown hair from his eyes with thin eager fingers.

"Yes sir?"

Grigsby sat back in his chair. "I got a job for you. Couple jobs."

"Yes sir?" Tall and slump-shouldered, the deputy stood at eager near attention in front of Grigsby's desk. One thing about Carver—he wasn't any great shakes when it came to brains, but he was eager as all get-out.

"Here." Grigsby handed him the sheet of writing paper. "I want you to take this over to the telegraph office. Talk to Mort.

Have him send it off to the mayors of these here cities." He handed Carver the list of cities he'd copied from Wilde's itinerary. "And also the mayors here." He handed over a second list, western cities that Wilde hadn't visited. "Have him sign all of 'em with my name, and make sure he puts down Federal Marshal."

Carver looked through the two lists. "Golly, Marshal," he said. "There must be thirty or forty of 'em." He looked down at Grigsby. "That's gonna cost more, probably, than we got in petty cash."

"That's why I want you to talk to Mort. He'll put it on the cuff."

Carver was reading Grigsby's message. He looked up. "How come you want to know about prostitutes, Marshal?"

"Somethin' I'm workin' on. Special survey for the attorney general. Top secret, Carver, so don't you go jawin' about it to nobody."

"No sir, Marshal. Mum's the word. You can count on me. How come the mayors?"

Grigsby frowned. "How come the mayors what?"

"How come you're sendin' it to the mayors?"

Grigsby swallowed some bourbon. "Well, Carver, some of those cities got sheriffs, and some of 'em got city police. Some, maybe, only got a justice of the peace. Take me forever to find out which was which. Now s'pose I send it to the sheriff, and there ain't no sheriff. Maybe no one'll ever read it. But they all got mayors. There's always some poor sonovabitch wants to be mayor."

Carver grinned. "Yes, sir. Reckon that's so."

Grigsby handed Carver another sheet of paper. "And I want Mort to send this off, too."

Carver read from the sheet. " 'The New York Sun.' What's that?"

"Newspaper."

Carver read slowly: " 'Par . . . tic . . . u . . . lars.' " He looked up. "What're they, Marshal?"

"They're like details. You go ahead now, Carver."

161

"Yes, sir. And I won't say nothin' about the survey to nobody, Marshal. Mum's the word."

"Good, Carver. Appreciate it."

As Carver loped quickly off, Grigsby stood and walked over to the window. Peering out it, looking down at Main Street, he rolled himself a cigarette.

There was an outside chance that the killer wasn't traveling with Wilde. Grigsby doubted this, but it was a possibility. Like Wilde had said, if even a single hooker had been killed in a town the tour hadn't covered, then everyone on the tour was pretty much in the clear. The cities on Grigsby's second list were close enough to the other cities, the cities where hookers had been killed, for the killer to reach them in the time available. If no hookers had been killed in any of them, then Grigsby was back where he'd started. With the people on the tour.

He snapped a match alight with his thumb.

Naturally, it was possible that if the killer wasn't connected to the tour, he could've killed off a hooker in some other town somewhere, some one-horse place too small for Grigsby's list. And Grigsby would never know about it.

But how many of those small towns had hookers anyway? And even if they did, how many of the hookers had red hair?

Grigsby puffed at the cigarette. He could hear the wind sliding around the corners of the Federal Building, growling low in its throat. Outside, down in the street, the gusts kicked flurries of dust at the bent figures who scurried along the sidewalks, their heads tucked low, their hands hooked at their hats.

Exhaling smoke, he glanced up at the rooftops opposite. Dark clouds, swollen and sullen, still bellied their way across the sky. The rain would arrive soon, curtains of it, each one swaying dull and cold behind the other.

A memory came to him then, a summer afternoon riding with Clara, a storm coming up, the two of them too far from town to make it back before the shower hit, but racing for it all the same, Clara laughing with excitement, her brown hair flung behind her like a banner. The downpour starting cold and shivery, fat round raindrops hard as pebbles slapping at his thighs, the smells of earth and grass suddenly draped across the cooling air, and he and Clara making a final sprint for an empty barn in a huddle of trembling pines. And there, standing in the opened doorway, both of them dripping wet, the horses softly shuffling in the shadows, they had come together, mouth to mouth, hip to hip, the clean smell of Clara's soap mingling with the sweet barn smell of hay, and right there, Clara's back arched against the pinewood jamb, they had taken each other.

Grigsby swallowed, sucked a quick staggered breath into a chest abruptly too tight. It still surprised him, the pain, by how swiftly it could sneak up on him, and how real it was, how physical, as though some great gray claw had lurched between his ribs and ripped away his living heart.

Even a storm could bring the pain. Almost anything could. They had so long been together, he and Clara, or maybe so intensely together, that everything in the world had been touched and shared by the two of them. They had left, the two of them, their imprints on everything. And now, in those hollows, a kind of poison had welled up, as bitter as acid, and the world had become a precarious place, crowded with dangers. A snatch of music. A child's laugh. A flicker of rose in the sunshine. A rainstorm. Almost everything he saw, or heard, or smelled, was tainted now.

He stepped over to the desk, lifted the glass of bourbon and finished it off. Setting it back down on the desktop, he heard footsteps in the anteroom. He turned. Carver, as usual, had left the door open.

A thin man walked into the office, holding himself as upright as if he wore a corset somewhere beneath his gray suit and topcoat. His bristly white hair was so short that the pink scalp shone through it. He looked at Grigsby, nodded stiffly, and said, "You are Marshal Grigsby?"

"Yeah."

"Wolfgang von Hesse. Mr. Vail suggested to me that I see you."

"Well now, Colonel," said Grigsby, sitting back in his chair. "That's a mighty fine story. I've always been a sucker for stories about graveyards and storms and such. But I'll tell ya, that corporal of yours, it doesn't surprise me none that he tried to claim he was innocent. Just about every lowlife I ever met tried to tell me the same thing. I know of a fella, Jake Lindstrum, five different people saw him gun down his partner in broad daylight, and he was still claimin' he didn't know a thing about it when he got hung. Prob'ly believed it himself by then."

"Ach, yes, of course," said von Hesse. "But I speak here of something quite different, Marshal. Consciously, this corporal would never have done what he did."

"Crazy people do crazy things," Grigsby said. "That's what makes 'em crazy."

Sitting across the desk from Grigsby, his back very straight, von Hesse had given him a precisely detailed account of his activities last night. Dinner with Wilde and the Countess from nine-thirty to eleven. Escorting the Countess to her room at eleven-ten. A single drink—a brandy—in the hotel bar, which he finished by eleven thirty-five. Reading in bed until twelve-thirty. Asleep by quarter to one.

While von Hesse talked, Grigsby had tried to picture the man wielding a knife over the body of Molly Woods, cutting and slicing. He hadn't been able to. But he hadn't been able to picture any of the others doing it, either. Even though he'd seen the results with his own eyes, he still couldn't picture anyone doing that.

And now von Hesse was trying to sell Grigsby on an idea that made no sense at all.

"There are many forms of madness," said von Hesse.

And this was one of them, Grigsby thought. "So what you're tellin' me here," he said, "is that any one of these people could be the killer, and not even know about it."

"Yes, exactly," said von Hesse, and nodded. He looked toward the bottle and the glass, full once again, on Grigsby's desk.

164

"Marshal, I see that you are a man who enjoys the occasional drink."

Grigsby looked at glass and bottle, smiled bleakly. "I been known to indulge."

"Have you ever, in the course of an evening, perhaps lost a few moments of time? I mean to say, have you ever, on the following day, been unable to recall certain events of the night before?"

Grigsby nodded. "Once or twice."

"But yet, during the time lost to you, you moved about, you spoke, you acted and reacted."

Grigsby shrugged. "Never killed no one."

"But still, in a sense, during that period your conscious self was somehow absent. In a sense, another part of you had taken over."

Yeah, Grigsby thought. My pecker.

He said, "So you think this fella's a big drinker." Like O'Conner.

"Ah," said von Hesse, sitting back. "I mention the drinking as an example only. Perhaps alcohol would have this effect, perhaps it would not. The corporal I spoke of, he drank nothing at all."

"So you could be this guy yourself. And not know it." Was this some crazy kind of confession? Was von Hesse the killer, and maybe playing with him?

"Exactly. If I were he, I would have no recollection whatever of committing these crimes."

"Which'd mean," Grigsby said, "that you'd be innocent in a way, that right?"

"In a sense, yes. But I believe, you see, that in a sense we are all innocent."

"Yeah. Well, Colonel, I been around too long to buy that. There are some folks in the world that're just plain evil, pure and simple. They got something missin', a conscience or whatever, and hurtin' other people don't mean a thing to them. Some of them even like it. This bastard that killed those women, way I read him, he's one of the ones that like it."

"But evil, I think, is a kind of ignorance."

"I don't give a damn what it is, tell you the truth. All I care about is stoppin' it. Now this corporal you're talkin' about, what happened to him?"

Von Hesse pressed his lips briefly together. "I recommended that he be hospitalized. My recommendation was ignored. He was executed."

"Well," said Grigsby, and shrugged, "there you go."

"Justice in this world is imperfect, Marshal Grigsby."

"Maybe so. But at least that fella wasn't out there diggin' up no more graves." Grigsby shifted in his chair. "But okay. Let's say you're right. Let's say one of the others is crazy the way you're talkin' about. Which one you figure it is?"

Von Hesse smiled a small prim smile. "But this is exactly my point, you see. There would be no way of my knowing. Outwardly, this man would appear perfectly normal."

Grigsby nodded. "Uh-huh. So try it the other way. Say this bastard knows exactly what he's doin'. All the time. So then who would you say it is?"

"I would say, then, that it was none of them."

"Way I figure it," Grigsby said, "it's gotta be one of them." And maybe you, scout.

"I am inclined to agree. That the murders were committed in each of the towns we visited makes this seem likely. But none of these men has at any time evinced any behavior that suggests his guilt. It is precisely this, you see, which leads me to believe that he may himself be unaware of it."

"Uh-huh. Well, Mr. von Hesse, I appreciate you comin' by and talkin' to me. I'll surely bear in mind what you say."

Von Hesse smiled. "And I thank you for your patience, Marshal, in listening to me."

The rain had started. It drummed steadily along the window, rattled occasionally against the glass like a handful of thrown stones. Now and then, muffled by distance, far-off thunder boomed and rumbled. Grigsby had lighted the oil lamp and,

166

ankles crossed, bootheels on the desktop, the glass of bourbon perched atop his stomach, he sat back in his chair and considered.

Wilde? O'Conner? Vail? Von Hesse?

He couldn't buy von Hesse's theory. Okay, you drink too much, you black out, you maybe act like a born fool (you grab Brenda from the saloon and drag her home). But you don't spend hours cutting a prostitute into careful bloody strips. You don't hang pieces of her from the mirror, from the dresser. That took an act of deliberate will. A completely crazy will, for sure, but a will. And enough physical strength and enough coordination to carry it out.

So how come von Hesse wanted him to buy the story? He was blowing smoke, maybe. Trying to confuse the issue.

Only reason to do that was if he was the killer.

But he really seemed to believe all that shit. And he even admitted that if he was right, he could've been the killer himself.

More smoke? Trying to flimflam the bonehead country marshal?

Just then, Grigsby heard a commotion out in the anteroom, beyond the closed door. He heard Carver's voice rising almost to a squeak as it called out, "You can't *do* that!" and then another voice, gruff and deep, bellowing, "*Out of my way, you fool.*"

Grigsby recognized the second voice as Greaves's. He frowned and remained where he was.

The door swung open, smacked against the doorstop, bounced back. Greaves slammed at it with his open palm and strode into the room. Behind him, Harlan Brubaker held his splayed hands to Carver's narrow chest, preventing the deputy from moving forward. Carver's face was red and his mouth was twisted in frustration.

Greaves stopped, still looking sleek and prosperous in his fur-lined overcoat, and he smiled broadly, theatrically, at Grigsby. "Well, my friend," he said, "you really fucked up this time."

Carver said, "Marshal, I told 'em you were busy, they couldn't come in, but they—"

"S'okay, Carver," Grigsby said. He took a swallow of bourbon. "Greaves, you tell your boy there to let go my deputy."

Greaves laughed, a deep booming baritone. He turned to Brubaker and nodded. Brubaker stood back away from Carver and put his hands in his topcoat pockets. Carver adjusted his black wool vest and then, glaring at Brubaker, elaborately brushed it off with his fingers. Brubaker smirked.

Grigsby said, "Go get some coffee, Carver."

Carver glanced at Brubaker, at Greaves, back to Grigsby. "You sure, Marshal?"

"I'm sure."

Frowning, Carver glanced again at the other two men, and then turned and walked away.

Grigsby looked at Greaves. "You got somethin' to say to me?"

Greaves grinned. "I've already said it. You fucked up."

"That right?"

"I told you to stay away from the Molly Woods killing. I told you, I *reminded* you, that you don't have any jurisdiction over a municipal homicide. I made that very clear this morning. Imagine how surprised I was when I found out, a few hours ago, that you've been snooping around, asking questions, disturbing people, sticking your fat nose in places where it doesn't belong. So I went and had a long conversation with Judge Sheldon. I have to tell you that the judge was shocked."

Grigsby smiled. The only time Sheldon ever got shocked was when someone forgot to slip him a bribe.

"But he agreed with me," Greaves said, "that this meddling of yours has got to be stopped." He reached into the inside pocket of his topcoat, came out with a folded sheet of paper. "This is an injunction ordering you to to cease and desist your interference in the Molly Woods investigation." He tossed it onto Grigsby's desk. "And I think it only fair to tell you that Judge Sheldon has sent a telegram to Washington, demanding your immediate recall."

Poor Mort would be earning his keep today. "Sheldon tried that once," Grigsby said. He shrugged. "Didn't get him very far."

Greaves grinned again. "Like I say, Grigsby, times have changed. Even at the attorney general's office. Your friend Danner is out. And by tomorrow, you'll be out too. Just another

168

saddle tramp." Still grinning, he added, "I'm going to enjoy that."

Grigsby nodded. "Fella's got to take his pleasure where he finds it."

Greaves smiled. "You know, Grigsby, the sad thing is, it never had to come to this. I'm a reasonable man—I told you that a long time ago. We could've worked together. We could've co-operated. But no, not you. You chose to go your own way. And after all this time, you still haven't learned that your way, the old way, is finished now. Forever. You're like one of those big lizards they dig out of the ground, so old they've turned into stone. And the pitiful thing is, you don't even know it. In a way, it's a real tragedy."

Grigsby smiled. "You want to borrow a hanky?"

Greaves grinned at him. "I've always admired your spirit." He turned to Brubaker. "Haven't I, Harlan? Haven't I always said so?"

Brubaker smirked. "Sure."

"But the fact is," said Greaves, "you're washed up. Look at you. You're a pathetic old drunk. A lush. A rummy. No good to anybody, not even yourself. No wonder you couldn't hold on to that pretty young wife of yours. No wonder she took your brats and ran off to California."

Behind Greaves, Brubaker snorted.

Greaves grinned. "And now, old man, you don't have any-thing. Not a wife, not kids, not even a job. Not anything at all. In six months time you'll be scrounging drinks in the nigger saloons."

Grigsby nodded. "Prob'ly. But I reckon you'll be wantin' the information on the other hookers." He swung his legs off the desk and stood up.

Greaves frowned. "What information?"

"About the other hookers. In all those other cities. Maybe *you* can make somethin' out of it. I surely can't."

Greaves was watching him, his eyes wary. Grigsby walked over to the file cabinet, opened the top drawer, took out a sheath of papers. Holding them in his left hand, he turned and offered

169

them to Greaves. As Greaves stepped forward, Grigsby dropped the papers and hit Greaves as hard as he could along the side of the jaw. Greaves went flying toward the wall, arms opening wide, and Grigsby turned to Brubaker.

Brubaker was going for his holster, a cross-draw rig on his left hip, below his overcoat. Grigsby took a step and grabbed Brubaker's wrist and squeezed. Brubaker's eyes winced narrow and then they closed completely and his mouth opened wide in a silent scream with his teeth showing and his lips white. Grigsby squeezed some more and Brubaker dropped to his knees. Grigsby brought up his own knee into Brubaker's face.

Brubaker banged back against the doorjamb and Grigsby turned again to Greaves. The chief of police was coming off the wall now and his hand was moving toward his gun, another cross-draw rig, and Grigsby took a step toward him and smiled. His own gun was hanging on the coat rack in the anteroom. He knew there was no way to get to Greaves before Greaves had the gun out, but he didn't much care because he also knew that no matter how many bullets Greaves put into him he was going to kill the man. "Yeah," he said. "Do it."

Greaves jerked his hand away from the holster and held it up, palm outward. "Hold on, Grigsby. You listen to me."

"No," Grigsby said. "I already did that. Maybe I'll be marshal tomorrow and maybe I won't, but I'm still marshal today and you're in my office and I don't want you here. Get out. And wipe up that gob of spit on the way." He nodded toward Brubaker, still slumped in the doorway.

Greaves opened his mouth to speak and Grigsby shook his head. "Out," he said.

Greaves pulled himself fully upright and tugged once at the lapels of his overcoat, settling the coat back over his broad shoulders. He walked around Grigsby and over to Brubaker. He kicked him lightly on the hip. "Harlan."

Brubaker groaned. Greaves bent forward and took Brubaker under the arms and levered him to his feet.

His left arm supporting Brubaker, he looked back at Grigsby. "Tomorrow," he said.

Grigsby nodded.

Greaves walked Brubaker out the door.

Grigsby stepped over to the desk and poured himself another drink. His right hand was shaking so badly that he had to use his left to steady the bottle. Even so, a half ounce of whiskey splashed across the desktop.

He raised the glass and swallowed. The rain rattled at the windowpane. Far off, thunder rumbled.

Grigsby took another drink. His hand was still trembling.

He looked down at the papers scattered along the floor. He set the drink on the desktop, then squatted down and gathered the papers together. He tossed them to the top of the file cabinet, returned to his desk, and lifted his glass.

Someone knocked at the door and Grigsby wheeled around. A few dollops of bourbon sloshed onto his hand.

A tall young man in an expensive tan topcoat. Curly black hair, a pale, narrow, clean-shaven face. "Are you Marshal Grigsby?" A soft fluting voice.

"Yeah?" Grigsby growled.

"I'm Wilbur Ruddick. Mr. Vail—"

"Get your ass in here!" Grigsby bellowed.

CHAPTER FIFTEEN

HE CEILING WAS LOW, made from unfinished planks of knotted pine supported by beams of stripped pine logs whose uneven, and dangerously splintered, lower ridges were no more than a few inches from the vulnerable top of Oscar's head. Smoke had stained the wood a dull tobacco brown. Three oil lamps, shaded by funnels of oiled paper and hung from the beams on sooty metal chains, provided most of the illumination, musty yellow pools of light in which sat some rickety tables and some rickety chairs and two or three rickety-looking people. Most of the customers stood at the bar, which ran the length of the narrow room and which, like the ceiling and the floor, was constructed of raw pine, now stained and drab. More sawdust was scattered everywhere—whoever owned the sawdust concession in Denver was doubtless a millionaire by this time—and the thick, still air was cluttered with the smell of stale beer and mildew and perspiration.

Oscar swept up to the empty space at the center of the bar, Henry following slightly behind him. The barkeep, a tubby little person who had been leaning over the low counter into a cluster of elderly men at the right, waddled slowly toward him, wiping his hands against the dirty apron, taut as a sandbag, that encased his belly. He glanced sidelong at Henry, bit his lip, and said to Oscar, "Sorry, mister, but we don't serve no coloreds here."

Oscar smiled engagingly. "But I didn't order one."

The barkeep shrugged, uneasy. "Sorry, mister."

"Mistuh Oscar," began Henry.

Oscar asked the barkeep, "Is that a local law?"

The barkeep shrugged again. "It's the principle of the thing. I'm sorry and all, but I got other customers to think of."

"Perhaps I should explain," Oscar said, smiling again as he put his big hands on the bartop and leaned forward to look down at the barkeep. "Henry here is my personal attendant. I'm subject to fits, you see. Really quite frightful fits that cause me to foam at the mouth and leap about the room. I tend to break things, I'm afraid. Tables. Chairs. These attacks can come upon me at any time, and for virtually no reason at all. Henry is the only person able to cope with me. It's a matter of precise physical pressure being applied to certain highly complicated neuralgic intersections. And, of course, in order to apply this pressure properly, Henry requires an occasional steadying drink of whiskey. Surely you can understand this?"

The barkeep was frowning. "You're not from around here," he said.

"Not originally," said Oscar, "no."

The barkeep nodded toward Henry, whose face was blank. "He's like a what? A nurse, kind of?"

"Something like, yes. He studied with Hegel in Germany."

The barkeep scratched at his jaw. "Well, shoot, mister." He shifted his glance, and then shifted his weight from one foot to the other. Once again he wiped the palms of his hands against his apron. He said, forlornly, "I got customers to think of."

"Of course. Foolish of me." Oscar turned to the three old men on his right, all of whom were staring at him with undisguised interest. "Gentlemen, would you mind sharing a bottle of the best with me and my attendant? My treat, of course."

Grins appeared, two of them entirely toothless, and Oscar was

173

suddenly reminded of the witches in *Macbeth*. "Set 'em up, by God!" "Get 'em a drink!" "Let 'em stay, Harry, let's see the big dude throw hisself a fit!"

"Drinks all round, then," said Oscar to the barkeep, and smiled again. "Two whiskeys for us. And something for yourself."

The barkeep nodded. "Yeah. Well. Just this one time, right? But I mean, look, mister, these fits you get . . ."

"Yes?"

"I mean, you get them, you know they're coming up ahead of time?"

"Certainly. Never fear. And Henry will have me right as rain in an instant."

The barkeep nodded, turned away.

Henry said quietly, "Mistuh Oscar, I don' drink no hard liquor. Only beer."

"Ah." Oscar smiled. "Well, Henry, under the circumstances, I think it might be best if we kept mum about that. Eh?"

"Yes suh."

As the barkeep poured their drinks, Oscar said to him, "I understand that some poor young woman was killed near here."

The barkeep nodded. "Molly Woods. Hooker worked down the road a piece. Got diced up like stew meat, they say." From his bored monotone, this might have been an everyday event. He leaned on the bar and said, with the seriousness of a Harley Street physician, "You been havin' these fits for a long time?"

"Since infancy. You knew her? Molly Woods?"

The barkeep shrugged. "Everybody did. It's kind of like that epilectics?"

Oscar shook his head. "The medical term for it is *pique*. Did she have any particular friends? Someone with whom I might be able to speak?"

"What for?"

"Well, you see, I dabble a bit as a writer, and I'm doing a small monograph on the subject."

The barkeep seemed puzzled.

"An essay," Oscar said. "An article. On the subject of murder."

"Yeah?" said the barkeep. "A writer, huh? Any money in that?" He asked this like someone who had lately been mulling over a change of career.

"Not really," Oscar told him.

The barkeep nodded sadly, as though his hopes, presumably never very high, had nonetheless been dashed. "Same thing everywhere, I guess." He shrugged. "Talk to old Larson over there. He knew her. He's the one found the body. Biggest thing ever happened to him."

"Splendid. Give us another bottle, would you? And another glass." These the bartender produced; Oscar took them. "Thanks very much. Come along, Henry."

Old Larson was old indeed, a small wizened man whose long white hair hung, limp and yellowish, from a freckled pink bald spot and snaked over the frayed collar of a ruined overcoat several sizes too large. Beneath the overcoat he wore two more coats and a number of sweaters, creating a bulky mass from which his scrawny neck poked at an angle, like a turtle's. He sat curled around an empty glass, holding it in a pair of hands ropy with veins and ligaments.

"Excuse me," Oscar said. "Would you mind terribly if we joined you?"

The man's head lifted and his eyes blinked, focusing. He looked from Oscar to Henry to Oscar again, and then to the bottle of whiskey. He sat upright. "You buyin?" he said, addressing the bottle.

"It would be my pleasure," said Oscar.

"Grab yourselves some seats then, boys." He licked his lips. Like the two at the bar, he was toothless. "Always happy to chew the fat."

Oscar and Henry sat, and Oscar placed the new glass in front of Larson and filled it. "The name is Wilde," he said. "This is my friend Henry."

The old man nodded, grinning. "Howdy, boys. Carl Larson.

175

Pleased to make your acquaintance.'' He held up his shot glass. "Here's to gals with loose morals and tight privates."

"Yes," said Oscar, raising his glass. "Absolutely." Henry raised his as well, and the three of them drank. When they set the drinks down on the table, Oscar noted that the level of whiskey in Henry's glass remained the same. Larson's was empty.

"Mr. Larson," Oscar began.

"Carl," said the old man. "Mr. Larson, that was my pa. Dead these thirty years. And good riddance, too. Stubborn as a mule and twice as dumb. What you say your monicker was, son?"

"My monicker?"

"Your handle."

Oscar looked at Henry. Henry said, "Your name, Mistuh Oscar."

"Ah. Oscar. Oscar Wilde."

Larson considered for a moment and finally shrugged. "Well, a fella's gotta take what his folks pass along, I reckon. Where you hail from, Oscar?"

"Ireland. Mr. Larson—"

"That a fact? We got a lot of Irish hereabouts. Good people, the Irish. Got nothing against 'em. Nigras, neither," he assured Henry. "Me, now, I'm from Arkansas. God's country, son. The sun hangs up in the sky twelve months at a shot and sometimes it don't come down till leap year's. Lakes're so deep that every now and then we get a Chinaman floatin' in one. Say now. That's some mighty fine whiskey you got there." He nodded to the bottle. "First one went down real good, I got to admit."

Oscar filled the man's glass. "Mr. Larson, I understand that you knew Molly Woods."

The old man tossed back his drink, grimaced, and shook his head. "Terrible. Plumb terrible what happened to that poor gal. I been all over the country, Oswald, been up and down the Mighty Mississippi on keelboats, rode with Quantrill, lived in the mountains with the Cheyenne and the Arapaho. I seen my share of killin' and blood-lettin', Lord knows, but I never seen nothin' like what happened to that poor gal. Seen a fella been half et by a grizzly once, and that was apple pie compared to what happened

176

to poor Molly. It was me what found her, ya know." He sat back and nodded once, a quick, self-important nod. "Yes sir. I was bringin' her a pint of milk like I always do, she had a hankerin' for her milk of a mornin', Molly did, and she don't answer like she always does. So I commence to open the door just a mite to see is she okay, and there she is—"

He grimaced again, lifted his glass, saw that it was empty, and glanced slyly toward the bottle.

Oscar lifted the bottle and filled the glass. He said, "What sort of woman was she, Mr. Larson?"

"All spread out on the bed. Chunks of her all over the room, blood ever'where—"

"Mr. Larson," Oscar said quickly, "I'm more interested, really, in what sort of woman she was."

Larson frowned in disappointment. He tossed back his whiskey and shrugged. "Well, son, she had a heart o' gold. Yes sir. That's the way I'd tally it up. A heart o' gold. Tell you one thing, Waldo. I ever find out who did her in, I'll shoot down the yellow-bellied varmint myself, right where he stands, and that's a brass-bound fact. An eye for an eye, the good book says. Exodus, chapter twenty-one, verse twenty-four. You know the good book, Waldo?"

"I draw succor from it often." Oscar refilled the man's glass. "How old a woman was she, Mr. Larson?"

Larson shrugged. "Middlin', I reckon."

"In her twenties, do you mean? In her thirties?"

Larson cocked his head and looked at Oscar curiously. "You know somethin', Waldo? You don't talk like no Irishman I ever heard before."

"I hail from the southern part of the country," Oscar said. "How old was she, Mr. Larson?"

Larson shrugged. "Pushin' forty, I reckon." He lifted his glass and drank down the whiskey.

"And what did she look like?"

Larson leaned toward Oscar. "Like I said, son, it was terrible. No face left a-tall, just this white ole skull a-grinnin' at me from the bed, and then *chunks* of her—"

177

"No, no," said Oscar quickly, holding out his hand. "I meant before the tragedy." He swallowed. "What did she look like then?"

"Oh," said Larson, frowning again. "Well, she was a right handsome piece of woman, son. Pushin' forty, like I say, but still a handsome piece of woman. Still had all her equipment." He frowned and shook his head. "A terrible waste. What kinda dirty, lily-livered, dung-suckin' polecat would do a thing like that, anyhow? I ever find out, that varmint is dead where he stands." He looked round the room with a determined glare, as though daring the killer to step forth and identify himself.

"Was she tall?" Oscar asked him.

Larson looked back at him, thought about this, finally said, "Middlin', I reckon."

"Was she heavyset? Slender?"

Larson thought about this. "Middlin', I reckon." He leaned toward Oscar. "Say now—" His face went momentarily slack, and then he frowned. "What was the name again?"

"Waldo."

"—Waldo. How come you wanna know so much about ole Molly?"

"I'm a writer for the *Times* of London, and I'm doing an article on murder in the American West."

Larson grinned happily. "That a fact? Well, Waldo, you came to the right man, you surely did. Why, in my time I seen just about every form of killin' that one varmint can create upon another. You name it and I seen it. Murder by gunshot and murder by knife, murder by rope and fire and dynamite. 'Their feet run to evil, and they make haste to shed innocent blood.' Know where that's from?"

"The good book," Oscar hazarded.

"Sure it is, course it is, but *where* in the good book?"

"I'm afraid I can't recall. But Mr. Larson—"

Larson turned to Henry. "How 'bout you, boy? You know?"

Henry nodded. "Yes suh. Isaiah, chapter fifty-nine, verse seven."

178

Larson's lower lip buckled, his eyes narrowed. "Now how'd you know that?"

"My father, suh, he was a minister."

Larson nodded and relaxed back into his chair. "Reckon that's all right then." He turned back to Oscar, expansive once again. "So what you want to know, Waldo? You want to know about killers? I seen 'em all. Rode with some of 'em. The James Boys. The Youngers. Doc Holliday. John Wesley Hardin. Billy Bonney."

"What I'd like to know, Mr. Larson, is whether Molly Woods preferred any particular sort of customer."

"Yessir, she surely did," said Larson, and grinned. "She took a real fancy to the ones what had cash money a-jinglin' in their pockets."

Oscar sighed. This was beginning to seem hopeless. Larson was more colorful than informative, and rather more fatiguing than colorful. "Was there anything about the woman, Mr. Larson, anything at all, that distinguished her? Any particular trait that would have enabled her to stand out?"

"Sure, like I tole ya. She had a heart o' gold."

"I was thinking, you see, more along the lines of some physical trait."

Larson shook his head. "Nope. 'Less you count her hair. Real proud of her hair, Molly was. It was red, and she had a mess of it."

"I don't drink in no saloon as got niggers in it."

Oscar turned and looked up.

Two men stood there. One was short and dark, with a lean wedge-shaped face in which a prominent bumpy nose jutted over a pair of narrow lips and a thin, receding chin. His beard, a few optimistic strands of brown hair curling along his narrow jaw, accentuated rather than concealed the pockmarks on his skin. He wore a black hat with a rounded brim, and a gray canvas duster, stained and battered, that reached from his narrow shoulders to the ankles of his mud-caked leather boots. His eyes were small and brown, like a stoat's, and they kept sliding left and right,

179

quickly, excitedly, as though they knew that something wonderful was about to happen and didn't want to miss a single moment of it.

The other man was enormous, a giant. Towering over the table in a long opened coat of dark, heavy fur streaked with grease, he stood with his thick arms akimbo and his big booted feet apart, his hard round belly ballooned against the soiled red plaid flannel of his shirt. A revolver was jammed into the top of his denim trousers. Below a matted thatch of brown hair, his head was globular, the massive forehead looming over the tiny, deeply set gray eyes and the hard, rounded ridges of cheekbone. His nose had been flattened back against his face, as though by a hammer, and two broad nostrils, bristling with black hairs, peered down at Oscar from above a wide fleshy mouth. He looked like the sort of person who would kill without a moment's thought. He looked like the sort of person who would do everything without a moment's thought.

"Say now, Biff," said Larson. "Leave it be, this boy's all right, his pa was a minister. And this here's Waldo, Biff, he's from Ireland. Biff here hunts buff, and he's from—where was it you was from, Biff?"

The old man was chattering, obviously trying to entangle the giant in a rush of words.

Without looking at him, his eyes and his nostrils still staring down at Oscar, the giant growled from the corner of his mouth, "Shut your hole." To Oscar, he said, "I said I don't drink in no saloon as got niggers in it."

Very much to his own surprise, Oscar felt a sudden bolt of fury go surging through him, as cold and as clear and as bracing as a mountain stream. Perhaps its source lay in the recent past, back in the confrontation with Vail, when he had (regrettably) refrained from hurling the business manager out the window. Wherever it had come from, it was definitely here now, a tumbling flood of it; and, with an eerie, cool detachment, he found himself sitting back comfortably in his chair, smiling blandly, and saying, "Well then. Why don't you just trot along and find another saloon."

From his previous experiences with bullies, at public school and at Oxford, Oscar expected a more or less prolonged exchange of incivilities—dull and banal on the part of his hulking adversary, witty and scathing on his own—which gradually grew more heated until at last the two of them squared off and Oscar, much to his opponent's astonishment, beat him to a pulp. Things here proceeded rather differently.

Later, he worked out what must have happened. The giant, moving with a sudden easy violence, and much more swiftly than Oscar would have thought possible, snapped his booted foot forward and smashed it into the rung of Oscar's chair.

At the time, however, all Oscar understood was that abruptly he was airborne and the room was spinning about him in a startling fashion. He crashed, chest down, into the sawdust.

He pushed himself quickly to his feet (speed—as he recalled from his previous encounters—being of the essence in these affairs). But when he wheeled around, bringing up his fists, he saw that someone else had entered the tableau.

Between Oscar and the other two, his back to Oscar, stood a third man dressed in a well-cut frock coat that seemed vaguely familiar. For some reason, the man had drawn the right side of the coat behind him, and this he held lightly with the fingers of his left hand, while his right hand hung down loosely alongside his hip and a large holstered pistol.

Oscar brushed sawdust from the velvet of his topcoat. Vexed by the interruption, and curious as to who had effected it, he stalked around the man, and heard him say to the giant, in an uncanny whisper, "Make your move, friend."

All at once Oscar recognized the whisper, and the handlebar mustache and the elegant nose and the dark wavy hair. Today the man was dressed almost entirely in black—shirt, tie, boots—the black nicely set off by a waistcoat of brilliant scarlet silk.

The giant laughed loudly. "And just who're you, little man?"

"The name is Holliday," the gunfighter whispered. For an instant, that chill ghost of a smile flickered beneath the mustache. "Folks call me Doc."

Slowly, as though a pale curtain were being drawn from his

181

forehead down to his jaw, color left the big man's face. His hands, slung down at his sides like lumps of meat, opened and closed.

No one spoke. Oscar, although not really certain what exactly was happening (not a gunfight, surely?), judged that discretion, just then, was the better part of ignorance. Into the silence, from overhead, came a low muffled patter; and distantly he realized that the rain had begun.

The big man took a step backward. "Hold on there," he said. "I got no quarrel with you."

Holliday's chill smile flickered once more. "Wrong."

The giant's beady gray eyes darted back and forth as he looked around the room. For an escape. For assistance.

Neither was provided. Even his friend, the man with the eyes of a stoat, stepped to the side, moving out of the scene and into the audience.

The giant lifted his big hands and held them away from his body, showing Holliday that they were empty. "I ain't no gunman, Doc."

Holliday nodded. "I am."

The giant glanced desperately around again.

"Maybe," Holliday whispered, "if you apologized to Mr. Wilde here." He jerked his head very slightly to the side.

Oscar understood that Holliday, without once turning, had known precisely where he was standing. Extraordinary.

"Sure, sure," said the giant. His smile looked sickly. "Sorry, fella, sorry," he said quickly to Oscar. "Didn' mean no harm." He looked back at Holliday, his small eyes opened wide.

Oscar discovered, with a start, that he was embarrassed for the man.

How on earth was it possible to feel sorry for a murderous oaf? Probably because, in an instant, he had revealed the simple terror that lay beneath his bulk, beneath his violence and anger. And sometimes, perhaps, even a monster should be permitted his mask.

"No harm done," Oscar said. Looking down, away from those frightened eyes, he brushed sawdust from the sleeve of his coat.

182

"Fine," whispered Holliday to the giant. Again, fractionally, his head nodded once. "Be seeing you."

"Sure, yeah, sure. Come on, Darryl." He grabbed the other man by his elbow. And without either of them looking back, the two men left the saloon, the giant's head tucked low—clearly to avoid the ceiling beams; but perhaps also, or so Oscar imagined, in shame.

Before Oscar had an opportunity to speak to Holliday, grinning old Larson had scuttled up from the table, bony hand outstretched from his bulky sleeves. "Howdy, Doc, maybe you remember me, Carl Larson outta Arkansas, we had a drink once, well, not together, I reckon, but over in Leadville at Pap's place—"

Holliday glanced down at the hand, ignored it, nodded, and whispered, "Mr. Larson."

"—last year it was," Larson continued, undaunted as he slipped his hand into the pocket of his coat, "—round about July. I just wanted to tell you I purely did admire the way you handled old Biff there, he's been lookin' for trouble since he blowed into town—"

Holliday turned to Oscar, and Larson trailed off, "—and now I reckon he got it."

Oscar nodded to the gunfighter. "Dr. Holliday."

Holliday nodded back. "Poet." His eyes were still as black and blank as the outer reaches of space.

"I suppose I should thank you for your intervention," Oscar said, "but you know, I really do believe that I should have acquitted myself quite well." He brushed a few more bits of sawdust from his coat front.

For a moment Holliday said nothing; he merely stared at Oscar with those bleak, empty eyes. Oscar thought, as his stomach sank floorward, that he had just made a dreadful mistake. And then Holliday's smile flickered briefly. "Maybe so," the man whispered.

"I'm rather good at boxing, you see," Oscar explained.

Holliday nodded. "Good. Keep an eye opened for your big friend."

"Ah? You think he'll be back, then?" Oscar's unwonted bloodlust was beginning to subside.

Holliday whispered, "I think he'll be keeping an eye opened for you."

Oscar shrugged. He and the tour would be gone from Denver by tomorrow. "Ah well. What will be, will be. Fancy a drink?"

Fractionally, Holliday shook his head. "Another time."

"But you've only just arrived."

"Another time," Holliday said, and smiled that small frigid smile. He looked once around the room, as though making sure that there were no more giants to be dispatched, and then looked back at Oscar and nodded. "Be seeing you," he whispered, and then, his slim back as straight and as supple beneath his coat as a matador's, he turned and glided from the saloon.

CHAPTER SIXTEEN

RUDDICK DREW HIMSELF UP and made a face that reminded Grigsby of someone who had just chomped down on a green persimmon. "Now just a *minute*, Mr. Marshal," he said. "I came here of my own free *will*, you know. I'm only trying to do my *duty*. I certainly don't expect to get *snapped* at."

Oh Jesus, Grigsby thought. This is one solid gold daffodil we got here.

But having just punched out Greaves (and Brubaker, too, a real bonus) Grisby now discovered within himself a sudden expansive tolerance. And the boy, daffodil or not, was right. No point in hollering. More flies with honey.

He sucked in some air. "Yeah," he said. "Been a rough day. Come on in. Take a seat." He jerked his thumb at the office's other chair, then shuffled around his desk and eased himself down into his own. The brief fight had left him exhausted and drained. Hanrahan was right—he was getting too old for that shit. His spirits might be a bit higher now, but his knuckles were throbbing and his hand felt like another fifteen minutes would see it the size of a boiled ham.

185

One thing, though—his hand probably didn't hurt anywhere near as bad as Greaves's jawbone.

Moving lightly, in a kind of leisurely skip, Ruddick floated across the room to the chair. He glanced down suspiciously, as though expecting to spot something nasty, and maybe poisonous, perched on the wood, then plucked a pink handkerchief from his jacket pocket and whisked it at the seat. The air was suddenly clotted with the smell of lilacs. He tucked away the handkerchief and sat down, his back straight but tilted a bit forward, his knees together, his hands folded primly in his lap.

Jesus, Grigsby thought. But, looking at Ruddick, he moved his mouth in a pleasant, empty smile; he was being tolerant.

The boy was in his early twenties, his eyes gray, his skin clear except for a small scattering of pink pimples along each pale cheek. Good bones, strong nose, a firm jaw. Grigsby decided that if he scrubbed away that stinkum, got himself some steady outdoor work, and stopped flouncing around like a dizzy school-marm, he could probably pass himself off as a normal person. So how come he had to act like such a lulu-belle? .

Well, it was a free country. And a big one. Room in it for lulu-belles, even.

"Right," he said. "Appreciate you droppin' by. I reckon you know about these hookers that got killed off."

Ruddick's face twisted in its persimmon pucker. "Mr. Vail told me all about it. I think it's absolutely *hideous*. I've never *heard* of such a thing. Mr. Vail said that you believe it must be one of *us*, but really, Marshal, that's just too *incredible* to consider."

"Maybe," Grigsby told the boy. "But I got to check out all the possibilities. You can see that, right?"

Ruddick shrugged. "Well. I *suppose* so." He glanced around the office, frowning as though he didn't much care for the green walls, the bare wood floors, the drab gray file cabinet.

That was fine with Grigsby. He didn't much care for any of it either.

"Thing of it is," Grigsby said, "I got to eliminate the innocent before I can determine the guilty.'' To himself, remembering the letter from the Scientific lawman of Leavenworth, Kansas, Grigsby smiled. ''You follow me?''

''Yes, certainly,'' Ruddick said, and crossed his legs, right knee over left.

''Right. So I reckon you can figure why I got to ask you where you were at last night.''

''Certainly,'' said Ruddick. He looked down and, mouth thoughtfully pursed, eyebrows thoughtfully raised, admired the sheen of his black patent leather shoe.

Grigsby waited. Ruddick said nothing, and then after a moment he looked up and smiled politely, as though he too were waiting. Patiently, Grigsby said, ''So where were you at last night?''

''Oh,'' said Ruddick. ''I was out.'' He smiled brightly then, as pleased with himself as the winner of a spelling bee.

Grigsby grinned, showing Ruddick all of his teeth. ''Ya know, Wilbur, I'm startin' to get the feelin' that you're funnin' with me.''

Ruddick's left eyebrow arched up his forehead at this curious notion. ''Funning?''

''Tell me somethin','' Grigsby said seriously. ''Haven't I been all nice and considerate while I been askin' you my questions?''

Ruddick shifted in his chair. ''I suppose so,'' he said, and looked down at his shoe again.

''I haven't hollered at you but the one time, now have I?''

Ruddick sighed. ''No.'' He glanced around the office with a sulky frown, like a small boy dragged before the principal.

''Appears to me,'' Grigsby said, ''that you're tryin' to get some kind of a rise outta me. Now most times I like a bit of funnin' as much as the next fella. But this here is a murder we're talkin' about, and I don't have my normal parcel of patience. So I calculate that this'd probably go along better for the both of us if you put aside the funnin' for a time and just answered the questions. You follow me?''

Ruddick shrugged. He nodded, then looked off, toward the window.

187

And then, as Grigsby was congratulating himself on his tact, he heard footsteps out in the anteroom. After a moment, Carver Peckingham appeared in the doorway, tall and anxious.

"Everything okay, Marshal?" he asked.

"Fine, Carver. Close the door now. We'll talk later."

Carver looked at Ruddick. Ruddick brushed his hand back over his black hair and smiled pleasantly. Carver nodded to him and backed out, shutting the door behind him.

"Right," said Grigsby, and slipped the tobacco pouch from his vest pocket. "So where were you at last night?"

Ruddick frowned, sulky and resentful again. "Where would you like me to *start*, exactly?"

"Start with suppertime," Grigsby said, and curled a sheet of cigarette paper with the tip of his left forefinger. "Where'd you eat at?"

"The Decker House. I had the trout in mushroom sauce." He frowned. "It was *awful*."

Tapping the brown flakes from the pouch, Grigsby nodded. "They never have worked out how to cook up a fish. What time you leave the Decker House?"

"Nine o'clock. Ten, possibly."

Grigsby glanced up at him from over the half-finished cigarette.

"I really don't *know*," Ruddick said. "Honestly. I don't own a watch. It was round ten, I suppose. But I really couldn't *swear* to that."

Grigsby nodded. He licked the paper, rolled it closed. "Where'd you go to afterwards?"

Ruddick shrugged. "*Really*, Marshal, I can't remember."

Grigsbye stuck the cigarette in his mouth, reached into his vest pocket for a match. "Saloons? A casino?"

Ruddick shrugged again. "A saloon or two, I suppose."

Grigsby snapped his thumb against the match, held the flame to the cigarette, puffed. Eyes narrowed against the smoke, he said, "Gimme a f'r-instance."

"The Palace. I *think*."

Exhaling smoke, Grigsby smiled. "You only been in town for

188

two days. Either you went to the Palace last night or you went the night before. Which one is it?"

Ruddick sighed again. "I suppose it must've been last night."

Grigsby smiled, nodded: See how easy it is? "And what time are we talkin'?"

A shrug. "Eleven o'clock, I think."

"How long you there?"

"An hour or so."

"Talk to anybody?"

Ruddick's eyelids fluttered. "Not really."

Grigsby inhaled on the cigarette, exhaled. Silently, he stared at Ruddick.

Ruddick shifted in his chair, uncrossed his legs, then recrossed them, left knee over right. "I had a few drinks and I got a little bit tiddly." He smiled now as he stared levelly at Grigsby. "That's probably why I don't remember much."

Grigsby flicked his cigarette ash into the ashtray. "You sure you didn't make yourself a friend?"

A frown, as though genuinely confused. "What do you mean?"

"A friend," Grigsby said. He smiled sociably, man to man. "Look, son. I ain't especially interested in your personal life." As far as Grigsby was concerned, the less he knew about that, the better. "I don't care whether you favor women, men, dogs, or rattlesnakes. I'm just tryin' to clear up a killin'."

Ruddick sat back and for a moment he stared at Grigsby. Finally he smiled a small bitter smile and he said, "*Son*? You're going to be my *father*, is that it?"

"Come again?" said Grigsby.

"Look, Mr. Marshal, if I wanted a big, brave, *manly* father, I'd use my own. Why don't we just admit that you're not especially fond of *me* and I'm not especially fond of *you*, and just leave it at that."

Grigsby frowned. "It don't matter here who likes who. I need to find out where you were last night. Can't you see that the best thing you could do for yourself is tell me?"

Ruddick smiled. "And what if I don't? What happens then, *Dad*? Are you going to *beat* it out of me? That's what fathers are *supposed* to do, isn't it?"

"It's an idea could grow on me," Grigsby said.

This was a mistake; he knew it as soon as he said it—from his smile, the boy took Grigsby's admission as a vindication, as a personal victory.

Grigsby said, "Okay. Let's stop fuckin' around. Who was it?"

Ruddick smiled again. "I guess that's for me to know and you to find out."

Grigsby sat up and stubbed out his cigarette. He looked at Ruddick. He said, "Now you listen to me. I told you, we're talkin' here 'bout a murder. Some sonovabitch sliced up a hooker, and I'm tryin' to find out if it was you. I don't give a damn about anything else. I don't give a damn if you whacked off every goddamn cowpoke at the Palace. What I wanna know is, who you were *with*, and how *long* you were with 'im, and if you don't goddamn tell me, and tell me *now*, I'm gonna sling your ass in the lockup."

Ruddick was staring at him, lips compressed, face flushed.

"Lockup'll be right up your alley," Grigsby said. "Got a guy in there name of André. Trapper. Ripe as a dead skunk. 'Bout seven feet tall, mean old fucker with a dose of clap, picked it up from some Cheyenne dog soldier, and young fellas like you are his meat exactly."

The threat of the lockup (a threat which was pretty much as empty as the lockup itself) hadn't worked with O'Conner, but it worked like a charm with Ruddick. Looking directly at Grigsby, the boy said, "Dell Jameson." He spit out the name as though it were a piece of tobacco caught on his tongue.

"Dell *Jameson*?" said Grigsby.

Ruddick smiled coldly, viciously. "You wanted to know who I was with. I was with Dell Jameson."

Grigsby exploded. "He's *married*, he's got *kids*. He's a goddamn *fireman*."

Ruddick's brief little laugh was brittle and shrill. "I met him at eleven o'clock," he said. "You can ask at the saloon, at the

190

Palace. *They'll* tell you. We left around twelve and went to my room at the hotel." He smiled a hard, nasty smile. The poisonous little shit was enjoying himself. "Poor Dell was a bit nervous about being seen, so I let him in through the service entrance. It didn't really matter, because the desk clerk was asleep. He stayed until two." He smiled again. "It's the truth. You can ask your friend Dell."

Grigsby lifted his glass, took a swallow of bourbon. "You leave the room afterwards?"

"No."

But he knew about the service entrance.

"Is that *it*?" said Ruddick. "Can I *go* now?"

"Yeah," Grigsby said. He waved a hand. "Take off."

As Ruddick, sauntering again, reached the door, Grigsby said, "One thing, Wilbur."

Ruddick turned.

Grigsby said, "I'm gonna be watchin' you. All of you. Like a hawk." But Grigsby's heart wasn't really in the threat, and it didn't sound, even to him, particularly threatening.

Apparently, it didn't sound too threatening to Ruddick, either. He only shrugged, and then he turned and flounced from the room.

Grigsby stood looking down through the window at the street below him, a shallow brown river dimpled with raindrops, shivering beneath gusts of wind. The storm was easing up, the clouds were feathering away. A few people, most of them in flapping yellow slickers, dashed along the sleek black sidewalks.

Poor Dell.

Poor Dell was right.

Grigsby had known Dell Jameson for nearly fifteen years. He was a good man, hardworking, dependable, and a good father to his kids. And brave as a bull—three years ago he had gone barreling through a burning house to grab old Mrs. Cartwright and carry her out to the street. He had come staggering onto the sidewalk and set her down soft as silk on the ground, then

191

taken a step or two back toward the house and keeled right over.

Jesus Christ. Dell Jameson.

How the hell was Grigsby supposed to handle this?

Hey, Dell, how's Barbara, oh, and by the way, about what time last night you finish cornholing the lulu-belle from San Francisco?

Grigsby frowned.

Goddamm it, Dell. How could you *do* this to me?

He sighed.

Well, shit. Maybe it was time to pack it in. Let Sheldon and Greaves take over like they wanted to. Looked like they were about to do that anyway.

He frowned again.

Greaves. Who had gone whining to Greaves?

Wilde.

It had to be Wilde. Couldn't have been von Hesse or Ruddick, because Greaves had known too soon. If it'd been O'Conner, he would've told Greaves about the shooting, and Greaves hadn't mentioned that. Henry had no reason to talk to Greaves, not that Grigsby could see. It had to be Wilde or Vail, and Vail and Grigsby had struck a deal.

So. It had been Wilde.

Grigsby tried to work up some anger at the Englishman, and discovered that he couldn't do it.

He really didn't care anymore. About much of anything.

It was beginning to look like he'd never get to the bottom of this Molly Woods thing. The whole business was a mess. Greaves and Sheldon butting in. Nances coming out of the woodwork, everywhere you looked. (Including, Jesus, poor Dell Jameson.) Drunken reporters and crazy German officers. French countesses.

French countesses. Grigsby remembered the round breasts, the pouty mouth, and felt a familiar tingling tightness in his crotch.

Leave it be, Bob, that one's too classy for the likes of you.

Right about now, Grigsby would've given his left arm for an uncomplicated shoot-out. Two drunken cowboys drawing down

192

on each other for the simple satisfaction of blowing each other off the face of the earth.

Someone knocked on the office door.

Grigsby turned. "Yeah?"

The door opened and Carver poked in his head. "Doc Boynton is out here, Marshal."

Sitting opposite Grigsby, Boynton raised his glass of bourbon in a hand that was small and stubby and yet somehow delicate. "Health and wealth and pretty women, Bob, and the time to enjoy them all."

Grigsby raised his own glass and smiled. "Too late for all of it, Doc."

The doctor was short, round, and bald. His eyebrows were bushy and gray and so was his mustache. His cheeks were red; his eyes, behind shiny round spectacles, were light brown. He wore—as he had always worn, for as long as Grigsby had known him—a gray three-piece suit. Only the lower portion of the trousers were wet, so he must've worn a slicker and hung it up on the coat rack out in the anteroom.

Boynton sipped at his glass, sighed happily, lowered the glass to his shelf of stomach, and held it there between his fingers, daintily, like a spinster careful not to spill a drop of sherry. He lifted his head slightly and sniffed at the air, then turned with a grin to Grigsby. "Are you wearing toilet water these days, Bob?"

Grigsby smiled. "Tryin' to improve myself."

Boynton grinned at him. "Or maybe you've got a fancy woman hiding in the closet?"

"Wish I did. Okay, Doc. What can you tell me about Molly Woods?"

Boynton frowned. "Well, for one thing," he said, "she couldn't get any deader than she is."

Grigsby smiled bleakly. "Yeah. I reckoned she wasn't gonna be makin' no recovery."

Boynton shook his head. "Jesus Christ, Bob. I've been a doctor

193

for more years than I care to think about, and I've never seen anything like that. Have you? Ever?''

"Nope. When do you figure she got killed?''

"Sometime early this morning.'' Boynton adjusted his spectacles. "Probably not much earlier than two or three, I'd say.''

Which meant that any of the men in Wilde's tour could've killed her. Including Ruddick, after Dell Jameson had left his hotel. Which meant that maybe Grigsby wouldn't have to talk to Dell Jameson after all.

"What's the latest time it coulda been?'' he asked Boynton.

Boynton shrugged. "Four or five, maybe. Not much beyond that.''

Grigsby nodded—any later than that and there would've been people up and about, even in Shantytown. "There were some parts missin' from the body?''

Boynton looked at him. "How'd you know about that, Bob?''

"Molly Woods wasn't the first hooker this sonovabitch has cut up.''

Boynton frowned, thought for a moment, took a sip of whiskey. "That doesn't really surprise me. It seemed to me that he knew what he was doing. He knew what he was looking for. Who else has he killed?''

"Three others. Not here in Denver. What do you mean, he knew what he was doin'?''

"He knows his anatomy, Bob. He cut out her uterus, cut it out and took it with him when he left. And did a fairly neat job of it, too.''

"You sayin' he's a *doctor?*''

Boynton took a delicate sip of bourbon. "I'd be inclined to doubt that. The wound was neat, but it wasn't professional. And a doctor would've used a scalpel, probably. The knife this fellow used had a narrow blade, about seven inches long. Single edged, something like a carving knife. Very sharp. He takes good care of his tools.''

Grigsby smiled bleakly again. "So how come he knows about anatomy?'' ·

Boynton shrugged. "If he's done this three times before, he's

194

had plenty of opportunity to practice. And the uterus isn't a difficult organ to locate.''

Grigsby swallowed some bourbon. "Why do you reckon he's cartin' away pieces?''

"Mementos?"

"Mementos? Somethin' to remember the hookers by? That's pretty fuckin' sick, Doc.''

"So is your killer.''

"But why the uterus?''

"I couldn't say. Did he remove the uterus from any of the others?''

"From all of em, looks like.'' Grigsby frowned. "How much time would he need to do that to Molly? Everything he did?''

"An hour at least. Closer to two.''

Two hours of hacking and slicing. "So what can you tell me about him, Doc?''

"Well.'' Boynton smiled faintly and adjusted his spectacles. "I'd say that he's not very happy with women, or at least with prostitutes. The others were all prostitutes?''

"One was a storekeeper's wife, but maybe she was hookin' on the side. Somethin' else, though. All of 'em had red hair.''

Boynton shrugged. "Then I'd say that he's not very happy with redheaded prostitutes.''

Grigsby said, "Some redheaded hooker maybe gave him a dose of clap?''

Boynton frowned thoughtfully. "I'd guess it was something more than that, Bob. He was like a kid with a brand-new toy. He really *enjoyed* himself. He was having *fun*. You saw what he did to her breast? On the table there?''

Grigsby nodded. He swallowed some bourbon.

"I can picture him,'' Boynton said. "I can see him dancing around the room with those strips of her—''

"Dancin'?''

"He left bloody footprints all over.'' Boynton frowned. "You were there, Bob. You didn't notice that?''

Grigsby shook his head. "Too busy forcin' myself to look at Molly.''

Boynton nodded. "Sure. Well, you could see from the prints that he'd been up on his toes, jumping from place to place. Like he was doing some crazy kind of dance."

Grigsby sat up. "Hold on there a minute. He took his shoes off?"

Boynton nodded "In places you could see the outline of each separate toe. I think he was probably naked the whole time he was working on her. Would've made it easier for him to clean himself off, afterward. There was bloody water in the basin under—"

"Anything funny about the feet? Missin' toes?"

"No. Just a normal pair of feet."

"Big feet? Small feet?"

"Average." He shook his head. "No help for you there, Bob."

"Did Greaves get somebody to trace an outline of the prints?"

Boynton shrugged. "I couldn't say. It'd be the obvious thing to do, though, wouldn't it?"

Grigsby nodded. If he could get hold of one of those traced outlines . . .

"Anyway, like I say," said Boynton, "I can picture him dancing around, and laughing and giggling while he played with pieces of Molly. This one is a real can of worms, Bob."

"So from the footprints, you reckon he'd be about average height?" That would eliminate Wilde.

Boynton nodded. "But footprints can be deceptive. I knew a miner once who was six foot six and weighed two hundred pounds, but he wore size nine boots. It was always a wonder to me how he managed to stand up without falling flat on his face."

Grigsby told himself to take a look at Wilde's feet next time he saw him. He glanced down at his own size twelve boot and he frowned. He looked up at Boynton. "You think this sonovabitch could be a nance?"

Boynton frowned. "A homosexual? What makes you ask that?"

"I got some suspects, and a couple of 'em are nances."

Boynton thought about it. "Why not?" he said finally. "I'm not saying that he is, now. There's nothing in what he did that

196

would indicate he was a homosexual. But I don't see any reason why he couldn't be.''

"What turns a fella into a nance, anyway, Doc?"

Boynton smiled. "Just the luck of the draw, I'd guess."

"You reckon they're born that way?"

"Probably. But I'd say that the culture has something to do with it, too. You know that in some societies, homosexuality was actually encouraged. In ancient Greece, for example.''

Grigsby smiled. "You ain't goin' nance on me, are you, Doc?"

Boynton laughed lightly, comfortably. "Not a chance, Bob."

Grigsby suddenly remembered that Doc Boynton had been a bachelor all his life.

CHAPTER SEVENTEEN

WHERE WAS SHE?

An entire day had passed and Oscar had neither seen nor heard from her.

It was all very well to go gadding about the slums of Denver, to spend time chatting with professionally colorful old dipsomaniacs about dead prostitutes, to bandy pleasantries with the mysterious Doctor Holliday (how on earth had the man managed to materialize just *then*?); but finally, desperately, he missed the violet eyes, the titian hair, the sly supple sensual smile of Elizabeth McCourt Doe.

Lying in his pajamas atop his bed, really quite spectacularly alone, he realized that this mission for which he had volunteered, establishing the identity of the killer, had actually been a means of busying himself, of distracting himself from the dull aching void within him.

Was there really any likelihood that he could discover who was killing these women? He had spent, after all, an entire hour with that muddle of an old man, and learned nothing more substantial than that the dead woman had possessed red hair. A snippet of information so irrelevant as to be utterly useless.

198

Could he really credit von Hesse's theory—that one of the men on the tour harbored, without knowing it, a homicidal self? Earlier, the notion had seemed persuasive, so much so that Oscar had appropriated it, made it his own. But now, at the close of a long and dreary day, it seemed as hollow as Oscar felt.

A long and dreary day indeed. He and Henry had gotten drenched when they returned to the hotel. With the wind sweeping great hissing gouts of water around the snapping cover of the carriage, the journey back had seemed to take fully as long as Oscar's crossing of the Atlantic Ocean. At the hotel, his hair sopping wet, his clothes cold and sodden, he had stood elaborately dripping onto the front desk, a minor storm shower himself, to learn that Vail had in fact arranged a change of room for Henry. Afterward, he had dismissed Henry for the day and tramped upstairs, his shoes squeaking, to his own room. There he had stripped, showered, scented himself with rose water, donned dry clothing (gray trousers, powder blue shirt, vermilion cravat, the *lune du lac* coat) and gone out in search of Vail. It was time, Oscar decided, for a bit of bridge mending.

He had found the business manager in the bar downstairs, slumped in a chair at the corner of the room. A nearly empty bottle of whiskey stood on the table before him, and Vail, glaring glumly off into space, appeared not to notice as Oscar sat down to his left. Vail's toupee was aslant, the halibut's head contemplating Vail's right eyebrow as though about to peck at it. Oscar found himself wanting to screw the thing round to the front; it was one temptation he was able to resist.

"Vail," he said, "I think we should talk."

His head resting back against the flocked red wallpaper, Vail turned to Oscar an unblinking pair of glassy gray eyes. "Have you come to attack me again?" he said in a low, resonant voice. "Have you come once more to heap iniquities upon my head? To smother me beneath the weight of your scorn?"

Oscar felt a chill go fluttering down his spine. The voice was so unlike Vail's in timbre and tone that it seemed to be issuing from some sinister stranger buried deep within the business manager. He said, "I beg your pardon?"

199

Vail blinked, frowned, sucked in his cheeks, and then smiled sadly. "Oscar boy," he said, his voice all at once Vailish again.

"What *was* that you were saying?" Oscar asked him.

Vail blinked again, like a man having difficulty awakening. "Huh? Oh." He spoke slowly, distractedly. "Something from a play I was in. A real stinker." He smiled sadly once more. "You didn't know, did you, Oscar boy, that I used to be on the boards myself?"

"No," said Oscar.

"No," agreed Vail. His eyes misting over, he sat forward, lifted the bottle, poured the remaining whiskey into his glass. "Course not. How would you know? Why would you care? Far as you're concerned, I'm just greedy old Jack Vail. Am I right? Sloppy old greedy old insignificant old Jack Vail."

"Come now, Vail, I've never thought anything remotely like that. But I do think that we should—"

"You can't judge a book by its cover, ya know."

Oscar smiled, sensing an opportunity. "Actually," he said, "I've always maintained that a cover reveals more about a book than—"

"I had dreams once too, ya know," said Vail to his whiskey glass. He turned to Oscar. "I was young once too, ya know."

"I've never doubted that for a moment." Never having for a moment given it a thought.

Vail nodded. "Yeah. Dreams. I wanted to play Hamlet. The Melancholy Dane." He raised the glass to his lips, swallowed some bourbon. "Alas, poor Yorick," he said.

"You'd have made a capital Hamlet."

"I would of been terrible," Vail said. "Fact is, I wasn't much good in the stinkers." He looked at Oscar. "But at least, ya know, back then I had my dreams. Dreams are important, Oscar boy. You got to hold on to them as long as you can."

"Nicely phrased."

Vail nodded and narrowed his eyes. "You're okay. You're okay, Oscar boy." His eyes misted over again. "But really, ya know, you shouldn't ought to talk to me like you did before. I mean, what I did, I did it for the tour, Oscar boy. The tour's the thing, am I right?"

"Well, yes, up to a point."

"Absolutely," Vail nodded. "I was only thinking of you, see, you and the tour. That's my job, isn't it? I didn't mean anybody any harm."

"Of course not."

"So're we friends again, Oscar boy? Huh?" Vail held out his right hand. Oscar took it, and Vail squeezed his hand and clapped him heavily on the shoulder. "We friends again?"

"Of course we are. But don't you think you ought to get some rest? Tonight's the last lecture here in Denver. Come along, I'll walk with you upstairs."

"Great," said Vail. "Great idea." He released Oscar's hand, started to rise, then sat back and looked at him mournfully. "Tell me one thing, though, Oscar boy."

"What's that?"

"What you said. Upstairs in Henry's room. You wouldn't really of thrown me out the window, would ya? Not your old friend Jack. You wouldn't really of done that to old Jack, would ya?"

Oscar smiled. "Well, yes, Jack, I'm afraid I would."

Vail looked at him for a moment and then he laughed. He slapped his hand down on Oscar's thigh. "That's what I love," he said. "That wit you got."

And so Oscar had escorted Vail up the stairs to his room, the business manager cheerfully bouncing from time to time against the wall, then watched almost fondly as Vail toppled into bed and immediately began to snore. (So helpless and harmless did he seem that Oscar completely discounted the small frisson he had felt when a stranger's voice had rumbled from Vail's mouth.)

Oscar had gone back downstairs to eat. After an extremely depressing meal of dismembered chicken drifting in a pasty gray gravy, he had gone to his own room to nap. But sleep did not come. His stomach gurgled and grumbled in protest at the swill fermenting inside it. His brain attempted, and failed, to visualize

201

any of the people on the tour as a deranged murderer. And images of old men in tattered overcoats and of burly bullying giants in buffalo fur blended with the recurring image of a smiling Elizabeth McCourt Doe in nothing at all. Finally, at seven-thirty, he had arisen and returned to Vail's room. No one answered when he knocked, and the door was now locked, so Oscar had proceeded to the Opera House alone.

The lecture had been a disaster. His wittiest sallies stumbled into a blank wall of silence. His most profound observations met with uneasy titters or, worse, with the pachydermal trumpeting of some dunce emptying his sinuses into a pocket handkerchief. (Or more likely, given the caliber of the crowd, into his fingers.) Throughout the evening, Oscar was unable to prevent himself from glancing over expectantly at the box on his right, as though one of the two desiccated old harpies slumbering there, mouths agape, might magically transform herself into a regal presence swathed in ermine.

After the spotty and perfunctory applause, Oscar had left the Opera House and trudged back to the hotel. He had wanted to see, had wanted to speak with, no one. (Except of course Her.) But his stomach had recovered from its battle with the chicken—curious, and a bit vexing, how it could remain utterly indifferent to its owner's personal tragedy—and he had stopped downstairs for a bite to eat. There had been only a few customers in the bar, but one of them had been O'Conner, sitting with a bottle before him in the same chair that Vail had occupied earlier, and looking every bit as glum. Oscar had joined him.

"What do you recommend tonight?" Oscar asked him.

O'Conner, wearing the brown suit he had purloined from some scarecrow, looked at him balefully and said, "The whiskey."

When the waiter arrived a moment later, however, Oscar ordered the night's special, something called meat loaf. (They had no tea here; he had asked before.) As the waiter left, Oscar asked O'Conner, "You've spoken with Marshal Grigsby?"

O'Conner made a sour frown. "Yeah."

"What do you think of all this? These women being killed?"

O'Conner raised his glass, drank from it. "Some hookers got killed. Happens all the time." He shrugged. "It's a rough line of work."

Surprised, Oscar said, "You won't be writing about it, then?"

O'Conner shook his head. "Not my kind of thing."

"I should've thought that any reporter would've found the story fascinating."

O'Conner shook his head. "It's not my kind of thing," he said again, then drank some more whiskey and stared off at the nearly empty room.

"What do you think of Grigsby's notion that it's one of us?"

O'Conner looked at him. "Can you see any of us disemboweling a hooker?"

"No," Oscar admitted. "I can't."

O'Conner shrugged.

Oscar said, "Von Hesse had an interesting idea."

O'Conner looked at him. "I doubt that."

"He believes that one of us may be the killer, without being aware of it. That the homicidal side of his nature is as unknown to him as it is to the rest of us."

O'Conner snorted lightly. "Von Hesse is good at believing in things he can't see."

The meat loaf arrived then, and turned out to be a thick slab of parched, overcooked ground meat studded throughout with limp fragments of unidentifiable vegetable and glazed with an oily tomato sauce. Beside it on the plate rose a lumpy mound of mashed potatoes. The waiter also set on the table an empty whiskey glass

O'Conner looked at Oscar's plate, frowned, and said, "I wouldn't eat that on an empty stomach, if I were you." He poured bourbon into Oscar's glass.

Tentatively, Oscar tasted the meat. *Execrable* was the first word that sprang to mind. It was followed closely by *vile*.

O'Conner grinned. "That's a pretty hefty portion you've got there. The cook must like you."

"Fortunately," said Oscar, "I've never met the man."

203

"It's a woman," O'Conner said. "The wife of one of the brothers who owns the hotel. Maybe she's after you. The quickest way to a man's heart is through his stomach." He frowned. "Who was it who said that?"

"Lucretia Borgia."

O'Conner snorted.

Oscar took a sip of whiskey. "How are your articles coming along?"

"Fine," O'Conner said, and swallowed some whiskey of his own.

"When will we get a opportunity to read them?"

The reporter shrugged dismissively. "I asked Horner, the editor, to send copies to Chicago. They should be waiting for me there."

Oscar tasted the mashed potatoes. Or rather, attempted to, for they had no taste at all. "And so you're really not going to write about these killings?"

O'Conner scowled. "Jesus, Wilde, I already said so, didn't I?" Abruptly he pushed back his chair and stood up. "I've got to get some work done. I'll see you at the train station tomorrow." And lifting his bottle and tucking it under his arm, he had stalked from the room.

Leaving a puzzled Oscar to finish what he could of his meal by himself.

After dinner, he had climbed up the stairs to his room and, dispirited, dejected, climbed out of his clothes and into his pajamas, then flopped with his cigarette case and his notebook onto the bed.

Tomorrow, he told himself. Tomorrow he would present himself at Tabor's mansion, using the excuse that he wished to say goodbye. He must see her. Even if disguised as merely a polite visitor, even if only for a few moments, he must see her.

As for this murder business, the more one thought about that, the less probable the whole thing seemed. It had been the novelty of von Hesse's theory, rather than its plausibility, that had attracted; and the novelty now had worn off. And having used the

204

theory to fill up the emptiness within him, Oscar now felt, without it, doubly empty.

And yet those poor women had been killed in towns where the tour had stopped. How to explain that?

An itinerant madman. This was the only possible explanation.

Still, it would do no harm to keep an eye opened. All the men were innocent, certainly; but assuming, simply for the sake of argument, that one of them *could* be guilty, then it might be wise to remain alert.

O'Conner *had* acted oddly tonight. Brusque and moody. Quite unlike himself. And how could a reporter ignore the journalistic possibilities of these murders?

And what of that queer voice emerging from Vail's mouth?

But perhaps once you set out to discover secrets, you discovered that there was no end of them. Each of us had his own; each of us had another face hidden behind the mask.

Who would've thought that Vail had once been an actor? That once he had, good Lord, wanted to play Hamlet?

To be or not to be, that's the question, am I right?

But Vail a madman, a murderer? Or O'Conner? Or any of them? Absurd.

One should keep alert, however. If any of them *were* a madman (which was of course impossible), then surely he must finally reveal himself to the alert mind. To the alert, penetrating mind of a poet.

Oscar lit a cigarette.

Where was she? Just now, just at this moment, what was she doing?

Her white breasts are perfectly rounded at the bottom, and they slope down along their upper surface in a graceful arc to broad, pale pink, puckered aureoles and stiff fragrant nipples the thickness of fingertips; and, kneeling upright and naked on the bed, she offers them to him . . .

Oscar's hand drifted down his stomach.

Ah, Freddy. Tonight we have only each other.

Tonight, naked, once again he was dancing.

Twirling, spinning, silently wheeling, feet darting, arms loose and free.

It had been better last night, *yes*, it had been oh so wonderful last night when the red came flying off those streamers of flesh at his fingertips and sailed through the air and pattered bright shining patterns along the wall. It had been glorious then, afloat in the brilliant tumbling spate of divine light . . .

. . . he was on the bed now—another of those disconcerting shifts, those inexplicable folds in the fabric of Time, but never mind, never mind, he was beyond Time now. He held the pillow to his face (a whisper of camphor uncoiling from the cotton, and the sour musty shadows left behind by each of the countless heads that over the years had rested there) and he giggled as he remembered *oh yes* red fingertips capering down the slickness of bone

There will be another.

and prying open *oh yes* the wet red secrets of flesh

Another. Soon.

. . . up again, dancing again, reeling, swaying. On the cast-iron wood stove before him sat the porcelain washbasin, filled nearly to the brim with brownish water. He pranced forward, dipped his fingers into the warm water, fished out the limp slippery lump of flesh, and slumped to his knees, not in supplication, oh no, but in bliss and gratitude, and he

There will be another soon.

sank his teeth into the meat and tore away a chunk of it and chewed, his body shuddering with pleasure

Soon.

while the silence trembled like the wings of angels behind him in the room.

Grigsby walks into the room and closes the door behind him. The air is heavy with a dank, slaughterhouse stench.

The thing on the bed, its upper half propped against the wall, was once Molly Woods. The thing wears a petticoat, pushed back to its waist, and its legs are drawn up. There is no skin or flesh on the legs: glistening white shinbones, a pair of round white kneecaps, white thighbones. Only the feet, splayed out against the bed, are intact. Each toenail is painted red.

The flesh has been stripped, too, from the ribs, and between white arches of bone he can see a dull film of pink tissue.

The arms are peeled as well, from shoulder to wrist. The curled fingers of both hands have been placed at the black savage rent in the belly, as though to make it appear, obscenely, that they are drawing back the wide lips of the awful wound.

The face is gone. The thick red hair, falling to the exposed shoulder bones, frames a leering skull from which empty sockets gape.

Grigsby closes his eyes. He wants nothing now but to sink into the embrace of his absent wife, bury his face in her neck. He hears himself mutter her name: "Clara."

"Clara!" he cried out, and he twisted his body away from the room, from the terrible thing on the bed.

And felt a hand at his brow and heard a soft voice murmuring in a foreign language. "C'est un mauvais rêve, chéri."

And opened his eyes and in the moonlit dimness saw the soft white shoulders and the curling blond hair and the troubled blue eyes, and he reached out and drew to him the warm enfolding body of Mathilde de la Môle.

BOOK THREE

CHAPTER EIGHTEEN

DEAR OSCAR

Baby and I wanted to tell you that we will be joining up with the noon train to Manitou Springs today. My private car will be hooked to the rear of the train. We hope you will join us for a *chat!* See you at the station! I remain

> Yours truly,
> H. A. W. Tabor

Pathetic, really, those exclamation marks.

And that sloppy childish scrawl.

And *my private car* indeed. As though to say, "I'm really quite appallingly rich, you know." Why hadn't the boor simply enclosed one of his bank statements?

Yet Oscar was inanely smiling as he thanked the desk clerk for the note. He felt potent, invincible: Ulysses rearing up, leonine, from the lobby of a Denver hotel.

She would be there. He would see her.

"Good news?" said a voice to Oscar's left.

211

Vail, looking today rather the worse for wear: sagging gray dewlaps and bloodshot eyes.

"From Tabor," said Oscar, folding the note and sliding it into his coat pocket. "To inform me that he'll be on the train today."

The bloodshot eyes grew wary. "Is *she* coming? The doxy?"

"I couldn't say. By the way, I looked for you last night, before the lecture. Where had you gone?"

"Nowhere. I was out cold all night." He shook his head ruefully, and then suddenly winced, as though the movement had sent a splinter of bone spearing through his brain. "Jeez," he said, and reached up and tenderly touched his temple. "That booze is a killer. I don't know how O'Conner does it."

"So you never went to the ticket office?"

"Not till this morning. Receipts were down, huh? A hundred and seventy-five tickets. That sound about right to you?"

Oscar waved an indifferent hand. "Somewhere thereabouts." He would have said a hundred and seventy-seven, but perhaps last night's distress had affected his reckoning.

"Yeah, well," said Vail, "I got a telegram today from Tabor's manager in Leadville. Tomorrow night is sold out already."

Oscar nodded, distracted. He must buy her something. A gift.

Vail frowned. "Hey. You should be happy. Four hundred tickets, that's eight hundred bucks."

"Hmm? Yes, of course. Delighted. You know, I think I'll trot over to the station and see if Henry's gotten the luggage safely on board."

Another frown. "The train doesn't leave for another three hours." The frown became a scowl. "Shit. She *is* coming, am I right?"

"I really don't understand why you're so prejudiced against the woman. At bottom, you know, she's rather shy and retiring."

At bottom: lovely phrase.

"Shy like a cobra," said Vail.

Oscar laughed. "Ah, Vail, you're too much the trusting soul. You really should acquire a little cynicism. It would go so well with your necktie."

Vail glanced down, frowning, at his checkered bow tie.

212

"Now," said Oscar, "you'll see to the others? The Countess and the rest? Make sure they get to the station? Oh, and give me one hundred dollars, would you?"

Vail squinted at him. "What for?"

"For cigarettes."

"Aw, come on, Oscar. Be fair. I'm the business manager. I got to ask questions like that."

"But I'm the business," Oscar smiled. "And I needn't answer them. One hundred dollars, if you please."

Vail reached into his jacket pocket, slid out his billfold, counted out the money. He handed it to Oscar. "You keep spending money like this and you're not gonna have any left when we finish the tour."

"But I shall have some lovely memories."

"Memories and a nickel will get you a ride on the streetcar."

Oscar smiled. "A gentleman," he said, "never rides the streetcar."

A ring was out of the question; he didn't know what size she wore, and he refused to turn their time together into farce by presenting her with one that didn't fit. "What do you have," he asked, "in the way of lockets?"

Behind the counter, the short, elderly German proprietor looked Oscar up and down from over the rims of his spectacles. Oscar wore this morning his dark purple velvet coat and a pale green shirt wrapped at the neck with a rakishly fluffed paisley foulard, and he thought that on balance he looked smashing. The jeweler said, "Dis vould be for yourself?"

"For a young woman," Oscar said in German.

In English, evidently unimpressed by Oscar's fluid German: "Sister, cousin, friend, sweetheart?"

"The latter." How very annoying: he was blushing.

"Sveetheart," said the jeweler.

Oscar cleared his throat. "Yes."

"So a sveetheart, she gets a heart."

Oscar frowned. "Haven't you anything else?"

The jeweler shrugged. "You vant to give her, vot, a liver? A kidney, maybe?"

"Ah." Oscar smiled. "A comic jeweler. Extraordinary. Are there many of you here in Denver?"

"The other vun, he died. Vot's de matter mit a heart?"

"It's fairly . . . ordinary, don't you think?"

"It's nice, is vot I tink. A heart is nice. A kidney, not so nice."

"What I want is something unique, something extravagant."

"You vant a Fabergé egg."

"Something like, yes. What do you have along the lines of a Fabergé egg?"

"Hearts."

"Yes. Of course. Let's have a look at these hearts."

"Hearts ve got." The jeweler bent forward, slid open a panel at the rear of the counter, and brought up a tray. He set it atop the counter. "All sizes."

Oscar studied the lockets. He said, "None of them speak to me."

The jeweler shrugged. "You vant it to talk, ve can't do business."

"What's that over there?"

"Vot?"

"Behind you there, on the shelf."

"Dis? Dis is a brooch. Nice, a very nice piece, but a locket it's not."

"May I see it?"

He handed the brooch to Oscar. "Dot's Indian. The Zuni tribe. From Arizona. A very nice piece. Vun of a kind."

"Expensive, in other words."

"Dot I could let you haff for eighty-five dollars."

"These Zunis of yours. Do they by any chance *own* Arizona?"

"Look at dot inlay vork. A lot of craft goes into making a piece like dot."

"Into selling it, as well."

The jeweler shrugged. "Ve could go back to hearts."

"Do you have something attractive to present it in?"

"I got a box."

"Metal? Lined with velvet?"

"Cardboard. Lined with cardboard."

"The jeweler who died. It was a natural death?"

"Something he ate, I heard."

"Not a bullet, then?"

"Who vould eat a bullet?"

"Indeed. Do you have a box in, say, violet?"

"In white, I got vun."

"Fine. Done."

"You vant ribbon, I got ribbon. Red."

Oscar smiled. "A ribbon then, by all means."

Although the train to Manitou Springs and Leadville wouldn't be leaving for another hour and a half, the platform was crowded with people. There were cowboys in long canvas dusters, miners in canvas capes, businessmen in suits and topcoats, entire families in homespun and gingham. Children, giddy with candy and anticipation, scampered up and down the steps, scurried along the planking, dipped and disappeared behind adult legs. Vendors hawked popcorn and roasted peanuts. The sunlight slanting below the wooden canopy was thin but clear, and the air seemed festive, expectant, pulsing with possibilities.

How thoughtful it was of the universe, once again, to mirror Oscar's mood.

He strolled down the platform. People were drifting in and out of the carriages, smiling and laughing, chattering at each other through cheeks plump with peanuts.

Oscar saw that the carriages were smaller—lower and shorter and more narrow—than those with which he was familiar. But they were exquisitely built and beautifully painted, the bodies a rich emerald green, the trim around the windows a bright cheerful crimson. If any vehicles could ferry pilgrims to the promised land in comfort and style, these could. A pity that poor Moses hadn't been able to hire a railroad train.

He found Henry at the baggage carriage, being harangued by

215

a fat man in an ill-fitting pair of gray overalls beneath an opened gray wool coat.

Oscar asked Henry, "What seems to be the trouble?"

Henry's expression was, as always, noncommittal, but his face was a bit drawn today and his dark skin glistened with a thin sheen of perspiration. Perhaps he had picked up a chill yesterday, when the two of them had plunged through the torrent.

"It's your coat, Mistuh Oscar," Henry said. "The gennaman says it got to go inside the trunk."

"Sorry, friend," said the fat man, who seemed neither particularly sorry nor particularly friendly. His face was closed and knobby, like a fist. "I already tole the nigger here. All items of clothing gotta go inside the luggage. That's the rules."

"But the coat is still damp," Oscar explained. "It got soaked yesterday. If it's packed away, it'll become horribly wrinkled."

"Tough luck, but that's the rules."

Oscar turned to Henry. "Well, then, bring it along to the carriage."

"Uh-uh," said the man. "No good. No coat rack in the carriages."

Oscar told him, "We'll lay it over one of the seats."

"Only paying passengers allowed in the seats." The man was clearly beginning to warm to the exchange. Each refusal was an additional token of his power and further proof of his skill at debate.

"Mr. Tabor has arranged an entire first-class carriage for us."

"How many people?"

"Six."

"Tough luck. Only six seats in the first-class carriages. It goes in the trunk." He had the bad grace then to grin.

Oscar turned to Henry, reached into his pocket, pulled out his remaining money, and handed it to the valet. "Go to the ticket office, would you, Henry, and buy a seat for my coat. No, buy two of them. It needs room to air."

"Hey," said the fat man. "You can't do that."

"Why ever not?"

"Because . . ." He groped for a reason. "Because you *can't*."

216

"My good man," Oscar said. "I can understand that here in this carriage you are the master of all you survey. Quite clearly you are the Ozymandias of Baggage. But I fail to see how you can prevent me from purchasing a seat for any article of clothing I choose to. Clothes make the man, as I'm sure you'll agree, and in this case, so long as the seat is paid for, they also make the passenger."

"Second-class seat's gonna cost you five bucks apiece."

"No coat of mine," said Oscar, "travels second class." He turned to Henry and nodded. "Thank you, Henry."

"Yes suh, Mistuh Oscar."

Oscar turned back to the man. "One day," he said, "when your own coat travels by train, I hope you'll find it within yourself to provide it a proper seat."

"You crazy? I'm not gonna send my coat on no train trip."

Oscar studied the man's threadbare coat for a moment. Looked up from it. Smiled. "But you really should, you know."

"Huh?"

"This has been a most edifying conversation, one that I'm sure we'll both recall with enormous pleasure. But I must run along now. *Au revoir*."

The man stared at him in befuddlement, a condition he had doubtless experienced before, and Oscar turned away.

At the rear of the train, as promised, he found Tabor's private carriage. He was able to deduce that it was Tabor's carriage because on the door, set midway down its length, in raised wooden capital lettering, painted gold, were the words H. A. W. TABOR, and below that, PRIVATE CARRIAGE.

While the other passenger carriages had been attractive and colorful, fine examples of American workmanship (which could sometimes be quite surprisingly good), Tabor's looked as if it had been put together by a demented Swiss clockmaker. Every square inch of it was overlaid in elaborate, almost maniacal, wood carving: moldings and gingerbread filigrees. Obviously, too, whoever was guilty of its construction had intended that it resemble his own deranged notion of an Alpine chalet, for its windows were provided with exterior shutters and its shingled roof was steeply sloped (presumably to prevent the snow from settling atop it while the train was traveling at speed). Taken in its entirety, the carriage achieved a level of bad taste that was very nearly sublime.

Oscar knocked on the door, half expecting it to be opened by an enormous mechanical cuckoo bird. He was greeted instead by Tabor's liveried butler, who told him haughtily, in his amusing nasal twang, that Mr. Tabor and Mrs. Doe had not yet arrived.

Oscar thanked him, turned, and was about to walk back to the front of the train when, just at the edge of his vision, he thought he saw a towering figure in a fur coat. He looked, suddenly alarmed; but no one was there.

No shambling black bear, at any rate. Only a pair of cowboys slouched near the corner of the building, each with a booted foot notched back against the wall, each rolling a cigarette with one hand and effortless skill.

But that big furry shape, that (perhaps imaginary?) lumbering form—could it have been the brutal giant from Shantytown? Buff?

No, Biff. *Buff* was what the man hunted. Buffalo, according to the old man.

Had he followed Oscar here? Seeking revenge? Hadn't Doctor Holliday suggested that he might?

But Oscar had been alone on several occasions since his visit to Shantytown: walking to the opera house last night, walking back to the hotel. Surely if the giant had wanted to attack him, he could have done so then.

And the fellow was hardly likely to attack him on a train station platform that held a hundred witnesses.

No, even if the half-glimpsed figure *had* been Biff the Behemoth—and, really, what was the likelihood of that?—Biff represented no threat whatever here. In only an hour or so Oscar would be putting Denver, and Biff and his bad temper, behind him.

Satisfied that he was perfectly safe (although, of course, had he actually been attacked by the oaf, he would have given him a sound thrashing) Oscar began again to stroll alongside the train.

And then he saw her.

Suddenly everything else, the station, the train, the milling crowd, the earth, the sky, became mere backdrop: cardboard props and painted sets.

She wore a long fox cape, dark and lush; but that thick cascade of titian hair, gleaming in the limpid sunlight, made the fur seem dull and drab. Beneath the cape she wore a long dress of silk, light green at the bodice, dark green at the skirt. The fabric— loose, cut on the bias—shimmered as it shifted across those superb proud breasts. (Along the palms of Oscar's hands, remarkably, he could still feel their porcelain texture.)

Tabor marched beside her, the balding top of his egg-shaped head barely reaching the level of her sculpted jaw, his hands clasped behind him, his round vested belly jutting importantly between the opened front of his vicuna coat.

Tabor saw him. "Oscar!" he called and, grinning, he held out his stubby arm in greeting.

Smiling pleasantly (an outstanding performance, considering that this bloated dwarf had kept Elizabeth McCourt Doe to himself for a full day now), Oscar shook the beastly little hand and then turned to Elizabeth McCourt Doe.

The glance from her eyes came as two uncanny beams of violet light that pierced to the center of his being, melting it. His breath left him and so, very nearly, did his panache.

He wanted more than anything in the world to sweep her into his arms. This pretense of mere friendship made him curiously uneasy: he feared that by denying their love they might somehow lose it; that the pretense might become, against both their wills, the reality.

"Oscar," she said, and offered him her hand. "You look wonderful today."

He bent over her hand, inhaled its dusky moonlit scent, and gazed up at her. "If so, madam, this is because I look upon yourself."

Tabor laughed—brayed, more like it: *haw haw haw*—and said, "Watch out, Baby. Pretty soon he'll be trying to take advantage. You can't trust these poetic types."

Oscar stood upright and lightly laughed. You twit. You insufferable clod. "Indeed you cannot," he said to Elizabeth McCourt Doe. "No form of beauty is safe from us."

"Haw haw haw. Come on, Oscar. Let me show you the car. Nothing like it anywhere in the world."

About that Oscar had no doubts.

Her hand still lay in his. With a small smile she squeezed gently at his fingers and slipped it free.

Oscar turned to Tabor. "By all means."

The interior of the carriage was predictably vulgar. Gold wallpaper, red carpets, red plush furniture tasseled at the hem with strands of gold rope. The gas lamps were frosted glass torches held out from the wall by human hands, realistically molded in brass, which gave one the impression that their muscular brass owners stood on the other side of the panel, rolling their eyes in stupefied boredom.

"Whatta ya think?" Tabor asked him proudly.

"The mind boggles," Oscar told him.

"Ten thousand dollars," Tabor grinned, "and worth every penny. Grab a seat," he said, indicating the chair that stood opposite the divan. "Want a drink? What'll ya have? A coniac? We've got sherry, too, if you want it. You name it, we've got it."

"A small glass of sherry, then." He glanced at Elizabeth McCourt Doe. Except (perhaps) for the small smile playing about her red lips, she gave no indication, none at all, that only two nights ago the two of them had rolled one atop the other for hours.

Grinning, Tabor took her hand in his. The two of them sat down on the divan and Tabor plopped both their hands into his broad lap. "What about you, Baby?"

She smiled. "A sherry."

"Right. Three sherries, Peters," Tabor told the butler, who had been standing off to the left, as still and silent and stiff as a plank. "Sit, Oscar, sit," said Tabor. "Make yourself at home."

As the butler glided toward a mahogany sideboard, Oscar lowered himself into the red plush chair. He had just realized, abruptly, and with a startling quiver of nausea, that he didn't

220

want to be here; that he didn't want to see her slender hand ensnared in Tabor's pink meaty paw. Didn't want to see any part of her anywhere near the vicinity of Tabor's lap.

For the first time, looking at Tabor, he realized that this lumpish pygmy who totally lacked taste and style and wit was lying, night by night, in the same bed with Elizabeth. This pompous *dwarf* was making *love* to her.

Intellectually, he had known this before: he had packed the information away in that obscure attic of the mind where he stored the odds and ends in which he had no immediate interest. (The island of Zanzibar produces twenty thousand tons of cloves per annum. The expenses for this tour were gnawing away, as relentless as rats, at the profits.)

But now, suddenly, he understood it emotionally. And the realization struck him with the force of a blow to the chest.

"So how was your stay in Denver?" Tabor asked him, grinning.

"I found—" Oscar's voice was threaded; he cleared it. "I found parts of it extremely interesting."

Every night, night after night, those fleshy lips went crawling like garden slugs down the peerless skin of her throat . . .

"Manitou Springs is a whole different story," Tabor grinned. "A real one-horse town. But wait'll you see Leadville."

That bushy mustache, every night, hovered over the splendor of her breasts . . .

"Leadville," Oscar said. "Yes. I look forward to it."

He glanced at Elizabeth McCourt Doe. She sat regally, regally smiling.

Did she do with Tabor the things she had done with him?

Did her smiling mouth move down the length of that roly-poly body?

Oscar's stomach twisted.

The butler offered her a tray and, regally, she lifted from it a glass of sherry. The butler offered the tray to Oscar; he took a glass.

"Listen, Oscar," Tabor said, grinning as he took the last glass from the tray and sat back against the divan. "If you're interested,

221

I could let you in on a deal or two in Leadville." He hadn't let go of her hand. "I've got a lot of irons in the fire. You could double your money in no time flat. Guaranteed."

"Yes," said Oscar. "Yes, perhaps."

Night after night, those pudgy pink hands of his pried and prodded at her white skin . . .

"You know," Oscar said, putting his glass down on the end table, "I really should get back and check on the others. Make sure they've all arrived safely."

CHAPTER NINETEEN

DON'T THINK ABOUT IT, Oscar told himself.

Beneath the carriage, the wheels of the train clattered and rumbled, rumbled and clattered against the narrow-gauge tracks; outside the window a pine forest slipped past, dark straight tree trunks neatly sliding one around the other in a clever but pointless and ultimately annoying optical illusion.

Simply do not think about it.

But again and again, perverse, willful, a single image would begin to coalesce at the back of his mind: the long lean timeless body of Elizabeth McCourt Doe pinned beneath the stubby provisional bulk of Horace Tabor. Poetry buried beneath Babble.

Think about the forest, he told himself. How deep did it extend?

Hundreds of miles, probably. Thousands, perhaps.

That was the problem with this country. Like Tabor's mansion, it was built on too big a scale. The forests went on forever, or until they reached the prairies, and then the prairies went on forever, or until they reached another interminable forest, and over everything yawned that pitiless blue sky. The size of the place was staggering. It was literally frightful.

No wonder the Americans were such an aggressive lot. The

aggression masked the fear at the bottom of their souls: fear of this immensity, those endless forests teeming with disagreeable animals and bloodthirsty savages.

Masked it even from themselves, as the homicidal self theorized by von Hesse masked itself from its hypothetical owner. Of course: what two-fisted, four-square, six-gunned American would admit to fear? An American, almost by definition, was fearless. No doubt even Tabor saw himself as an intrepid Knight of Commerce.

(Tabor's bleak balding head bobs like a babe's at her perfect breast; her slender arms, sinuous as snakes, encircle his blunt bearlike shoulders: No. *No*. Absolutely not.)

And so, yes: and so . . . denied, disowned, left to itself in the darkness of the American psyche, the fear grew twisted and deformed; but still it grew, like a cancer. Until finally it broke through to the surface. Where it emerged as violence. The violence that the Americans directed at each other, the violence they directed toward the land.

(Bearlike? Why bearlike?)

But this *fear* . . .

Oscar sat up suddenly.

This *fear* might prove a partial explanation for these horrible murders.

If one assumed, with von Hesse, that the human mind could indeed be split into secret compartments, then perhaps fear was somehow at the basis of the split.

He looked around the carriage.

The baggage handler had lied about the number of seats. (Typically American; a British baggage handler would have played fair even while he cheated you.) There were six sets of two seats each, making a total of twelve. Those in the first two sets, right aisle and left, faced rearward. The seats of the two middle sets could be swung forward or back, to face front or rear. Both were arranged now to face the front, and it was in the window seat here, on the right side of the aisle, that Oscar sat. Vail sat slumped beside him, still looking worn and haggard.

224

In point of fact, nearly everyone in the carriage looked worn and haggard.

Young Ruddick lay sprawled along the first left-hand window seat, his eyes closed, his arms folded across his stomach. O'Conner sat opposite him, glowering sourly out the window. Von Hesse and the Countess sat opposite Vail and Oscar, facing them, and only these two seemed relaxed and rested. Von Hesse read quietly from a German translation of Chuang Tsu; the Countess gazed quietly out her own window, apparently lost in some pleasant reverie, for from time to time she smiled softly to herself.

No one had spoken since the train had left Denver. And even then, when they greeted one another, all of them had been subdued, their glances sliding uneasily away—and then furtively, speculatively, sliding back. All of them, of course, but von Hesse, who as a former German officer was seemingly indifferent, was perhaps immune, to the suspicions that troubled the others.

It was not surprising that the rest might be uneasy. This was the first time they had all been together since they had talked with Grigsby. All of them—presumably even the Countess— knew that Grigsby believed that one of them was guilty of a particularly grisly series of murders.

That might make for a difficult trip.

But it also—and here suddenly was another brilliant idea: it might also make for interesting theater.

Not only interesting. Something altogether new, something revolutionary.

One would need only a small stage, rigged out to resemble a train carriage and arranged in such a way that the audience could see all the players.

Bit of a problem there. The seats of the audience would have to rise in tiers, up from the stage, so that their occupants could look *down* onto the set, and so see everyone. Something like the old Greek amphitheaters. Oscar knew of no London theater with such an arrangement.

No matter. One would be found. Or, if necessary, constructed.

The audience would learn, from the passengers' conversation, that one of them was a murderer; but, like the passengers themselves, it would not know which.

A Poet, a German Officer, a Countess, a Journalist, a Businessman, another Poet—no, too many poets spoil the broth: make him a Disciple of the Poet.

A nicely representative selection of humanity. Commerce and Art. Europe and America. Aristocracy and Commoner. (Hamlet might be beyond Vail, but surely a Commoner was something he could manage.)

Six different perspectives, six different points of view brought together in a passenger carriage trundling through the vastness of the American West.

It would be the Poet, of course, who dominated the conversation, whose intelligence would illuminate the darkness, whose flashing wit would leaven the obligatory solemnity. And perhaps, by following his brilliant but infinitely subtle lead, so subtle as to pass unnoticed by its participants, the conversation would slowly, inexorably, reveal the identity of the killer?

THE POET: Herr von Hesse? Excuse me.
The German Officer lowers his copy of Chuang Tsu. (That would never do; no West End audience would have any idea what a Chuang Tsu was; change it to a copy of the Bible.)
THE GERMAN OFFICER: Yes?
THE POET: I've been mulling over your theory.
THE GERMAN OFFICER (*raising his eyebrows slightly*): Yes?
The Poet looks around the carriage, smiling fondly at the other passengers.
THE POET: Colonel von Hesse has come up with really quite an interesting theory about these murders. He believes that if Marshal Grigsby is correct, that if one of us is the killer, then perhaps this man is himself unaware of his homicidal urges. He kills without consciously knowing that he kills.
The response is a good deal less dramatic than the Poet had hoped for. The Countess merely tilts her blond head slightly to

226

*the side, her French mouth moving in a small moue of . . . what?
Concern? Distaste? The Businessman continues to stare balefully
at the floor of the carriage. The Disciple continues to slumber.
Only the Journalist reacts in a way that could be considered
theatrical, although not greatly so: he loudly snorts, and then he
reaches into his coat pocket for his flask of whiskey.*

THE POET (*turning back to the German Officer*): Yes. Well. As
I say, I've been thinking about this, and it occurred to me that
perhaps the force that has caused a separation within the man
may be a kind of *fear.*

THE GERMAN OFFICER: Fear? How so?

THE POET: Is it not possible that this "hidden being," as you put
it, might be a part of himself that our murderer actively *fears*?
A part which frightens him so badly that he has, in effect, walled
it off from himself?

THE GERMAN OFFICER (*nodding with a slow deliberate Teutonic
thoughtfulness*): Possible, yes, I should think. You have in mind
a particular aspect of his personality?

THE POET: Yes. That seems to me obvious from the nature of his
crimes. His sexuality.

THE BUSINESSMAN (*looking over at the Poet in alarm*): Jeez,
Oscar, we got a lady present.

*He nods toward the Countess and, from the exuberant blush that
washes even beneath his gray toupee, a puddle lapping beneath
a doormat, he is clearly embarrassed.*

THE COUNTESS (*smiling at the Businessman as though to reassure
him*): A lady, perhaps, but also a woman, Mr. Vail, and a French
one. In France we are, I think, more open to discussing sexuality.

THE JOURNALIST (*leering*): More open to having it, too. But I
guess that's only in France, eh, Countess?

THE BUSINESSMAN (*blustering*): Now just a minute there,
O'Conner—

THE JOURNALIST (*wearily*): Yeah, yeah. Sorry, Countess. Look,
Wilde, are you saying you agree with Grigsby? You think it was
one of us who killed those women?

THE POET (*smoothly, refusing to be drawn*): I say, only, that Herr

227

von Hesse's theory has merit. If one of us *is* the killer, and if the killer is in fact unaware of his identity, this would explain why none of the others have suspected him.

THE BUSINESSMAN (*shaking his head*): That's crazy.

THE POET: Precisely. The situation I describe would be a form of insanity.

THE JOURNALIST (*heatedly*): *I'll* tell you who's crazy. *Grigsby's* crazy.

THE POET: How so?

THE JOURNALIST: Yesterday he pulled a gun on me.

THE POET (*shrugging lightly*): He "pulled" one on me, as well. It's an old western tradition, I believe. Very much like shaking hands.

THE JOURNALIST: He *shot* at me.

THE POET: Perhaps he was especially pleased to see you. He seems a very demonstrative man.

THE GERMAN OFFICER (*to the Journalist*): Why would he do such a thing?

THE JOURNALIST: Because he's crazy!

THE GERMAN OFFICER: Troubled, perhaps. I think he is a troubled man. But insane? I think not. I found him very reasonable. (*He turns to the Countess.*) You spoke to him, did you not, Mathilde? What did you think?

THE COUNTESS (*smiling softly and, under the circumstances, inexplicably*): I found him most *sympathique*.

THE POET (*ignoring, for the moment, the unlikelihood of anyone finding Grigsby sympathetic, and deciding that it was time for him to begin his infinitely subtle direction of the conversation*): Grigsby's personality doesn't really enter into this. The fact is, women *have* been killed in precisely those towns in which we stayed, and I think that this is something we should all address.

THE JOURNALIST: Coincidence. How do we know some other women didn't get killed, the same way, in some other town hundreds of miles away?

THE POET (*who had himself brought up this precise point with Grigsby*): Presumably Grigsby will be looking into that possibility.

228

THE JOURNALIST: I wouldn't count on it. Grigsby's got a bee in his bonnet.

THE POET: That bonnet of his has room for an entire hive of bees. But, as I say, I think we should discuss this matter. Countess, it suddenly occurs to me that your presence here brings up an interesting question.

THE COUNTESS: And what is that, Oscair?

THE POET: You've spoken, you say, with Grigsby. You understand the possibility that one of us may be a murderer. And yet you continue to travel with us. Should we take this to mean that you disbelieve in Grigsby's notion?

THE COUNTESS (*after a fetching moment of deliberation*): I think that Marshal Greegsby is most probably correct.

THE JOURNALIST (*scornfully*): You think one of us is a killer?

THE COUNTESS (*turning to him with her chin upraised, a small smile on her lips, very nicely done indeed*): Regrettably, yes.

The Businessman shifts uncomfortably in his seat. The German Officer looks upon her earnestly. The Journalist snorts and takes a swallow of whiskey from his flask. The Disciple continues to slumber. (Perhaps later we could enliven this particular role.)

THE POET: And yet you continue to travel with us.

THE COUNTESS: From what Marshal Greegsby has told me, the murderer seems to prefer women of only a certain type.

THE JOURNALIST (*leering*): He could always branch out. Diversify.

THE COUNTESS (*smiling again*): A de la Môle fought beside Charlemagne. De la Môles have fought beside the kings of France ever since. I have committed myself to making this journey. I will complete it.

THE JOURNALIST: Too bad the king of France isn't coming along.

The German Officer looks at the Journalist curiously, as though he were a novel species of water bug.

THE DISCIPLE (*finally opening his eyes*): Just where *is* Grigsby anyway? He told me he'd be watching us like a hawk.

THE POET: I shouldn't worry about Grigsby. I have a feeling that he'll turn up at some unexpected and probably inopportune moment, like the chaperone at a costume ball.

229

The Disciple laughs merrily. The others smile their appreciation of this flash of wit.

THE POET: But returning, Herr von Hesse, to this interesting little idea I had. That our hypothetical murderer has walled off the sexual side of his nature. Do you think that his denied sexuality might provide a motive force for these killings?

Once again the Businessman shifts in his seat. Nervously, he glances at the Countess.

THE GERMAN OFFICER (*nodding thoughtfully once again*): Yes, of course. We know from de Sade that sexuality and violence can become intimately connected, yes? But even granting your point, Mr. Wilde, how does this bring us any closer to the identity of the murderer?

THE POET: If we could somehow establish the psychological characteristics of the man, then perhaps we will have gone some way toward identifying him.

THE GERMAN OFFICER: But this is all speculation. We do not *know* that his sexuality is the cause of his bifurcation.

THE POET: Nor do we know that he is in fact bifurcated. We know *nothing* about him. If we did, we shouldn't need to speculate.

THE GERMAN OFFICER: But I believe that this exercise of yours could become a dangerous undertaking. To add one unverified—and unverifiable—hypothesis to another is not, I think, the way to discover truth.

THE POET: And yet we do it every day, all of us. We live our lives amid a wilderness of unverified hypotheses. About the world, about our fellow man, about ourselves. I merely suggest that for a moment we do so deliberately, and see where it leads us.

THE GERMAN OFFICER: Into great troubles, I fear.

THE POET (*smiling, unfazed*): Those are the only sort worth troubling over. So, let us assume that the man *is* unconscious of this other self. And let us assume that this other self is, in some way, his own tormented sexuality. Let us assume that he has walled it off because he is positively terrified of the sexual side of his nature.

230

THE JOURNALIST (*rudely interrupting*): Well, that lets me out.
He slaps his stomach vulgarly and leers at the Countess.
THE POET (*suavely ignoring all this*): The question then becomes,
what would cause him to take such an extraordinary psychological
step? What would cause him to so fear his own sexuality?
THE DISCIPLE (*blurting it out*): His parents.
*All heads turn toward the young man, who blushes and flutters
his eyelashes, as though himself startled by his statement, or as
though embarrassed at having interrupted the Poet's methodical
Socratic presentation.*
THE DISCIPLE (*rather defensively*): Well, it's *obvious*, isn't it? I
mean, they're the ones who give approval from the *start*. Or who
don't. And if they disapproved *strongly* enough, of the way he
was, if they were really *vicious* about it, wouldn't that somehow
change him?
*For an embarrassed moment no one says a word. It is as if all
the others share, with the Poet, the feeling that the Disciple has
revealed more about himself and his own family life, and more
about his own sexuality, than he intended to. It is the Countess
who comes to the young man's rescue.*
THE COUNTESS: I think that I should agree. I spoke of this yesterday with Marshal Greegsby. I think that madness of this sort,
perhaps of any sort, can be traced back to the early years of life.
But I believe that the important element in this matter is vicious-
ness. The more physically brutal are the parents, the more likely
they are to produce brutality in their offspring. I have seen this
happen, many times.
THE POET: What, then, of Gilles de Rais? He appeared perfectly
normal until the death of Joan of Arc. It was only after this that
he embarked upon a life of utter wickedness and depravity.
THE BUSINESSMAN (*looking confused*): Who was Jeels da Ray?
THE POET (*lucidly explaining*): A knight of France. He was evidently in love with Joan. After the English burned her at the
stake—an old English tradition, one that they have never really
forgiven themselves for abolishing—Gilles retired to his estate
and began a career of really quite astonishing cruelty. He tortured
young peasant boys, hundreds of them, apparently, and then,

231

with the help of his servants, savagely raped and murdered them.

THE BUSINESSMAN (*looking ill*): Aw, jeez. Aw, come on, Oscar.

THE COUNTESS: But we know nothing of the early years of Gilles de Rais. Perhaps he had been brutally ill treated himself. Perhaps his madness lay dormant until the shock of Joan's death.

THE POET: I've always believed, about Gilles, that after Joan's death he became not so much mad as unmoored. What sort of a world was it, I think he asked himself, whose God could allow the execution of a woman he loved, a woman who had saved France, a woman he believed to be a saint? I believe that by his wickedness he was trying to determine the limits, the boundaries, of this new universe. And perhaps the same might be true of our murderer. Perhaps he too is testing for, probing at, the limits of his world.

THE GERMAN OFFICER: Murder as a philosophical inquiry? But Mr. Wilde, you cannot have it both ways. You cannot on the one hand assume an insane hidden self, and then assume that this hidden self is conducting an investigation into the nature of reality.

THE POET: I assume nothing. I merely, for a time, play with an idea or two. (*Ideas being, at the moment, all the Poet has to play with.*)

THE JOURNALIST: This is garbage. (*Heads turn.*) First of all, you don't know anything about this murderer. You said so yourself. You haven't got a single fact to start making up theories with.

THE POET: Facts would only confuse us.

This clever sally is met with a gratifying set of smiles from the Countess, the German Officer, and the Disciple. The Businessman still looks fairly ill.

THE JOURNALIST: Second, it looks to me like you're all forgetting that what you're talking about here is one of *us*. Me, or von Hesse, or Vail, or Ruddick, or *you*, Wilde. Everyone's being real civilized and sophisticated about it, but what you're all saying is that one of us is a murderer. A killer. You can really believe that after we've been together all this time?

THE GERMAN OFFICER: It has not been actually for long, Mr.

232

O'Conner. A few weeks is hardly time enough for any human being to know another. An entire life, perhaps, is not time enough.

THE JOURNALIST (*speaking with a vehemence and a venom that seem uncalled for*): I don't buy that. I think you can size a person up, good or bad, in a couple of hours. And I don't buy this "hidden self" thing either. I think this guy, whoever he is, and I *don't* think he's one of us, is killing these women just because he *wants* to. You don't need any fancy psychological theories to figure him out. Killing is what he *does*. It's what he *wants* to do. But if you really buy the idea that he's one of us, then you'd be better off forgetting theories, and start trying to decide what you're going to do about it. And it looks to me like there's *nothing* you can do about it. Nothing at all.

THE GERMAN OFFICER (*quietly*): There is one possibility. (*Heads turn once again. The Poet is reminded of spectators at a tennis match.*) We could divide ourselves into pairs. Each of us would remain, at all times, with his assigned partner. This way, at least, none of us would have an opportunity to commit any further atrocities.

THE JOURNALIST (*with another leer*): Great. I'll take the Countess.

THE BUSINESSMAN: Hey!

THE GERMAN OFFICER (*faintly smiling*): What you suggest is impossible. And Countess de la Môle is of course beyond suspicion.

THE JOURNALIST: Why? You don't know *anything* about this killer. If it could be one of us, it could just as easily be the Countess.

THE BUSINESSMAN: Listen, O'Conner, I'm warning you—

THE JOURNALIST (*disgustedly*): Ah, forget it. Pairing up is a crazy idea anyway. Think about it. Who wants to spend the rest of the tour shackled to anybody here? (*Yet another leer.*) Except to the Countess, naturally. And the other thing is, if I really believed that *one* of you was a murderer, I for damn sure wouldn't want to sleep in the same room with *any* of you.

THE GERMAN OFFICER: The killer has never struck against a man.

THE JOURNALIST (*once again speaking with an untoward vehemence, as though interpreting the German Officer's remark as*

233

a personal attack): How do we *know* that? Maybe there are dead men rotting away back in El Paso and San Francisco. Maybe they haven't been found yet, or maybe Grigsby just doesn't *know* about them. And even if this guy hasn't killed a man, so *far*, how do you know that he's not gonna start? How do we know that one night he's not gonna go even crazier and kill his roommate, just so he *can* go out and kill another woman? You *don't* know it. Like I said, you don't know *anything*. Do any of you really want to take a risk like that?

The Disciple and the Businessman look at one another and then, in unison, their glances fall away.

THE GERMAN OFFICER: I would of course accept this risk.

The Journalist snorts and opens his flask to take a drink.

THE JOURNALIST: Yeah, but who's gonna accept it with you?

More silence. No one moves. The German Officer looks at the others and, after a moment, sadly frowns. And the Poet abruptly realizes that although the trip may continue, although they may all remain together over the countless miles that stretch from here to New York City, the tour as it has been constituted—seven people sharing meals and transport and time and also a simple, a commonplace, really a rather banal belief: a belief in the essential humanity of one another—all that is over. The killer, whoever he is, has killed this as well.

And killed, too, this particular dramatic piece. Pity. Exeunt the Poet, pursued by a bear.

CHAPTER TWENTY

A FTER DOCTOR BOYNTON LEFT Grigsby's office, Grigsby walked out into the anteroom and strapped on his gun. Behind him, Carver Peckingham swung his long legs down to the floor and lowered his chair—quietly, maybe thinking that if he did it softly enough, Grigsby wouldn't notice that his feet had been perched atop the desk.

"You goin' out again, Marshal?" Carver asked him.

"Yeah." He pulled the sheepskin coat up over his shoulders and turned to the deputy. "I'm not gonna be back again today, prob'ly, and tomorrow I'm goin' outta town. You mind the store for me, okay, Carver?"

Carver was leaning forward eagerly in his chair. "Sure, Marshal. Where you goin'?"

"Not sure yet." Best that Carver didn't know. The deputy couldn't tell a lie to save his life, and tomorrow, one way or another, Greaves would be looking for Grigsby.

Grigsby looked around the anteroom, glanced at the door to his office, and wondered whether he'd ever see any of it again.

He turned to Carver. "Greaves'll maybe give you a hard time tomorrow."

When he discovered Grigsby gone tomorrow, Greaves would think that he'd run out. That bothered Grigsby some, Greaves thinking he'd turned yellow. But with all the tour members, including the killer, leaving town, Grigsby knew he had to follow them.

Another thing. Maybe Judge Sheldon would be able to get Grigsby recalled tomorrow, and maybe he wouldn't. But if he did manage it, the only way Grigsby might be able to get his job back (which maybe he'd want to, and maybe he wouldn't) was to figure out who the killer was.

Carver smiled up at him. "Don't you worry none, Marshal. I can take care of myself."

Grigsby nodded. "Know you can. But don't be no hero, Carver."

"Greaves don't scare me none."

Gruffly, Grigsby said, "Don't you be no hero. That's an order. Greaves leans on you, you bend. Hear me?"

Carver nodded, abashed. "Yes sir."

Grigsby glanced around once more.

In June it would be twelve years since Grigsby had first stepped into these two rooms, and they looked exactly the same today as they had then. From time to time Clara had begged him to fix them up, hang pictures on the wall, lay carpets on the floor. But Grigsby had liked them the way they were—plain, simple, functional. They made the place look like a marshal's office, and that was the way a marshal's office was supposed to look.

It seemed to him now that his twelve years here had left no mark at all. He might never have been here; might never have hung his coat on the coat rack; might never have lowered his painful hip behind the big broad wooden desk . . .

"Anything else, Marshal?"

Grigsby looked at him.

Anything else.

What could he say to Carver's eager young face?

Time passes. Things change. Life goes on but sometimes we don't.

He shook his head. "Nope. See you, Carver."

Mary Hanrahan opened the door, her bony shoulders stooped, her long face so pale that the freckles across her nose seemed gray. She wore a brown cotton frock, much washed and often ironed, and against her gaunt frame it looked almost as worn and tired as she did. Her gray hair was pulled into a bun at the back of her thin neck. Resignation was etched into the lines at the hollows of her cheeks, smudged into the circles below her eyes. But when she saw Grigsby, her face tightened— it folded up, like a flower when the sunlight left it.

"Mary," Grigsby said, nodding.

"Bob," she said, her voice flat. She didn't nod.

"Sorry, Mary. I got to talk to him."

"He's asleep." Cool and curt, offering the words with the reluctance of a miser handing out gold coins.

"It's important. I wouldn't bother him unless it was."

"He needs his sleep," she said.

"It's important," he repeated.

She folded her arms below her small parched breasts and she shook her head, less in refusal than in disappointment. "You're still the same, Bob Grigsby. Some people have it in them to change, but not you. You're still the same selfish man you've always been. Does it matter to you, the horror he had to face this morning? Does it matter to you that he was hours getting to sleep, he was so sick at heart?"

"It matters," Grigsby said. "But I got a job to do."

"*It's not your job,*" she said. Her eyes narrowing, she leaned toward him and put one hand on the door, the other on the jamb, effectively blocking his way. "Greaves wants you out of it. Gerry told me so. And nothing good will come to him by helping you. Isn't it enough you ruined your own life, and Clara's? Do you have to ruin his as well?"

Grigsby looked down. Whatever happened, whatever was said here, he was going to talk to Hanrahan. If listening to a lecture from Mary was the price he had to pay, then he would pay it.

237

"Oh Bob," she said, and her voice had softened. Grigsby looked up and for a moment he saw, hovering like a ghost before her present-day self, the Mary she had once been, tall and slender and proud. "Won't you leave him be?" she said. "You know he can't refuse you, whatever you ask him. Bob, if you've any fondness for the man at all, *please* leave him alone. We've enough trouble without the sort you'll be bringing us."

But it was too late, even if Grigsby could have turned himself, magically, into some other person. Because just then he heard Hanrahan's voice behind her: "Let the man in, Mary. In this house we don't keep no one standin' on the doorstep, not even the divil himself."

Mary glanced over her shoulder. She turned back to Grigsby for a moment with a look of naked fury; and then, all at once, her face sagged back into its usual look of resignation.

She stood aside and Grigsby stepped into the small parlor.

Wearing his uniform pants and the top of his union suit, his feet bare, Hanrahan stood in front of the curtained doorway that led into the kitchen and the bedroom. The light in the room was dim; the shades were drawn at the windows and only a single small oil lamp burned on the end table. Grigsby suspected that the room was always like this, blurred and indistinct in the grayness of a perpetual dusk.

Behind Grisgsby, Mary slammed the door shut.

"It's all right," Hanrahan said to his wife. "I wasn't sleepin' anyhow. Fetch us a bottle, would you, Mary?"

Mary's face was closed again. "You fetch your own bloody bottle," she snapped, and stalked past them. She whipped the curtains aside and stormed through them.

Hanrahan turned to Grigsby. He smiled apologetically and ran a hand back through his disheveled hair. "She's not feelin' herself today," he said. "Have a seat, Bob. I'll be back directly."

As Hanrahan slipped through the curtains, Grigsby lowered himself into one of the two frayed armchairs that faced the sofa. He could hear, through the curtains, the sharp serrated hiss of their whispering.

Over the sofa hung a rectangle of needlepoint, framed in wood,

238

set beneath glass. Grigsby could just make out the words: GOD BLESS OUR HAPPY HOME.

Grigsby sighed. Maybe Mary was right. Maybe he shouldn't have come here.

Ducking his head, Hanrahan emerged through the curtains carrying a bottle of Irish whiskey and two glasses. He set the glasses on the end table, filled them halfway with whiskey, then set down the bottle and picked up the glasses. He handed one to Grigsby. "Health, Bob."

Grigsby raised his glass. "Health, Gerry."

Hanrahan drank from the glass, sat down on the sofa and looked for a moment around the room. Grigsby sipped at his drink and waited; this was Hanrahan's home, happy or otherwise, and Grigsby would discuss no business here until Hanrahan was ready for it.

Hanrahan turned to Grigsby. "Have ye heard from Clara?" He shrugged, smiled apologetically again, and said, "I neglected to ask ye this mornin'."

"Got a letter a while ago. She's fine. The kids are fine."

Hanrahan nodded. He looked around the room once more, turned again to Grigsby. " 'Member when we all of us went up to the Springs? You and Clara, and Mary? How long ago was that now, Bob?"

"Ten years," said Grigsby. "Eleven."

Hanrahan nodded. He sipped at his whiskey. "Good times," he said.

Grigsby nodded. "Good times."

"At least you had the kids," Hanrahan said. "We shoulda had kids, me and Mary." He sipped at his whiskey. "She blames herself. There wasn't anything in the world Mary wanted more than kids."

Grigsby nodded. The air in the tiny parlor was growing heavier as it filled up with the smoke of losses and regrets. He took another sip of whiskey.

Hanrahan studied the threadbare oval rug in the center of the floor. He looked at Grigsby. "Doesn't take long for things to turn to shit, now does it?"

Grigsby shook his head. "Nope." He smiled. "Happens over-night, seems like."

Hanrahan nodded. "You think Clara's ever comin' back?"

"Nope." He wanted a cigarette; Mary didn't allow them in her house; never had. He sipped some more whiskey.

"You could go off to San Francisco," Hanrahan said.

"Get me a job as a sailor boy?"

"Police work."

Grigsby smiled. "I'm fifty-two, Gerry. You reckon they hire many fifty-two-year-old patrolmen?"

"You're an experienced lawman, Bob. You could do better than patrolman."

Grigsby shook his head. "Too late. I made my choices. I can live with 'em."

Hanrahan nodded. He drank some whiskey. He sighed. "Ah well. What can I do for ye?"

"I talked to Doc Boynton. He said there were footprints in Molly's room."

Again Hanrahan nodded. "There was. Gone now."

"Gone?"

"Greaves had me clean 'em up."

"Did he make a trace of the prints?" And then, in a kind of delayed echo, Grigsby heard what Hanrahan had actually said. "He made *you* clean 'em up?"

Hanrahan smiled faintly. "Told me I could order young Tol-liver to help me." He shrugged. "Better me than him. Kid woulda never got over it. I put her pieces in a couple of wicker baskets. Washed down the floor and the walls."

"Aw Jesus." Grigsby tried to picture it; his mind skittered away. "Jesus," he said, and realized that this had been his fault. "Because you were talkin' to me. Because I was there."

Hanrahan shrugged. "Someone had to do it. Might as well be me."

"Jesus, Gerry," Grigsby said. "I'm sorry."

Hanrahan swallowed some whiskey. "What's done is done."

A couple of wicker baskets. "Aw *shit*, Gerry."

"It's over, Bob. I wouldna done things no different anyhow."

240

Grigsby took in a deep breath, let it slowly out. "Did he make traces of the prints?"

"No. They wasn't much good, Bob. None of them was a whole entire foot, and all of them was smeared. They wouldna been no help a-tall."

"Boynton says they were average size."

Hanrahan nodded. "Average," he said.

"When did Greaves . . . What time did you clean everything up?"

" 'Bout an hour after you left."

"How come so soon?"

"Greaves said he didn't want no panic." He shrugged again. "I hate to say it, Bob, but could be he was right."

Grigsby took a sip of whiskey. Whether Greaves had been right or wrong, the footprints were gone now. "Listen, Gerry. I'm takin' off tomorrow mornin' for the Springs. Anything happens to me, I'd appreciate it, you do me a favor."

Hanrahan frowned. "What's gonna be happenin' to ye?"

Grigsby shrugged. "Long way to the Springs. Anything could happen."

"Yer takin' the train?"

"Thought I'd take it down to Colorado Springs and hire me a horse from there. Nice piece of road along the way to Manitou. Haven't seen it for a while."

Hanrahan smiled. "Cowboys and Indians and wide open prairies?"

Grigsby smiled back. "Somethin' like that."

"What's the favor?"

"There's a key to my house on the porch, under the flower pot on the rail. Key fits the back door. I got a big dresser in the bedroom. You pull out the bottom drawer and there's some letters and stuff inside. Take 'em, and then you'll know everything I know about all this."

"About all what?"

"It's all in the letters."

"You wouldn't want to be givin' me a little hint, now would ye, Bob?"

"Letters'll tell you everything you need to know. If I'm not back by Monday night, you go ahead and get 'em."

"And what do I do with them, exactly, once I got 'em?"

"Whatever you want. Whatever you think is right."

Hanrahan nodded. "How come yer tellin' me all this?"

"Greaves and I had kind of a set-to this afternoon."

Hanrahan looked at him for a moment. "Ye didn't, by any chance, cause the man some physical damage?"

"Some."

"What sort?"

Grigsby smiled. "Well, Gerry, it was kind of an accident."

"An accident."

"Yeah. I had my hand out and he walked smack into it."

Hanrahan nodded. "And I suppose yer hand was all balled up into a fist at the time."

Grigsby nodded. "Now you mention it."

Hanrahan nodded. "And where was Mr. Brubaker durin' these proceedin's?"

"On the floor. Some kinda problem with his head, it looked like."

Hanrahan suddenly laughed. He shook his head. "Jesus, Bob."

"Anyway—"

"What about Sheldon?" Suddenly serious. "Greaves goes to Sheldon with that, and yer up shit creek entirely."

"He already went to Sheldon. Reckon I'll find out tomorrow what happens. Maybe I'll get to be a sailor boy after all."

"Jesus." He looked at Grigsby. "You're thinkin' that Greaves might be layin' for ye? Lookin' to cause ye some physical damage of his own?"

Grigsby shook his head. "It's only that I'm gonna be away for a while, and if anything happened to me, nobody'd know about those letters."

Hanrahan frowned. "You need some help?"

Grigsby shook his head. "I'll be fine, Gerry. Like I say, this is all just in case."

242

Hanrahan sat in silence for a moment. Finally he said, "Tell me one thing, Bob. You figure it was worth it? Givin' Greaves a taste of knuckle?"

Grigsby thought about it for a moment. Finally he smiled. "Yeah, Gerry, I got to say it was."

Hanrahan stared at him for another long moment, and then he grinned. "Greaves and Brubaker both." He shook his head. "I'd give me right arm to see a thing like that."

"You keep your right arm. Things work out, I'll see you on Monday."

"And if things don't work out?"

Grisgby smiled. "Then maybe I won't."

When he left Hanrahan's house, Grigsby was surprised to see that the real dusk, of vanishing sun and blending shadows, had come and gone. Night had fallen. He slipped his pocket watch from his vest, saw that the time was nearly a quarter to eight. He climbed on his horse and rode over to the telegraph office.

No telegrams addressed to him had arrived. He wasn't surprised; it was early yet. Mort had gone home, so he told Peters, the night operator, to hold any telegrams addressed to Grigsby that arrived tonight, and hand them over to Mort in the morning. He left Mort a note, asking him to forward his telegrams on to the Woods Hotel in Manitou Springs tomorrow, and to the Clarendon in Leadville on Sunday. Mort, Grigsby knew, would tell no one, not even Greaves; Mort believed that a telegraph operator took the same oath of silence as a doctor.

Afterward, Grigsby rode to Wilde's hotel.

Ned Winters, the desk clerk, told him that Wilde had left for the opera house. Except for Vail and the French woman, the others, too, were gone.

Grigsby nodded. "Okay, Ned. Give me the passkey."

Winters hesitated. He was a round little man in a baggy checked suit who grew the left side of his hair long and troweled it up over his bright pink scalp and plastered it in place. "I don't know, Marshal."

Grigsby smiled. "What is it you don't know, Ned?"

"If I should do that. Lonny—Mr. Laidlaw—he told me he don't want me ever to give out the passkey."

Grigsby nodded. "And what did he tell ya about sleepin' on the job?"

Winters looked quickly around the lobby. "Like I told you this morning, Marshal, I musta just closed my eyes for only a minute."

"You want to explain that to Lonny?"

Winters sighed. He opened a drawer in the desktop and pulled out a key, handed it to Grigsby. "What happens if one of them comes back?"

"Tell him the maid's in there cleaning. Buy him a drink and come up and get me. Bang on the door twice."

"How will I know which room you're in?"

"Bang hard on any one of 'em. Walls up there ain't that thick."

Winters nodded. He leaned confidentially toward Grigsby. "What's goin' on, Marshal?"

"How's that?"

Winters adjusted his bow tie. "Well, I mean, you wanted to know where they were all at last night. Woke me up to find out. I figure it must be something pretty important."

Grigsby nodded. "Reckon there's not much slips past you, Ned."

Winters smiled, pleased. "Well, you know how it is, Marshal. I been in the business a long time."

Grigsby put his elbows on the counter and leaned toward the clerk. "I ever lie to you, Ned?

Winters shook his head. "No sir, Marshal. Not that I know of."

Grigsby nodded. "Then I reckon there's no reason for me to start now."

Winters stared at him.

Grigsby said, "I'll be back down in a little while."

Upstairs, no one was wandering along the carpeted hallway. Grigsby unlocked the door to Wilde's room, stepped in, locked it shut behind him.

The room smelled, in the darkness, like roses.

Figured.

He lit a match, cupped it in his hand as he carried it over to the oil lamp, used it to set the lamp's wick aflame. He blew out the match, stuck it in his vest pocket. He adjusted the flame, then held the lamp up and looked around the room.

He stepped back and nearly dropped the lamp. Over in the corner, somehow sprawled along the room's two chairs, was a dead man.

No.

No, he realized, and blew air from his lungs. Not a dead man.

Only a long black topcoat spread atop the chairs, its long limp arms hanging loose.

Jesus, Grigsby thought. Spooked by an overcoat. He really *was* getting too old for this shit.

His heart still pounding, Grigsby walked over to the coat and touched it.

Wet.

Wilde had laid it out to dry.

Grigsby thought: *bloodstains*? Wilde had washed away the bloodstains?

Or had he worn it today, in the rain?

Grigsby walked over to the closet and opened the door.

Arranged neatly along the floor were more shoes than he had ever seen together at one time, in any one place outside a shoe store. Beneath him they gleamed and glimmered in the flickering lamplight, boots and brogues and some dainty, delicate things that looked like slippers for a fairy godmother.

But she would have been a fairly hefty fairy godmother. The slippers were dainty only in construction. In size they were larger than Grigsby's boots.

245

No one could call those feet average. Except maybe an elephant.

So. The shoes cleared Wilde.

In a way—and it surprised him—he was glad to learn it. He didn't much care for nances, but Wilde, at least, had some style. Some balls, too.

He looked around the closet. Suits, jackets, topcoats, trousers, enough fancy-dan clothes for a regiment of lulu-belles. Pushed against the wall was a large metal steamer trunk, its hasp unlocked. For a moment Grigsby considered opening it. But Wilde's shoes had proved him innocent of the murders, and anything he happened to be toting along on his travels was none of Grigsby's business.

O'Conner's feet *were* average, and Grigsby spent some time going through the reporter's things.

He found three full bottles of liquor hidden around the room, one under the bed, one in the otherwise empty suitcase in the closet, and one in the bottom drawer of the dresser. This made sense—if you were a drinking man, you made a point of keeping some spare bottles handy.

There was also a half-filled bottle of liquor on the table by the bed, and Grigsby, being a drinking man, drank some.

In the top drawer of the dresser he found a cheap cardboard notebook. Opening it, he discovered that only the first page of it had been written upon.

In cramped, scratchy handwriting, it read:

O. Wilde.

Oscar Wilde.

Oscar Fingal O'Flahertie Wills Wilde.

That was all.

What kind of garbage was that? Where were his notes, where were the articles he was supposed to be writing?

Grigsby flipped through the notebook again. Empty.

He went back to searching. He found no single-edge knife with a seven-inch blade, and he found no mementos of Molly Woods.

246

Like O'Conner's, Ruddick's feet were average, and Grigsby spent a fair amount of time searching through the boy's room. In the closet, as he riffled the pockets of the suitcoats and jackets, the smell of lilacs was so strong that his eyes began to water.

On the top of the dresser, beside the empty water basin, he found a small painting in a gilt frame that showed a sleek young man, his hands tied above his head, who was naked except for a pair of diapers, and who seemed pretty indifferent to, or maybe even pleased with, all the arrows sprouting from his muscular arms and chest, and the blood trickling elegantly down his oiled flanks. Clara, raised by nuns, had owned a book of Saints; and, from the arrows, Grigsby recognized the young man as St. Se bastian. The patron saint of lulu-belles?

Inside the dresser, in the top drawer, he found a notebook. He opened it, flipped through pages filled with a rolling ornate handwriting. Scratched-out words and phrases made a scattered pattern like buckshot wounds amid the lines. Poetry, it looked like.

He read one.

> *Beloved, when I, beside your silken skin,*
> *Trapped in the longitude and latitude*
> *Of passion, consider that our attitude*
> *And history are nothing like akin,*
> *I fear that one day our deepest mood*
> *Will differ, and you, brood-*
> *Ing, will see crime where there is only sin.*

Crime? Sin?

Was he maybe talking about murder?

Or maybe just about cornholing?

It occurred to Grigsby that the poem might have been written about Dell Jameson, or someone like him, and he felt suddenly a bit queasy, as though he were holding a piece of dirty underwear. He closed the notebook and returned it to the drawer.

247

He searched some more, but he found no knife, and no organs belonging to Molly Woods.

Von Hesse's feet were average, too, and Grigsby went over his room carefully. In the closet, a suitcase filled with books, all of them in German. Clothes hanging neatly on their hangers.

More clothes, more neatness, in the dresser. Two small perfectly rectangular stacks of shirts, each perfectly folded shirt perfectly aligned atop the perfectly folded one beneath.

Grigsby glanced around the room. It was immaculate, nothing out of place, not a speck of dust anywhere.

Wilde's room, clean as it was, hadn't been this spotless. Neither had O'Conner's. Von Hesse could've had a different hotel maid, but Grigsby doubted it. And the maid hadn't arranged the shirts.

Clara hadn't kept their own house neater than von Hesse kept his room. Maybe Grigsby should hire the German to help him shovel out the place.

Grigsby searched. No knife, no bits and pieces of Molly Woods.

Henry's tiny cubicle of a room was even neater. It was empty. No shoes, no clothes, no suitcase, nothing.

Had the valet moved to another room? And if he had, why?

Find out from Winters at the front desk.

Grigsby pulled shut the door to Henry's room, locked it and started down the empty hallway.

When he came to 211, the Countess's room, he paused.

She's not for you, Bob.

But maybe she remembered something. She's had all day to think about it. She *told* me to come back.

Bullshit. You just want to see her.

She *told* me to come back.

248

What was that you said today to Wally, the day clerk? No fool like an old fool?

Grigsby rubbed the toe of his right boot against the back of his left trouser leg, then the toe of his left boot against the back of his right trouser leg. He took off his hat and knocked on the door.

CHAPTER TWENTY-ONE

FF TO THE WEST, immense even at this distance, the big bold pyramid of Pike's Peak shouldered aside the lesser mountains as it bullied itself toward the sky. Beyond the dusky pines that fringed the folds of foothills, it lurched up against the milky blue of early morning, the bright snowfield along its flank glazed golden by the light of the rising sun.

Shifting in the saddle against the slow rhythm of his horse, Grigsby winced. He'd come a mile since leaving Colorado Springs and already his hip was aching.

The road was empty. The only sound was the dull steady clop of the horse's hooves against the dirt. To the right, a pine forest still held, between tall straight trunks, below stacked green parasols of needled branch, the dark cool shadows of night. To the left, a hundred yards away, thin sunlight angled along the railroad tracks that ribboned over the rolling green prairie, heading west to Manitou Springs, and then up into the mountains, and over them, to Leadville.

The air was clear and clean, strung with the scents of pine and grass and reawakening earth. To Grigsby it was nearly as sweet, and nearly as intoxicating, as bourbon whiskey. He hadn't been out of Denver for weeks, hadn't been into the mountains for months; and, despite the pain gnawing at his hip, he was glad he had decided to hire a horse for this part of the trip.

If only his hip wasn't bothering him.

But the horse and the saddle weren't responsible for all the aches and pains. A large part of them had been caused by his time last night with Mathilde de la Môle.

She had answered the door wearing another long silk robe, this one pink and belted at the waist. (Altogether, these people were carting around enough duds to dress up a good-sized town.)

She smiled when she saw him. "Marshal Greegsby. What a lovely surprise. Do come in." Peeking from below the robe, at its front, was a slim black blade of delicate lace gown.

"Howdy, ma'am," said Grigsby. "You sure I'm not intrudin'?"

"Not at all. Please come in."

Grigsby shuffled into the room. She shut the door, turned to him, and, still smiling, she cocked her head and held out her hand. "May I take the famous hat?"

Grigsby surrendered the Stetson. Tonight her hair was piled up, blond and shiny, on the top of her head. A few loose strands arched down along her elegant neck.

"Please," she said, and waved an arm toward the chair. "Sit."

He crossed the room and sat in the same chair he had used that afternoon, and immediately he discovered, once again, that his hands were big lumpy things at the ends of arms a couple of yards too long. Once again, he crossed the arms over his chest. His right hand, the one he'd used to punch out Greaves, was still throbbing.

"Would you care for a drink?" she asked him. "I have a Calvados which is rather nice, I think."

Grigsby didn't know what a Calvados was, but if it was alcoholic, he was ready for it. A full day of drinking, a nip here, a nip there, another nip here, and yet now that he was alone in the room with this woman he felt, all at once, stone cold sober. "Yes ma'am. Thank you."

She smiled again. "Good." She turned and went to the dresser, her robe whispering softly. Along the curve of her hip, the swell of her buttocks, the lamplight rippled like sunshine on creekwater. Grigsby could see no indentations in the smooth flesh, no sign of confining corset or girdle.

Underneath that thin silk robe, that wispy black gown, she was bareass naked.

It was at her ass that Grigsby realized he was staring, like a stooped old man sitting outside a saloon, gaping at the passing ankles. And, trapped in this patch of sobriety that had somehow sprouted in the middle of his familiar, friendly, whiskey fog, he suddenly *felt* like an old man. Old and spent and drained. Washed up, like Greaves had said.

He didn't belong here.

She laid the Stetson down on the dresser, opened the top drawer, took out a leather box that was maybe a foot high and a foot wide, and placed it beside the hat. She opened the box. Inside it was a flat green bottle and, set back in red velvet compartments on either side of it, four balloon-shaped glasses. She removed two of these, put them on the dresser, removed the bottle, uncorked it, and poured a pale brown liquid into each glass. She stood the bottle on the dresser, carried the glasses over to the chairs, and handed one to Grigsby, who took it between fingers that were swollen and stiff. She sat down. She smiled again and raised her glass. "Cheers," she said.

"Right," Grigsby said. He was trying to decide what to do with his left hand, which at the moment was lying on his thigh like a large dead squirrel.

Coming here had been a mistake. Like going to Hanrahan's had probably been a mistake. Like hitting Greaves had probably been a mistake.

He was making a lot of mistakes lately.

He took a sip of the drink. It went down almost like water, but when it hit his stomach it expanded with a comforting, fa-

252

miliar, potent glow. The taste, too, was familiar, but it was one that Grigsby had never before associated with liquor.

He smiled at her, surprised and pleased. "Apples," he said.

She smiled back. "Apple brandy, yes. Do you like it?"

"Yes ma'am. Real nice. Real smooth."

She bobbed her head once. "Good. Now, please, you must tell me to what I owe this pleasure."

Grigsby crossed his long legs and pain flamed down his thigh. "Well, ma'am. I just came by to find out if maybe you remembered anything. About the trip and all. What we talked about before."

She frowned sadly. "Ah, but no, alas. I have racked my brain all through the day, and I can remember nothing that would help. I am so terribly sorry."

"Well, ma'am. No call for you to be sorry. I'm obliged to you for tryin'."

She cocked her head. "Marshal Greegsby—" She smiled suddenly. "But I cannot call you this. Your given name is Bohb?"

"Bob. Yes ma'am. Short for Robert."

Another smile. "Ah. *Robair*. I once had a very good friend with this name. But you know, I think I prefer the other. *Bohb*. Yes. I like very much the sound of this. It suits you somehow, I think." She leaned forward and lightly touched his knee. "And you must call me Mathilde."

Grigsby knew that a week from now he would still be able to locate the exact spot on his knee where she had touched him.

Suddenly, from out in the hallway, Grigsby heard a loud urgent banging—*slam slam*—and then a muffled clatter as someone went clomping down the stairwell.

Ned Winters, the desk clerk, warning him that one of the others had returned to the hotel. Wilde or Vail or O'Conner. Or Henry. (And just where was Henry staying, anyway?)

Winters would get nervous if Grigsby didn't show up soon. Start seeing Grigsby cramped up in some closet or hunkered between the dust balls underneath some bed.

Good. Maybe if Winters was sweating some, he wouldn't fall asleep on the job.

The woman was smiling. "This is not the most quiet of ho-tels," she said. "This morning, do you know, I actually heard a gunshot."

"Yes ma'am," said Grigsby, who had fired that particular shot. "It can be a pretty rowdy place sometimes."

"No, no, no," she said, waving a slender finger, playacting at being cross. "No more of this *mayam*. You make me feel one hundred years old. You must say it. *Mathilde*."

"Mahteeld," Grigsby said. Damn. He was blushing like some dumb farmboy with straw growing in his ears.

Annoyed with himself, he gulped down some apple brandy. What the hell was he hanging around here for? Finish up the drink and go.

"Thank you," she said, cocking her head once more, serious again. "Now," she said, "Bohb. Have you learned anything thus far?"

"Well," Grigsby said, "looks like it's a pretty safe bet that whoever this fella is, he ain't your friend Mr. Wilde."

She cocked her head and smiled. "But this is wonderful, no? You are making progress. And I am so very glad to hear of it. I have a great fondness for Oscair. However did you learn this?"

Grigsby shrugged. "Pokin' around," he said. Poking around in closets, looking at shoes. The irresistible juggernaut of Sci-entific policework.

"Tell me something, Bohb. Are you a married man?"

Grigsby nodded. "Me and my wife are separated."

"She is where?"

"San Francisco."

She raised an eyebrow. "That is quite a separation."

Grigsby nodded again. "Yeah."

"You have children?"

"Two of 'em. Boy and a girl. They're with her."

She sighed and smiled sadly. "Love, eh? It seems such a simple thing, and yet for all of us it creates such complications."

"Yeah." Grigsby didn't want to talk about this. He uncrossed his legs, recrossed them, and again the flame flared down his thigh.

254

She leaned slightly forward. "What is it, Bohb? You were in pain this afternoon as well."

Grigsby shook his head. "Just a touch of rheumatism."

"Would you like a massage?"

She asked this with the same matter-of-fact politeness that she'd shown when she asked him whether he wanted a drink.

"You mean like a back rub?" Grigsby asked her, uncertain.

"Yes," she said, and smiled. "This."

Grigsby discovered, once again, that the skin of his face was hot and tight. Goddammit, she was only a woman. How could she keep making him feel like some bumpkin who'd just arrived in town inside a suit three sizes too small? "No, ma'am," he said. "No thank you. It's right kind of you, though."

"But no," she said. "I insist." She placed her drink on the table and stood. "I am very good with this. Come. You must remove your shirt."

Grigsby surprised himself—amazed himself—by grinning. Maybe he'd gone so far into embarrassment that he'd come out the other side of it. Maybe he'd just given up. And then, before he could stop them, the words came tumbling from his mouth: "You gonna take off yours, too?"

And instead of smacking him across the face, or leaping to her feet, or simply fainting dead away, the Countess Mathilde de la Môle suddenly smiled widely, her brown eyes flashing as she showed all her bright white teeth, and she said, "But of course."

➤   ➤

Sitting with his back braced against a ponderosa pine, his knees drawn up, Grigsby rolled himself a cigarette. His right hand still hurt, the fingers were still stiff and clumsy. Across the small brown sunswept pasture, just where the pine forest painted dark shadows at its edge, old man Jenner's small herd of goats nibbled at some stubbly weeds.

Pretty soon Jenner would have to fence them off. He'd need that barbed wire they were using down in Texas—nothing else would hold in goats—and he'd need a lot of it. Grigsby didn't envy him the job of stringing that prickly, twitchy stuff around his land.

The old man had been living alone up here for at least twenty years, just him and his goats, and for all that time he'd let them roam wild. But more settlers were moving in, trying to scrape a living off rocky scraps of property that had been ignored till now. And no farmer wanted a pack of goats grazing near his crops. They could strip a field cleaner than a flock of locusts.

The country was changing. It was crowding up. The West was disappearing. Cowboys and Indians and wide open prairies—all of that was dying out. But maybe it had begun to die the moment it was born. As soon as you got some people standing around and admiring the wide open spaces, the spaces weren't so wide open any more.

Maybe none of it had never really existed after all, not as a real place. Maybe, all the time, it had only been an idea, something that people moved toward but never actually arrived at, like the line of the horizon.

Grigsby lit the cigarette, inhaled the smoke, blew it out. Too nice a day to worry on it.

The goats, ten of them, maybe sixty feet away, hadn't moved when he swung down from his horse and ambled over to the shade of the ponderosa. But they'd been watching him ever since, each of them chewing with one eye cocked in Grigsby's direction. Now one of them—curious, maybe—began to wander toward him across the field.

The leader, Grigsby realized—he could hear the tinkle of its bell.

The goat came to within five feet and stood there staring at him with those weird yellow rectangular eyes that always seemed to Grigsby more knowing than any animal's eyes had a right to be.

"You know what, goat?" Grigsby said aloud. "You smell just like a goat."

The goat was a male and at his forehead were the two small bumps that would one day be horns. It took another few steps toward him and lowered his head.

"They itch, huh?" Grigsby said. He reached out and scratched the goat's forehead, rubbing his fingertips against the bristly skin stretched taut above the bone. Twisting its neck, the animal leaned its head against his fingers, as insistent as a cat, and Grigsby laughed.

The goat, in its need, reminded him of himself last night, with Mathilde de la Môle.

Damn. She was some kind of a woman.

She knew tricks that Grigsby had never heard of, had never even imagined. She was like eighteen different women all at once, and she made Grigsby feel like eighteen different kinds of men, all of them as horny as billy goats. She moaned and sighed and purred and chuckled deep inside her throat, and she whispered instructions and endearments and breathless little gasps of pleasure into his astounded, disbelieving ear. She offered her body and she took his, sometimes with abandon and sometimes with practiced, almost diabolical skill.

And then afterward, just like she promised, she had given him a back rub. And, just like she promised, she had been damned good at it.

While her strong shrewd hands kneaded the flesh and the muscle above his aching hip, Grigsby sighed happily. From time to time he remembered to close his mouth, so he wouldn't drool all over her sheets.

"It is good?" the Countess Mathilde de la Môle had asked him after a while. He could hear the smile in her voice.

"Good don't even come close," Grigsby said. He sighed again. "My God."

Her fingers were prodding at the pain, locating it, enclosing it somehow, capturing it and then pushing it deep down below awareness.

"But it don't hardly seem fair," Grigsby said. "Me just lyin' here like a lump on a log while you work at me."

"Quiet," she said. "You were not just lying there a while ago. As I recall, you were quite active."

Grigsby grinned against the pillow, ridiculously pleased with himself. Despite his eagerness (and he had been as eager as an sixteen-year-old buck), he had pleasured her three times before taking his final pleasure himself. And now, inside his head, a small excited thought capered like a circus dwarf: She's a goddamn *countess*, from goddamn *France*, and she's giving you a goddamn *back-rub!*

She kissed him gently on the spine, between his shoulders. "Better?"

"Better," he said. "I thank you."

She swung herself off his thighs and lay down beside him. With an effort—he was so limp that he felt he might melt into the mattress—Grigsby rolled over onto his side to look at her.

Her right elbow against the pillow, her head propped against her hand, she lay with her tousled blond hair loose along her smooth white shoulders. Her red lips, slightly more pouty now, were parted in a smile. Her skin was misted shiny with sweat, and she wore her naked body as proudly as most women wore a brand new dress.

He grinned. "I'll tell you one thing, Mathilde," he said. This time he didn't blush; nothing like a roll in the hay to smooth the edges off a fellow's embarrassment. "You surely do take the cake."

She laughed. "Take the cake? This is good?"

"Damn good."

Smiling, she inclined her head. "Then I thank you for the compliment."

"This is the first time," he said, "bein' with you, it's the first time all day I been able to forget about those killin's."

She smiled sadly. "And now," she put her finger to his chin, "you remember them again."

"Yeah," said Grigsby. "Well. They ain't gonna go away."

She pursed her lips. "It is a pity that you cannot learn something of the childhood of all the men traveling with Oscair."

"What good would that do?"

She moved her shoulder lightly in a shrug. "It all begins there, does it not? We spend the rest of our lives attempting to make right the wrongs which we suffer in childhood."

Grigsby grinned; he thought she was joking. "Get revenge, like?"

She said seriously, "Sometimes, I think, yes. A child who is beaten by his parents becomes, very often, a parent who beats his child. But I believe that we all suffer, that we all become wounded. Even with the best intentions in the world, our parents cannot always be there when we stumble, cannot always console us when we hurt. And so we grow up, all of us, somehow knowing at the core of our selves that we are completely alone."

"Yeah, well, sure," said Grigsby. "That's just the way of the world."

"But no," she said. "I speak now not of a conscious awareness, a philosophical position. I speak of a flaw, a wound that lies concealed in the structure of the soul. And I believe that throughout our lives we will be attracted to situations, and to people, that will sooner or later cause us pain. And the result will be that the wound, the fundamental pain of the soul, reemerges."

Grigsby frowned. "You're sayin' we pick people who're gonna *hurt* us?"

"Or who will cause us to hurt them, which will of course hurt us as well."

Grigsby thought then of Clara. Her face twisted in pain, her voice unraveling, ragged, as she shrieked at him: Bob, how could you *do* this?

He pushed away the image. "That don't make much sense," he said.

"You have read Stendahl?" she said.

He frowned. "That a book?"

She smiled. "An author. He talks about the phenomenon of crystallization. We meet someone—a man, let us say, meets a woman. He is attracted to her, and soon he discovers that all the qualities he most admires in a woman have begun to crystallize around this particular female. She is not only beautiful, but also intelligent, and kind, and loving. She is altogether perfect."

Thinking of Clara, Grigsby said, "Some women can come pretty close to bein' perfect."

"Perhaps," she said. "But the point I make here is that frequently our minds crystallize, they *construct*, this perfection. And I believe that the mind constructs the perfection around an individual whom the soul, the spirit selects. Someone who is in fact perfect for the spirit's purposes."

"Somebody who's gonna hurt us?"

"I believe that the spirit, the soul, wishes to heal itself of its wound. You cannot heal a wound unless you are aware that it exists. And so the spirit seeks out those people who will, sooner or later, cause us exactly the sort of pain which already we suffer, but at a level below consciousness."

Grigsby smiled. These folks from Europe surely did like their theories. "And you're sayin' everybody does this?"

She smiled at the gentle mockery in his voice, and she tapped him on the chin. "I believe so, yes."

"What about the folks who get married and live happily ever after?"

She smiled again. "Apart from fairy tales, do you know many of these?"

"Some," Grigsby said, but offhand he couldn't think of any. Him and Clara? Gerry and Mary Hanrahan? Dell and Barbara Jameson? He asked her, "And what about this sonovabitch who's killin' the women? How do you work him in?"

She shrugged. "This man, this killer, perhaps in a sense he is trying to heal *his* wound by the murder of these women. Something quite horrible must have happened to him when he was a child. If you could learn what it was, you might better understand him."

"I don't gotta understand him. All I gotta do is catch him."

"But perhaps you must understand him in order to catch him."

"Hope not," Grigsby said. "I don't reckon I'll ever understand him. Don't reckon I really want to." He frowned.

She smiled. "Perhaps we should try to make you forget this matter again."

Grigsby grinned. "What you got in mind?"
She told him.

Afterward, without intending to, Grigsby had slipped off to sleep. Only to come thrashing out of it, soaked with sweat and crying Clara's name as he scrambled from the horror of Molly Woods. The oil lamps were off; Mathilde must have blown them out. Pale moonlight streamed through the window. For a few minutes, before he could pull himself together, he trembled like a baby against her body, and in the darkness she held him.

At last, his breathing and his heartbeat back to normal, the image of Molly Woods finally fading, he eased himself away from her shoulder. Ashamed at the weakness he had revealed, he forced a hollow chuckle through a throat that was still thick and tight.

"Bad dream," he told her.

She said nothing, only stroked his cheek.

Grigsby rolled over and fished his watch from his vest pocket, struck a match. Three o'clock.

"I gotta go, Mathilde," he told her.

She nodded. "If you must."

Grigsby dressed himself, keeping his back to the Countess— acting the fool like that, hollering and shouting in his sleep, had made him feel lumpish and clumsy once more.

Buttoning up the sheepskin jacket, he turned to her and said, "Am I gonna be able to see you again?"

She smiled. "But of course. If you wish it."

"I do. And listen." He felt his face reddening once more. Too dark for her to see it—good thing. "Well," he said. "I'm real sorry about all the commotion. Wakin' you up and all."

She shook her head. "We all have our terrors, Bohb."

He looked down at her. He felt suddenly that he was leaving her with something left undone, something left unsaid; but he couldn't think what they might be. He nodded. "Thank you, Mathilde. I'll see you soon."

She smiled again. "Good night, Bohb."

Out in the hallway, Grigsby remembered that the the hotel's passkey still lay in his pocket. Quietly, holding his breath, he unlocked each door in turn and peered inside. Vail, O'Conner, Ruddick, and Wilde were all asleep, Wilde snoring away like a sawmill.

Downstairs, when Ned Winters saw Grigsby, he looked like someone who had just been told that he wouldn't be getting hanged today after all. Breathing an explosive sigh of relief, he took back the passkey. "Thank *God*, Marshal! Where *were* you?"

"Pokin' around."

"Holy Hannah! When you didn't come back down, I didn't know *what* to think."

Grigsby nodded. "Listen, Ned. There's a colored fella travelin' with Wilde. Servant name of Henry. He move into another room?"

Winters nodded. "He's in room 201 now. Wally said the manager, Mr. Vail, ordered him a new room."

"He up there now?"

Winters nodded. "Went out around eight, came back at ten-thirty."

"You sure? You didn't maybe have yourself a catnap or two?"

"No sir, Marshal. Not a one. I been awake all night. They were all up in their rooms by midnight." He leaned toward Grigsby. "But, come on now, Marshal, you sure you can't tell me what's goin' on?"

"Positive. See you."

From the hotel, Grigsby had ridden the mare back to his house, where he'd cleaned himself up, dressed in fresh clothes, and thrown some spare shirts and an extra union suit into his saddle-bag. After leaving the horse at the livery stable, he had set off for the railroad station. He had arrived in Colorado Springs at six in the morning.

And now, as the horse jounced and rocked beneath his aching hip, Grigsby could see, over the tree line, against the bright blue of sky, the smudge of smoke that hung above the chimneys of Manitou Springs.

He realized, abruptly, that he hadn't had a drink since the apple brandy in Mathilde's room. Been so tickled with himself, probably, that he hadn't even thought about it.

He tried to remember the last time he'd gone three or four hours without taking a single drink. Without *thinking* about a drink. Not since before Clara left.

Damn, he thought. That was cause for a little celebration.

CHAPTER TWENTY-TWO

"**D**AMN FINE LECTURE, Mr. Wilde," said the mayor of Manitou Springs.

"Don't cuss, Cleveland," said his wife.

From over their heads, beyond the now empty chairs aligned in precise rows beneath the glittering chandeliers, Oscar could make out Elizabeth McCourt Doe chatting with Mathilde de la Môle and a gaggle of Manitou Springs luminaries beside the closed French windows that led onto the ballroom's veranda.

"Good turnout, too," said the Mayor. "Almost as good as that fella Dickens got."

This snared Oscar's attention.

"Dickens spoke here, did he?" he asked, and sipped at his champagne. Appalling stuff, flat and sulfurous.

"Sure did," said the mayor. "He read from that book of his, about the death of Little Nell. Damn fine writing. Nearly brought a tear to my eye, I don't mind telling you. Isn't that right, Mother?"

"Don't cuss, Cleveland," said his wife.

"You know Dickens, Mr. Wilde?" asked the Mayor.

The mayor of Manitou Springs—Mr. Mudds, or Muggs, or

something equally glum—was a jolly personage in a poorly tailored but extravagantly tailed dress coat who seemed utterly unaware that in the center of his round red face, roughly where his nose should have been installed, there bloomed an entity the size of a pomegranate, veined and gullied and carbuncled. He was short and portly, with skin as taut as a sausage casing. Mrs. Mudds (or Muggs) was a small desiccated woman, prodigiously creased, like a gnome left too long in a pickling vat. She wore a low-cut dress which flaunted an expanse of what probably she believed to be décolletage, but which to Oscar more nearly resembled erosion.

A scrum of Manitou Springians stood huddled about, all of them leaning slightly forward, as though Oscar were standing at the bottom of a shallow crater in the parquet floor. All of them wore evening dress, and all of them looked at least as well fed as Mr. Muggs. No watercress and celery for this lot, except perhaps by the troughful.

They were all wealthy enough to have paid twenty dollars apiece for the lecture and for this "intimate" champagne party. With the others milling about the ballroom, they were the elite of Manitou Springs—according to Vail, everybody who was anybody in the town. ("In other words," Oscar had said, "nobody.") And at the moment none of them, alas, was Elizabeth McCourt Doe.

"Not personally," Oscar said to the mayor. "Although of course I know his works. I find them admirable. But I do sometimes wonder at the unusual number of pathetic little waifs he dispatches. In a novel by Mr. Dickens, one has only to come upon a pathetic little waif to know that the poor moppet is doomed. Sooner or later, usually after wasting away for several months, and for several chapters, he will breathe his last wretched little breath." Oscar frowned thoughtfully. "Do you suppose it possible that Mr. Dickens secretly dislikes children?"

The mayor turned to his wife, she evidently being the authority on literary matters.

"But I thought I read," she said, frowning, "that he's got children of his own? A lot of them, I believe. A big family."

"Ah," said Oscar. "Perhaps that explains it."

As Mrs. Muggs (or Mudds) assimilated this (or failed to), and as a few uneasy chuckles, all of these male, sputtered through the crowd, a female voice to Oscar's right asked him, "Do you mean to tell us, Mr. Wilde, that *you* dislike children?"

Oscar turned. Beneath a sculpted mass of blue-white hair which possessed the dull seamless glow of a conquistador's helmet, the woman's jowly face was eloquently puckered in distaste. She was all combative shoulders and cannon-barrel breasts, and for a moment he felt like the owner of a skiff who looks up and discovers that a frigate is bearing down upon him on a collision course.

"On the contrary, madam. I think they are one of life's great treasures. A joy to us when we are in our prime, and a solace in our decline. As soon as I can afford to do so, I intend to hire several of them."

More laughter this time, some of it shocked. The frigate's face remained shuttered.

Oscar glanced over at Elizabeth McCourt Doe.

Still gaily smiling with her entourage.

The least she could do was look over in this direction.

He swallowed some champagne. What was it that Holliday, the dentist-gunman, had called that bourbon? Donkey piss.

"Mr. Wilde?"

Oscar turned. A small silver-haired man, warm brown puppy eyes peering out from a tracery of amused crinkles. "Jim Cathcart, editor of the *Sentinel*. I'll bet you've heard this before"—he smiled an engaging deprecatory smile—"but I guess you can understand that I've got to ask you anyway. What are your feelings so far about America?"

Oscar beamed down at this pleasant little man. "I can scarce describe my feelings. And of course I can scarce describe America. How *could* one describe a thing which by its very nature is indescribable? The vastness, the richness, the splendor—they boggle the mind and beggar even my own powers of description."

Around him, heads nodded in complacent agreement. His

266

puppy eyes shining, Cathcart asked him, "Would you like to comment on which parts of it you've liked best?"

"I can answer you without hesitation," said Oscar. "More than any other I've enjoyed this Colorado country of yours, filled as it is with splendid vistas and noble prospects." Not likely that anyone in this flock knew Johnson's comment to Boswell.

Clearly not. The remark had set more heads abob, and had apparently even taken some of the wind from the frigate's sails. Her jowls had unclenched appreciably.

"Does that mean," casually asked Cathcart, his brown eyes still warm and shining, "that you don't care for the cities of America?"

Oscar smiled again. So: not a puppy after all: a fox. Ah well, Reynard, no nasty quotations from me tonight. "Not at all," he said. "I found Denver, for example, altogether fascinating."

Heads nodded, indicating that this was not an unpopular opinion. Everybody seemed (rather annoyingly) content to let Cathcart continue playing the part of inquisitor.

"Is it true, Mr. Wilde," Cathcart asked him, "that you're traveling with a servant and two steamer trunks packed with clothes?"

Probably none of the Manitou Springs gentry gathered round would be in any way ruffled by the idea of Oscar's traveling with a servant. Those who didn't employ servants themselves doubtless envied those who did. Some of them, possibly most of them, doubtless looked back with fondness to the good old days of slavery. Cathcart was plainly pursuing some plum he could present the rest of his readership, the simple untutored yeoman, the honest untutored laborer.

"No. I have only one steamer trunk," Oscar said. And then, on an impulse which he knew he might later regret, but could not now resist, he added, "The other four were unfortunately lost at sea. As for my valet, he's a charming fellow. His name is Henry—he's floating about here somewhere—and we often sit together by the fireside and discuss the merits of republican democracy."

267

"Excuse me," said a familiar voice.

Cathcart, who had opened his mouth again, suddenly clamped it shut as Elizabeth McCourt Doe appeared at Oscar's elbow.

She was, of course, stunning. Tonight she was swathed in clouds of bright beaming scarlet, like a rising sun. The color should have clashed with her titian hair; but nothing in the world could have clashed with her titian hair. And when she looked smiling up at Oscar with those luminous violet eyes, and laid her slender hand upon his arm, he felt a curious weakness at the knees, as though his joints were liquefying.

"Excuse me," she said to the group. "But may I steal Mr. Wilde away from you for just a moment?"

Immediately, and without physically moving, the group had divided itself into two separate camps. Among the men, Cathcart smiled a courtly smile and graciously lowered his silver head in a small bow. Mayor Muggs beamed in delight around his pomegranate and announced, "Ah, Mrs. Doe!" Among the women, Mrs. Muggs lifted her meager chin and, disdain making her bones shrink away from her skin, miraculously acquired additional creases. The frigate, sails snapping, ponderously wheeled her heavy guns about.

"I'll bring him right back," said Elizabeth McCourt Doe, and, with a gentle pressure on Oscar's arm, she led him off.

Her silks rustling beside him, her scent fluttering beneath his nostrils, they passed several chattering coveys of *lumpen* aristocracy. (Silver barons, cattle barons, timber barons and their respective baronesses, some of the men in costumes so stiffly starched that their occupants appeared to have petrified.) By the time the two of them had located an open space, a pocket of privacy, Oscar had remembered that he was an aggrieved party. His knees were still weak, but he had determined to himself that the weakness was galling rather than curious.

He must maintain his aloofness; he must firm his resolve.

She stopped and he turned to face her.

She smiled and tapped him with the hand she held upon his arm. "Oscar, you've been ignoring me all evening."

Coolly he said, "I ignore you? Madam, I assure you I have

268

not." How dreadful. He sounded like a butler. But his pride could see no way to escape the role which circumstance, and Elizabeth McCourt Doe, had thrust upon him. "Permit me to point out that it is you who have been ignoring me. For two days, I might add." Dreadful. Worse than a butler. An insufferable prig.

She leaned toward him, leaning on his arm, and she smiled. "This is fun, isn't it? Can we do this in bed sometime?"

In a flash, firmness drained away from his resolve and began to trickle into another (potentially more visible and embarrassing) part of his person. "Ah, Elizabeth," he said, and in his voice he heard passion and yearning, which he was pleased to convey; but also a kind of tremulous whimper, which he was not.

"Oscar," she said, and canted her head to the side, her brilliant curls trembling along her scarlet shoulders. "I couldn't get away. Horace had all sorts of horrible business meetings and he needed a hostess."

"A hostess?" So perhaps they had not been, she and Tabor, skidding naked one atop the other for the past thirty-eight hours. As Oscar, for the past nine, had been busily imagining them; or busily attempting to avoid imagining them.

"You can't believe how boring it's been," she said. She smiled and put her hands behind her hips, which caused her pert perfect breasts to lift up and strain against her bodice, as though reaching out for him like the hands of a child. "Have you missed me?"

"Of *course* I've missed you. Elizabeth—"

"I talked to your friend, the Countess." Smiling her Gioconda smile, she narrowed her eyes slightly. "Should I be jealous of her?"

"Jealous?" He produced a laugh which he intended to sound light and airy; it came out giddy and shrill, nearly hysterical with relief. *She* jealous?

"She's a very beautiful woman, Oscar." Still smiling. "And French. And ever so much more cultured than I am."

He laughed again. More successfully this time: blithe, debonaire, almost avuncular. "My dear Elizabeth. No. I promise you. There is no woman, anywhere in the world, of whom you need

269

be jealous. I only wish that I could prove that to you, just now, just at this very moment."

Her smiled widened. "How?" she said. "How would you prove it?"

Oscar glanced to his right. The nearest bevy of barons and baronesses stood twenty feet off, all their pink faces staring frankly at Oscar and Elizabeth McCourt Doe. Instantly, in unison, like a troupe of minstrels, they turned away. Oscar glanced to his left. Saw Ruddick leaning earnestly forward as he talked to a young waiter with a silver tray tucked beneath his arm.

Oh dear. Discretion, Wilbur.

He turned back to Elizabeth McCourt Doe and lowered his voice. "I prefer showing you to telling you. May I see you tonight?"

She sighed sadly. "I'm sorry, Oscar. I can't tonight. Horace has another boring meeting."

Oscar felt his facial muscles wilt.

"Poor Oscar," she said. "And poor me." She smiled. "But tomorrow morning let me show you the sights of Manitou Springs. I'll rent a carriage."

"You're the only sight I care to see."

"I know a place, up in the mountains. It's beautiful. It's shaded and quiet and there's a little brook nearby. We can lie down on the pine needles."

Oscar was willing to lie down in the brook. "But the train to Leadville leaves at one o'clock."

"I'll come pick you up at nine, at the hotel."

"Nine o'clock, then."

He smiled, delighted.

She smiled, reached out, put her hand lightly on his arm. "I've missed you, Oscar. I'll see you tomorrow."

"I look forward to it. There's something I wish to ask you. Something rather important."

She smiled again, gently pressed his arm with her fingers, then turned and rustled off.

Tomorrow!

The ballroom, despite its size, was suddenly too small to contain both Oscar and his elation. He glanced around once more. Ruddick had gone missing, but after an anxious moment (SCANDAL IN MANITOU SPRINGS!) Oscar spied the young waiter serving champagne to Colonel von Hesse. Four or five yards to their left, O'Conner stood talking to Mathilde de la Môle, the Countess wearing a lovely blue gown of taffeta and lace and an expression of heroic politeness. O'Conner had dressed for this occasion, as he did for all others, in his brown scarecrow suit.

At the moment, no one seemed to be paying Oscar any attention. He crossed the room, nodding politely to the gaggles and bevies and coveys. He opened the French door and stepped out onto the veranda.

But someone *had* been paying attention. As Oscar spoke with Elizabeth McCourt Doe, an intense pair of eyes had watched the two of them.

I know you, slut. I know you, harlot. For all your expensive clothes and your expensive perfumes and your red red hair, you're no better than any streetcorner whore riddled with pox. No better than any alleyway trollop sour with stale liquor and the stink of a thousand squalid couplings.

I know you, Elizabeth McCourt Doe. I know you. I've learned about you. Left your husband. Ruined one marriage already, and now you're ruining another. And still you you prance and whinny with Oscar Wilde.

Shameless bitch.

You sicken me.

Whore.

Oh yes, walk away. Walk away while you can, you vile stinking hole. Walk away now. One day you won't be able to walk away.

One day, perhaps, I'll show you the flame that roars at the center of the universe.

The moon, nearly full, splashed white light across the flagstones. Overhead, the bare branches of oak trees clucked and sighed.

Oscar looked up through them to the sky. The Milky Way swept across the blackness, an extravagant scattering of diamonds hurled against velvet. And over there was Orion. And there was Ursa Major. Or was it Ursa Minor? One of them, he remembered, had some sort of chummy relationship with the North Star.

No matter. What did stars signify?

Tomorrow! Tomorrow amid the whispering pines he would ask her to come away with him! They would sit on the banks of the babbling brook and dip their feet into its laughing water. Tomorrow atop the pine needles they would pledge their troth.

But didn't pine needles cling to one's clothing? Didn't they irritate one's skin? Well, presumably a woman like her, as practical as she was beautiful, would ferry along a blanket.

Yes, tomorrow he would tell her his plans, show her how the two of them, together, would become the toast of London.

Tomorrow—

He heard a faint rasp to his left, a foot scraping against stone, and he turned.

The figure by the balustrade, looming out of the shadows of the nearby oak, was monstrous. Something inhuman, something gross and foul that came lumbering toward him like a beast, *like a bear . . .*

Oscar's heart juddered.

And then a voice came from the shadows, an uncanny whisper: "Poet."

And as the man stepped out onto the moonlit veranda, hands in his frock coat pockets, Oscar heard himself exhale a hiss. "Dr."—his voice was strangled; he cleared his throat—"Dr. Holliday. I didn't see you there."

So. Only a trick of light and shade. Ursa Accidentalis.

Acci-dentalistic.

But the wordplay was desperate, defensive: Oscar's heart still clapped against his chest.

Why all these bloody *bears*?

"I came for the lecture," Holliday whispered.

"Ah." Oscar cleared his throat again, something he seemed

272

to do quite a lot whenever Holliday was in the vicinity. By now the man must be convinced that Oscar was consumptive. "This wasn't the one you heard, then, while you were in San Francisco."

Holliday nodded. "One of them."

Oscar raised his eyebrows. "You've heard it before?"

Holliday nodded. He wore tonight, below his beautifully cut black frock coat, a three-piece suit, this just as black and just as beautifully cut. Oscar wondered who his tailor was. Patently, not the same man who dressed the majority of Coloradans. This one obviously had taste. And eyes and fingers.

He smiled. "Well, it's very flattering that you'd come to listen to it again." Dentist or gunman, Holliday was clearly a man of discernment.

Holliday smiled his ghost of a smile. "When I find something I like," he whispered, "I stick with it."

"Do you?" Oscar smiled. "Personally, when I find something I like, I immediately attempt to find something else. One should avoid habits of any sort, I think, and especially the good ones. But if one *must* have habits, then attending my lectures is, I suspect, a habit of the forgivable kind. I thank you. And, by the way, I thank you again for your intervention back in Denver. It's difficult to believe, I know, but I have a feeling that the large furry gentleman was beginning to take a dislike to me."

Holliday nodded his ghost of a nod. "Seen him again?"

Oscar remembered the shambling figure he had seen, or fancied he had seen, at the Denver train station. "No." And realized: *bear*. And realized that since he had left Denver, down some dark corridor at the back of his mind, the figure had continued all along to shamble.

This was why he had lately been suffering an invasion of bruins.

"Keep your eyes opened," Holliday whispered.

"I shall, yes. But I do thank you."

Holliday nodded faintly once again. In the moonlight his black clothing, his black hair and black mustache, those jet-black empty eyes—they all conspired to make him seem somehow a creature of the night. An almost elemental being who in some unaccountable way shared the night's substance, its darkness, its mystery, its promises and its threats.

How, exactly, did one converse with such an individual? What, exactly, did one say?

But it was Holliday who renewed the conversation. "Saw you talking to Mrs. Doe," he whispered. "A handsome woman."

"Isn't she? Do you know her?"

Faintly, Holliday shook his head.

"An extraordinary woman, I think. Not only handsome, as you say, but remarkably perceptive as well."

Faintly, Holliday nodded.

"Totally unlike any of the women one meets in London. I wonder what they'd make of her there. I mean, if she were ever to travel to England. Which is thoroughly unlikely, of course— why would she? But I should think that if it ever did transpire, she'd go over rather well in London."

Holliday nodded.

"She's engaged, I gather, to that fellow Tabor. Do you know him?"

Holliday shook his head.

"Splendid chap, I suppose. But somehow, you know, he doesn't seem quite right for her. I can't imagine why I say that. I barely know him—or her, either, of course. It's merely a feeling I have. Call it an intuition."

Holliday nodded.

All at once Oscar realized that he was seeking Holliday's approval, trying to pry from him an opinion that would validate his own. It was Holliday's stolid indifference, his ultimate lack of opinions of any sort, which had suddenly made Oscar uncomfortably aware of what he had been attempting.

Yesterday Holliday had rescued him, and today Oscar was turning him into a father confessor.

Well, *rescue* was perhaps too strong a word; certainly, Oscar would have done a creditable job of Biff-bashing, had that proven necessary. And *father confessor*, too, was a bit off the mark. Oscar was hardly confessing, or even admitting, to anything. He

274

was merely attempting to elicit Holliday's judgment of Tabor and Elizabeth McCourt Doe.

But why on earth would he *want* to elicit the judgment of this . . . *gunman*? A gunman of discernment, perhaps, when it came to clothes, and to lectures, but still a gunman.

"Ah," he said. He cleared his throat once more. (Soon the good doctor would be prescribing lozenges and syrups.) "Well," he said. "It's been, as always, a great pleasure chatting with you. I hope—"

The French doors opened behind Oscar. He turned.

Young Ruddick stepped onto the Veranda. He glanced at Holliday, turned to Oscar, and said, "Oscar, that awful Marshal *Grigsby* person is here. He *has* to talk to you, he says." He glanced back at Holliday and frowned slightly.

Oscar said to Holliday, "Well, I must run. I hope that one day we'll have another opportunity to chat."

Holliday nodded. "Be seeing you."

Inside, Ruddick closed the door. As they walked across the floor, he said, "Oscar, who *was* that man?"

"Dr. Holliday," Oscar told him. "He's—"

Ruddick abruptly stopped walking, causing Oscar to do the same. Irritating. "*Doc* Holliday?" Ruddick said. "The *gun-fighter*?"

"Yes. Fascinating chap. Quite a raconteur. Where's Grigsby?"

"But he was in El *Paso*," Ruddick said.

"Hmm?" Oscar looked around, couldn't spot the marshal anywhere among the Manitouians.

"And in Leavenworth, too," Ruddick said. "I *saw* him there. I thought he was a *reporter* or something, like O'Conner."

Oscar turned to him. "What are you saying?"

"Doc *Holliday*. I saw him in El Paso, and then a few days later in Leavenworth. He was in the audience both times."

And Holliday had been, by his own admission, in San Francisco.

"Are you certain?" Oscar asked him.

"Of *course* I am."

275

Oscar looked back at the French door. He could see nothing through the glass. He could only make out, framed like a photograph along its surface, brightly lit beneath a spectral chandelier, looking sleek and dashing and more than a little alarmed, his own reflection.

CHAPTER TWENTY-THREE

"HOWDY, MATHILDE," GRIBSBY SAID to the ringlets of gleaming blond hair, the opposed white arcs of naked shoulder blade fanned above the band of bright blue satin.

She turned, a glass of champagne held between both hands, and she smiled broadly up at him. "Bohb!" She reached out and touched his arm. "How are you?"

He grinned, deeply pleased by how deeply pleased she seemed to be. "Just fine. Yourself?"

"Very well, thank you. When did you arrive?"

"While ago. I was over at the hotel, thought I'd step out and take a gander at this blowout here."

After checking into the Woods and learning at the front desk that he had received no telegrams, Grigsby had drunk a quick bourbon in the bar and then limped painfully upstairs to his room. He had lain down—for only a moment or two, he had told himself, only time enough to rest up his hip a bit. Almost immediately he fell asleep. He had slept away the entire afternoon, the first time in years he had been able to sleep in the daytime.

She was good for him, this French countess.

In more ways than one—when he awoke, the pain in his hip

277

had contracted to a memory of itself, a dim trivial blur, meek and powerless. And, even more surprising, he hadn't felt the need for a drink to get his head cleared and his stomach settled. (He had put one away anyhow, of course, down in the bar; but that had been just a bracer, what he called a heart-starter.)

At the front desk, the clerk had handed him a packet of telegrams.

One of these in particular, Grigsby thought, just might hold the answer to all the questions he'd been asking lately.

At the moment, his pain in retreat, his hopes advancing, he felt strong and fit and convinced that he could go without drinking for the rest of his life. If he wanted to.

And maybe he would. Maybe he'd do exactly that. Clean himself out, stay off the booze. Maybe even stop smoking. Why the hell not?

Mathilde was laughing. "Gander. Blowout. I once believed that I knew the English language."

"Seems to me you know it just fine."

With her glass, she indicated the rest of the room. "Are you familiar with all these people?"

He nodded. "Some of 'em."

He and she were standing near the entrance to the ballroom, beside a long trestle table supporting platters of food and iced silver buckets of champagne. Grigsby glanced around, at the men plump and stiff in their penguin suits, the women plump and stiff in their billowing gowns.

They might look dumb—they did look dumb—but these were the movers and shakers of central Colorado, the mine owners, the cattlemen, the railroad men, the bankers. These were the solid citizens who had brought industry and civilization to the frontier. Naturally, along the way, they had raped the land, killed off the Indians and the buffalo, fouled the rivers with poisons and sewage; but they reckoned that this was a fair price to pay for progress. And, since they were the ones setting the price, the deal had gone through.

"Would you like some *champagne*?" Mathilde asked him.

She smiled. "I warn you, it is like no *champagne* I have ever drunk before."

Grigsby smiled. "Don't mind if I do." A little champagne never hurt anybody. Stuff was like soda pop, not like real liquor at all.

"Allow me," she said, and smiled.

As she moved around the table, Grigsby looked once more toward the crowd. He didn't like these people. Never had. They had grown rich, most of them, through swindle and fraud and outright theft; and yet they were the first to bitch and bellyache about law and order. *Their* law, *their* order. Once they had their pile together, they didn't want anyone else messing with it.

Grigsby felt the bitterness within himself, recognized it, and smiled ruefully.

Yep. No question. He was getting too old for this shit. Time to find himself a new line of work. Maybe start giving lectures. Famous Outlaws I Have Known.

"*Monsieur*," said Mathilde, smiling as she handed him a glass of champagne.

"Much obliged." He raised his glass.

She smiled and raised her own.

Grigsby sipped at the champagne. He frowned. Watery and kind of rotten-eggy. Shame they didn't have any good bourbon whiskey on hand.

He spotted Wilde and Ruddick winding toward him through the thickets of crowd, Wilde nodding grandly right and left, like the king of Siam waltzing along a street packed with adoring riffraff. Well, if he could get these yahoos to fork out twenty bucks to hear a lecture and drink sheepdip, more power to him.

Grigsby turned to Mathilde. "Can I come by and see you tonight?"

She smiled. "I shall be in my room by midnight. Room 204 at the Woods Hotel."

Grigsby already knew her room number; he had asked at the front desk. "I'll be there."

He turned to face Wilde.

"Marshal Grigsby," Wilde said. "Your arrival is fortuitous. Young Ruddick here has just told me something that may possibly be important."

Grigsby nodded to the lulu-belle. "Wilbur."

Ruddick smiled a bitter-persimmon smile.

Jesus, Dell, why did it have to be *this* one?

"You're familiar with Doctor John Holliday?" Wilde asked him. "The gunman?"

Grigsby nodded.

"Well, young Ruddick—" Wilde stopped, glanced around, leaned toward Grigsby and lowered his voice. "Perhaps we should discuss this in private."

"Fine by me." He tossed back the rest of his champagne, then turned to Mathilde and nodded. "Ma'am." Turned to the lulu-belle. "Stick around, Wilbur. Might wanta talk to you later."

The gravel drive outside the Hardee mansion was packed with carriages, their liveried horses sighing bored white puffs of vapor that feathered away in the moonlight. As Grigsby followed Wilde across the lawn, he wondered where all the drivers were hiding. Probably in the kitchen, along with the mansion's servants. And probably drinking, all of them, better stuff than watery sheepdip champagne.

Wilde stopped beside an oak tree. "First," he said, "I should tell you that I've met Doctor Holliday on several occasions, and found him an absolutely charming man."

Grigsby nodded. *Charming* wasn't a word he'd use himself, and especially not for Doc Holliday, but never mind. "What's Doc got to do with anything?"

"If the situation weren't such a serious one," Wilde said, "I shouldn't be bringing this to your attention."

Grigsby nodded.

"I mean to say, I quite like the man."

"Uh-huh," Grigsby said. "This story gonna start sometime soon?"

280

Wilde sighed sadly. He nodded. "Yes. Quite right." He inhaled deeply, exhaled a bit, like someone about to squeeze a rifle trigger, and he said, "Dr. Holliday told me, when I first met him, that he had attended one of my lectures in San Francisco. This evening, when young Ruddick saw him, he recognized him. According to Ruddick, the man was present both at the lecture in El Paso and the lecture in Leavenworth. He was also, as you may know, in Denver at the time of this most recent killing."

Grigsby frowned. Doc?

Suddenly he remembered that Earl, the sheriff down in El Paso, had mentioned Doc. In the same letter he had mentioned the murder of Susie Morris, the hooker. In the same letter he had mentioned Wilde's visit. Grigsby hadn't paid much attention at the time, because Doc tended to wander. One week he might be in Tuscon, the next in Dodge City.

But Doc killing hookers?

He shook his head. "Nope," he said to Wilde. "Don't see it."

"Well, as I say, I like the man. But he was *there*. In San Francisco, El Paso, and Leavenworth. And in Denver. I spoke to him myself on the very night that poor woman was killed."

Grigsby shook his head again. "Don't see it."

"Well, no matter what either of *us* sees, or doesn't see, the fact remains that Ruddick is convinced that *he* saw the man. In both cities. In every city where a woman was killed, Dr. Holliday was present. Surely that makes him at least as suspect as anyone traveling with me."

Wilde was right. If Doc had been in all those cities when the hookers got cut, Grigsby owed it to himself to talk to the man.

He said, "Ruddick saw him tonight?"

Wilde nodded. "I was speaking with him on the patio. Not ten minutes ago."

"He still there?"

"I don't know."

Grigsby nodded. "I'll find him. Is O'Conner inside?"

"O'Conner? Yes. I saw him a few minutes ago. Why?"

Grigsby considered telling him. Decided not to. "Just got a few questions for him, is all."

281

"Ruddick said that you wanted to speak with me."

Grigsby had planned to let Wilde know that he was no longer a suspect—he felt he owed him that, for coming on so strong yesterday, for shoving his Colt up the Englishman's nose. But now Grigsby was pissed off. By handing him this business about Doc, Wilde had thrown him off his stride. Just when he thought he might be getting to the bottom of things, Wilde (and his lulu-belle buddy, Ruddick) had tossed in some more things.

"It'll keep," he said.

O'Conner wasn't in the ballroom and Doc wasn't on the patio. Grigsby left the mansion and went looking for them both. Wouldn't be too hard to find either one of them in a town the size of the Springs.

Doc he found within half an hour at the Whirligig Casino, playing stud poker at a corner table. He was sitting as he always did—with his back to the wall, so he could cover the room, and with an empty chair to his right, so no one could crowd his gun hand.

The game was five-card, and as Grigsby approached the table, Doc was getting his fourth ticket. The dealer and one other player, a cowboy, had folded their hands. Doc was playing head to head against a sawed-off little dude—plaid suit, shiny slicked-back black hair, probably a traveling salesman. The salesman held his cards up against his vest with the fingers of both hands, and he was showing a pair of nines and the queen of hearts. Doc's cards were lying on the table, and he was showing a pair of eights and the ace of clubs.

Doc looked up at Grigsby. "Bob," he whispered.

Grigsby nodded. "A word, Doc."

"Right with you," said Doc.

"Pair of nines has the bet," said the dealer.

The drummer looked down at his hole card, glanced at Doc's cards, and he grinned. He pushed a blue chip forward, into the pot. "Pair of nines bets ten simoleons," he said.

A loser, Grigsby thought. Even if he did have the other queen tucked away in the hole.

Without looking at his hole card, Doc picked up two blue chips and tossed them in. "Up ten," he whispered. He had used his left hand to throw the chips; his right hadn't moved from the arm of his chair.

The drummer glanced at his hole card, grinned again. He pushed two chips into the pot. "I'll just see that," he said. He pushed two more chips forward. "And I guess I'm gonna have to raise another twenty."

Doc picked up four chips and tossed them in. "Up twenty."

The little drummer grinned. "Question is, my friend, do you got the other ace under there or not?"

"Question is," whispered Doc, "are you going to see the twenty?" No irritation, no anger, nothing. Just a group of words strung out in a flat, indifferent line.

The salesman chuckled. He pushed in two chips and said, "I see your twenty."

Grigsby knew then that the man didn't have the queen. And he reckoned that if he knew that, Doc had to know it, too.

The dealer dealt the cards. An ace of hearts for Doc, a nine of hearts for the drummer.

"Three nines and two pair," said the dealer. "Three nines bets."

The salesman chuckled. He pushed some chips forward. "Those three lovely nines bet thirty."

Doc picked up a stack of chips, moved them forward. "Up a hundred."

The salesman chuckled. But his face was shiny now with sweat. Grigsby counted the chips in front of him, saw that a hundred dollars would just about wipe him out. The salesman chuckled again. "It occurs to me that you're bluffing, my friend."

Doc nodded. "I do that from time to time."

Quickly, abruptly, the drummer pushed in the chips. "I see you," he snapped. "Whatta you got?"

Using his left hand, Doc turned over his hole card. The ace of spades.

"*Damn!*" said the drummer, and he hurled his cards to the table.

Doc stood up. To the dealer he whispered, "Cash me in, Vance. Be back in a minute."

He turned to Grigsby. "Drink, Bob?"

"Sure."

"The bar?"

"A bottle and a table."

Doc nodded. Together they walked to the bar, where Doc picked up a bottle and two glasses from the barkeep, and then over to an empty table at the far side of the room. Doc took the wall seat, Grigsby sat to his left.

Doc filled their glasses, lifted his. "To dying in bed," he said.

Grigsby raised his glass and smiled. "But not tonight, Doc, if it's all the same to you."

They drank, emptying their glasses. It was good whiskey. Warm and smooth and tasting like a trip back home. Better stuff, for damn sure, than that champagne at the mansion.

Doc filled their glasses again.

"You cleaned him out pretty good there," Grigsby said.

Doc shrugged, just a small movement at his shoulders. "If you're playing poker," he whispered, "and you haven't figured out who the chump is, you'd better start figuring it's you." It was a long speech for Doc. "What's up, Bob?"

Doc's eyes, Grigsby thought, were like glass. Shiny black glass, so dark you couldn't see into them. They didn't tell you a damn thing more than Doc wanted you to know, and that was nothing.

He said, "The poet fella, Oscar Wilde. You know him?"

Doc nodded.

"Some hookers been getting killed. Killed and cut up. Whoever's doin' it, he's doin' it in the same cities where Wilde is giving his talks. Same time, too. One in San Francisco, one in El Paso, one in Leavenworth, and one last night back in Denver. Molly Woods. You know her?"

Doc shook his head. He sipped at his drink.

"I heard tell, Doc, that you were in all those cities. The same time Wilde was." Grigsby sipped at his drink.

Doc moved his mouth, quickly, just a little bit, a twitch that could've been a smile. "Heard tell from where, Bob?"

Grigsby shook his head. "Don't matter. Were you there?"

Doc sipped at his drink. "You asking me if I'm killing hookers?"

"Not yet."

Doc shrugged. "I was there. All those places."

Grigsby nodded. "Kind of a coincidence."

Doc sipped at his drink. "Killing hookers." His head made a small negative shake and he smiled his twitch of a smile. "Not my style."

"I wouldn'ta thought so, Doc." Grigsby sipped at the bourbon. "So how come the coincidence?"

For a moment Doc was silent, staring at Grigsby with those glassy black unreadable eyes. Then he whispered, "How long have we known each other, Bob?"

"Five years. Six."

It was true that for six years, off and on, Doc had drifted in and out of the territory, and Grigsby had known him well enough to say hello and shoot the breeze. He had even played cards with him once. (Once had been enough.) But truly know him? Did anyone truly know Doc Holliday?

Doc said, "I ever give you any trouble?"

Grigsby smiled. "Not yet."

Doc nodded. "Seems to me, Bob, that a man who doesn't cause trouble has a right to go just about anywhere he wants to, without having to answer for it."

Grigsby nodded. "Seems to me, Doc, that when people start gettin' themselves killed off, a marshal's got a right to ask some questions."

Another twitch. "Conflicting philosophies, sounds like."

Grigsby nodded. "Maybe."

Doc sipped at his drink. "How far do you want to go with this, Bob?"

"Far as I got to."

Again, Doc was silent for a moment. Then he said, "It's the wives want to hear the lectures."

Grigsby frowned. "So?"

"The husbands get dragged along. Afterwards, they're looking for a game."

Grigsby smiled. "If they can afford a lecture, they can afford a game of stud."

Doc smiled his twitchy smile. "Some of them seem to think so."

Grigsby nodded. "You been followin' the tour."

Doc nodded.

"Business is good?" Grigsby asked him.

Doc smiled again. "I get by."

Grigsby finished off the last of his bourbon. "I don't s'pose you know anything about the folks travelin' with Wilde."

Doc shook his head.

Grigsby stood up. "Okay, Doc. 'Preciate it."

"Be seeing you, Bob."

O'Conner opened the door and his face sank.

"Howdy, Davey," said Grigsby, grinning happily. "Good to see you again. You gonna invite me in?"

"Do I have a choice?"

"Not a one."

O'Conner stepped back and Grigsby shuffled into the room.

"It is Davey, ain't it?" Grigsby asked him. "I got that right? I mean, we never did get properly innerduced."

"David," said O'Conner. He crossed the room and sat down on a straight-backed wooden chair beside the small wooden table in the corner of the room. The table held a half-empty bottle of whiskey and an empty glass.

Grigsby said, "The same David O'Conner who's a hotshot reporter for the *New York Sun*? The one who's gonna get the president of the United States to start sendin' me telegrams?"

O'Conner lifted the bottle, poured whiskey into the glass. "You have something to say to me, Marshal?"

"Just so happens," Grigsby said, "I did get a telegram about you today. Wasn't from President Arthur, though." He reached into his vest pocket, slipped out the telegram, unfolded it. "Was from a fella name of Jackson B. Martindale. Ever hearda him, Davey?"

O'Conner drank from the glass. "You telegraphed him."

"I did. I did that little thing, Davey. I asked him for particulars about this hotshot reporter of his, David O'Conner. And you know what he wired back?"

"You're enjoying this," O'Conner said. He seemed neither surprised nor alarmed. He seemed only resigned.

"Some," Grigsby admitted. "What he wired back, Davey, was this—OCONNER A LIAR AND A DRUNK. STOP. NO LONGER A REPORTER THIS OR ANY OTHER NEW YORK NEWSPAPER. STOP. INFORM HIM LEGAL ACTION IF HE CONTINUES MISREPRESENTA-TION. SIGNED, JACKSON B. MARTINDALE, EDITOR, NEW YORK SUN." Grigsby looked over the telegram at O'Conner, and smiled. "Doesn't sound like a very friendly fella, now does he?"

CHAPTER TWENTY-FOUR

"HAVE YOU TOLD WILDE yet?" O'Conner asked Grigsby with what looked like, and sounded like, casual curiosity. Grigsby knew it wasn't.

He sat down opposite the reporter. "I reckoned you and me oughta talk it over first."

O'Conner nodded. "Then I guess I owe you something." He smiled. It was a small, sickly smile, bitter and inward looking. "Would a drink do?"

"For starters." No point in Grigsby's quitting now; he already had a good strong buzz going. He'd quit tomorrow. If he decided tomorrow that he wanted to.

O'Conner stood, walked to the dresser, found another glass, brought it back to the table, sat down. He filled the glass, handed it to Grigsby. He raised his own glass, drank from it, and sighed. He looked away.

"Well now, Davey," Grigsby said. "Why don't you tell me why you're pretendin' to work for the *New York Sun* when you're not doin' any such a thing."

Without looking at him, O'Conner said, "It's a long story."

"That's the best kind."

O'Conner took another swallow from his drink. Still looking away, his voice flat, he spoke as though he were talking to the floor. "My wife and I moved to San Francisco last year. Things hadn't been going very well for us in New York, and Sonia had some money, so we decided to try California for a while. Get a fresh start." He smiled the bitter smile. "Well, things didn't go very well for us there, either. My fault. I admit it. I was hitting the booze a little too heavily. I made a few mistakes." He turned to Grigsby, and now some emotion slipped into his voice: defensiveness. "Nothing big, nothing spectacular, but the newspaper business is like a great big dragon. As long as you're doing the job, getting in your stories, feeding the dragon, it lets you ride on its back. You're way up there, in the clouds. But make a mistake, and the dragon turns on you. It chews you up and then it spits you out."

Grigsby nodded. He didn't know much about the newspaper business, but as a lawman he did know a little bit about people making excuses for themselves, and he was pretty sure that he was hearing someone do that now.

O'Conner took another drink. "But it would've worked out. I had plans. I had a couple of good things lined up, a couple of real possibilities. I could've turned it all around." He shrugged. "And then Sonia died."

Grigsby nodded. "How?"

"Pneumonia. She went to bed with it one Monday morning and by Wednesday night she was dead."

"When was this?"

O'Conner smiled his wan, bitter smile. "Oh, you can check on it, Marshal. It's all on record. Sonia O'Conner, beloved wife of David. Died on November Seventeenth, Eighteen Eighty-one." He drank some more whiskey. "A week before Thanksgiving."

Grigsby nodded.

"Anyway, I went a little crazy there for a while." Another smile, one that tried for sarcasm and almost succeeded. "Not killing hookers. Just drinking too much. And then—in January, I don't even remember exactly how it happened—I met Vail. He

289

remembered me from New York." Another small smile, bitter again. "From my days of glory. Anyway, we talked, and he came up with an idea. Why not write a book about the tour—this tour, Wilde's tour across America. Write a book showing how Wilde reacts to the country, and how the country reacts to him. The Poet meets the populace. Why not, I thought. A living dog is better than a dead lion. And besides, it *was* a good idea. No one's ever done it before."

"So Vail knows you're not working for the *New York Sun?*"

O'Conner nodded. "We've got a contract. He pays for the rooms I stay in, and he'll get forty percent of the money from the book." He drank some bourbon. "I pay for my own food and liquor. I had some money left. From Sonia."

"Wilde doesn't know about this."

"No."

"How come?"

"Vail's idea. He's afraid that Wilde'll want a percentage of the book."

So there was more to Vail—or maybe less—than met the eye.

O'Conner looked at him. "Listen, Marshal. I asked around, back in Denver. I found out about you. I heard about your wife leaving. You and I, we've got a lot in common. We've both lost our wives. Other people don't understand about a pain like that. They don't know what it can do to a man. How you can feel it all over your body, like the weight of the world, when you get up in the morning."

He raised his glass of whiskey and held it up between him and Grigsby. "And we've got this, too. Our one real friend. The balm of Gilead. The wine that maketh merry. Other people, when they get up, they don't know what their day's going to be like. Happy or sad, long or short. But you and me, we know exactly how its going to go. All we've got to do is look at our bottle. We can measure the day, before it even happens, by the amount of liquor left."

"Don't worry," Grigsby said. "I'm not gonna tell Wilde about your deal with Vail, if that's what you're leadin' up to. It's none of my business. But as for drinkin', scout, you speak for yourself." It was a shame about O'Conner's wife, a tragedy; but where did the reporter get off comparing himself to Grigsby? Grigsby had a job to do, and he did it. He had responsibilities, and he lived up to them. He wasn't lying around in a hotel room feeling sorry for himself and pretending to be something he wasn't. "Liquor's no big thing with me. I can take it or I can leave it alone."

O'Conner smiled. "When was the last time you left it alone?"

Today, Grigsby thought. For part of the day, anyway. A good chunk of it. And tomorrow, for sure, he was definitely going to quit. "Now listen, Davey," he said, "you just let me be the one asks the questions here, okay?"

O'Conner shrugged. "Whatever you say. And listen, I'm grateful. I mean it. For your not telling Wilde."

"Fine." Grigsby reached for his glass, stopped himself. "Tell me this. You're not even a reporter nowadays. Why'd you get so steamed up when I told you not to write about these killin's?"

O'Conner nodded. "That's right," he said, and his voice was flat again. "I'm not a reporter these days." He looked off, smiled to himself, then looked again to Grigsby. "But I thought, for a moment there I thought maybe I could pull it all together. It's a good story, Marshal. I can still recognize one when I see it. I thought, maybe, if I put my mind to it, I could write it and sell it to one of the New York papers."

He swallowed some whiskey. "And maybe I will." He smiled at Grigsby. Sarcastically again, and this time the sarcasm came off real well. "Later, of course. After you catch the killer."

Irritated, Grigsby said, "You think I won't?"

O'Conner's face went blank and he held out his hands. "What do I know?"

Grigsby reached for his drink, nearly stopped himself once more, and then snatched it up and tossed back what was left of the whiskey. Why the hell try to prove anything to O'Conner. "How's the book going?"

O'Conner, watching Grigsby drink, had been smiling. Now he frowned, puzzled. "What?"

"The book you're writin' about Wilde."

"Oh." The reporter nodded. "Good. Damn good, I think. I've already written a couple of chapters. Taken a lot of notes. I think it's really going to turn things around for me."

He sounded convincing, maybe because he had convinced himself. But Grigsby remembered what he'd seen in the reporter's notebook, the only thing he'd seen in the reporter's notebook:

O. Wilde.

Oscar Wilde.

Oscar Fingal O'Flahertie Wills Wilde.

He said nothing. Lying about some book you were supposed to be writing wasn't against the law.

Neither was self-deception. If it had been, probably everyone in the world would be in jail.

Grigsby felt sour and sad and used up. The night had started off so goddamn well. The telegram had lifted his spirits by suggesting an ulterior motive for O'Conner's joining the tour. And in fact there had been an ulterior motive; it just hadn't involved killing hookers.

Of course, the whole story could be a passel of lies. Tomorrow Grigsby would talk to Vail. And send a telegram to San Francisco to check up on the rest of it.

And even if the story turned out to be true, that didn't mean that O'Conner was off the hook. Maybe his wife's death had unbalanced him; maybe he'd decided to start taking revenge against the world by cutting up women.

But Grigsby was discouraged. He'd traveled from possibilities to likelihoods and back again to possibilities. And O'Conner depressed him. Grigsby felt both sorry for the reporter and angry at him. He wanted to grab him by the shirt front and shake some sense into him. But he knew that self-pity was as unshakable as self-esteem, maybe more so. There was nothing he could do for the man; and nothing, right now, he could do about him. Besides, it was nearly twelve o'clock and Mathilde would be waiting. "I'm gonna check up on all this," he told the reporter.

O'Conner nodded. "Like I said, it's all on record."

"Telegrams?" said Mathilde.

Propped up against the pillows, they both lay naked on the bed, each holding a glass of calvados. Grigsby was smoking.

"I sent a bunch of telegrams to the cities Wilde stopped in before he got to San Francisco. And I sent others to cities where he didn't stop, out West here. Askin' if any . . . uh, prostitutes got themselves killed."

"Yes? And?"

"None, so far."

"Which would mean?"

"Which'd mean that so far the only killin's are the ones I already know about. San Francisco, El Paso, Leavenworth, and Denver."

"So. This suggests that the killer, he is indeed one of us. But also—no?—that he must be Mr. O'Conner. It cannot be Wolfgang, and Mr. O'Conner joined with the tour in San Francisco."

Grigsby shook his head. "Nope. See, I haven't heard yet from all the cities I sent the telegrams to. One problem, see, with the cities that Wilde didn't visit, is I'm tryin' to prove that something *didn't* happen in any of 'em. That's generally a pretty tough row to hoe. You're always gonna have your element of doubt. And second, this fella coulda come all the way from New York to San Francisco before he decided to start cuttin' up women."

"So he could, then, be Mr. Vail."

"Yeah. Or even Henry."

"*Henri?*" She smiled, her eyebrows furrowed in surprise. "You suspect Henri?"

"I gotta suspect everyone till I know different." Grigsby sipped at his apple brandy. "But, fact is, I can't really picture Henry. I reckon he's a little too slow on the uptake to pull off a thing like this."

"Ah." She set her glass on the bed table and then rolled herself over to face Grigsby. "You still believe that some other person could not be responsible? Someone not traveling with us?"

"Be a pretty big coincidence."

And yet Doc Holliday, for example, had been in all four cities at the same time as Wilde and the tour.

But Doc was a gambler before he was anything else, even before he was a gunman—he was a gunman, mostly, so he could protect himself and his winnings. And it made sense to Grigsby that Doc had followed the tour in order to light onto some high-stakes games.

It made sense, but naturally it didn't have to be the truth.

Problem here was that Doc was a wild card. Unreadable, a mystery. There was no way to know what went on inside his head. That was why Doc *had* winnings to protect.

So the story about the games might be pure bushwah.

But if it was, why would Doc invent it? And in the six years that he'd been floating through Colorado, no hookers had got themselves cut up, that Grigsby knew of.

Suppose Doc had gone off the beam for some reason? Suppose he'd gone crazy? Suppose . . .

Nope. Doc was strange, maybe, but as far as Grigsby could tell, he wasn't crazy.

It had to be someone on the tour.

But who? Didn't seem like any of them were crazy either.

The more Grigsby learned, the less he knew. The more he thought about it, the more tangled the whole thing became.

Mathilde said, "If you are convinced that one of these men is responsible, why do you not assign some people to watch each of them?"

Grigsby smiled. "I got one deputy workin' for me, Mathilde. Just the one. No way the two of us could cover all of 'em."

"But what about here? Could you not ask the police of this town to assist you?"

"I don't get along real well with the sheriff here." Tim Drucker, the county sheriff, was a friend of Greaves's.

Grigsby sucked on the cigarette, exhaled a long slow sigh of pale blue smoke.

Mathilde said, "You are troubled tonight, Bohb."

"Just frustrated, I reckon."

294

"Tell me something." She put the tip of her finger against his chin.

"What's that?"

"Why did you and your wife separate?"

Grigsby's chest suddenly clenched up on him. He inhaled some more smoke, exhaled it. He shrugged. "Things just didn't work out."

"And why not?"

"It's a kinda boring story, Mathilde."

She smiled. "Which is to say, you do not wish to tell it."

He shrugged again. Why not? The whole town of Denver knew. "She found out I was seein' another woman."

She looked puzzled, head tilted, lips pursed, eyes narrowed. "Seeing?"

"Sleepin' with."

"She learned that you were making love to some other woman? And for this she left you?"

Grigsby didn't think it was fair to Clara for him to talk about her behind her back, even though her back happened to be a thousand miles away; but on the other hand he didn't think it was fair to Clara for Mathilde to start judging her, either. As nice a woman as she was, Mathilde was a stranger to the situation, and a foreigner to boot, with a foreigner's funny notions. "Well, see, what you gotta understand about Clara is that she was just naturally a real jealous woman. She's one of the smartest women I ever knew, maybe the most levelheaded woman I ever knew, except for this one little thing. This jealousy."

"You think of jealousy as a little thing?"

"Well, yeah. It was. At first, anyway. Everything else about her was . . . just what I wanted." He had nearly said *perfect*, but in his experience it was seldom a slick move to call one woman perfect to another woman's face. Especially when the other woman's face was attached to a body you happened to be lying in bed with.

"If she was everything you wanted, why then did you make love to someone else?"

"Well, see, I didn't. Not for a long time." Grigsby turned, stabbed his cigarette out in the ashtray and lifted the tobacco pouch and a match from the table. He sat back against the pillow.

"After a while, see, it started to bother me. The jealousy." He drew up his feet and propped the balloon glass against his thigh, then poured tobacco into a slip of paper. "Every time I was a few minutes late for supper, she was sure I was off screwin' around."

"And were you?"

"No. Leastways not at first." He rolled the paper, stuck the cigarette between his lips.

"For how long were you faithful?"

He snapped the match alight, held it to the cigarette. "Five years."

"You were unfaithful only once?"

Grigsby inhaled, exhaled. "Nope. Maybe once a year for the next four years. I never looked for it, never went out huntin' it, but when it showed up on my doorstep, I didn't go runnin' away from it, neither."

"Five years," said Mathilde, "is a long time to be faithful."

He exhaled. "It is when you're hangin' by your thumbs. 'Cause the thing of it is, see, this faithfulness, it's not an item comes real easy to me. Problem is, I purely do love women. It's like a sickness with me, almost. Shoot, maybe it *is* a sickness. Clara surely thought it was."

"How do you mean, exactly, love them?"

"What I say. I love everything about 'em. I don't just mean the stand-out things, breasts and butts and all, although Lord knows I love all that, too. I mean everything. Their hair and their mouths and their ears. Their eyelashes, even. Their chins. Their noses."

He inhaled, slowly exhaled, and smiled at her. "You take noses now. Women got all kinds of noses. Big ones, small ones, narrow ones, thick ones, pointy ones, ones with a kind of bump in the middle, ones that got a kinda sideways turn to 'em, left or right. And the thing is, I love all of 'em. The only kind I'm not real partial to is the kind that twists up at the end and makes a woman look like she stands a good chance of drownin' in a downpour.''

"*Retroussé.*"

"Huh?"

"In French we call this type of nose *retroussé*. Turned up. Upturned.''

"Whatever. But even there, see, I been known to make exceptions. It's just one little ole thing, and they got so much else, and I love it all. Like I say, everything. The way their eyes move and the way they hold a cup of coffee. They way they talk and the way they think and the way they smell. Smell, Lord, I'll tell ya. Sometimes I'll be walkin' along on the sidewalk, in the springtime, say, and the wind'll kick up a whiff of perfume and carry it on over my way and, God's honest truth, it's like I got kicked in the chest by a horse.''

"Perhaps," she said, "you want their approval. Perhaps you feel you need it.''

Grigsby grinned. "I want everything they got, and I'm plumb grateful for anything I get.''

She smiled. "Did your wife not understand this about you?''

"Course she did. And that just made the jealousy worse. I'm walkin' around thinkin' I ought to be gettin' some kinda congressional medal of honor for bein' such a hero—for *not* screwin' around. And instead, ever' time I get home, she jumps all over me because she thinks I *am* screwin' around.''

"So you decided, finally, that if you were going to be accused of infidelity, you might as well commit it.''

Looking at her sideways, Grigsby smiled. "You heard this story before, huh?''

She smiled back. "Several times. Bohb, do you not see that this is exactly what I was talking about yesterday? How we are attracted to precisely the people who will provide us with pain?''

"Don't see it that way. I mean, I fell in love with Clara in *spite* of how she was jealous, not *because* of it.''

"And she fell in love with you in spite of your womanizing, and not because of it.''

"Right.''

She nodded. "And now that you are separated, both of you are miserable."

"I can't speak for Clara. But me, I tell ya, sometimes I feel like I got a hole in my chest the size of Nebraska."

"But I believe, you see, that perhaps this hole was there even before you met your Clara. And that perhaps a part of you wished you to become aware of it, and so selected Clara."

Grigsby smiled. "And Clara chose me because I was gonna screw around on her?"

"Perhaps, yes. I think that jealousy has nothing to do with love. It has to do with fear, with the fear of betrayal. And I think that for many of us, our private wound is exactly this—a sense of betrayal, deep within us. It is perhaps common to all of us. Perhaps your Clara dealt with her fear of betrayal by expressing it as jealousy. Perhaps you dealt with yours by an inability to remain with only one woman."

"But I *did* remain with just one woman. I mean, for five years I was as faithful to Clara as an old coondog."

"And the woman with whom you remained was a woman of great jealousy. Do you not perceive that, on one level, a jealous woman is the safest of wives? If she is so preoccupied by the possibility of your betraying *her*, she is unlikely, herself, to betray *you*."

"Well, now—"

"And yet, of course, sooner or later the tensions become unbearable. The situation explodes. You betray her by making love to someone else, and she betrays you by leaving you. And you see, my belief is that, in a way, this was precisely the point of the entire exercise. For both of you to experience your inner pain. To feel it."

Grigsby shook his head. "I don't buy that." He smiled sadly. "But I'll tell ya, if that *hadda* been the idea of the whole thing, it surely did work like a charm."

"Ah," she said, and the smile on her lips looked as sad as his own smile felt. "But did it?"

"How do you mean?"

"For us finally to remove the pain, we must actually experience it, penetrate it. Have you done this, or have you avoided it?"

"Doesn't seem to me like it's the kind of pain a body can avoid real easy."

She frowned slightly. "And yet I notice, Bohb, that you drink quite a lot of alcohol."

What was it today? Everybody and his brown mule was after him about his drinking. "Yeah, well," Grigsby said. "Maybe. But the funny thing is, I been drinkin' a lot less since I met you."

She smiled. "So perhaps you are using me, rather than alcohol, to escape your pain."

Grigsby returned her smile. "Gives me less of a hangover."

She tapped his nose. "So far."

Grigsby laughed. He realized, smack in the middle of his laughter, that he hadn't laughed for a long time. "Well, tell me this," he said. "If ever'body's lookin' to get hurt by the people they hook up with, how do you figure you're gonna get hurt by hookin' up with me? I mean, where's the pain come in?"

She shrugged. Grigsby very much admired the way her breasts shivered when she shrugged. "Soon I will be leaving," she said. "Even after only this short time, I will find it painful to part."

"Well," Grigsby said, "first off, seems to me that you're talkin' about a whole 'nother thing there. You didn't get hooked up with me just so's you could get unhooked, and then suffer for it. Leastways, I don't think so. And second, you know there ain't no law of nature says you got to be leavin'."

She smiled. "Bohb." Once again she placed her fingertip against his chin. "I enjoy you very much. I liked you from the first time I saw you. I sensed your kindness, and your concern. You are, I think, a good man. Truly. But we are very different, you and I. I have my plans and you have yours. I must continue with my journey. And you must continue with your own. You have unfinished business, I believe. You are still deeply in love with your wife, and this is something with which you must contend. You must either return to her somehow, or you must at last move on."

Grigsby took a sip of his brandy. "But accordin' to you, if me and her got back together, we'd just mess each other up all over again."

"It is possible, I think, for two people to work together, to help each other with this."

Grigsby smiled sadly. "I don't think Clara would go for it."

"Then perhaps it is time for you to continue with your life."

Grigsby sighed again. "I purely do hate it when a woman starts makin' sense."

Mathilde smiled. "But for now, we have some time together, you and I. We have, not love, perhaps, not exactly. But affection." She smiled. "And lust, too, of course."

Grigsby grinned. "Sounds to me like you got one hell of an idea there." He stubbed out his cigarette, set his glass on the night table, and turned to reach for her.

CHAPTER TWENTY-FIVE

YING IN BED, HE sang it softly to himself:

Doe, Doe, Doe.
Doe Re Mi Fa Sol La Ti *Doe*.
Doe Re Mi . . .
Doe Re *Mine*. Elizabeth McCourt Doe is
    mine.
You are *mine*, harlot. You are *mine*, slut.

Somewhere, perhaps right at this moment, she was writhing and squirming beneath some slobbering male, Tabor or Wilde or some other; somewhere she cooed and grunted, gasped and groaned; *and she did not know*. She did not know that she had been chosen. Did not know that her destiny had been immovably fixed. Did not know that the passing hours were carrying her toward them, toward him and the Lords of Light, as surely, as inexorably, as the currents of a river swept refuse and carrion to the waiting sea.

But of course getting her would require every particle of his cunning. She was different from the rest. Although at heart she was as corrupt and foul as the others, as lost as they, finally as doomed, on the surface she was successful, prosperous, one of society's darlings. She had a sponsor: Tabor. She had friends, she had money. She had a lair into which she could retreat, like a scorpion, like a snake.

And Grigsby was still hanging about. Bumbling and inept he might be, a drunkard and a clown; still he was persistent. He was watching. He was waiting.

How infuriating it was to be forced to take that slovenly dullard into account.

Sometimes the pressures and the tensions of the work seemed nearly overwhelming. Sometimes the difficulties, the dangers, seemed nearly too much to bear, crowding around him, looming black and weighty overhead. Sometimes, even, he doubted.

She *will* be mine?

She will be yours, came the deep, raspy, magisterial voice. *She will be ours*.

What comfort those voices provided him! The absolute certainty throbbing in their tones—how it inspired him!

He

had learned that if he stopped fighting it, if he embraced it as a friend, the pain from the ropes would become a part of himself. Instead of lingering at the chafed strips of skin where the hemp bit into his flesh, it would slowly expand, slowly drift through tissue and bone, slowly fill his entire being with a dull red glow, as hot and potent as a smoldering ember of coal. To contain the glow, to prevent it from seeping off, his skin would harden, stiffen, become shiny and brittle, like the shell of a beetle.

The darkness no longer frightened him. Often, in the beginning, he had heard things moving through it. He had heard the feathery whisper of scales as something slithered along the wood of the floor, he had heard the rustle of fur beneath his bed, the click of sharp tiny claws.

But over time he had learned to use it. Now he was not only in it, but of it. While his body lay armored and protected atop the mattress, his soul merged with the darkness, and together he and the darkness billowed out beyond the confines of the narrow room, out beyond the confines of the house, out into the night sky, out to the very ends of the universe.

He had begun, almost, to dislike the light. Where the darkness was powerful and boundless, the light was frail and petty. Limited. And with the light came the Preacher. And, sometimes, the Harlot, the Red Bitch. And, always, each time, a new and different pain.

As now:

He heard a door slam, down below. They had returned. His soul swept back into his body and hid itself beneath the sleek smooth shell of his skin.

He heard the footsteps on the stairs, and the unmodulated murmur, the jerky rise and fall, of drunken voices. Both of them were coming.

The door swung open and light swung across the room. In the yellow rectangle at the doorway stood the dark towering form of the Preacher. Swaying slightly, he advanced toward the bed. The floorboards creaked beneath him. In the background, her arms crossed as she leaned against the jamb, her disheveled red hair burning like a flame, stood the Harlot. At the bottom of her round white face, her painted red mouth hung open in a leer.

The Preacher leaned over, put out his hands to feel the mattress. His black bulk blotted out the ceiling.

"Wet again," said the Preacher, and his breath was thick with liquor. "Train up a child in the way he should go: and when he is old, he will not depart from it. You must learn, boy."

His hand moved between the boy's legs, and then pain like a bolt of lightning rattled up the center of the world. "You must learn, boy."

From far off, the boy heard the wild jangling laughter of the Harlot. He

stood at the very center of a flat featureless field of pale parched grass that extended in every direction out to the horizon. Overhead

303

the sky was booming with light, the sun so fierce it had scorched away the blue. In the distance wheeled a small flock of crows, black hieroglyphs sliding down the white of sky. The boy watched until they seemed about to slip between the thin line that separated sky and field.

And just there, just at the point where they vanished, the fissure began. It slashed upward from the horizon into the bare bleached sky, as straight and true as though sliced by a razor, and it stopped directly overhead, where the sun had burned only a moment before. The lips of the gash trembled for a moment, then buckled earthward, splitting apart, and from between them gushed a glistening tumble of entrails. Gigantic coils and loops of pink shiny intestine, monstrous red gleaming chunks of liver and spleen and kidney, gray lumps and strands of brain, spilled in a vast torrent to the field and splattered against it, slopping over one another, heaping themselves in slick steaming piles. The boy

sometimes felt the need for comfort now. All too often now those strange periods of blackness would overtake him and sweep him away into that mysterious, timeless limbo. Minutes or hours might pass before he returned to himself. Fortunately he had learned to sense their approach. He could feel himself becoming attentuated, becoming somehow less real, less substantial, thinning into a pale gray mist within his clothes; and before he allowed himself to slip altogether into transparency he would retreat to the safety of his room. But sometimes, still, when he returned, he would discover himself pacing down a sidewalk he had never seen before, or eating a meal he had not ordered, or engaged in a conversation he had not initiated. On one or two occasions, only his supreme skill at dissembling had saved him.

It was, yes, the result of fatigue. The enormous energy he expended on his mission. The difficulties and the dangers he daily faced and daily defeated.

And yet, paradoxically, it was the mission which provided him with energy, which brought him into contact with the pulse that beat at the very center of creation. Without the mission, he might

304

wisp away entirely, his body disintegrating, dissipating, its isolate atoms floating off into the ether forever. Without it, he might disappear.

He

danced, he reeled, he spun like a dervish as he chanted in a language he did not recognize but one he knew was sanctified by the Lords of Light. Sometimes he laughed and sometimes, when he considered how he had been blessed, how he had been graced, he sobbed in gratitude. He

required the mission as surely as the mission required him.

Soon.

Yes. And soon he would have her, this Elizabeth McCourt Doe. Soon he would show her the world of wonders that lay just beneath this one, separated from it by a veil that was the thickness, merely, of human skin.

And, yes, it would need every particle of their cunning, his and that of the Lords of Light. But cunning had been needed before and always, from his inexhaustible store, and from theirs, he had supplied it.

Like Grigsby, but of course with infinitely more subtlety and intelligence, he would watch and he would wait. The time would come; that was fated. And when it did, he would be ready.

Soon, yes, he would have her.

Soon.

Elizabeth McCourt Doe.

Doe.

Doe Re Mi.

Doe Re Mine.

CHAPTER TWENTY-SIX

"ISN'T THE FOREST LOVELY?" asked Elizabeth McCourt Doe.

"Sorry?" Oscar turned to her. With the reins held loosely in his hand, he had been blankly staring at the nodding heads of the plodding pair of horses that drew the carriage.

"The forest. Isn't it lovely?"

Oscar glanced around, noted the large number of pine trees that loomed up rather aggressively on both sides of the narrow dirt track. It was, to be sure, a forest. But lovely? It was a bit too gloomy for his taste, and the trees were a good deal too large; it resembled a typical Teutonic woodland, brooding and dim, which had somehow undergone a lunatic surge of growth.

"Ah," he said. "Yes. Charming."

"It looks primeval, don't you think?" Poised and regal in her red fox coat and matching muff, a wide-brimmed bonnet shading her cascade of titian hair, she appeared today—as she always appeared—stunningly beautiful.

"Primeval, yes," said Oscar. "My very thought."

She put her hand lightly on his forearm. "Oscar," she said, "you seem distracted."

306

"Not at all." He smiled. "I am merely speechless with pleasure at your company."

She smiled, slid her hand down his sleeve to the back of his hand, squeezed it, and then withdrew her own and slipped it back into the muff. Still smiling, she looked off into the tall glowering pine trees.

Normally her touch would have enflamed him, sent all the nerve ends of his body migrating to the patch of skin beneath her fingertips; but at the moment Oscar *was* in fact distracted. An hour ago, when he had clambered up into the driver's seat of the carriage, he had glanced toward the alleyway across the street from the hotel. And there he had seen (or imagined?) a large shadowy figure suddenly lurch back into the darkness. Only a glimpse it had been, lasting no longer than the blink of an eye.

Since then, he had been trying to persuade himself that the figure had been merely a phantasm, merely one more illusory member of that illusory band of bears which had lately been stalking him.

For why on earth would Biff the Behemoth follow Oscar all the way from Denver to Manitou Springs? Oscar had done him no harm. Indeed, during their encounter, it had been Oscar who was the injured party—having been lobbed through the air to tumble into that disgusting heap of sawdust. If anyone had a right to harbor a grudge, clearly it was he. And he, for his part, was perfectly happy to let bygones be bygones.

If Biff, somewhere deep within the murky corridors of his mind, nursed a desire for revenge, would he not have sought out Dr. Holliday? It was Holliday, not Oscar, who had been the author of Biff's humiliation. Surely even Biff could grasp that fact?

As he had done three or four times since leaving Manitou Springs, Oscar leaned from the carriage and peered behind them. With its twists and turns through the somber pines, the track was visible for only a hundred yards. But those hundred yards were empty. No one, apparently, was following.

Of course not. That lurching shape had been only another trick of nature, a mirage, one of those droll sleights produced by the interplay of light and shade. Like the huge ursine apparition last night—which had metamorphosed into the quite human (if admittedly still somewhat mysterious) form of Dr. Holliday.

He glanced off into the trees. Really, this *was* a dreary place. Dark, broad, towering trees rising to quite preposterous heights from pools of sunless gloom. It seemed silent and empty; but who knew what sort of creatures were skulking through those sullen depths, following the passage of the carriage with hungry yellow eyes? Wolves. Coyotes. Mountain lions. Rattlesnakes the thickness and length of fire hoses.

And of course bears.

No. No bears. The bears were an illusion.

He sat back against the rigid seat of the carriage. Perhaps the portentousness of the occasion had made him a tad uneasy. It was not, after all, every day that one asked a young woman for her hand. (Mother would have said it was not *any* day that one asked a young woman for her hand when the young woman was a penniless divorcée. But Mother would come around. She must come around, and therefore she would come around.)

The silver brooch Oscar had purchased in Denver lay in his topcoat pocket, and now it seemed to him inadequate, trivial, as tawdry as a piece of costume jewelry. It should have been gold; and it should have been a ring.

He would buy her a ring later. Today. As soon as they returned to town.

Could one buy a diamond ring in Manitou Springs?

"There," said Elizabeth McCourt Doe. She pointed to a small clearing along the left side of the track. "There's room for the carriage."

Oscar tugged the reins to the left and the horses drew the carriage off the track. As the animals approached the end of the clearing, he pulled the reins back. The carriage stopped. He set the brake lever, tied the reins to it, then stepped down and assisted Elizabeth McCourt Doe to the ground.

How could he worry about someone as insignificant as Biff

when someone as breathtakingly beautiful as this stood (both physically and metaphorically) within his grasp?

She *had* brought along blankets (admirable woman!) and also a large wicker hamper. She placed her muff on the seat and scooped up the blankets. "You can bring the basket," she said, smiling.

Oscar looked around him, at the forest crowding in, vast and bleak. Lightly—no apprehension here, just a simple, manly curiosity—he asked, "Is it terribly far?"

She shook her head. "A short walk."

He lifted the hamper, which he found to be somewhat on the heavy side, and set off behind her.

The air today was mild. Back in Manitou Springs it had been almost warm. Here, higher up, along the slope of the mountain, it was cooler but still comfortable.

As he trailed behind Elizabeth McCourt Doe, he could smell the dusky fragrance of her perfume, blended now with the drab, prosaic odors of the forest: earth and pine, and also something dank, something heavy and oppressive which must have been mold or fungus, and which reminded him of graveyards and crypts.

Despite his admiration for the woman, her notion of a short walk was one to which he could not wholeheartedly subscribe. They marched for what seemed like miles through the shadows, over glum gray hillocks and around them, deeper and deeper into the dusky wood. (However had she found this place of hers? Guided there by some local Chingachgook?)

Beneath a slippery cover of brown pine needles, the ground was soft and spongy, threatening now and then to engulf his shoes, and possibly his entire body. He began to perspire elaborately. The wicker hamper grew increasingly heavy and cumbersome, and he had run out of arms into which he could shift the thing. Perhaps, he thought, he should perch it atop his skull, like a cheerful native bearer, and begin to sing cheerful native bearer songs. Whatever they might be.

Finally the two of them emerged from the gloom into a small sunlit glen. A blue patch of sky hung overhead, stretched taut between the faraway black treetops. At the clearing's opposite side ran the promised brook. It was not, however, babbling. On some earlier occasion it might perhaps have babbled; but to-day—swollen, presumably, by meltwater—it thundered like a small but determined Niagara. Gushing, whooshing, it slapped and slammed against its banks as it blundered down the slope.

So much for the idea of dipping their feet into its laughing water. Any foot dipped into that current would be wrenched off at the ankle.

Elizabeth McCourt Doe spread out one of the blankets and sat down on it, arranging her skirt about her. She looked up, smiling, and patted the blanket. With aching arms, Oscar lowered the basket and sat down beside her, disguising his small gasp of exhaustion as a sigh of pleasure: "Ah!"

She leaned toward him, kissed his cheek, then sat back. "Isn't it perfect?" she asked. Oscar could just make out her voice over the roar of the stream.

"Perfect," he said, and swallowed. His breath was coming in frantic little puffs.

"Wouldn't it be wonderful to live in a place like this? Away from all the crowds, all the bustle and noise?"

"Yes," he said. For a day or two, if one had a wealth of provisions and virtually no other choice. "Delightful. You don't care for Denver, then?"

She made a face, shook her head. "It's so dirty and crowded." She turned to him. "Is London like that?"

He laughed, suddenly lightheaded with relief. This was evidently going to proceed more easily, with far less awkwardness, than he had dared hope. (Why, then, had his heart vaulted from his chest to his head, where it now hammered against his ears?) "Not at all. There are areas in London that are sublime. Filled with gracious homes and lovely parks." And, alas, with spiteful estate agents.

"Parks? Really? There are trees?"

"Masses of them. And Ireland, where I've a small piece of property, has still more. A plenitude of trees. A positive welter of trees. You'd very much like Ireland, I think."

310

She smiled. "I'd love to see it one day."

Once again Oscar felt as though he were hovering at the brink of a precipice.

And once again he leaped. "Then you must permit me to show it to you."

She turned to him again. She laughed. "I don't think I'd be able to persuade Horace to take a trip to Ireland."

Oscar smiled. "Well, naturally, the invitation doesn't extend to Horace."

Her smile became quizzical.

Oscar said, "Elizabeth, since the first moment we met I've known that you and I were destined for something grand. There are some souls so finely attuned to one another that instantly, when they meet, they fuse. They become a single entity. I've known, since I saw you that first night, that we were such souls. I flatter myself that you've known this as well."

Now the smile was pleased—no, delighted. She put her hand along his thigh. "It *has* been grand, hasn't it?"

"And it will be grander still. You'll love London, I know you will. The galleries, the shops, the restaurants, the parks, the homes. We'll find ourselves something modest at the start—" He laughed. "Which will no doubt astound everyone who knows me. But this modest little haven of ours, Elizabeth, together we'll transform it into something wonderful, something so stylish it shall become the envy of the entire city. And that shall be, as I say, only at the start, only for a year or so, perhaps. I have great prospects, Elizabeth. Glorious prospects. Soon my play will be produced in New York. Afterward, it's certain to be produced in London. And then, as soon as possible, we'll move into something still more suitable."

Her smile had gone from pleased to quizzical again, and then it had simply gone. "Oscar," she said, "Horace and I are going to get married."

He put her hand over hers. "I understand how you must feel. He seems a good man—a bit limited, of course, but essentially good—and I know how it must trouble you, the idea of bringing him any pain or distress. But you needn't worry, Elizabeth. I'll

311

speak with him myself. I accept the responsibility, and I accept it gladly. Once he learns what's passed between us, what we've become to one another, I'm certain that he'll free you from any promises you may've made. It's what any decent chap would do."

"He already knows what's passed between us."

Oscar looked off. "Perhaps," he said thoughtfully, "perhaps it's not a matter of our *becoming* something. Perhaps we were conjoined even before we met. Perhaps the Hindu sages are right—perhaps through countless lives, countless millennia, you and I—" He turned to her. "What? What did you say?"

"He already knows what's passed between us."

He frowned. "You've told him, you mean?"

"Of course."

He smiled, hugely pleased. "But that's splendid! He knows, then. He understands. And surely he'll set you free? He wouldn't stand in the way of your happiness?"

Her hand was still lying on his thigh, his own still lying atop it. Now she used hers to push lightly at him, once, twice, like a gentle mother trying to rouse a sleeping child. "Oscar, Horace and I are getting *married*."

"But Elizabeth, haven't you heard what I've been saying? There's no need for you to marry Tabor. I shall provide for you. Admittedly not on quite the lavish—one might almost say extravagant—scale that Tabor does. As I mentioned, for a short time, possibly for as little as a month or two, we shall be forced to live perhaps a shade more modestly than either of us would like." Perhaps a shade more modestly than a beggar would like. But he would sell his prints and his Meissen pottery. They were all such beautiful things, all so carefully selected, each in its own way a small masterpiece. But no sacrifice, finally, was too great.

Still, it was a pity about the Meissens.

"But afterward," he said, "once the play is produced, I'll be rich, Elizabeth. We'll find exactly the sort of house we both deserve, and we'll furnish it with the most lovely furniture in London." New prints, new Meissens! "We'll travel to Paris and we'll buy art. There are some brilliant artists working now in Paris. We'll travel to Italy for tapestries. We'll—"

"*Oscar*," she said forcefully. Her beautiful face as rigid as a mask, she spoke to him slowly, deliberately: "I am not going with you to London. Horace and I are engaged. As soon as he gets his divorce, we're going to get married. Don't you understand? I *love* him."

"You *love* him? Elizabeth, that's quite impossible. The man's a *gnome*!"

"He's the richest man between here and San Francisco."

"The richest man?" Why did he keep repeating, like some buffoon, everything she said? "What on earth does money have to do with love? Elizabeth, what we have, you and I, is something that no amount of money can buy. The union of two exquisite souls, the joining of two poetic temperaments—this isn't a thing that can be *purchased*."

Her face softened. "Oscar," she said, and again she placed her hand on his thigh. "I'm extremely fond of you—"

"Fond!" He was doing it again; he could not stop himself.

"And the time we've spent together has been a tremendous amount of fun—"

"*Fun!*"

"But I love him, Oscar. You have to understand. Before I met Horace, I didn't have a dime to my name. All my life, from the time I was a little girl in Minnesota, I've had to scrimp and save just to get by. I've cleaned other people's houses. I've taken in laundry. I've spent the whole afternoon sweating like a pig while I was boiled dirty shirts and stinking underwear. I've worked until the blisters on my hands split open and I left bloody fingerprints on everything I touched. Horace has saved me from all that. For the first time in my life I'm free. I can go where I want, do what I want. I can *be* what I want."

"But I'm trying to tell you, Elizabeth, that very soon, in a matter of *weeks*, I'll be rich myself. Not so rich—I admit it— as Tabor, but rich enough to support you with style and grace and comfort."

She smiled, shook her head. "Oscar, I love him. He lets me be myself."

Wounded now, he snapped, "And who else, pray, could you possibly be?"

"He gives me complete freedom. He knows who I am, and he loves who I am. He lets me *be*, Oscar. How many men are like that? How many men are strong enough to give their women complete freedom?" She smiled suddenly. "How many men would let their women carry on an affair with a handsome young poet?"

He stared at her, aghast. "He *knows*? You're saying that he *knows*?"

"Of course he knows."

"Of course," he repeated stupidly. "*Wait*, yes, you said before . . . You *told* him?"

She nodded. "We have no secrets."

"About us? About everything? You told him about *everything*? Our time together? At the house? And the other night, at the place with the Chinese person?"

She nodded.

Oscar was dizzy with shock. All the secrets of his soul, the heights and depths of his existence, the crushing pains and the ineffable transports of childhood—he had told her everything. He had emptied himself, disemboweled himself, into her slender white hands—and she had danced off to Tabor and the two of them had picked over the entrails. To Tabor! To that insufferable swine, that boar, that bore, that *boor*!

"How?" he said, and he heard his voice crack. "How could you do it? How could you betray me like that?"

She smiled softly, patiently. "Oscar, I didn't betray you. I never told him what we said, what we talked about. And I never went into any details about what we did."

"*Details?* Good Lord, woman, it's not something that *requires* details."

"Oscar, Horace knew that night, the night we met you, that I'd be making love to you the next day. We talked about it."

"You *talked* about it?" Perhaps he was going mad. Perhaps

for the rest of his life he was doomed to repeat everything that was said to him.

"I told you, Horace lets me do what I want. He could see that I was attracted to you. He knows I love him, and he knows that I'll never leave him. So we discussed it. He promised not to return to the house until late the next day."

"My God! The two of you sat there *talking* about this? Like some dreary shopkeeper and his wife planning a holiday in Brighton?"

"Oscar, why are you so upset? Nothing has changed. We still have time to spend with each other. We have this morning and we have this evening in Leadville, after your lecture."

Stunned, he could only stare at her. Nothing had changed?

The woman couldn't see that his entire world had changed?

She lifted his hand to her breasts. Only a determination not to appear ridiculous stopped him from ripping the hand away.

Again she smiled. "Life is short, Oscar. Do you really want to throw away the few moments that you and I have left?"

"Madam," he began.

She opened the front of her coat and slipped his hand between the folds of fur. He could feel, against the back of his knuckles, the silken fabric that encased her breast; and he could feel, beneath it, the shape and density of her flesh.

And then he could feel, beneath his own trousers, the acute and rising interest taken in all this by Freddy Phallus.

Absurd! Betrayed first by the woman, and now by his own wobbly glands!

"Oscar," she said, and she moved his hand up along the arc of breast. "Make love to me. Here. Now."

"*Better do it, boy,*" said a loud gruff voice across the clearing. "*Gonna be the last pussy you ever get.*"

He wheeled about, felt her fingers curl like talons into his hand.

It was, of course, Biff the Behemoth, Biff the Bear. Beside him stood his friend with the eyes of a stoat. Both of them were wearing the same clothes they had worn back in Denver (probably the same clothes they had worn for the past decade)—the friend

315

looking thin and sly in his gray canvas duster, Biff looking immense in his greasy black buffalo fur. Biff had added a piece of apparel today: an old top hat, bent at an angle midway up its stovepipe length. Both men were grinning in dull, stupefied anticipation, and both were holding revolvers, and both of these were pointed at Oscar.

CHAPTER TWENTY-SEVEN

OSCAR WAS SURPRISED to discover that he was not the least bit surprised. The bears who had shambled into his life over the past twenty-four hours—he saw now in a burst of understanding—had clearly been portents, prefigurings of the bulky, burly, bearlike giant who stood twenty feet away across the clearing, holding a large gun in his large meaty hand.

And even supposing that those other bears had never appeared, Biff's arrival here, after what Elizabeth had said, seemed fitting and inevitable. It was part of a natural progression: first you learn that you have been betrayed, and then you learn that you are about to be plugged.

But Oscar also discovered, an instant later, that despite having just realized that the remainder of his life was destined to be empty, desolate, a vast trackless waste of crushing loneliness and despair, he had no wish to surrender it to anyone, and particularly not to an oaf like Biff.

He slipped his hand free from Elizabeth's, and he stood.

"Ah, Biff!" he said heartily. "Splendid! I was afraid, for a moment there, that you might not turn up. But better late than never, eh?"

Above Biff's flat broad nose, below his swollen, misshapen forehead, his beady brown eyes narrowed in puzzlement.

Oscar unbuttoned the front of his velvet topcoat. "You're looking, by the way, absolutely smashing. Is that a new hat?"

"Hey now," growled Biff. "Don't you move."

Oscar shrugged the topcoat from his shoulders and kept talking. "It suits you, I must say. Simple, uncluttered, just the thing for an evening's amble on the prairie. And you wear it with considerable élan." He folded the topcoat and, bending over, laid it alongside the blanket. Beneath his tweed suit coat his skin suddenly felt the cold: the chill pinched at his nipples and sent a shiver rippling over his flesh. But perhaps it was not only the chill which was responsible.

He saw that Elizabeth McCourt Doe was watching him, her beautiful violet eyes opened wide. Standing upright, he continued: "And you know, Biff, I don't believe I mentioned how much I admired that fur coat of yours."

Biff growled, "You listen here, boy—"

Oscar clapped his hands, rubbed his palms together, turned to Biff's friend. "Now Darryl—it is Darryl, isn't it?"

Darryl nodded his narrow, sparsely bearded head, then he frowned and turned to Biff as though seeking instructions.

Oscar said, "You've a watch, haven't you, Darryl?"

Darryl looked at Oscar, looked back to Biff. "How come we don't just shoot him, Biff? And then we can go ahead and pork the bitch."

"Listen, boy," Biff growled at Oscar.

"No watch?" said Oscar. "Well, here—" Oscar unhooked the watch fob from his belt loop, tugged the watch from his pocket, and tossed it lightly toward Darryl. Clumsily, head back, using his left hand and nearly losing the gun from his right, Darryl caught it, slapped it up against his chest.

"Mind you don't drop it now," said Oscar. "It isn't worth much intrinsically, but it has an enormous sentimental value. I stole it from my father." Once again he clapped his hands together. "Right. What I propose are rounds of three minutes each. We should fight for a total of, oh, I think perhaps ten

318

rounds. That ought to be sufficient. Darryl, you'll act as time-keeper.''

Darryl had been studying the watch. Now he looked up, frowning again, at Biff.

"Biff," Oscar said, "you might want to remove that coat. I think you'll find it a bit restrictive. And naturally you won't need your gun."

Biff produced a guffaw. *Guffaw*, Oscar decided, was definitely the only word for the sound Biff made, low and moist and throaty: huh huh huh huh. "Dude," he said, and shook his big bulbous head, "you are one fuckin' crazy asshole."

Oscar shrugged. "Well, Biff, if you feel that ten rounds aren't enough, I've no objections to fifteen."

Biff guffawed again. "First thing," he said, "Darryl here can't tell time nohow." Another guffaw—either at Darryl's deficiency or at Oscar's presumption. "Second thing, I ain't gonna fight you, dude. I don't got to. I got a gun." He held it up slightly sideways, as though thinking that Oscar had not yet noticed the thing. "See, what I'm gonna do is gut-shoot you. Drill some lead right into yer belly. Two shots, I figger. Take you least an hour to kick off, an' it hurts like blazes the whole time. I gut-shot a fella once in Laredo, and he was beggin' me somethin' horrible to finish him off. And then, see, while you hold onta yer guts and watch us, me and Darryl here, we're gonna prong your woman every ole which way, back and front and sideways. And then I'm gonna gut-shoot *her*.''

Oscar crossed his arms over his chest and he nodded. "Well, Biff, I think that's an excellent plan. Really top drawer. You fulfill my every expectation. I was just saying to Elizabeth— Elizabeth, this is Biff, the chap I spoke about—I was just saying to Elizabeth that if I know my Biff, he'll have devised something truly inventive for the two of us. And you know, funnily enough, the subject of gut-shooting did come up. I said—didn't I, Elizabeth?—I said, I wonder whether Biff has given any thought to the idea of gut-shooting? I mean to say, gut-shooting has a purity, a classic simplicity, that might elude the average chap. But it hasn't eluded you, eh, Biff? Well done!''

319

Biff was looking puzzled again.

"Naturally, though," said Oscar, "before we get to all that, I know you'll want to continue where we left off, back in Denver. Believe me, Biff, the interruption of our boxing match was as distressing to me as it was to you."

"You don't listen good," Biff said. "There ain't gonna be no boxing match. I'm gonna shoot you. Right smack in the belly."

"Oh, I know that, Biff. I expect nothing less from a man of your caliber." Oscar chuckled. "Caliber, eh? Isn't it wonderful the way our words will sport with themselves? But Biff, seriously now, there's a time and a place for everything. And clearly this is the time for us to finish what we began back in Shantytown. I know how you'd hate for Elizabeth or for your good friend Darryl to think, even for a moment, that you were perhaps *frightened* by the idea of a boxing match."

Biff guffawed once more. Without taking his eyes off Oscar, he said, "Darryl?"

"Uh-huh?"

"You figger I'm ascared of this pissant windbag?"

"No sirree, Biff. You ain't ascared-a nobody."

"Then I guess it won't bother you none if I go ahead and put a bullet in his guts."

"Well, shit, Biff, that's just what I been sayin' all along."

Biff shook his head in mock sadness. "Gee, dude, I'm real sorry about it, but looks to me like it's okay to blow yer belly out."

Beside him, Darryl hooted with laughter.

Oscar slipped his hands into his trouser pockets and shrugged. "Fine, then, Biff, if you insist. But I'm astonished, I confess, to see you reveal this timidity. Particularly in front of a lady whose charms you covet. There you are, a true-blue American, a man obviously in the prime of health, and yet you quake in your boots at the idea of a few rounds of fistfighting with an English poet. Biff, I'm dreadfully sorry to have to say this, but your behavior leaves me no choice. You, sir, are a coward."

Shaking his head, Biff guffawed again. "You figger you get

me riled enough, I'm gonna do somethin' dumb. Maybe *yer* dumb enough to figger you can whup me. But none of it makes no never mind to me. You're a dead man, dude.''

"Come now, Biff. It's your country and not mine. I didn't invent the rules.''

"Rules?'' Another guffaw. "There ain't no *rules*. Darryl, seems to me like the dude here is downright harda hearin'.''

Darryl grinned. "How you figger that, Biff? He's the one doin' all the talkin'.''

"That's what I mean,'' said Biff. "He can't hear how dumb he sounds.''

Biff guffawed and Darryl hooted. In different circumstances Oscar might have relished the *mot* himself.

"Okay, dude,'' Biff said. "Time's up.''

Oscar knew then that the scene had played out. His one chance, and not a very good chance at that, had been to provoke the giant into a fight. That chance now was gone. That chance had never existed.

So it came to this. He had traveled some eight or nine thousand miles, over the sea and across the prairies and the forests, to meet Death in the form of an ignorant lout wearing a greasy buffalo fur coat. He should have been frightened, should have been awash in the clammy sweat of terror; he was not. When all hope goes, he perceived, fear leaves with it.

He was, however, sorely disappointed. That his life would end like this, in farce, seemed to him perhaps the most tragic of tragedies.

And what of Elizabeth? Although at the moment his fondness for her was somewhat diminished (she and Tabor *discussing* him as if he were a packet of lamb cutlets!), certainly he had no wish to see her ravished and murdered by this mindless brute.

And what of Mother? Who would entertain the old dear?

Where was Dr. John Holliday when you really needed him?

Biff was broadly grinning. He glanced for a moment to Elizabeth McCourt Doe, then looked back at Oscar. "Tell you what. You get down, right now, on your hands and knees, and you beg

321

me for it, and I'll shoot you in the head insteada the belly. That way you die quick, without watchin' your guts spill out for an hour. But see, you gotta beg me for it.''

Here was an opportunity to tack an artful ending onto this sorry comedy, to give it one small note of nobility and panache. He raised his head and stood at his full height. "It's an extraordinarily generous offer, Biff. It does you credit. But much as I'd like to oblige you, I'm afraid I can't. I learned years ago that kneeling wreaks havoc with the creases of my trousers. It's one of the reasons I left the Church of England.''

"Too bad," said Biff, and cocked his pistol.

And, off to the right, stepping from around the gray trunk of a pine tree, wearing his sleek black topcoat and holding in his hand a bright silver revolver, Dr. John Holliday said in a whisper that somehow carried across the small glen with perfect clarity, "Drop the guns, children, and grab yourselves a cloud.''

With a small startled squeak, Darryl tossed his gun away, and shot his hands toward the sky.

Biff hesitated. His revolver still pointing at Oscar, he glanced toward Holliday without moving his head.

Holliday whispered, "I hate to repeat myself.''

Biff wheeled toward him, moving his big body into a crouch, bringing his gun to bear, and Holliday's gun exploded. Oscar watched Biff as several things happened simultaneously. Biff's gun went off and so did his hat, popping straight up into the air as a small black hole appeared in the exact center of his forehead and pennants of gray and brilliant red fluttered for an instant from the back of his skull. He stood upright and then, with a look of utter amazement on his face, his arms opening wide as though he were about to embrace an old friend, he toppled backward and crashed to the ground.

Stunned, Oscar felt his stomach roil. He stared stupidly at the lifeless bulk of Biff as Holliday approached.

To Elizabeth McCourt Doe, Holliday said, "You all right, Mrs. Doe?''

"Yes," she said softly, her voice hushed. "Who are you?''

"Elizabeth," muttered Oscar, still staring at the recumbent

322

Biff, "this is—" He stopped, suddenly overcome by the preposterousness of introductions at a time like this.

"John Holliday, ma'am. A pleasure."

Oscar turned to him, gaping. *A pleasure?*

"Best thing now," Holliday whispered, "would be for you folks to head back to the Springs. I'll take care of this." He nodded to Biff's body. He held the gun loosely, down at his side—he was no longer worried, evidently, about Darryl (who, eyes darting, seemed to be trying to disappear within his gray duster).

Oscar said, "But . . . the man is *dead*. Surely, the police . . . the authorities, Grigsby, *someone* . . . surely *someone* should be notified."

Fractionally, Holliday shrugged. "More trouble than it's worth. Means the two of you testifying. A trial. Might take weeks. And it comes to the same thing in the end. He's dead, and we walk away. Self-defense. But you'd be using up a lot of time." Another faint shrug. "Up to you, though."

"Oscar," said Elizabeth McCourt Doe, "help me up. We're going back."

Moving slowly, as in a dream, Oscar offered her his hand. She took it and arose from the blanket. Oscar turned to look back at Biff. He was still dead.

Elizabeth handed him his coat. He took it and, without thinking, without quite knowing that he did so, he put it on.

Biff's angled stovepipe hat lay on its side in the pine needles a few yards from his body. For some reason the hat, battered and abandoned, seemed more poignant, more emotionally resonant, more *final* than the man's lifeless form.

Oscar turned to Holliday. "How did you know? How did you manage to get here in time?"

Another faint shrug. "Saw the two of them headed this way from the Springs. Thought it might be a good idea to follow them. Lost the trail for a while after they left their horses, back on the road." Below the handlebar mustache, he smiled his ghost of a smile. "I'm not much of a tracker."

"Oscar," said Elizabeth McCourt Doe.

He turned to her.

She was squatting down, her hands along the hem of the blanket, the wings of her fur coat spread out atop the pine needles. "You're standing on it."

"Oh. Sorry." He stepped off the blanket.

"What about the basket?" he asked her. This was insane. A man had been shot to death, his brains splashed across the forest floor, and the two of them were jabbering about the picnic paraphernalia.

Standing now, folding the blanket, Elizabeth McCourt Doe looked at Holliday. "Do you drink champagne?"

Holliday nodded his infinitesimal nod. "Now and again."

"Then you're welcome to it," she said. "The basket, too. With my compliments."

A similar nod. "Obliged."

Oscar turned to Darryl. He stood, silent and still, his glance darting from Oscar to Holliday to Elizabeth McCourt Doe to Biff, and then back to Holliday.

Oscar said to Holliday, "What about him?"

Holliday looked at Darryl, looked back to Oscar, shrugged slightly. "He won't be saying anything to anybody."

"No sir," Darryl ventured eagerly. "No sir, I surely won't."

Oscar said to Holliday, "You're not going to—"

Holliday faintly smiled. "Kill him? Don't expect so." He asked Darryl, "You won't be giving me any grief, will you, Darryl?"

"Uh-uh, no sir, no sirree, not a speck of it."

Holliday said to Oscar, "Soon as he helps me get rid of that"—a small nod toward Biff—"I'll send him on his way."

"Oscar," said Elizabeth McCourt Doe. "We have to go."

Oscar nodded numbly. And then remembered: "My watch."

Holliday looked at Darryl. "Give the man his watch, Darryl."

"Yessir, yessir," said Darryl quickly, reaching into his duster. "It just plumb slipped my mind." He sprang forward and handed the watch to Oscar.

Elizabeth McCourt Doe turned to Holliday. "Thank you, Mr. Holliday. For everything."

Holliday nodded.

Pocketing his watch, still feeling somewhat numb, Oscar said, "Yes, well, I suppose . . . thanks . . . are in order . . ."

Holliday nodded. "Be seeing you, Poet."

Twenty or thirty yards from the glen, as they walked through the forest back to their carriage, Oscar muttered, "It's Doctor."

"What?" she said.

"It's Doctor Holliday. Not Mister."

"He has the strangest eyes," said Elizabeth.

"Sorry?" Oscar was distracted once again. Nearly back in Manitou Springs now, the two of them had not spoken since they climbed into the carriage.

"Doc Holliday. He *is* Doc Holliday, isn't he?"

Oscar nodded. Again and again he had watched Biff's absurd hat levitate from his hair as the lead slug pocked his forehead. Again and again he had seen the flurry of tissue spurt from the back of Biff's massive skull; had seen the giant open wide his heavy arms to enfold Death in his embrace before he toppled to the earth.

"I've never seen eyes like that," she said. "They seem so melancholy. He must've suffered terribly in his life."

Oscar turned to her. "Well, now that the two of you have been properly introduced, you can invite him to breakfast. I'm sure he'll be happy to have you clasp him to the comfort of your bosom. Of course, you'll need to discuss it with Tabor first."

She slipped her hand from her muff and placed it on his arm. "Oscar. Don't."

"If you'll recall, you once made a similar remark about *my* eyes."

"Oscar," she said, "you'll spoil everything."

"Spoil it? How can one spoil a thing which is already rotten?"

She removed her hand from his arm. "Oscar. Listen to me. What you and I have together takes nothing away from what Horace and I have. And what we have, Horace and I, takes nothing away from us, from you and me. Horace is staying over

325

in Manitou Springs tonight. I have a room to myself at the Clarendon, in Leadville. We enjoy each other, you and I. We get along. This'll be our last chance to spend some time together.''

He faced forward. ''I had been hoping,'' he said, ''for rather more of your time than merely another night.''

''But that can't be. Things are the way they are, Oscar. The world is the way it is. Wishing and hoping and dreaming doesn't change it any.''

''Then I prefer to live among the wishes and the hopes and the dreams.''

''You prefer illusions to reality?''

''Infinitely. Reality is tawdry and dull.'' He turned to her. ''And treacherous.''

''That's not fair. I never made you any promises. And you knew from the beginning that I was engaged to Horace.''

Against these statements, both true, Oscar had no defense. He said stiffly, ''A man has been killed, Elizabeth. It seems to me that you're displaying a signal lack of dismay at that fact.''

''He was going to kill *us*, remember? And you're the one who brought up the subject.''

All of this was true, as well. It was infuriating, arguing with a woman who persisted in dealing with facts.

Oscar chose to withdraw himself from the contest—which clearly served only to drag him down to her level—by turning away in disdainful silence.

From the corner of his eye he saw her reach into the pocket of her fur coat.

''Oscar, this is the key to my hotel room. It's on the third floor, room 303. You can get to the third floor of the hotel directly from the Opera House, without going out into the street. There's a connecting passageway at the back of Horace's box.''

''How convenient that must be. For both of you.''

''Here, Oscar. Take the key.''

''No, thank you. I already possess an abundance of keys.''

''Oscar, come and see me after your lecture tonight. I'll be waiting for you. Here. Take it. I have another one.''

''I daresay. Many more of them, I'll wager.''

She laughed, surprising him. "No," she said, "just the one."

He felt her hand dip into his pocket and then slide out. "If you change your mind," she said.

"I frequently do change my mind. A mind is a thing, like a cravat, that is designed to be changed. But about this I am adamant."

"I'll be waiting," she said.

"You shall wait, I'm afraid, in vain."

Neither of them spoke again until they arrived at the Woods Hotel. There, wordlessly, Oscar handed her the reins and stepped down from the carriage. He turned and looked up, at the beautiful mass of titian hair, the beautiful violet eyes, the beautiful wide red mouth, and he felt something wrench, irrevocable, within his chest. "I shall probably never forget you," he said. "I will, however, attempt to do so."

It wasn't as eloquent an exit line as he would've liked; but after having discarded four or five others over the past ten minutes, this was the only one which remained.

The wide red mouth smiled at him. "I'll be waiting," she said, and softly flicked the reins against the backs of the horses. The carriage wheeled away.

Upstairs in his room, Oscar saw that Henry had already packed everything. An hour remained before he had to catch the train to Leadville. He spent most of it retching into the toilet; and he did not know, he could not tell, which sickened him the most: his horror at the death of Biff, or his grief at the loss of Elizabeth McCourt Doe.

CHAPTER TWENTY-EIGHT

WHAT HAD FALLEN AS rain three days ago in Denver had fallen here, in the jumbled heights of the mountains, as snow. Alongside the railroad tracks it lay dingy and dirty, peppered by the cinder and grit sprayed from the smokestacks of passing trains; along the steeply sloped ground before the steeply sloped pine forest, it lay a brilliant white, dazzling in the late afternoon sun. It draped the drooping boughs of the trees and it lay blue and gray beneath them and, even muted by shadow, it turned the tall shaggy trunks to silhouettes.

The carriage was climbing at an impossible angle, the trees all leaning drunkenly in the direction of the train's passage, the entire world atilt. This seemed to Oscar, after the events of the morning, altogether appropriate. A universe that so easily admitted, so easily permitted, betrayal and sudden death was a universe which was patently askew. He would not have been surprised to look out the window and see the trees dangling, topsy-turvy, from the sky.

He glanced around the carriage. Once again, most of the others had withdrawn into themselves and their silences. Opposite him, von Hesse and the Countess were reading: von Hesse, his Chuang Tzu; the Countess, Stendhal's *Charterhouse of Parma*.

Sitting in the left front seats, facing back, were O'Conner and Ruddick. Ruddick was scribbling across the pages of his notebook; at the window a subdued O'Conner was playing gin rummy with a subdued Vail, who sat opposite him in the window seat to Oscar's left.

Oscar sighed. (Discreetly; he had no wish to advertise his distress.) All the others, even the perpetually inebriated O'Conner, appeared complete within themselves. Whole. Entire. Sound. None of them seemed to be, as Oscar felt, adrift and rudderless, storm-shattered, bobbing and yawing mindlessly, helplessly, hopelessly. *Le Bateau Ivre.*

He looked out the window at the crazed, canted trees of the forest as they dropped down the slope behind the slowly moving train. Perhaps he should retreat to some hermitage in those woody depths. Perhaps he might find, deep within the hushed forest, a lasting peace. He could build himself a small comfortable cell amid the pines, and there, surrounded by only a very few beautiful objects—his Bokhara rug, his Meissens, possibly a lovely brass samovar like the one he had seen last year at that cunning little shop in Belgravia—he could commune with nature. He would have for company only the birds and the squirrels.

And the bears. The dead bears.

Once again, Biff's battered hat sprang skyward and a third eye winked open in wonderment at his forehead. (The Eye of Wisdom this was called in certain Oriental traditions which at the moment Oscar was unable, precisely, to identify.)

And now, buried (presumably) beneath damp earth and brown pine needles, that unblinking eye stared up at . . . what?

At nothing. At the Void.

It stared at the Void and the Void stared back. One mirror contemplating itself in another.

"Oscar?"

Ruddick, looking up from his notebook.

"Yes?"

"When we're in Leadville, will you be going to see the Ice Palace?"

"I beg your pardon?"

Evidently pleased to be the bearer of good (or at any rate hitherto unborne) tidings, Ruddick enthusiastically fluttered his long eyelashes. Sometimes, truth to tell, Ruddick could be a bit much. "You mean you don't know? Oh, well, really, I heard all about it in Manitou Springs, and it sounds *wonderful*. It's a real *palace*, with rooms and towers and courtyards, like a Norman castle, but it's all made out of *ice*. They cut the blocks out of the lake up there, and they had a big celebration, ice sculptures and a band and *everything*. That's all over, naturally, but the palace is still there. It's *huge*, I heard, absolutely *enormous*—three whole *acres* of it. Can you imagine? A whole great big *castle* made out of ice? It's definitely the first thing I'm going to go see tomorrow."

The idea of a castle constructed of ice—cold, bleak, and transient: like life—nicely complemented Oscar's mood. Perhaps whoever owned the thing would lease him a room. The dungeon, perhaps.

"Wilde's got better things to do with his time," said O'Conner, looking up with a comfortable leer from his cards.

Oscar turned to him. "Have I, indeed. And what might they be?"

Still leering, O'Conner said, "I saw you last night, after the lecture. I couldn't help noticing that you were getting along real well with Baby Doe."

"Mrs. Doe," Oscar said, "is an acquaintance only. And scarcely even that."

"Yeah," said O'Conner, nodding with mock earnestness, damnable man. "Right. Then I guess you didn't know that Tabor's carriage is hooked up to the train we're on, and that she's in it, but he isn't. He's staying over in Manitou Springs. And I guess you didn't know that she's got a permanent room at the Clarendon Hotel, room 303. And I guess you didn't know that the third floor of the hotel, her floor, is connected by a passageway

330

to the Opera House, where you'll be lecturing tonight.'' He nodded again. ''I guess you didn't know any of that, right?''

Vail was glaring over at Oscar, a scowl on his round pink face.

''No,'' said Oscar. ''As a matter of fact, I didn't. And if I had, I should have utterly forgotten it. But tell me. How did you learn so much about Mrs. Doe?''

O'Conner shrugged. He produced a variation on his leer, an extremely irksome smirk. ''I'm a reporter. I ask people for information, they give it to me.''

''Ah.'' Pity he hadn't asked, with the same success, for lockjaw. Or coma.

Still smirking, O'Conner said, ''You ever notice that when people say *as a matter of fact*, they're usually not telling the truth?''

Oscar smiled. ''No,'' he said. ''As a matter of fact, I haven't.''

O'Conner nodded. ''So you're saying there's nothing between the two of you?''

''Only distance. Which is as I prefer it.'' As soon as he said this, he knew he had said too much.

''Oh yeah?'' said O'Conner, looking interested. ''Why's that? She turn you down?''

''Excuse me, gentlemen,'' said the Countess. Heads turned.

''I do not wish to interrupt, but I find myself suddenly quite hungry. Oscair, would you be so good as to accompany me to the dining car?''

''With great pleasure,'' he said, and realized that this was the first true statement he had made in some time.

''Now, Oscair,'' said Mathilde de la Môle as she sat down opposite him, across the white linen of the dining table and facing the rear of the train, ''you must tell me what is wrong. You look entirely disconsolate.'' She sat back in her seat and put her hands in her lap.

''It's nothing,'' he said. ''Something I ate must have disagreed

331

with me." This was, he realized sadly, yet another statement of fact—although several days had passed between the occasion of his eating and the occasion of Elizabeth McCourt Doe's disagreeing.

"Oscair," she said, gently chiding, "Come now. Mr. O'-Conner was not the only person to see you with the beautiful Madame Doe last night. You seemed so happy then, both of you. What has happened?"

"Ah," he said sadly. If only he *could* unburden himself, accept her sympathy, halve his pain by sharing it. Impossible, of course. A gentleman never complained about a lady.

"Get you folks some food?" The Negro waiter hovered beside their table, looking as resplendent in his whites as a society surgeon about to perform wonders in the operating theater. Teeth agleam, eyes asparkle in the friendly black face, he was really quite appallingly cheerful.

"Only some coffee, please," said the Countess.

"Have you any tea?" Oscar asked him.

"No sir, we surely don't."

"Coffee, then."

As the waiter left, Oscar looked back at Mathilde. "Ah," he sadly said again.

She smiled softly. "Tell me, Oscair. Perhaps I can help."

Well, after all, Elizabeth McCourt Doe was no lady . . .

Oscar told her slowly at first, elliptically, avoiding specific details; and then gradually, as though for some curious reason he needed to feel his own pain even more acutely, as though he needed in fact to flaunt it, he began to elaborate and embellish his grief and humiliation (pausing only to accept the coffee when it arrived, and then impatiently to thank the smiling waiter). He told her of the house in Grosvenor Square and in the telling he made the cherished dwelling seem so real—its extensive and expensive wooden furnishings all gleaming with beeswax and lemon oil, its mortgage paid off—that its loss now was as crushing as if he had sipped sherry beside its cozy fireplace for a lifetime. He told her of those splendid trips to Italy and France and Germany; and to Greece, where, although he

332

had not realized it before this moment, he and Elizabeth McCourt Doe would have sat on the steps of the Erectheum and gazed in mutual love and shared awe at the sun-soaked pillars of the Parthenon.

Finally, omitting any mention of Darryl and Dr. Holliday and the (presumably) buried Biff, he told her of the woman's treachery. Of how, all along, she had kept Tabor informed about her relationship with Oscar. Of how she had permitted Oscar to lose himself, his heart, his soul, in visions of their future together when, all along, from the very beginning, they had had no future together.

"And not much of a present, either," he said forlornly. "A few stolen hours here and there. And those, as it turned out, had not been stolen at all. They had merely been borrowed, with his consent, from Tabor."

The Contess had listened in silence, merely nodding her head sympathetically now and then; or, from time to time, pursing her lips thoughtfully. Now she said, "But Oscair, of what, exactly, do you complain?"

"Mathilde," he said, "how on earth can you ask that? I *loved* the woman. I wanted to spend the rest of my life with her."

"But you barely knew her, *n'est-ce pas?*"

"I barely knew her, yes. Now I know her all too well."

She leaned forward and put her hand over his. "Oscair, do not judge her so harshly. Did she ever promise to share your life with you?"

"She never promised *not* to." He took a sip of coffee, sadly shook his head. "You know, Mathilde, in matters of the heart, I've always been able to rely upon the fact that deep down, I'm rather a shallow person. If a particular flower were unavailable, forbidden, promised to another, why then, I could always wander on and pluck the next. The fields are full of lovely flowers, are they not? But somehow this wretched woman has managed to worm her way *beneath* my superficiality. I find even her treachery less disturbing than this. Treachery, after all, one expects. Elephants grow tusks, dogs chase cats, human beings betray each other. I'm sure this is precisely what Jesus was trying to convey

333

to poor Judas Iscariot at the Last Supper. But to penetrate into the core of my being the way she's done—that is something that I doubt I can ever forgive."

"But Oscair, you placed her there yourself."

"But I wouldn't have placed her there, *couldn't* have placed her there, if she hadn't been the sort of woman she was."

"Or the sort of woman you believed she was."

"Exactly."

"Oscair," she said, "you are in pain now—"

"In agony," he corrected.

With a small smile, she nodded. "In agony, if you like. But it will pass."

"But when? The woman has moved into my mind and taken up residence, like some dreadful relative who arrives for Christmas dinner and never leaves. I *cannot* stop thinking about her. It's absolutely intolerable."

"Will you be seeing her again?"

"You heard O'Conner? What he said about her private room at the Clarendon? Well, she had the nerve to suggest that I visit here there tonight, after the lecture." He reached into his pocket, fished out the key. "You see? She gave me her key. Room 303."

"Will you be seeing her?"

"Of course not," he said, slipping the key carefully back into his pocket. "Seeing her is the last thing in the world I intend to do. No, what I must do now is forget her entirely. I must find some way to remove her from my mind, my heart, my life."

"You know, Oscair," she said, "the only way to remove a pain is to suffer through it."

"Rubbish. The only way to remove a pain is to ignore it. To divert oneself. Write a poem. Climb up an Alp. Or, better still, fall off one. Or catch a cold. Catching a cold is probably the best diversion of all. Who can worry about a broken heart when his nose is bright red and stoppered with phlegm?"

She was gently smiling. "Oscair, do you really believe everything you say?"

He smiled sadly. "I should be exceedingly credulous if I did.

334

But I do believe, Mathilde, that I need a diversion of some kind. Any kind.''

She shrugged. ''Then you must discover one.''

''But I can't, you see. My mind is stoppered with Elizabeth McCourt Doe.''

She pursed her lips. ''Wolfgang told me that you were attempting to discover who among us might have committed these horrible murders.''

''Ah.'' In fact, he had been so preoccupied by Elizabeth's treachery, and by the murder he had witnessed that he had very nearly forgotten the murders of the prostitutes. ''Well. I did take a stab at that.'' He heard the words after he spoke them, and added, ''No pun intended, I assure you.'' He shook his head. ''I wasn't terribly successful.''

''But what did you do?''

He told her of his wasted trip to Shantytown, his fruitless conversation with the crapulous old man. ''All he was able to tell me about the dead woman, this Molly Woods, was that she had red hair.''

The Countess nodded, then slightly narrowed her lovely brown eyes. ''But perhaps, you know, this is significant.''

''I shouldn't think so. Quite a lot of woman have red hair.'' He frowned, remembering the tumbling titian tresses of Elizabeth McCourt Doe.

The Countess was smiling. ''Like your Mrs. Doe.''

''Hardly *my* Mrs. Doe.''

Her face serious now, she looked off for a moment, toward the rear of the train, and then said, ''But Oscair, red hair is not so commonplace after all. Perhaps you should discuss this with Marshal Grigsby.''

''Whatever for? Presumably he already knows she had red hair. And besides, he's still back in Manitou Springs.''

''Indeed he is not. Here he is now.''

''Howdy,'' said Grigsby, still wearing his battered sheepskin jacket and his silly Kilimanjaro hat and looming over their table like a . . . like a burly forest animal of some indeterminate sort.

Oscar was suddenly awash in sweat and guilt. He was absolutely certain that Grigsby had come here to cart him off to the federal lockup—masked jailers, iron shackles dangling from damp stone walls, rats squeaking with hunger—for the murder of Biff the Behemoth. He leaped up and shot out his hand. "Marshal Grigsby," he said, his own voice a bit squeaky; and, as Grigsby grabbed Oscar's right hand, nearly pulling him off balance, Oscar put out his left for support and smacked the head of the passenger sitting in the seat behind him.

He looked down, reflexively muttered "Terribly sorry," and turning, saw the long black expressionless face of Henry Villiers.

"Henry! Good Lord! Sorry about that."

Henry nodded. "That's okay, Mistuh Oscar."

Oscar turned to Grigsby. Perhaps an exuberant show of friendship would convince the marshal that he had the wrong man; or would at least confuse him. "Well, Marshal Grigsby, fancy meeting you here! Join us, won't you?"

Grigsby, who did seem mildly confused, or at least uncertain, or at least not actively hostile, took off his twenty-gallon hat and turned to the Countess. "If that's okay with you, ma'am."

"But of course," she said, smiling. She moved over to the window and patted the seat she had just vacated. "Please."

As Grigsby sat, Oscar watched him carefully. The marshal hadn't arrested him yet, but perhaps this was in deference to the feelings of the Countess. Or perhaps he was playing at cat and mouse, deliberately trying to put Oscar at his ease before he attacked.

Well, it would take more than these bumbling efforts to hoodwink Oscar Fingal O'Flahertie Wills Wilde.

He noticed that Grigsby was looking rather more wholesome today than he had at their first, memorable, meeting. Beneath the sheepskin jacket and the leather vest, his red plaid shirt was clean and seemed freshly pressed. The whites of his eyes so longer displayed, at their corners, the deltas of tiny red Niles. He no longer gave off the penetrating reek of stale alcohol. Instead, he smelled of something herbal and faintly sweet, perhaps the fragrance of whatever grease he had used to slick his gray hair back into a shiny skullcap.

Possibly the marshal had a sweetheart in Leadville. Some earnest little thing in gingham, some cowgirl hausfrau redolent of baked bread, steamed apples, and outdoor plumbing.

Grigsby and the Countess were exchanging pleasantries: *Quite well, thank you, and you? Mighty fine, ma'am*. Then Grigsby turned to Oscar. "Wanted to talk to ya," he said.

"Yes?" said Oscar, blinking only once and keeping his face superbly bland.

Grigsby nodded. "I found out it couldn'ta been you, killed off them . . . women. Just wanted to tell ya. I reckon I came on a little strong, that time up in your room."

"Not at all," said Oscar. What, after all, was a loaded revolver between friends?

"I was pretty well steamed up at the time," said Grigsby. "Reckon I owe you an apology. Anyways, like I say, you're in the clear."

The man seemed guileless; surely this was no trick? Oscar asked him, "And how did you make this determination?"

Grigsby gave him a small smile. "Your feet."

"My feet?"

Grigsby nodded. "They're too big."

"Too big," Oscar said, "for what?"

"To belong to the killer. He left some tracks at Molly Woods' place. His feet are average size. Couldn't help but notice, when I took a look, that yours are a little on the largish side."

The waiter was hovering at the table. "Howdy do, Marshal," he grinned. "Get you a drink?"

"Howdy, Edward. Not today, thanks. Cup of coffee?"

"Yes sir, coming right up.

"I've always thought of my feet," said Oscar, "as rather nicely sized in proportion to my height."

Grigsby smiled again. "Never said they weren't. They fit *you* just fine. They just don't fit the killer."

"I see. Well, thank you for telling me." Still rather nettled:

337

his feet were, in his opinion, one of his finest features. "Have you also examined the feet of the rest of the men on the tour?"

A nod. "Took a look or two. Average size, all of 'em."

"Marshal," said the Countess, putting her hand briefly atop Grigsby's arm, "Oscair has, like yourself, been trying to discover the identity of the killer."

Grigsby turned back to Oscar. A small smile. Amusement? "That right?"

Oscar shrugged. "A few questions here and there. Nothing terribly elaborate. A sort of intellectual exercise, really."

"Yes, but Oscair, you did learn something about the poor dead prostitute."

Why on earth was she pursuing this?

Grigsby said, "What's that?"

Oscar shook his head. "Nothing, really. Only that she had red hair."

Grigsby nodded, his face unchanged, and said nothing.

But by rights he should have belittled the information; laughed at it; after all, it was useless. Unless . . .

"Which of course," said Oscar, "would be significant only if the other murdered women also had red hair."

His face still unchanged, Grigsby still said nothing.

"Here you go, Marshal," said the grinning black waiter.

" 'Preciate it, Edward." Grigsby looked at the Countess, looked back at Oscar.

Oscar said, "They did, didn't they?"

Grigsby sipped at his coffee, set the cup carefully back down on its saucer, looked back at Oscar. "You can keep your mouth shut?"

"I can be," said Oscar, "and often am, the soul of discretion."

"I want your word on it. That you won't go gabbin' about any of this to the others."

"That goes without saying."

"My experience, things that go without sayin', they go better when they're said."

"You have my word. But by now it's obvious, isn't it. They did have red hair."

338

Grigsby nodded.

"All four of them?" asked the Countess.

Grigsby turned to her. "All five of 'em. There was another one. Just got a telegram this mornin'."

"Where?" Oscar asked him.

"San Jose, California."

The Countess turned to Oscar. "We were in San Jose, were we not?"

"At the beginning of February."

"February the sixth," said Grigsby.

"When was she killed?" Oscar asked, already knowing the answer.

"That night."

Oscar felt the breath leave his lungs. Its departure weakened him, and he sat back.

The Countess said to no one in particular, "Then there is no doubt at all. It is one of us."

Grigsby nodded. "Looks like."

Listlessly, Oscar said, "What about Dr. Holliday?" Not really believing in the possibility, and feeling curiously disloyal even for suggesting it. After all, the man had saved his life, and Elizabeth's. "He might've been in San Jose that night."

"Prob'ly was. Doc's a gambler. He's been followin' your tour. Been settin' up poker games with the high rollers who come in to see ya."

"He told you this?"

Grigsby nodded. "And I got no reason to disbelieve him."

Yes. It could be. And perhaps, too, this explained why the gunman seemed so concerned with Oscar's welfare, why he had saved him twice from possible—no, admit it, from *certain* disaster. He had been protecting the farmer who gathered the geese who laid the golden eggs.

For some reason this notion—that Holliday had all along, and without Oscar's knowledge, been using him—disturbed him nearly as much as learning about the additional murder. He felt rather as though he had been betrayed yet again, not by a friend or a lover, which one might expect, but by a stranger, gratuitously.

But why should this bother him? Elephants grew tusks . . .

"What will you do now?" the Countess was asking Grigsby.

He shrugged. "What I been doin' all along. Keep watchin'. Keep waitin' for someone to make a move on a prostitute."

"They've all been prostitutes?" asked Oscar, more out of politeness now than out of any real interest. He felt flat, exhausted, defeated.

"All but one," Grigsby said. "And maybe that one was workin' on the side. Or maybe this fella just figured she was. I got the feelin', readin' about her, that maybe she was a little loose. Maybe that was enough for him."

Oscar nodded. He wanted to lie down in a bed and pull the covers over his head. He wanted, failing that, to complain some more about his heartache, which he could hardly do in front of Grigsby. Grigsby, a man as sensitive as a piano bench, would never understand. "Countess," he said, "shall we go?"

She leaned forward. "Oscair, would you mind very much if I spoke to Marshal Greegsby for a few minutes longer?" She smiled at Grigsby. "If, Marshal, you do not mind my company?"

"No, ma'am, be a pleasure."

"Of course not," said Oscar. Still another betrayal. It was an epidemic. He stood. "Marshal. Countess."

As he entered the first-class carriage, Oscar realized that he did not want to sit with the others. Not only because one of them was probably a murderer. (And now, with the news of an additional killing in still another town where they had stayed, this seemed an absolutely certainty.) But also because what he most wanted in the world at the moment was solitude.

He sat in the empty seat at the back of the carriage and stared out at the deranged trees leaning over the blue blanket of snow.

CHAPTER TWENTY-NINE

MY DEAR MRS. DOE,

Would you please be so kind as to meet with me this evening
at the Ice Palace? I will proceed directly there after my lecture
in the hope of finding you. The lecture will end at ten o'clock.
I have something of great weight and pointedness to share with
you. I think it would be best if you discussed this meeting
with no one. I very much look forward to your coming.

Sincerely,
O. Wilde

He reread the letter.
He giggled.
Truly, it was perfect. *Perfect*.
He especially liked *something of great weight and pointedness*.
The slut would think that this was a sly sexual allusion, and she
would never suspect that it might refer just as well—no, *better*—
to a sacramental knife.
Yes, the letter was perfect. It was certain to lure the bitch from
the safety of her lair, out into the darkness where he could act,

341

where he could show her, could become with her, the Light that flared at the center of the cosmos.

(*The splitting of taut pink flesh, the rush of red saps, the bright iridescent shimmer of meat.*)

From the train, he had seen the huge castle of ice, its slick translucent sides stained orange by the slanting light of the setting sun. Sprawling on a broad promontory to the west of town, it had appeared, at first glance, like something from a child's fairy tale. A wide portcullis yawned between two lofty crystal towers; the massive crystal walls, topped with delicate crystal parapets, rose dizzily skyward from the bright orange field of snow. It had seemed at once dreamlike and substantial, fanciful and concrete; something that had been imagined rather than constructed, but something that, having been created by an impossible feat of magic, would endure, magically, until the end of time.

But when you looked more closely, you saw that one of the huge towers was listing very slightly toward the other; that the parapet here and there showed gaps, like missing teeth, where sections had toppled to the ground. The entire structure was melting now, crumbling beneath the weight of time and temperature. In å few days, in a week at most, it would collapse upon itself, become a tumble of shattered, splintered blocks; and in another few weeks it would be gone entirely, leaving behind nothing but a small rill or two of turbid water gurgling over the black mud.

Well, in point of fact, there *would* be a little something else remaining. A delightful little surprise for the good people of Leadville. Damp fragments, choice thawing segments, lovely strips and chunks of what had been the wicked slut, the vile strumpet Elizabeth McCourt Doe.

(*Threads of scarlet streaking the brown meltwater.*)

He giggled again. He had spoken with some of them this evening, with some of the good people of Leadville. (Fools, fools! Not a one of them had guessed!) He had learned this: that because of the danger posed by the rotting ice, no one entered the Palace now. During the day, a few visitors to the town might wander up to marvel at the vast frozen construction, perhaps to frown at the futility, the enormous effort wasted on a thing so ephemeral, so fugitive. But at night, in the cold, in the darkness, no one went there.

Except the sort of creature driven by her own vile lusts, by her need to spread corruption and depravity.

She would come, yes. She would come to offer her rank, stinking, poisonous body to Wilde.

And, oh, she would suffer, this one. She would *pay*. This one he would keep alive for as long as possible. This one would know exactly what was happening, this one would *see* it happening, *hear* it happening. The glide and whisper of the knife, the pluck and prod of knowing fingers.

She would scream, oh my yes, she would beg for mercy.

Let her. Yes, let her. No one would hear her.

Her hair. Her red red hair. He would slice it off, skin and all, tear it in one piece from her skull as the wild Indians did, and then, oh yes, and then he would *wear* it for her. What a fine joke that would be! What a magnificent jest! And then, with it damp against his head, draped and dripping from his shoulders, he would dance for her, round and round in the silvered moonlight, holding the knife high so she might see it, so she might know that soon she would taste it again.

A shudder of pleasure ran through him.

It was too much, almost, to contemplate. A faint glow, a promise of the Flame to come, pulsed along the sides of his vision. And then . . .

. . . for a moment, for only a moment, the darkness overtook him, rushed over him with the roar of a typhoon, and he was back once again in the attic, listening to the footfall of the Preacher rising up the stairs . . .

. . . and then once again he was back in the endless empty field, watching the sky split apart and send entrails spilling to the parched earth . . .

But then he was back in his room at the Clarendon. He was all right. He was in absolute control.

He was in absolute, utter, control. Of his destiny. Of the unthinkable, unstoppable force that throbbed within him.

Tonight he would have her. Tonight she would be his. No one would, no one could, stop him.

And if someone *should* come, if some interloper should enter the Palace tonight, he was ready.

He picked up the revolver from the bed and turned it over, admiring its solidity, its clean forceful lines.

How easy it had been to obtain. You merely walked into a store, made your selection, paid your money, took your gun and your ammunition, and you left. As easily as purchasing a box of chocolates.

In the light of the oil lamp the blued steel gave off a soft, lovely glow.

Yes. He was ready.

He looked at his watch. Eight-thirty. Wilde would be starting his lecture.

Time to go. Time to find room 303 and slip the note beneath her door.

He picked up the note, reread it once more.

He giggled.

CHAPTER THIRTY

ENRY, COMING DOWN WITH a cold, coughing and wheezing, had asked for the evening off; and so Oscar was alone in the dressing room as he sat slumped in the red plush chair and watched himself smoke a cigarette in the mirror.

The lecture had gone well: the miners, in their simple, good-natured way, had roared with merry laughter at his wit. This had been rather a surprise, for Oscar's heart had not been in his performance.

No, his heart had been floating somewhere behind the seats in the box to stage right, Tabor's box. It had been fluttering and hovering somewhere there in the shadows, where behind a red velvet curtain a door led to the passageway which connected the theater to the third floor of the Clarendon Hotel. Outside the Opera House, on his way here, he had looked up and seen it: a long windowless brick structure, graceless but utilitarian, obviously an afterthought, poised in midair between the two buildings.

All he need do was take an oil lamp, walk up into Tabor's box, pull back the curtain, open the door, amble down the passageway, open the door on the other side, find room 303, use

345

the key she had given him, and straightaway he would be with her.

She would be awaiting him, she had said.

Probably she would already be lying in bed, her remarkable red hair atumble on her pale white shoulders, one perfect pert nipple peeking (perhaps) above the sheet . . .

He would not go to her.

To go to her was to admit that he *must* have her; that to have her, he would accept her even on her own, impossible, terms. To go to her was to validate her worldview at the expense of his own. To go to her was to surrender his dreams to the sordid reality of her arrangement with Tabor. To go to her was to diminish himself.

But in his pocket, heavy inside its cardboard box, was the silver brooch he had purchased in Denver. He had not given it to her this morning (what with revelations and revolvers, he had not found the time); and for some reason, not thinking about it, when he dressed this evening he had slipped the box into the pocket of his green velvet jacket.

He didn't want the bloody thing. It would serve, forever, as a reminder. Of his foolishness. Of his stupidity.

He could, of course, throw it away. But that seemed a terrible waste.

What he should do, perhaps, was go to her room—for only a moment or two. Give her the brooch. Here. Something I picked up for you in Denver, before you tore out my heart and hurled it to the ground and performed a mazurka atop it.

No. No bitterness. Bitterness would lose her forever.

Idiot. You've already lost her forever.

No. What was needed here was a light touch. A casual, airy insouciance.

Just stopped by for a minute, must run, but I thought I'd pass along this little bauble. Nothing special, but I thought it might amuse you. Well, cheerio, do drop me a line if you get the opportunity. You have the address?—The Rambles, Grosvenor Square, London. Oh, and make sure you write *private* on the envelope. Otherwise one of the servants might open it, they're hopeless really.

She would be naked under the sheet.

He sat forward, stubbed out the cigarette in the ashtray.

He would go to her, yes, but only for a moment. Only to give her the brooch.

In his carpetbag, lying in the shadows beside him, he had everything he needed. A coil of rope. A change of clothes. An oil lamp. A square of soap and a large bottle of warm water, so that afterward, when he had done with the creature, he might wash the stains of it from his body. And afterward, he would use the oil remaining in the lamp to burn the clothes he wore now.

The knife was in the inner pocket of his jacket. The gun was in his topcoat pocket.

He was ready.

The night was perfect. The full moon was nearly at the center of the sky and by its light, had he wished to, he could have read a newspaper. He had not needed the oil lamp to search through the chill, empty hallways of the Palace. The room he had chosen was ideal for his purposes: splashed with moonlight, ceilingless but for the spidery metal framework which had once held sheets of ice. Part of one wall had already collapsed. In one corner lay a ragged jumble of ice and snow, and there, afterward, when he had finished, he would bury it. He had never felt the need before to hide them, to conceal the bits and pieces; but with Grigsby still prowling about, concealment was the wisest course. No one would find it for weeks, and by then he would long be gone.

The earth beneath his feet was a frigid, semiliquid muck which now, in the cold, was beginning to solidify. His toes were aching, tingling—an indication that once again all his senses had been brought to a preternatural sharpness.

He could hear his breathing, soft and steady. Always he was surprised and pleased by how calm he could remain. Anyone else might, right now, be panting with fear and tension. He—

He heard, and then he saw, the carriage. Led by two prancing black horses, it rolled across the empty field of snow. Even from a hundred yards away, so extraordinary was the accuracy of his vision, he could see her clearly, sitting upright in the seat, her long red hair trailing in the wind behind her, black now in the moonlight.

Always, before, he had gone in search of his prey. Stalking it. Tonight it came to him.

He giggled.

How convenient this was. He must use this method again.

The carriage drew closer, the thudding of the horses' hooves, the rattle of the wheels, growing louder in the still night air.

Come to me, bitch. Come to me, slut.

Come to us.

Oscar knocked on the door to room 303.

No answer.

He slipped the key into the lock, turned it, pushed open the door.

"Elizabeth?"

He shut the door behind him. The only light came from the oil lamp he held. He was in the empty sitting room of a suite—bookcases, a dining table and some chairs, a long sofa behind a dark-wood coffee table. A door stood open to his right. The bedroom.

She would be in there, naked, lying on the bed.

Just stopped by for a minute, must run . . .

He entered the bedroom. The room was empty, the bed was empty.

Another betrayal.

A cruel joke.

Somewhere she was laughing at him, filled with wicked mirth as she pictured him standing here, the lamp in his hand, an expression of doltish disappointment on his face.

Enough. He had played the fool for far too long.

348

He was turning to leave when he saw, lying open on the dresser top, a sheet of paper.

Perhaps she had been called away, perhaps she had left him a note.

He crossed the room, lifted the paper, read, "My Dear Mrs. Doe . . ."

He frowned. A joke, yes; but a joke played on *her*. By someone else. Someone masquerading as him.

Was the woman a ninny? How could she possibly have believed that he had written this drivel? Declarative sentences so simple as to be almost moronic. Could she really accept that he was capable of such limp, pedestrian prose?

And *I have something of great weight and pointedness to share with you*. Only a dull, lewd mind could have produced that.

Nasty, really. Repellent.

Who could have written it? And why had he done so?

Suddenly he knew.

Not who, but why.

He remembered what Grigsby had said in the dining car. When Oscar had asked if all the murdered women had been prostitutes. "All but one. And maybe she was working on the side. Or maybe he thought she was. I got the feelin', readin' about her, that maybe she was a little loose. Maybe that was enough for him."

Maybe that was enough for him.

Red hair. All the women had red hair.

All the men traveling with the tour had seen her last night; all of them knew that Elizabeth McCourt Doe had red hair.

And, thanks to O'Conner, all of them knew that she was staying in room 303 of the Clarendon.

He set the oil lamp carefully on the dresser, and then he ran from the room.

"Oscar?"

The creature was down from the carriage, standing in the slush at the entrance to the Palace, calling out Wilde's name. It stood close enough for him to see the color of its hair, a deep dark red in the moonlight, the color of blood.

The snow crunched beneath him as he came up behind it, and the creature turned.

He brought the gun down, hard, against the side of its head. It flinched, tried to bring up an arm to protect itself, and he brought the gun down again.

Grigsby was drunk and he was no longer a United States marshal.

The drunkenness wouldn't have happened at all (so he had told himself several times, back when he was still capable of telling himself anything) if he hadn't learned that he was no longer a United States marshal. He'd been doing damned well—not a single drink all day, not even a heart-starter in the morning. He'd been stone cold sober when he talked to that little weasel, Vail, and confirmed O'Conner's story. He'd been stone cold sober for the entire train trip from Manitou Springs. When the train pulled in to Leadville, he'd been feeling so proud of himself that he nearly stopped to celebrate in the saloon beside the station. He'd caught himself in time.

The telegram had been waiting for him at the Clarendon. Mort, the Denver telegraph operator, had addressed it to U.S. Marshal Robert Grigsby—even though Mort had known that no such a person existed anymore.

SHELDON RECEIVED WIRE TODAY CONFIRMING RECALL STOP WIRE ME IF QUESTIONS STOP SORRY MORT.

Only Mort had known where to reach Grigsby, and Mort had been cagey enough to word the message in such a way that the operator here in Leadville wouldn't figure it out. No one here in town, and probably only a few people in Denver, knew that he was out of a job.

But Grigsby knew. He folded the telegram neatly into quarters and slipped it into his left back pocket, thinking, as he did, that this thin scrap of paper was far too fragile, far too flimsy, to carry the weight it carried. A few words penciled across its front, and a life was ended. A career was finished. Twelve years of

350

work went spinning into the gutter. He paid the desk clerk for his room and then he walked over to the bar and ordered a drink.

That had been the first. Since then, over the past three hours, he had downed at least a quart of whiskey. After the first five or six drinks, he had stopped telling himself that the drunkenness was a considered, reasonable response to bad news. He drank, he realized, because he was a drunk. Other people were lawyers, bakers, candlestick makers. Farmers. Mine owners. Poets. United States Marshals. He was a drunk.

With the knowledge had come a kind of liberation, a sense of pressure lifted, tension eased. He was a drunk, he had always been a drunk, he would always be a drunk. So what if he wasn't marshal anymore. Who gave a shit. No one in Denver. No one here in Leadville. Not him. He still had his other identity, his true identity. That he would always have. Tomorrow, or maybe the next day, or maybe next week, he'd go back to Denver, sell the house, and then take off for Texas. Lots of good whiskey down in Texas. Good place for a drunk.

He had been in Hyman's Saloon, next door to the Opera House, for an hour. (An hour and a half?) His legs were wobbly and his mouth was numb and slack, and he knew, dimly, that it was time to go. He bought a bottle from the barkeep and staggered off.

Shuffling along the wooden planking of the sidewalk with a flat-footed lurch, the bottle tucked under his arm, he smiled blearily when he saw people watching him from the corners of their eyes, taking care to step well around him as they passed. Citizens. The good citizens of Colorado. The good citizens he had sworn to protect, back when he had been a U.S. marshal.

Assholes, all of them. Petty, money-grubbing assholes. What did they know? Nothing, was what.

Mathilde. Maybe he should go see Mathilde.

No. Not like this. Tomorrow, after he sobered up. Plenty of time tomorrow. Plenty of time now for everything.

As he was reeling into the entrance of the Clarendon, some large bulky shape exploded from within and slammed into him. He stumbled backward and the whiskey bottle went slowly sailing from beneath his arm, lazily spun in the air once, then somehow sped up just before it smacked against the sidewalk. It shattered, whiskey splashing everywhere.

Grigsby wheeled around, his big hands coming up to destroy. *"Asshole! Sonovabitch!"*

Wilde grabbed him by the front of his jacket. "Grigsby! He has her! The killer! The madman! He has Elizabeth!"

Grigsby tried to focus. Clumsily he grabbed Wilde's wrists, tried to wrench the hands away, discovered that he couldn't. Sonavabitch was strong for a lulu-belle.

Wilde was shaking him. "Damn it, Grigsby! Don't you understand! Mrs. Doe! He wrote a note, he pretended he was me! The Ice Palace! He's *there* with her!"

"Mrs. Doe?" said Grigsby. His mind was clearing, and he was beginning to understand that he didn't want it to clear because when it did he would learn something horrible. About the killer. About himself. "The killer?"

Wilde's mouth curled with contempt and he pushed Grigsby away. *"Drunk!"* He looked quickly around him, turned back to Grigsby. *"Your gun! Give me your gun!"*

Grigsby had never handed his gun over to anyone. Now he didn't, even for an instant, consider refusing. He fumbled at the hammer strap, finally slipped it free, fumbled the gun from its holster. Holding the weapon by the barrel, its butt wavering, he forced his loose lips to move around the words: "You know how . . . use it?"

Wilde snapped it away, shoved it into his waistband. "You point it and you pull the bloody trigger."

He spun away and Grigsby called out, *"Wait!"*

Wilde looked back.

Grigsby pointed to the horses tethered to the hitching rail in front of the hotel. "Horse. Take a horse."

Wilde nodded, sprang from the sidewalk, ripped loose a set of reins, and then awkwardly but swiftly scrambled up into the saddle. The horse reared, forelegs clawing at the air, but Wilde leaned forward, knees clenched against its flanks, and kept his seat. He jerked the reins to the right, and the horse came down and then bolted off in a gallop, kicking up black clods of mud behind it.

Weaving, Grigsby tottered to the hitching rail. He put his shaking hand atop it and lowered his head.

Fucking useless old man. Fucking useless old drunk.

You swore to yourself you'd get this bastard, stop him before he killed again, and then when it comes to the crunch you're blind stinking drunk, slobbering with booze and self-pity, can't ride a fucking horse, can't even fucking walk.

Useless.

End it, old man. Pack it in. Put a bullet in your head and get it over with.

Something grabbed at his arm, wrenched him around.

"*Bob.* What's going on?"

Doc Holliday. The fingers of his hand digging into Grigsby's upper arm.

Grigsby shook his head, trying to shake away the cotton.

"Bob, where's Wilde going?"

Grigsby scraped his tongue against his teeth. He brought his glance into focus, found Holliday's cold, glassy eyes. "The killer. At the Ice Palace. Mrs. Doe."

Holliday's fingers squeezed. "Get to the police, Bob. Tell them."

And then he was gone.

The saddle was bigger, broader than an English one, and the stirrups were set far too high for Oscar's long legs. But the horse was moving in a fluid gallop as it raced down the wide muddy Leadville street, powerful muscles smoothly bunching and unbunching; and Oscar, right hand holding the reins, left hand clutching at the saddle horn, had no trouble staying on.

Earlier this evening, when he had arrived in Leadville, he had thought it the ugliest city he had ever seen, as dreary and desolate as the Tenth Circle of Hell. The hills around it for barren miles had been stripped of their trees, black stubble sticking up everywhere through the gray slush. The slush was gray because the air was gray, thick with the smoke that belched day and night from the smelters and the refineries. And from the smoke that belched day and night from the stacks of the ore trains—thousands of them, it seemed—that crisscrossed the bleak, denuded land and ferried countless tons of rock ripped and blasted from the earth.

The city itself was a drab black sprawl of soot-sown wooden shacks and shanties, each huddled up pathetically against the next. In a way, it was more depressing than Denver's Shantytown. In Shantytown, one felt that the inhabitants had never been given a choice: that they had been swept there by the unforgiving tides of fate. Here, one understood that the inhabitants, seeking their fortunes in the silver fields, had made a deliberate decision. They had elected to live here, amid the smoke and the sad, sinister squalor. The monochromatic ugliness of the place, its gross deformity, was the consequence of human greed, and the monument to it.

Now, racing down those black mean streets atop an unfamiliar horse, Oscar thought of none of this. He barely saw the tawdry, tatty huts and hovels as they slipped past.

He could not get his breath. At ten thousand feet the air was too thin; there was not enough of it. Earlier, when he had first climbed up the stairs to his hotel room, he had nearly collapsed. Now his ribs were clawing at his lungs; his heart was flailing against his sternum as though it might burst.

He rounded a corner and saw the Palace, asprawl across the top of a broad, low, moonlit hill. He thumped his heels against the horse's sides and willed himself to keep breathing, willed himself to arrive on time.

A carriage was parked at the entrance to the castle. Oscar hurled himself to the ground, stumbled, pulled the gun from his waistband.

His heart pounding madly, his chest heaving, a whine shrilling in his ears, he stalked into the portcullis. The ground squished and squirmed under his feet, like a jelly, and water gushed over the sides of his boots into his socks, stinging cold.

In the moonlight the crystal walls of the palace seemed to glow from within, a ghastly, unearthly radiance.

The place was huge, enormous—how would he find her in time?

He heard—from up ahead, off to the left—a scream. He ran.

A courtyard. An opening to the left. Another scream. From inside there.

He flew across the expanse of slush, plunged through the opening in the wall of ice. Saw Elizabeth lying on a pile of rubble, her hands behind her back, her coat and dress torn open, her naked body splashed bright white by the moon. Saw a smear of something back and shiny across her pale face.

Saw the black form leaning toward her, an object in its hand.

The figure whirled to face him.

Oscar gasped. *"You!"*

CHAPTER THIRTY-ONE

AILED SLIGHTLY ASLANT to the wall above the old upright piano was a handwritten sign that read: *"Please don't shoot the piano player, he's doing his best."*

His best was clearly not very good. The tune he was torturing at the moment had perhaps been, when it was written, a light, bouncy, frivolous piece. It sounded now, its notes warped, its tempo wavering, like a prolonged wail of pain.

No one in the crowded saloon appeared to mind. The women, most of them grossly overweight, bulging from the tight red bodices of their dresses like sacks of flour from shop shelves, laughed raucously as they danced and drank and flirted with the miners, the cowboys, the shopkeepers. The miners and the cowboys and the shopkeepers laughed raucously back. The place was a bedlam, noise and smoke and the bright bilious blare of gaslight. It seemed impossible to Oscar that only a few hours before, less than a mile away, an utter horror had taken place.

Dr. Holliday asked him, "How's Mrs. Doe?"

"She seems all right," said Oscar glumly. "He hit her in the head and she bled rather a lot—well, you saw. But the doctor believes that it's nothing serious." Lying on her hotel room bed,

356

pallid and beautiful, she had asked Oscar to telegraph Tabor in Manitou Springs and request that he come as soon as possible. Even after Oscar had saved her life, she still preferred that horrid little man to him. He had sent the telegram anyway, one of Love's brave martyrs.

"Would've been a lot worse," Holliday said, "if you hadn't gotten there in time."

"Umm," said Oscar.

"Have another drink," said Holliday, and poured from the bottle into Oscar's glass."

"You don't suppose," he said, "that they've any tea here, do you?"

Holliday smiled his ghost of a smile and shook his head.

"Umm," said Oscar. Dispirited, feeling drained and infinitely weary, he sipped at the whiskey

"If you hadn't shown up," Holliday said, "he would've killed her."

Oscar slowly shook his head. "I still can't credit it, you know. That it was *he* who killed those women. I never for a moment would've thought it possible."

Holliday moved his shoulders faintly in a shrug. "Sometimes you can't figure people."

Oscar shook his head again. "But *him.*"

Holliday drank some bourbon, looked up over Oscar's shoulder, and nodded. "Bob."

"Doc. Wilde." Grigsby's face was ashen and he moved his big body slowly, like someone recuperationg from a long illness. Oscar noticed, as the man sat down, that his hands were trembling. Perhaps sensing Oscar's scrutiny, he folded his arms over his chest, hiding the hands.

"Just finished with the chief of police," he told Oscar. "He's gonna keep the thing quiet. No need for the newspapers to hear about all this. Reckoned you ought to know."

"Umm," said Oscar. That was, yes, probably for the best. The news that someone in his entourage had brutally killed five women might—as Vail had tonight suggested—"really punch up ticket sales." But it would turn the tour into even more of a

357

circus than it had been so far. And besides, Oscar wanted no reminders of what had happened tonight. Probably, he would never need any. "Thank you," he said.

"I'll send some telegrams out, tomorrow mornin'," Grigsby said. "To the towns where the others got killed off. Let 'em know the thing is over."

"Umm," said Oscar.

For a few moments no one spoke. Holliday's empty black eyes were watching Grigsby, who sat with his head and his large, silly hat tipped forward, staring down at the tabletop.

It was Grigsby who broke the silence. He turned to Oscar and said, "I fucked up."

"Well, now, Marshal . . ." Oscar began.

"I fucked up. I got stinkin' drunk when the most important thing I shoulda been doin' was keepin' a clear head. Shoot, I'm still drunk. Swallowed near enough a gallon of black coffee and I'm still drunk. I let you people down, you and Mrs. Doe. Let myself down. And I wanted you to know that I'm right sorry about that."

"Well, Marshal," said Oscar, embarrassed and—surprisingly, reluctantly—touched. "Really, you know, if you hadn't told me that all the women he killed had red hair, I should never have rushed off as I did. I should never have reached Mrs. Doe on time."

"That don't count for much, my tellin' you," Grigsby said. "But you did good, Wilde. You did real good."

Oscar shook his head. "If only it could have ended some other way."

Grigsby said, "Probably best it ended the way it did. Cleaner."

Cleaner? All that blood splashing on the snow?

Again, for a few moments, no one spoke. Again, when someone did, it was Grisgsby.

"Where'd you learn to ride like that? You handled that mare like a rodeo champ."

"In Ireland. I've been riding since I was a child." Oscar shrugged modestly. "I should have done better if I'd had a proper saddle."

358

"You did just fine."

"Thank you for saying so, Marshal."

Grigsby smiled ruefully. "You can stop callin' me *Marshal*. That don't apply no more."

"How do you mean?" said Oscar.

"I'm out of a job. I'm not Marshal no more."

"Because of this? Because of me?"

Grigsby shook his head. "Nothin' to do with you."

Holliday said, "Greaves and Sheldon?"

Grisgby nodded.

Holliday said, "So what're your plans, Bob?"

"Don't rightly know yet. Maybe head down to Texas." He turned to Oscar. "Do all the others know yet? About what happened?"

"Yes. I've spoken with all of them."

"How's the Countess makin' out?"

"Distressed, of course. How would you feel if you learned that the man who'd been acting as your escort was an insane killer?"

Grigsby smiled slightly. "Never had me an escort. But the best thing for her, I reckon, is to put it behind her. Best thing for you, too."

Yes. But how? So long as he lived Oscar would remember von Hesse's face as it looked in the Ice Palace when the man whirled to confront him.

"*Hau ab!*" he had snapped. *Go away!* His lips were twisted back in a fierce rictus and his eyes were narrow vicious slits. His voice was a stranger's: thin and querulous, like that of a very old man, or of a young, furious boy.

"Von Hesse," Oscar said. In German. "Let her go."

"Go away! You'll spoil everything." The object in his hand, Oscar realized, was a knife.

Elizabeth McCourt Doe watched them, her glance sliding from Oscar to von Hesse. Oscar could see shudders running down along her naked body.

"Let her go," he said.

"*No! She is mine! She is ours!*"

"Von Hesse. Wolfgang. I don't want to shoot you. But I will, I promise you. Get away from her."

"You fool! You silly shallow man! You don't understand *anything!* She is mine!" He looked over Oscar's shoulder, then suddenly moved with a speed and power Oscar could scarcely believe. His left hand darted forward and grabbed Elizabeth by the hair and he ripped her up from the pile of shattered ice, her mouth wide open in a silent scream, and he swung her before him. He wrapped his left arm around her throat and pointed with the knife to something behind Oscar's back. *"Who is he? Who is he?"* And then the tip of the knife was against the woman's skin, just below her breast.

Oscar turned.

Dr. John Holliday stood there, a gun in his hand, looking in the pale spill of moonlight like some black angel of death. How had he gotten here without Oscar's hearing him? How had he gotten here at all?

Oscar turned back to von Hesse. "Von Hesse. Don't you see? You can't escape. There's nowhere for you to go. We know now. Don't you see that?"

"Don't talk," Holliday said in his uncanny whisper. "Shoot."

Elizabeth McCourt Doe spoke. Her voice was quite calm. "If anyone's asking for my vote," she said, "I'd say shoot the crazy bastard."

"No!" Oscar said. "Don't shoot!" He softened his voice. "Wolfgang—"

"You're spoiling it!," von Hesse shrieked. Again, he sounded like an angry, frustrated child, and the note of petulance in his voice, which at some other time might have seemed discordant, even comical, was horribly chilling now. "You're spoiling everything! This is *my* moment! This is my *destiny*! You stupid, ignorant people!"

"Wolfgang," Oscar said, "do you remember when we spoke, you and I, about the young corporal you knew in Germany? The one who had dug up the women's graves? Do you remember what you told me?"

"No! Go away! Leave us!"

"Wolfgang, you told me you believed that at bottom we are all good. Do you remember? You told me that we're all tiny pieces of the infinite, all of us connected, each to the other, and to everything in creation. Do you remember, Wolfgang?"

Von Hesse shook his head as though clearing it. "You are trying to trick me."

"I'm not, Wolfgang, I'm not. I'm trying to help you remember who you are. *What* you are. Wolfgang, you understand me. I know you do. I know that, at basis, you *are* good. Do you remember what else you told me? You said that we cannot do violence to another without doing violence to ourselves. The other *is* ourself. Remember, Wolfgang?"

Von Hesse shook his head again. But slowly this time, almost tentatively.

"Wolfgang, I want you to remember who you are. Think, Wolfgang. Each of us is connected, one to the other. Each of us is a piece of the infinite. You are. I am. That woman is."

Von Hesse's glance darted round the room.

Very softly, Holliday whispered, "Keep it up, Poet."

Oscar said, "Wolfgang, the young corporal. You told me you believed that a part of him *wanted* to be caught, *wanted* to be stopped. Wolfgang, *you* wanted to be stopped. Otherwise you wouldn't have written that letter to Mrs. Doe. A letter that anyone might have found. A letter that I *did* find."

Once again, von Hesse shook his head.

Oscar said, "We cannot do violence to another without doing violence to ourselves. You know this. You know that the other is ourselves. Wolfgang—"

Von Hesse closed his eyes for a moment. His shoulders sagged. His body moved slightly forward, forcing Elizabeth McCourt Doe's to do the same. Then he threw back his head, his face to the moon, and he screamed.

The scream filled the room, filled the night, a scream of horror and dread and endless, agonizing pain. It seemed as though it had gone on forever, it seemed as though it would go on forever: that all of them, all four, would be trapped within that scream, frozen within it, until the end of time.

Finally, slowly, it dimmed, cracked, diminished, died. In the vast, trembling silence, Oscar heard von Hesse's labored breath.

And then, in a single swift movement, von Hesse released the woman, stepped back, and slashed the knife across his own throat. A bright black gout of blood surged from the wound and reached out like a liquid arm for the shoulder of Elizabeth McCourt Doe. She made a choked, gasping sound and Oscar rushed for her as von Hesse fell to his knees, blood still spurting from his neck and slapping against the snow.

"Elizabeth."

"I'm all right, I'm all right." But then she collapsed against him, all her weight in his arms. Oscar embraced her. He realized that he was still holding the gun. He dropped it.

Holliday was kneeling beside von Hesse, the man's wrist between his fingers.

Oscar said, "He's dead?"

Holliday nodded. "And then some."

Holliday stood. He indicated Elizabeth McCourt Doe with a single inclination of his head. "Let's get her back."

And so Holliday had untied her hands as Oscar held her, and then the two of them had walked her, each supporting her by an arm, to the carriage. Oscar had driven it back toward Leadville, with her sitting against him in the seat, her head at his shoulder. Holliday had followed on horseback. Along the way, they had met a party of policemen coming from the town. Holliday had sent Oscar on, had remained behind to deal with them.

And now Grigsby said, "He came to my office, von Hesse, and gave me a story about some corporal in the army. Diggin' up graves without knowin' he was doin' it. Fella's mind was all jumbled up, von Hesse said. What I wonder is, you reckon he knew what he was doing? Von Hesse? Or was he crazy in the way he was talkin' about? Killin' em all without knowing he was doin' it?"

Oscar had wondered this himself. "The latter, I believe. I believe that the von Hesse we knew was truly a good man, a religious man. At some level, deep within his consciousness, he must have been under a terrible stress. Suffering terrible guilt.

Perhaps this was why he felt it was so important to tell us about the young corporal."

Grigsby frowned. "Maybe. Reckon we'll never know. There's one other other thing I'm still not real clear on."

"Yes?"

"Why would a note from you send Mrs. Doe way out to the Ice Palace at night?"

"Mrs. Doe writes poetry. She had asked me if I might read some of it and give her my opinion. When she received the note, she assumed that I wished for her to bring me her verses." This was the story that Elizabeth had insisted he tell, a tale which Oscar found utterly absurd.

Grigsby apparently agreed. "To the Ice Palace? At ten o'clock at night?"

"She has, evidently, something of a romantic bent."

"Uh-huh." Dubious. "And von Hesse knew about the poetry?"

"He knew that Mrs. Doe and I had become friendly. If he hadn't seen us talking last night, in Manitou Springs, then he would've learned from O'Conner, on the train today. He mentioned the woman."

Grigsby nodded. He studied Oscar for a moment. "Good thing there won't be a trial. I wouldn't want to hear you use that story on a jury."

"It's quite true, I assure you."

Grigsby was studying Oscar again, speculatively. At last, having apparently made up his mind about something, he shook his head. Firmly, definitively. "Don't matter now. It's all over. So what're your plans?"

"Tomorrow we leave for Kansas City."

"All of you?"

"Except for Countess de la Môle. She told me that she wishes to stay here for several days, and then join with us later."

Grigsby nodded. "Well. If I don't see ya tomorrow, you have yourself a good trip."

"Thank you," said Oscar.

Grigsby stood up. "Time for me to mosey on."

"Where you off to, Bob?" Holliday asked him.

"The hotel. Maybe get some rest." He turned to Oscar. "You take care now, hear?"

"Thank you, yes. You, too, Marshal."

Grigsby smiled faintly again. "Just Bob'll do."

Oscar watched him walk slowly away. Even after the man himself had disappeared among the crowd, the big white hat bobbed for a time over the heads of the women, the miners, the cowboys, the shopkeepers.

Oscar turned to Holliday. "He seems . . . depressed." He would never have thought it possible that Grigsby, a monolith, might become depressed.

"He is," said Holliday. "Like he said, he let himself down." He poured more whiskey into Oscar's glass. "What about you, Poet?"

"How do you mean?"

"How're you feeling?"

"Exhausted. I'm glad, I suppose, that it's over, that we can all get on with our lives." All of them, of course, but von Hesse. "But, as I said, I wish it could have ended some other way."

"Just stick with being glad that it's over."

Oscar nodded. He reached into his pocket, pulled out his watch. One-thirty in the morning.

And then, abruptly, as he stared at the watch, a thought came to him. He looked at Holliday. "You knew that Darryl had my watch."

His eyebrows raised ever so slightly, Holliday looked at him.

"This morning," Oscar said. "Yesterday morning. When you appeared, there in the clearing. As we were leaving, Mrs. Doe and I, you told Darryl to return my watch to me. You could have known that he had it only if you'd been there, watching, all along."

Holliday smiled that ghost of a smile. "Makes sense."

"You were there? The entire time?"

Holliday nodded.

"Why didn't you . . . intercede before?"

364

A faint shrug. "You seemed to be doing all right on your own." A faint smile. "I figured maybe you'd talk him to death."

"But he could've *killed* us."

Holliday shook his head. "Not fast enough."

"And how did you get here so quickly tonight? When we saw you last, you and Darryl were—"

"Didn't take long to bury him. Darryl did most of the work. I caught the same train you did."

"Darryl is all right? He's still alive?"

Another faint smile. "As much as he ever was."

Oscar sipped at his whiskey. "Tell me something, Doctor."

"The name's John."

"John. Yes. Tell me. Marshal Grigsby—you know, I'll never be able to think of him as anything but Marshal Grigsby—in any event, he told me that you'd been following the lecture tour in order to arrange poker games with the men who attended. Is that true?"

Holliday smiled. "Partly," he said.

"Partly?"

Holliday finished the whiskey in his glass, refilled it from the bottle. "The games were the icing on the cake."

"What, then, was the cake?"

Holliday's black empty eyes looked levelly into Oscar's. "You were."

Oscar frowned. "*I* was? I don't know what you mean."

Below the handlebar mustache, the quick ghost of a smile flickered once. "Sure you do, Poet."

And suddenly Oscar did. And suddenly, astonishingly, so did Freddy Phallus, who stirred slightly, like a child beneath the blankets about to awaken from a long slumber.

"Ah," Oscar said. "Ah. Well. I see."

Holliday's stare hadn't wavered.

"Well," said Oscar. "Yes. Well. Doctor. John. If I understand you aright—"

Holliday nodded. "You do."

"Yes. Well, then of course, yes, I'm very flattered. Very

365

flattered. Of course. But you see, I'm not, well, I don't . . . As it happens, you see, I'm very much attached to a particular person. A young woman, actually.''

Holliday nodded. ''Mrs. Doe.''

''Well, let us simply say a young woman. And you know, well, it's my loss, probably, but I've never actively engaged in . . . the other.''

Another flicker of a smile. ''So far.''

''Indeed. So far, yes, exactly. Who knows what the future may bring, eh?''

Holliday nodded. He lifted his glass, drank it down in a single swallow, set the glass back on the table. He smiled once again. ''Well,'' he said, ''when you change your mind, you let me know.''

''Absolutely,'' said Oscar. ''The very instant.''

''Like I said,'' Holliday said, ''when I find something I like, I stick with it.''

He stood, looked down at Oscar, nodded. ''Be seeing you, Poet.''

As he walked away, a dark, slim, lithe figure moving with the grace of a toreador, the crowd parted to let him pass—out of respect, or awe, or simply out of fear.

What an extraordinary man.

What an extraordinary few days these had been.

Had it truly been only five days since he had met Elizabeth McCourt Doe in Denver?

Between then and now, he had fallen in love. He had been battered about inside a madly driven carriage, been given opium to smoke, been bored by drunken old men, been hurled into sawdust and then stalked for days by a bearlike buffalo hunter. He had watched the bearlike buffalo hunter die. He had suffered a broken heart. He had been at the receiving end of two revolvers, and at the discharging end of one. He had been propositioned by a legendary gunman. He had learned that a man he had liked and respected was a killer, and he had seen him open his own throat with one savage swipe of a knife.

Perhaps it was the sheer number of events, or perhaps it was the velocity with which they had arrived. Or perhaps it was his horror at von Hesse's death. Whatever the reason, Oscar was too worn and weary now to worry about his betrayal by Elizabeth McCourt Doe. She was a beautiful woman, and very probably, at some time in the future, he would mourn the death of his love, and of his hopes.

Farewell my love, and remember me . . .

Just now, Oscar wanted, he needed, a respite.

Grigsby was right. The best thing to do was put it all behind him. Everything. Elizabeth McCourt Doe. Biff. Von Hesse.

And what of the brooch that still lay in his pocket, the brooch he had purchased for Elizabeth McCourt Doe?

Give it to Mother.

Put the rest behind.

Think of it as a book. One chapter closes and another begins. Tomorrow, and in the tomorrows which followed, there would be new cities, new adventures, new people. Perhaps new women.

No. No new women for a while, if you please.

Perhaps he should take up Dr. Holliday's offer.

Extraordinary man. He ought to meet Wilbur.

"Sure you do, Poet."

Fancy that.

Enough. This chapter is over.

It was, as Grigsby said, time to mosey on.

EPILOGUE

From the Grigsby Archives

November 7, 1890

MY DEAR GRIGSBY,

It was with great surprise and greater pleasure that I learned, in a letter sent by Mr. Jack Vail, that he had seen you recently in San Francisco, at a lecture given by Vail's current charge, someone called Lysander Richards (which must be, surely, a *nom de route?*). According to Vail, you were accompanied by a lovely wife and two lovely, nearly grown children, all of whom you successfully concealed from us when we met you eight years ago in Denver.

Vail says that you've become something of a luminary in the San Francisco Police Department. I'm delighted for you, of course; but somehow I shall always think of you astride a noble palomino, with the serried, snowbound peaks of Colorado looming magnificently in the background. To bring you up to date on myself, I should tell you that I am married also, and also to a lovely woman, and also the father of two lovely children. My writing career has proceeded rather well of late. I've a novel coming out this month—*The Picture of*

371

Dorian Gray, I shall send you a copy when I receive some—and I've been toying with an idea or two for a play. So it seems that, despite some early setbacks, I shall become something of a luminary myself. He who laughs, lasts. He who lasts, laughs.

But to come to my reason for writing you. You will remember, of course, the terrible events of that March in 1882, when you and I met. Two years ago, on a trip to Germany, I was in the town of Kürten, not too many miles from Berlin. This was, so I recalled being told by Wolfgang von Hesse, the town in which he had been born and raised. Now, one might have thought that after so many years, no one remaining there would have any memory of Herr von Hesse, who, so he told me, had left it back in 1836. But, still curious about the man, I initiated enquiries.

To make a long story short, something I seldom do, I discovered a woman who had lived next door to the von Hesse family. A bitter old thing of some eighty years, blind as a bat and smelling rather like one as well, she had been a young girl then.

Wolfgang's mother, I was told, died in childbirth and he, an only child, was raised for several years solely by his father. The father was a sort of unordained minister. He was quite mad, according to my bat-woman—all hellfire and brimstone, one of those Christians who discover in the Bible license for bitterness, bigotry, and warped brutality. "The Devil can cite scripture for his purpose." (*The Merchant of Venice, I, iii*)

In any event, apparently he beat the boy, severely and often. Wolfgang kept—or was kept, by his father—very much to himself, but when he was old enough to attend school, the other children noticed on his wrists terrible scars that could only have come from ropes.

It was about this time that the father brought back with him from Berlin a female who, said my bat-woman, was obviously a prostitute. She was blowsy, slovenly, and *her hair was bright red*. She lived with father and son until 1836. In February of that year—bat-woman cannot be more precise—

the neighbors were awakened by dreadful screams coming from within the von Hesse house. Investigating, following the screams, they found all three in a tiny attic room. The boy—it was he who was screaming—was tied to a narrow cot. Both the father and the woman were lying on the floor, dead. Her throat had been cut—by the father, presumably, before he had committed suicide by plunging the knife into his own heart. The father and the woman had been dead for at least a day. No one ever understood why the boy had not screamed earlier.

The boy, who fell into a kind of faint when he was untied, was put under a doctor's care. He remained in a vegetative state for several days, and, when he recovered, had no recollection of anything that had occurred in the attic. Later, evidently returned to normalcy, he was sent to live with a distant relative in Berlin. The bat-woman had heard nothing further of him since.

It occurred to me when I learned all this that one day I should write to you and inform you of it. None of this, of course, in any way provides a pardon for what von Hesse did in the United States. (And perhaps—who knows?—elsewhere.) None of it reveals whether he committed his murders consciously and deliberately. (Although I am more than ever inclined to believe that he did not.) But all of it does, I think, provide the beginnings of an explanation. I have a theory that children, when brutalized, become brutal themselves. Von Hesse's history seems instructive in this regard.

As for the others whom you met that fateful March, Vail, as you know, is still managing his touring artistes. O'Conner, you may have heard, disappeared when we arrived in Chicago. It transpired, much to everyone's surprise, that he was not working for the *New York Sun* after all, and had been traveling with us under false pretenses for some unknown reason of his own. No one, so far as I know, has ever seen him again.

You remember, perhaps, the Frenchwoman, Mathilde de la Môle? Well, it transpired that she, like O'Conner, was not what she claimed to be. She was no countess, and her name was not de la Môle. She was, rather, Mathilde Horlec, the daughter of a bourgeois of Boulogne. But the most delicious part of her story is this: three years after our tour, she wrote a book describing her adventures, and the book, quite a success in France, was read with fascination by a certain Count d'Angiers, who promptly sought her out, wooed her, and finally married her. And so the pretend countess becomes a genuine countess, and Life, once again, imitates Art, or at any rate strives to.

I've read the woman's book and it's not bad of its kind. She doesn't mention the murders. But it may amuse you to learn that she claims to have conducted long and involved conversations, *in French*, about literature with my valet, Henry Villiers (the black man who assisted me; I believe you met him). She goes so far as to hint, very delicately of course, that at the end of the tour he and she conducted a brief liaison.

I couldn't tell you whether she actually had an affair with poor Henry. But as to his speaking French—he traveled with me for many months and, despite his French-sounding name, he never spoke a word of it to me.

I suppose what all this—the careers of Mathilde, von Hesse, O'Conner (and perhaps even Henry?)—proves is that, finally, no matter how much we might like to believe otherwise, no one of us ever truly knows anyone else. Or even ourselves. And that perhaps these are things for which we ought all be grateful.

I hope this letter finds you and your family well. I should very much enjoy hearing from you, should you ever find the time to write.

By the way, if you ever happen to see Dr. John Holliday, please tell him for me that I've reconsidered his offer. Until I hear from you, then, I remain,

Yours sincerely,
Oscar Wilde

Paros, September 22, 1990